SLIP

OF

THE

TONGUE

JESSICA
HAWKINS

© 2016 JESSICA HAWKINS
www.JESSICAHAWKINS.net

Editing by Elizabeth London Editing
Proofreading by Underline This Editing
Cover Design © OkayCreations.
Cover Photo © Tyler Seielstad Photography

SLIP OF THE TONGUE

ISBN: 0-9908728-9-0
ISBN-13: 978-0-9908728-9-4

TITLES BY
JESSICA HAWKINS

SLIP OF THE TONGUE

NIGHT FEVER SERIES
NIGHT FEVER
NIGHT CALL
NIGHT MOVES
NIGHT EDGE

THE CITYSCAPE SERIES
COME UNDONE
COME ALIVE
COME TOGETHER

STRICTLY OFF LIMITS

ONE

The man who just stepped out of 6A doesn't notice me staring. He shakes out his honeyed-brown hair like a boy after a bath and wipes his temple with his sleeve. He rolls his neck. Watching him, I feel like an intruder in my own apartment building.

It's the jingle of Ginger's dog tags that makes him look over. He tilts his head, studying me. "Hello again."

I squint. The sixth floor has never been well lit. Warm light bathes the beige walls and a carpet the color of dead leaves. I let Ginger pull me down and across the hall. She wants to smell this new person, and I want a better look. When we make eye contact, my heartbeat snags as it might for a new lover. Because he isn't familiar. I don't know him. "Sorry, have we met?" I ask.

He doesn't respond, as if he's waiting for me to go on, but it's a pretty straightforward question. I'm not sure where to look—his soulful green eyes, or a bottom lip that sticks out like his default expression is a pout. He licks it with an easy smile and once again, I'm staring. "I must've mistaken you for another neighbor," he says. "Just moved in yesterday. You're 6B?" He points to his chest. "6A."

I stick my coffee thermos under my arm and shake his paw of a hand. He then ruffles Ginger's polished-penny red fur but watches me. And I forget that just moments ago, I was sad. Lonely. Confused. Now, I'm still a little confused, but not in the way that makes my brain and chest hurt.

"Welcome to the building." Since I'm already behind schedule thanks to this unplanned dog walk, I tug the leash. "Let's go, Ginger."

"If you wouldn't mind," he says as I continue to the elevator, "can you point me in the direction of a good breakfast spot? Something hearty."

I glance back. His back is arched, his large hand spread over his stomach. The corner of his mouth is quirked. He's kind of a hunk, and I think he knows it. I contain my smile, even when I realize it's my first genuine one in days. "There's a diner on the corner." I begin to sweat, my hands in my gloves, my neck under my scarf. I hadn't planned to be indoors this long. His expression is eager, though, like he's asking an old friend for help. "Don't be scared off by the smell. It's good."

2

"Which corner?"

"Lexington." Ginger whines. I shouldn't even be standing here. I'm verging on late for work. Suddenly, though, that seems less important than welcoming a new neighbor. "We're headed downstairs. I'll show you."

"That'd be great." He heads past me down the hall to get to the elevator first, where he pushes the button. Ginger and I catch up as it arrives, and he holds the door open for us. The space feels small with him in it. He's big, one of those guys who could jump and knock his head on the ceiling of the subway. One of those guys who can make the whole city feel small.

He glances up at the digital numbers, his hands stuck in the pockets of his hoodie.

"Won't you be cold?" I ask, eyeing the thin material.

"Nah. My heater's busted. It won't turn off. It has to be over eighty degrees in my apartment."

I had the opposite problem when I moved in. It shouldn't make me smile to remember that, but trying to stay warm can be fun when it involves a ridiculous amount of cozy blankets and endless, stovetop hot chocolate.

"I can deal with the cold," he continues, then groans, "the heat, though—Jesus. I could *not* sleep. I've been up for hours, moving boxes around the apartment. Finally, I had to come out for fresh air. You can only remove so much clothing, you know?"

3

Heat creeps up my chest. I scold myself. So what if he's naked in his own apartment? I try to think of a witty response to cover the fact that I'm blushing, but I come up short. I sip my coffee instead. We exit the elevator with his last comment hanging between us.

"So, these are the mailboxes," I say with flourish, breaking the silence, as we cross the small lobby. "Yours is next to mine."

He smiles politely and gets the door. We're blasted by cold air. I try to pull my collar up around my neck, but my hands are full.

"Need some help?" he offers.

I give him Ginger's leash and my thermos so I can bundle deeper into my coat. "The diner's to the right," I tell him. "I'm going that way too."

He gives me back the coffee but takes Ginger down the sidewalk as if she were his own.

Despite the cold, the sun is shining. I get a better look at him. He has a five o'clock, butter-blond shadow at seven o'clock in the morning. It's a shade lighter than his coppery lips and shows off his high cheekbones. His is the kind of face you'd see in a movie. One I might've gone to as a teenager just because he was on the poster.

"Shit," he states.

Because I'm paying attention to him and not where I'm going, it takes me a moment to understand. Literally—*shit*. I hop sideways just in time, narrowly avoiding a pile of dog poop. "Ugh."

He grins. "Mondays."

"Lazy assholes is more like it."

"Spoken like a true city girl." He smiles bigger. "Have you lived in the building long?"

"Four years yesterday." We stop so Ginger can pee on her usual tree. "But I went to NYU. I've lived on the east side for over ten years."

"So you hate it here."

I laugh, and God, does it feel good. My dry cheeks crack like they're made of concrete and I've hit them with a hammer. We continue walking, Ginger looking back at us every few seconds, as if we might disappear on her. My mood has lifted. Sometimes, in this city, talking to strangers is a burden. They want something—directions, money, time. I'm glad I stopped for my new neighbor, though. He's chasing off the dark clouds that've been hanging around lately.

But then, he stops abruptly and groans. I get the sudden, intense feeling this walk is over. "I left my wallet in the apartment. Think they'll let me open a tab?"

"Not a chance." We're a few feet from the crosswalk, and I nod across the street. "There's the diner."

"Okay." He wipes his nose on his sleeve. Mine is also running a little despite the fact that the walk has warmed me up. I don't believe he isn't the slightest bit cold. "I better run back. I'm about to eat my hand."

5

I don't have to think twice. He's helped me out just by making me feel better, and I want to return the favor. "I'll spot you," I say, digging in my pocket for cash. I keep forty bucks in my coat in case of dog-walking emergencies. Since I can hear his stomach grumbling from here, I give him both twenties. "Get the hash browns. Trust me."

He takes the money. "You're an angel. I'll pay you back."

"No problem." I nod at Ginger, who pants, giving us her signature Golden-Retriever smile. "Consider it a thanks for your services."

"For a ten-minute walk? Expensive pooch." He hands me back the leash, then adds, "Unless you want to join me? My treat," he teases.

I'm surprised by his invitation but even more so that I'm disappointed to turn it down. Hash browns and good company sound like a great way to spend the morning. "I should get to work," I say with some reluctance. "Not everyone can make rent walking dogs."

"Good point." He grins. The walk signal begins to count down. Last chance to change my mind and play hooky from work. He holds up the money. "Thanks again."

He jogs across the street toward the restaurant. I wonder what his name is. And why he isn't also on his way to work on a Monday morning.

Except for him, the view from this corner is familiar. I've stood here more times than I can count.

Ginger pulls on her leash. She knows this is where we turn back for the apartment. The sun is still out, but clouds edge the city. Alone again, any humor in my morning dissipates. My mood creeps back down to where it was earlier—where it's been for months.

TWO

After work, I shower longer than necessary. Some days, working PR in New York City leaves a layer of grime on my skin. And the hot water just feels good. I could stand here all night. I don't really have anything else to do. It's already been dark an hour, and the apartment is cold. Eventually, I reach one arm beyond the shower curtain and take a handful of terrycloth. Getting out is like pulling off a Band-Aid, same as always this time of year. In studied form, I turn off the faucet and have a towel around myself the next second.

I'm at the bathroom counter, getting out my blow dryer when Ginger barks. She doesn't stop, so I head to the door, tying the sash of my worth-every-penny cashmere robe. It takes me a moment to figure out I'm looking at my new neighbor through the peephole. The hallway seems to shine a spotlight right on him.

"Is this a bad time?" he asks when I open the door.

I'm not much warmer, and my hair is wet. My nipples whisper against the inside of my robe like a secret. "For what?"

"So, apparently you have curly hair," he says, ignoring my question, letting his eyes wander over me. "It's like I don't even know you."

I hesitate, and then let my smile happen. I don't know what I've done to deserve his teasing, but I think I like it. "I wear it straight most of the time."

"Aha. A rare glimpse of the elegant 6B in her natural form," he says. "Lucky me."

I don't know whether to laugh or blush. For a charged moment, it's as if we're both going to speak, but neither of us does.

"Sorry," he says first. "I shouldn't have said that. I read too much *National Geographic*."

I wave a hand. "No—it was funny."

"I'm just trying to say I like it curly—I mean, it was nice earlier too, when you had it straight. So, just in general, it's . . . nice." He scratches his jaw. "You're probably wondering why I'm here." He produces two twenty-dollar bills from his pocket. "You saved me this morning."

I thank him and stick the money in my robe. "How was it?"

"Words can't describe."

"What'd you have?"

"All the breakfast," he says.

"Did you get the hash browns like I said?"

He raises his eyebrows. "I'm not exaggerating. I ordered every breakfast item they had."

I gape at him. "Seriously?"

"Toast, oatmeal, fruit, orange juice . . ." He pats his stomach. "And while it was mostly good, I can now definitively say, hash browns are the best thing on the menu. Dipped in egg yolk—"

I bounce on the balls of my feet. "I do the same thing."

"You're a sunny-side-up girl?" he asks.

I nod. "If I wanted my eggs scrambled, I'd go to a tanning booth."

He has the decency to laugh at my obscure joke before his expression turns serious. "Don't even get me started on over easy."

"Never trust anyone who orders their eggs over easy."

This time, we both laugh. Ginger's tags clink as she sticks her nose between us. Water drips from my hair. "Do you want to come in? I'm about to start dinner."

It's not entirely true. Monday nights, I usually raid the freezer or heat up leftovers from the weekend. Cooking for myself feels decadent, but tonight, I'm not cooking for myself. My neighbor is here.

He glances down the hallway, toward his apartment, and sticks his hands in his pockets. "I, ah . . . I really shouldn't," he says. "I still have a lot of unpacking to do."

"Oh. All right." I try not to let the sting of his rejection show on my face. I barely know him. Surely, he has friends of his own to eat dinner with. I pull Ginger out of the doorway by her collar. "Okay, then. Thanks for paying me back so fast."

He smiles. "Sure."

I shut the door and return to the bathroom, but I only dry my hair until it's no longer dripping. It's been a while since I wore it curly. It'll be a nice change. I mentally list what's saved on the DVR. Even though I watch plenty of TV, there's a lot to choose from. I should probably find a hobby of my own, but sometimes, nothing beats staying in. Especially on a cold Monday night.

Once I'm in my sweats, I pour myself a glass of red wine and open the fridge. I could make something nutritious, but now all I can think of is breakfast food. Cinnamon Toast Crunch. Sunny-side-up eggs. Hash browns. I wonder gleefully about the look on my favorite waitress's face when the man across the hall ordered everything on the menu.

Ginger perks up from where she's lying in the middle of the kitchen floor. A second later, there's another knock at the door. She barks once and leaves the room.

I react the same way. Straighten up. Get wary. I don't know the neighbors very well. At thirty-one, everyone on this floor is nearly twice my age anyway. We say hello, and that's it. It's intentional.

Except for this man, who's on my doorstep for the second time in twenty minutes. It's possible I've said more words to him than anyone else in the building. I don't open up all the way since I'm not wearing a bra. Yes, I decide—he *is* a hunk. It's a good word to describe him. "Hello again, 6A."

"So," he says, "I thought it over. I haven't unpacked the kitchen yet. It's not really my domain. Plus, my heater is still blowing like I'm made of plastic and it wants to melt me." He billows his t-shirt, the same one from earlier. He looks ready for summer.

"Mine's off," I warn. "It's cold in here."

He groans. "You might as well be talking dirty to me."

I arch an eyebrow and invite him in. "I'm making stir-fry." I hadn't planned on it, but there are vegetables in the fridge and leftover Thai ginger chicken from last night. "Are you a vegetarian?"

"Babe, no."

I suppress a smile at his deadpan response. I wouldn't have believed him if he'd said yes. "I didn't think so."

"Good old-fashioned carnivore here. Hunting, gathering, bring it back to the cave—" He puts one foot in the apartment before he enters, as if the floor is water and he's testing the temperature.

"I get the idea." Ginger's happy to have him here, but she'd wag her tail for an axe murderer. I close the door behind him.

"Nice place," he says when we're out of the entryway. "Like mine but livable."

"Thanks." I point to the couch. "Make yourself comfortable. I'll be right back." I go into the bedroom, shut the door, and throw on a bra under my sweatshirt.

When I come out, he's flipping through Vogue magazine, his long legs spread out in front of him. He wrinkles his forehead. "Some of these outfits . . ."

"I work in fashion and beauty PR," I explain. "My clients are on the beauty side—make up, skin cream, that kind of thing—but I have to keep up with the trends."

He shuts the magazine and replaces it under the coffee table. "I won't pretend to understand it."

I walk into the kitchen, and he follows. Some of the vegetables in the fridge look questionable. I take out a bag of wilting spinach. He won't know the difference. "Can I get you some Pinot Noir?"

"Not much of a wine drinker," he says from behind me. "I wouldn't turn down one of those, though." He points to a six-pack of Sorachi Ace on the shelf.

I hesitate a second. They don't belong to me, but I don't think it matters. I pull one out and hand it to him. "Opener's in the drawer left of the sink."

"Thanks. Never had this kind. Is it good?"

"I wouldn't know. I don't drink a lot of beer." I line up the vegetables and start chopping.

It's quiet for a few seconds, except for his gulp-gulping as he drinks and the tap-tap of my knife on the cutting board.

"How is it?" I ask.

"Just what I need. My apartment is depressingly alcohol-free at the moment." He pulls out a chair, but seems to change his mind and stays standing. "I need to make a trip to the grocery store."

"It's from Brooklyn Brewery. The beer." I slide mushrooms from the board into a wok. "What brings you to Gramercy Park anyway?"

He coughs. "Work."

I don't ask what he does. I still don't even know his name. "Are you new to the city?"

"Actually, I went to NYU, just like you."

I look up from the bell pepper I'm about to julienne. "You did? When?"

He shakes his head. "Don't make me answer that," he says, but he does anyway. "I graduated ten years ago."

"I'm almost there too." I return to the vegetables. "Then what?"

"Then I did some things. Moved to the 'burbs. Now I'm back."

15

"Most people go to the suburbs and stay."

"I'm aware." I sense a hint of bitterness, and then it's gone. "I'm one of those rare birds who's happy to be back in the chaos."

"Well, you picked a good neighborhood. I never want to live anywhere else." I put the vegetables in the wok and get the chicken ready. It might not be enough food for him. One of the only things I really know about this man is that he has a large enough appetite to work his way through an entire meal group. You might guess it by his height and muscular physique, but there doesn't seem to be an ounce of fat on him.

"So, how do you even order everything on a menu?" I ask, pushing things around the pan with a spatula. I think I would've laughed my ass off to see it with my own eyes. "Do you start at the top and have the waitress write each thing down? Or does she just hand the cook a menu?"

When he doesn't respond, I turn around. He's wandered over to the desk in the corner. There's nothing special about it—it holds the typical office items. Neon Post-It notes, a mug of pens, a pile of mail. He isn't looking at any of that, though.

He picks up a framed photo of my husband and me on our wedding day. Nathan, tall and broad in his tuxedo, gazes down at me while I smile at the camera. Our dark hair and eyes complement each other and contrast my wedding gown.

"Let me guess—your twin sister?" he asks.

I glance at him. His green eyes, sweet and warm up until now, are narrowed on me. I've known him less than a day, but I can read the shift in his mood. Because I'm married? He shouldn't be disappointed, but judging by his closed expression, I think he might be. If so, I'm not wrong that there's been some strange electric charge between us today. And I wonder if I should've invited him in.

My laugh is forced, uncomfortable. "No. That's me."

"You didn't mention—" He looks back at the frame. "Divorced?"

"No." I hold up my left hand and wiggle my fingers. "I'm wearing a ring."

He looks. "You weren't earlier."

"This morning? I had gloves on. Or you mean after my shower?"

He clears his throat and gently returns the photo to its spot. "Where is he?"

I focus back on our dinner. "Not sure."

I haven't checked my phone since before my shower. I forgot. Most likely, there's a text waiting. I don't know why Nathan continues to let me know where he is when he goes out, though. That small communication will probably shut down soon.

"Either out with his friends or at a homeless shelter," I guess. Realizing how that sounds, I quickly add, "Serving food, I mean."

"Of course he is," he mutters. He comes back to my side of the kitchen. "Is it court mandated?"

I smile, even though I'm not sure if he's joking. "No. He volunteers once or twice a month." It's an automatic response, but come to think of it, it's no longer accurate. Lately, he's been there every week.

Nate does good work as a grant writer for the Family-kind Association, a youth-oriented nonprofit with homeless shelters and soup kitchens around the city. Earlier this year, he turned down a promotion to Communications Director a few days after we found out about his dad's lung cancer. Me, I sold out the first chance I got. I was offered a promotion months ago, and I accepted on the spot. I never had money growing up, and I want to help myself. Nathan never had money, and he wants to help others.

My neighbor takes a swig of his beer—Nathan's beer, actually. My husband brought it home from Brooklyn after a tour of the brewery this weekend. It occurs to me Nathan might not want this man in his kitchen drinking his beer. I brush the thought away. Unlike me, Nathan enjoys being social. If I let him, we'd have company over more often.

"Does he normally go out on Monday nights?"

"Mondays and Wednesdays he goes bowling with friends—sometimes he'll go by the shelter first."

"And you stay here by yourself?"

"Why not? I enjoy the alone time. I'll read a book or whatever." I don't mention that *whatever* normally means watching Project Runway or binging on Netflix shows. For some reason, I don't want him to think I'm a couch potato.

"This happens two nights every week?" he asks.

"Yes. And sometimes weekends."

"Weekends?" A pause. "What do you mean?"

I shrug. "Like, some Sundays, he plays pick-up basketball."

His silence is telling. It encroaches on my good mood like fog. We never really agreed to weekends, Nathan and I. A year or so ago, I read somewhere separate hobbies are good for a relationship, and Nathan and I were always glued at the hip. Nathan didn't like the idea of spending even one evening apart. Which is why I catch myself wondering when his absence spread into the weekend and became a regular thing.

"And that works?" he interrupts my thoughts. "For your marriage?"

I pull two plates from a cupboard. "Yes, I suppose it does."

"Really?" He sounds unconvinced. "You prefer to spend time away from each other . . .?"

I set the dishes on the counter and pause. "When you put it that way, no."

"How else would you put it?"

"We have our own lives." And those separate lives are bleeding into places they shouldn't. Like the bedroom. My husband hasn't touched me in two months, and he hasn't given me a reason why. When I ask, he shuts down, and I'm afraid pushing him will make it worse. But how can he stop wanting me all of a sudden, practically overnight? At first, I'd convinced myself it was stress. Unlike me or most people I know, Nathan gets emotionally attached to his work. I never thought it would last this long. It's hard not to take it personally, two months without fucking.

"What did you do this weekend?"

"Yesterday, Nathan went beer tasting with friends. I went to a movie with my brother and his daughter. Nathan—that's my husband. He hates matinees. He'd rather be outside."

"And you hate breweries?"

"No."

"You hate his friends?"

"No." I dump stir-fry from the pan onto the plates. Ginger hears the scrape of the spatula and comes in to lie under the kitchen table. "Couples don't need to spend every minute together. We can have our own lives."

He holds out his hands, and I pass him our meals. He sets the dishes down, opens the takeout menu drawer, and closes it. He finds the silverware in the next one.

"You don't need to—"

"Will he mind that I'm here?" he asks.

I open my mouth to respond. When it comes to other men, Nate usually just teases me. I give it right back to him. Plenty of women have shown interest in him, some even in front of my face. I've never had to worry, though. "He's not really the jealous type. I don't think."

"You don't think?" he asks. "Don't you know?"

"Not really. I don't give him reason to be." We look at each other a moment. My face warms. I don't want anyone other than my husband. Nathan knows that. And I know he only wants me, even if he hasn't shown it lately.

"All right," he says. "If he doesn't mind, then I'll stay."

I'm being silly. It means nothing that he's here. Nathan would love to come home and meet a new neighbor our age. He'd probably invite him out. I wave him off. "Yes, of course you will. I insist."

Somehow, he's already set the table with placemats, silverware, and napkins. I'm not used to having the table set for me. I'm not sure I even like it. Nathan loves to come in and start eating right away. He can never get enough of anything I make him.

I refill my wine. My shoulders are loose. "Would you like another beer?"

"Please."

I pass him a bottle, then top off each dish with cilantro and lemon juice.

Once he's opened his second beer, he takes a seat. My seat.

I laugh, and he pinches his eyebrows together. "What?"

"That's where I sit," I tease. "You claim to know me so well."

His mood visibly lightens. He smiles and stands, looking sheepish. "I knew that. I was just trying to shake things up." He gestures behind me. "Aren't you

21

tired of looking into kitchen night after night? Why not give the living room a try?"

The Pinot makes me giggly. "I don't know . . ."

"Come on." He sits back down in my seat, newly confident in his decision. "You need a change of scenery."

"Do I?" I take Nathan's chair. It's strange to be in a different spot, looking at someone else. "It's like Opposite World."

"I like it," he says, peering at me. "Personally, I could get used to the view."

I look down at my food. Is he flirting? I can't tell. I don't trust my judgment. It's been a long time since I flirted with anyone other than Nathan, and I know him so well, it's easy to get him worked up. Or, it was. Until recently, I barely had to try.

"I'm talking about the kitchen, of course," he adds, his mouth quirking into a smile. "It's a lovely room."

I half roll my eyes. Now, I hear it in his tone. He's definitely being playful. "Are we going to eat sometime tonight?"

"After you," he invites. He waits for me to take the first bite. Judging by the way he digs in, I don't have to ask if he likes it. "Oh," he says, "and *breakfast*."

I stop. "Sorry?"

"That's how I ordered this morning. I pointed to the word on the menu and said, 'I'll take breakfast.'"

"Just . . . breakfast? And she knew what you meant?"

"I must've looked hungry." He eats another forkful. "She knew."

I laugh with my mouth closed. For some reason, that's funny to me. "So, if I'd come along, then what? 'We'll take two breakfasts?'"

He shrugs. "Come with me next time, and we'll see."

"All right," I agree. I don't mean it, but it's fun to think about.

He glances around the kitchen, chewing. "You do keep it cold in here. Not that I'm complaining."

"We don't turn on the heater until November twenty-first."

He arches an eyebrow. "That's specific. Why not the twentieth? Or the twenty-second?"

"It's kind of a tradition."

"Strange tradition."

"Our friends think so too." I take a bite. The chicken is dry. I wonder if he notices, but I try not to look disappointed. "It's something only Nate and I can appreciate. We spent our first three weeks here without heat."

"Are you kidding?"

I smile down at my plate, shaking my head. "We slept on a mattress on the floor until our bed arrived."

Our first night in the apartment, we'd made love on the wood floor, then gone downstairs for food. On the same corner I stood on this morning, Nate had freed some curls from my knit cap and touched his lips all over my face. We'd walked across the street and eaten sunny-side-up eggs at one in the morning, bundled into one side of a booth at the diner.

I swallow my food, chicken sticking in my throat. That seems like a lifetime ago now. Nathan's been cold lately. Not toward others—just me. I'm still trying to figure it out. I don't come from an affectionate family. Everything I know about love and true intimacy, I learned from Nate. It's jarring to watch him take that away a little more each day. He's told me never to give him space. He always said that was what came between his parents. I think he wants his space now.

"What took so long?"

I look up again, wondering if it's pity I see in his eyes as he watches me. I sit up straighter. "You mean why did we sleep on the ground? The furniture store—"

"No, I mean what took so long to get the heat fixed? I won't last until next month with the heater blasting like it is. I have to stop what I'm doing every twenty minutes to stand by an open window."

I welcome the shift in subject, however small. I'd rather get wrapped up in his problems than my own. "What do you think's wrong with it?"

"I don't know. I'd give it a look, but I don't have my tools."

"Where are they?"

"Greenwich."

"Oh." I wait for him to explain. Instead, he takes a massive bite. Recalling our earlier conversation about the suburbs, I ask, "Connecticut?"

He nods. After he swallows, he says, "I left the tools behind in case I have to fix anything up before the deal closes."

"You're selling your house there?"

"It's in escrow."

He isn't exactly volunteering information, but I'm curious. It is unusual to move to the suburbs on your own for your twenties and return out of the blue. "Why are you moving back?"

"I miss it. Let me tell you, it's a tough life here in the city, but at least it's alive, not like Connecticut. Four years I went back and forth between Wall Street and Greenwich. It's a grind."

"You work on Wall Street?" I set my fork down. Men in finance don't spend their Monday mornings in t-shirts and shorts, and they don't spend them in diners. I'm fairly certain they have more important things to do. "So you moved to be closer to work?"

"No. I quit my job."

I tilt my head. If I was intrigued before, now I'm rapt. "You quit? Just like that?"

He sits back in the chair and wipes his mouth with a napkin. "Pretty much."

"I thought you said you moved back to the city for work."

"I did, but not for that job," he says quickly, confidently. "I'm here to make some career changes.

Did you know commuting the way I was costs weeks of your life *each year*?"

I raise my eyebrows at him. His expression is bright. "No. I didn't."

He nods. "Four hundred and eighty hours a year. That's almost three weeks. Time is our most precious resource, don't you think? What can you do in three weeks?"

I take a sip of my wine. I understand time best in segments. Eighteen years under my parents' roof in New Jersey. Four years undergrad at NYU. Eight years bullshitting in marketing and PR. Seven years with Nate, five of them legally bound to him. Two months since he's begun to pull away. Two months I've been utterly confused. Twelve hours I've known this man sitting across from me.

"But you can relax on the subway and read the paper while you commute," I point out. "Or if you're driving, listen to NPR. Maybe an audiobook."

"It wasn't a rhetorical question," he says. "What have you done these last three weeks?"

It's embarrassing how hard I have to think. I can feel the lines deepening in my forehead, leaving their mark. Another way to measure time: wrinkles. "I secured one of my clients a significant feature in *New York Magazine*. I finished one of the books in the *Game of Thrones* series." Or watched a season on HBO. Whatever. "I took my niece trick or treating."

"What else?"

"That's all I can think of."

"There must be more. They don't have to be big things."

I roll a carrot over on the plate. I haven't done anything worth mentioning the last three weeks. Spending Halloween with Andrew and Bell made me happy. Except that usually when I'm around Bell, Nathan is there. He adores and spoils her. He wants to see Bell more than we already do. Without him, what became painfully clear was his absence. And how I've failed Nathan because of what I haven't given him. May never be able to give him.

"What's on your mind?" he asks. "You look sad."

I glance up at him. His voice is soft, but he doesn't sweeten his words. Do I look sad, or does he sense it in me? Even if I tried, I couldn't explain the tornado of emotions working its way through me. I don't even really know what they are. Inadequacy? Hopelessness? This is what happens when I go where I shouldn't. For a second, I wish Nathan were across the table. He knows our story. Except that he doesn't—not everything. And the moment passes, because if he were here, I still wouldn't tell him there's a piece of the puzzle he doesn't know about.

Again, I try to think of something worth mentioning, and again, I come up short. "It is sad," I say, "how much time we waste."

"I didn't ask how you wasted time. What made you happy these last few weeks?"

"Hanging out with my brother and his daughter. He's single, so he doesn't get a lot of help." Ginger rolls onto her side at my feet. "Ginge and I have had more quality time together lately. Sometimes, it's like she's the only one who gets me."

"Why does anyone own a dog?" he asks. "For that reason, I think."

"Maybe." His plate is empty. "There's a little more in the wok," I say. "Why don't you take the leftovers?"

"What about your husband?"

"He'll eat at the bowling alley—God knows what kind of junk they serve—and that's one less meal for you at the diner."

"Thanks," he says. "It's nice to have a friendly neighbor."

"Sure, just not *too* friendly," I joke and immediately wish I hadn't. It wasn't funny, and if anything, it might be misconstrued. Isn't that why I said it, though? I've had too much wine.

He laughs, though, and picks up his plate. I turn away so he won't see that my face is red. Partly from the alcohol, but mostly from that comment. I stand up and get the leftovers into a Tupperware container.

He's standing at the sink with the faucet on. "Don't even think about it," I tell him.

"The dishes are the least I can do."

"Absolutely not." Nate doesn't do the dishes. It's our routine, and I like it that way. The kitchen is where I get to take care of him. Everywhere else,

Nathan puts me first. Cooking is one thing I don't think he'll ever ask me to stop doing for him, no matter how upset he is. "Seriously. I'm one of those rare birds who enjoys doing the dishes."

"Well, then." He turns off the water and walks over. He stops right in front of me. I have to tilt my head back a little. "Aren't we just a couple of rare birds?"

We haven't been this close yet in here. I still sense the playfulness between us, but I think my bad joke has tipped it into new territory. I'm painfully unable to think of the right response. I like our easy nature. I don't want to send the wrong message. "I guess so."

"You left your hair curly."

"You . . ." The wine has made the inside of my mouth tacky. I run my tongue along the roof. I could drink another glass or two. It's getting a little late for company, though. "You don't like it straight?"

"I like it both ways. I just find it interesting. Have you always worn it straight?"

"More as I get older. It's no different than wearing makeup or heels. Most women color their hair. I just straighten it."

"I'm not accusing you of anything."

"Good," I say. "Because that would be weird. I don't even know your name."

"Do you want to?"

"No." I'm surprised by my response, quick and cold. That simple *no* is a confession. Knowing your

29

JESSICA HAWKINS

neighbor's name is a pillar of our culture. To deny it
means more than to accept it. I should want his name,
and I do. I want to know him better. From the lifted
corner of his mouth, he knows it too.

We stand in silence for a moment. The parts of
me closest to him get warmer. His body must run hot,
like my husband's. A noise in the hallway makes me
move away. I listen for Nate's key in the door, even
though he wouldn't be home yet. I wish he would
come home now, but Ginger doesn't bolt for the
entryway.

"It's Finn," he says, a hint of beer on his breath.
"Finn Cohen."

"Okay."

"What's yours?"

"Sadie."

"Sadie," he repeats.

"Finn." I hold out the Tupperware. "Here."

He accepts it and walks a few steps back.
"Thanks. See you around . . . *Sadie.*"

My heart beats too hard to ignore. He stirs
something in me, something I've been forced to bury
for months. I don't like it. I don't like the fact that if
it weren't for Nathan, I'd invite Finn for another
drink. Let the lines blur, the conversation get intimate.
I'll never know where it would go from there.

I lock the door behind him.

THREE

Nathan makes no secret of his late-night arrival home from bowling. The front door slams. The bedroom lights come on. At first, I think I'm dreaming. I sit up and rub my eyes to see the clock. The red digital numbers sear my eyeballs—it's after two in the morning. "Nate?"

He fills the doorway, standing there as if he forgot what he came in the room for. "Yeah?"

"You woke me," I say.

"Sorry."

He doesn't look or sound sorry. His tie is balled in his fist, the collar of his button-down open. He's been wearing his hair in a smooth wave lately, like a dark chocolate truffle. Different. I like it. It's almost survived whatever he's been up to, except that a few stiff pieces sag over his forehead.

My husband is dark, with olive skin and brown-black hair that matches his eyes. But I don't think of him that way. To me, he's idyllic and warmhearted. That's his personality. Tonight, though, there is a darkness about him.

"Where've you been?" I ask.

"Same place as every other Monday night."

Still gauging his mood, I hide my disdain for his snark. "Yes, I know. I meant after."

"No after. Just came straight home."

"You got this wasted at a bowling alley?"

He rubs the bridge of his nose. "I've tried telling you, it isn't just a place you go roll a ball. It's—" He sighs. "Never mind. I'm not *wasted*. We had drinks. Is that okay with you?"

"It's fine. When have I ever said you can't go out drinking?" I glance at the clock. "I mean, it *is* late for a Monday night, but . . ."

He throws his arms up in frustration and goes to our walk-in closet. His tie and suit jacket end up on the floor before he undoes his belt and begins to undress. Nathan has always had a nice, solid ass. The first time I watched him walk away, my friend Jill called me out for staring. That was before he worked out consistently. Now, he's in the gym four days a week, and I'm definitely not the only woman enjoying the view.

"Nathan . . ." Considering our up until now healthy sex life, I still have a hard time accepting the fact that we've slept side by side for this long without touching each other. "Come to bed."

"I am," he says over his shoulder.

"I mean now. Like . . . *right now.*" I take my bottom lip between my teeth. Our high-thread-count sheets are suddenly silkier. The hour is no longer of any importance to me. Two months is a strange amount of time to go without sex. After a week passed, I started to go a day or two without even thinking of it. But sometimes, out of nowhere, my need will burn me up from the inside out. Two months isn't long enough that I've forgotten how good it is with him.

Nathan keeps his back to me, piling his clothes at his feet. "I'll take care of this in the morning."

Even drunk, Nate is worried about making a mess. I've never had to beg him to put his socks in the hamper or pick up the dry cleaning like some of my friends do with their husbands. He's tidier than anyone I know. "I don't care," I say. "You have plenty of suits. Come to bed."

"I said I will," he says shortly.

We both go quiet. Nathan's head is over his shoulder, but his eyes are on the floor. I slouch back against the bed. It doesn't concern me that Nate goes drinking with friends. I encourage it. He's social. I'm not as much. When he's happy, I'm happy. Tonight, though, there was no text or phone call like I'd assumed there'd be. Nathan and I used to be in continuous touch—virtually and physically. He'd text me just to say hi or tell me something about his day. He'd take my elbow when we crossed the street and leave me love notes in unexpected places. He got hungry for me at unexpected times. We were always in touch.

To go from one extreme to another is jarring. Before now, when Nathan went out with his friends, it was with reluctance. He didn't want me to be lonely. He wanted me with him, but when I'm there, he goes out of his way to make sure I'm having a good time. None of his friends do that with their wives, and that's part of why I stay home two nights a week. He should have fun with them, not worry about me.

When it becomes clear Nathan isn't going to apologize for his tone, I slip back under the covers and pull my pillow under my head. "Excuse *me* for wanting my husband to fuck me."

He says something under his breath. My temperature rises as I try to guess his comeback. I think it's "*give me a break*." Uncalled for and unoriginal. Neither of us is good at fighting. We don't do it often. I should be better considering my parents fought on a weekly basis when I was a kid and still do. My dad started drinking when I was a kid, and his unhappiness soon spread through the family. My mom picked up the addiction next. She was a shy drunk. During a fight, she'd run into their bedroom. It was the scrape-click of the door's deadbolt that would send my dad over the edge. When my brother was older, my dad picked fights with him. Andrew would barge into my room and lock the door. Although Dad never came after me, Andrew'd find me under the bed or in my closet. Coloring when I was younger. Playing music or reading magazines when I was older. Escaping. He'd kiss me on the forehead before climbing out my window and speeding off on his motorcycle. Like my mom, I hid until it blew over, which it always did.

I turn to my side, away from Nate, and take a meditative breath. I don't want to go there with him. He's sensitive, and I'll probably say something I don't mean. "Turn out the lights, please," I tell him. "And don't touch me tonight. Or any night until I say you can."

I expect a retort, maybe some more muttered, passive-aggressive attitude. It doesn't come. The floor creaks. Nathan turns out the light but doesn't get into bed. Seconds later, I hear a burst of voices in the next room before it gradually lowers to a soft hum. TV glares flashes into the bedroom. My side of the mattress sags.

"You're like the goddamn princess and the pea," Nathan told me once over breakfast. We'd been dating a month or two and had slept in the same bed a handful of times. "I had to hug you all night just to keep you still."

I blushed, smiling. "How do you know I wasn't faking so you'd cuddle?"

"Because you already know I don't need any excuse to cuddle with you . . . Princess."

"Princess?" I asked, surprised. He'd never called me that before. "Says who? I'm no princess."

He grinned. "Then I guess that makes you a pea."

Six months later, when he affectionately referred to me as 'pea' for the third time, I stopped him. "I don't like that nickname."

"Why not?" he asked, serious. "You don't want to be a pea?"

"A shriveled green ball that people pretend to like but actually hate?" I stuck out my bottom lip.

He laughed and laughed. "Yeah. That's exactly it. That's you."

Every few months, after I thought he'd mercifully forgotten about it, he'd call me pea out of nowhere. "More wine, Pea?" he'd shout in a crowded restaurant, or, another time, when we were alone, "My dear Pea, I took out the trash so you won't have to."

Tonight, I stare at the wall, unable to sleep. My problems are little green veggies under the mattress. I never could get him to shake that dumb nickname, but now I can't remember the last time he used it. It's just one more addition to a growing list of things I took for granted.

I get out of bed. Now, I'm not just hot for him, but nostalgic too. It's a lonely combination. I stand in the bedroom doorway. It's dark, except for the flash of the TV, and I know he can see me from where he lies on the couch in his boxer briefs. There are tools I haven't used on him yet, and I think it might be time to get them out. When he looks over, I strip off my dowdy pajama top, then slowly peel my panties off.

"Nathan," I try again. "Come to bed. You know what I want."

He stares. If he doesn't answer, I might have to beg. I'm not above it. Nathan's never made me doubt his attraction to me until now, and two months isn't enough to extinguish my confidence.

After a moment, he responds, his voice raspy. "What do you want?"

"You know," I repeat. I run a hand between my breasts, down my stomach. As I reach my mound, ready to do whatever it takes, he rises fluidly from the couch.

Briefly, I think of Finn, who sat there not hours ago. His beer-breath, later, as he told me his name.

I forget all about him when Nathan stalks toward me.

Suddenly, I'm nervous—to have sex with my own husband. He stops in front of me. The only sound is our breathing. I can't wait any longer. I rise onto the balls of my feet and press my lips to his. I wait there. Finally, he slides his hands in my hair and kisses me back. I hug his neck. And he thaws—right there in my arms. This is the Nathan I know, the one who adores me no matter what's going on his head.

On an inhale, he picks me up by my middle and walks me backward toward the bed. "Christ, baby," he says between frenzied kisses. "You taste so—"

I moan, "*Nathan.*"

He stops. Without warning, he releases me like my skin's on fire.

I stumble to catch my balance. "What's wrong?" I ask breathlessly.

I can see his expression darkening. I don't want to lose him, but he looks at me as if he doesn't know me. The silence grows uncomfortable. He engulfs my shoulders with his large hands and slowly turns me around. "Are you sure?"

I keep my gaze forward and swallow dryly. "Sure . . . about what?"

He steps forward, pulling my back to his front. "You sure you're ready?" he asks hoarsely into my ear. His rigid length jabs my lower back. There's no question *he's* ready. "Because two months is a long time to stay away from something I want. I'm going a little crazy."

I nod breathlessly. "I'm ready. You don't have to hold back."

"All right. I won't." He pushes me. It catches me off guard, and I fall forward onto the bed. I grip the comforter. He's so hot for me, I barely recognize him. Even his voice is different. And I fucking love it. I'm right where I want to be, at Nathan's mercy. Months' worth of desire courses through me. I'm almost trembling with anticipation. He feels me between the legs. I'm wet. He's hard. We don't need foreplay. "Fuck me," I demand.

He removes his hand, and his cock takes its place. The blunt tip presses against me. He folds over my back, sliding in slowly. I turn my head to kiss him just as he thrusts into me.

I cry out, dropping my forehead to the mattress. "Yes," I groan as he drives into me.

"Yes?" He pulls my hair until I'm looking up at the headboard. He takes me fast, greedy, knocking the bed against the wall. "You like that?"

"Oh, God, Nate—"

He clasps a hand over my mouth and with his hot, whispered *shh*, my skin pebbles. He breathes on the curve between my shoulder and neck. He feels too good. It's been too long. Neither of us will last when he's going at me like an animal. I want it. I want to explode into a million pieces and when it's over, I want him to sweep me up like shards of glass and put me back together.

His grunts come louder in my ear. My own orgasm builds, within reach. He slaps me firmly on the ass. With the unexpected sting, I shudder around him. He's rougher tonight, unbridled from staying away. Nathan can make love to me for hours, but the fact that I can still make him lose control in minutes turns me to jelly.

He tightens his hand in my hair. "You love getting fucked from behind, don't you, you little slut?"

I bite down on my lower lip with a sharp gasp. Nathan's never in his life called me a slut. Out of pure shock, my pussy contracts around him, drinking him deeper.

"*Fuck*," he bites out.

With two more thrusts, and with my face hot as the sun, I come—already—and I come hard. More intensely than I thought possible for so little time.

"Someone likes to be a slut," he murmurs appreciatively from above.

There's no hiding how turned on I am by the new pet name. I'm speechless and gushing on his cock. I could come again. "Uh-huh," I breathe.

He straightens up, takes my hips in his hands and pulls me onto him fast and brutal. Another orgasm closes in on me already. Before I can catch it, he plunges deep and releases into me, filling me with everything he's got.

We stay that way a few seconds. He continues to move in and out of me, slower now, leisurely. He touches my lower back. My eyelids droop. This—the burst of a long-contained climax followed by a lover's touch—is true bliss.

Nathan pulls out of me. I drag myself up the bed as he flops down next to me. We lie there, panting in the darkness. My body's still thrumming. He was raw. Carnal. I've never been his little slut, and after seven years together, a surprise in the bedroom can be a turn-on.

It can also be alarming.

Why did he call me that? Does he want a slut? Should I ask?

I wait a few seconds to see if he'll speak. "Nate . . .?"

He just hums. His breathing slows. I understand—it's late, and he's had a lot to drink. It isn't the best time to bring up anything serious. If it'd been any other night, I would ride this kink wave. I can be his bad girl. But considering he's been different lately, I'm not sure if it's cause for concern.

I get beneath the covers. Maybe the spell is broken, and tonight was a breakthrough, and tomorrow will be different. I tuck into my pillow and release any anxiety with my exhale. Even though nothing has really truly changed, I cling to the hope that tomorrow will be a new start.

FOUR

The next morning, Nathan wakes up before me. I touch my hair, tangled from his fingers in it. I want today to be fresh. A clean slate, as if the last two months never happened. I won't even make him tell me what all this was about, not right away at least. Marriage isn't easy. Everyone goes through rough patches.

I get up and put on my robe. His side of the bed looks undisturbed. I find him in the kitchen, already showered and dressed. When we were younger, it was a struggle to get him in a suit. Now, he wears one during the week, and the girl in me finds him grown-up sexy. "Morning."

His back is to me. He clears his throat. "Hey."

My mug waits on the counter as it does every morning. No matter his mood, Nathan is smart enough not to cut off my caffeine.

I pick a question that will let him lead the conversation. "How do you feel?"

"I drank too much last night." It sounds like an apology—but for what? Snapping at me, or sleeping with me? I hate that I can't tell. For so long, he was an open book.

I lean my shoulder against the doorframe. "Did you have fun?"

"Bowling? Not really." He glances over his shoulder and opens his mouth as if he's going to launch into some story about how dumb his friends act when they're drunk. I've heard it before. Instead, he says, "It was fine."

"Oh. Did you move to the couch last night?"

"No. Why?"

"Your side of the bed is made."

"That's what you get for marrying a neat freak. Almost made it with you in it."

I smile a little. He hands me my coffee and gets milk out of the fridge. As he's shutting the door, he stops and looks back inside. "You drank beer last night?"

I take a sip from my mug. He wouldn't question me if I said yes, but why would I lie? Our neighbor came over for dinner. Our neighbor, whose name I didn't want to know, and who is noticeably, ruggedly handsome, came over to avoid a second trip to the diner in one day.

If our roles were reversed, though, I'm not sure I'd be so understanding. Women love Nathan, his boyish charm and infectious smile. A fool could see why. If he had someone in my apartment while I was gone, I wouldn't like it. Not that he'd turn anyone away. I was being polite, and Nathan would've done the same.

"*And* wine?" Nate asks, picking up the half-empty bottle of Pinot Noir from a shelf inside the door. "Should I be worried?"

"Someone came over," I say.

"Who? Jill? She hates beer."

"No. We have a new neighbor in 6A, finally someone our age." I drink more from my mug. Nathan meets my eyes over the lip. "He hadn't unpacked his kitchen yet, so I invited him in for dinner."

"He?"

"Yes. Is that okay?"

He slowly replaces the wine in its spot. "Of course. It's fine." He shuts the door, and I can practically hear him thinking.

"What?" I prompt, curious. Seeing as I don't really talk about other men much, it isn't often I get to see his reaction when I do.

"You cooked for him?" he asks.

Aha. Nathan and his meals. He eats with love what I make with love, always. Even now, it's one thing we haven't lost. I shuffle a little closer to him, taking advantage of the chance to comfort him. "I felt bad," I say with a shrug. "Also, his radiator something-or-other broke, and he can't shut it off. He doesn't seem to be dealing well with the heat."

"Huh. Playing phone tag with the super?"

"Sounds like it."

He laughs to himself. "Just like when we moved in, only the opposite. Bastard should be thankful he's got heat at all."

"That's what I said." With a tiny bit of hesitation, but still more than I'm used to, I wrap my arms around Nate's middle. It's not the least bit soft—he dedicates a weekly gym session to abdominals, after all—but it's my happy place. I smell his aftershave. There's a new, subtle scent too, though. It must be the styling pomade that appeared on the bathroom counter a few weeks ago. "I was thinking about that too. Thank God I was sleeping next to a human heater. Remember how cold it was?"

"Not really," he says. "I was too happy to notice."

I look up. From this angle, I can clearly see the dark circles under his eyes. The lines around his frown. They make me ache from my core, because I know something is keeping him up at night. Part of it must be his dad's declining health. But there's more too, and it has to do with me.

"Our first real place together," he says. "We were so happy."

"*Are* happy, honey. It's a good memory, but I'm just as happy now as I was then." We may be going through a rough patch, but it isn't enough to erase the last seven years. "Aren't you?"

"This apartment is just—cramped." He flexes his muscles against me. "It would be nice to have more space."

"You think? We'd be hard pressed to find anything bigger for what we're paying."

"In Manhattan, yes."

"Yes," I repeat, "but where else is there?"

"I don't know." He checks his watch. "I have to go. Can you take Ginger out?"

Ginger is already sitting by the front door, ready for her morning walk. Nate started the tradition when she was a puppy. Back then, it was an excuse to smoke a cigarette. He quit years ago, though, worried tobacco could lower sperm count. He and Ginger continued their morning routine.

I sigh. "If this is going to be a habit," I say, since it's the same argument we had yesterday, "I need to know so I can wake up a few minutes earlier."

"And I've walked her almost every morning the last four years without complaint." He tries to pull away, but I hold fast. Argument or not, I'm not ready for the moment to end. "I've only asked you to do it a few times," he says.

"But you love it. You used to joke she was the only woman you'd been on more dates with than me."

He tenses. "Sadie. I have to go."

47

"All right, all right. I just want to stand with you a minute and tell you I love—"

"Sadie—can you—" He pushes my shoulder a little harder than I think he means. I stumble back. He whirls around to brace himself against the sink. "I think I'm going to be sick."

I'm shaken by the shove, but it vanishes when he heaves. I've only seen him throw up once or twice since I've known him. I touch his back. "Honey?"

He takes a couple deep breaths. "Hang on. It's passing."

Once I see it's not serious, I lose my fight against a smile. "So," I tease, "not wasted, huh?"

He shakes his head, his knuckles white.

I run my hand down his spine. "Call in. You must have a ton of sick days saved up. You never use them."

"I'm saving them. In case my dad—you know. He might need me." He pushes off the counter and turns, his hand at his stomach. "I can go over to the neighbor's after work and take a look at the radiator."

Nathan and I used to talk about his dad's cancer more. I haven't asked him how he's dealing, and he hasn't offered. I let the subject change slide. "You'd do that?" I ask. Since we spent those three weeks without heat, Nate has become good with fixing things around the apartment himself.

"Sure."

"That's nice, babe." I hesitate. Even though I think Nathan might like Finn, there's always a possibility a friendly neighbor could intrude on our alone time. "It's not our problem, though."

"It's the neighborly thing to do." He moves to go around me, but I have him cornered.

"I'm sorry about your beer," I say. "Should I swing by Brooklyn Brewery and get another six-pack?" I don't know where the offer comes from. I've never been good with guilt—feeling it, dealing with it. Sometimes it manifests in weird ways.

"Don't be silly. Beers are meant to be drunken." He wrinkles his nose. "Drunk? Drank? Whatever."

I laugh a little.

"I would take leftovers, though. It'll save me a trip downstairs at lunch."

"Oh." I scratch behind my ear. "There weren't any, actually. Sorry."

He just nods once. "No big deal."

"I'll take Ginger out," I say, a consolation.

"Okay."

I make no move to let him by. We're physically closer than we've been in a while outside of our bed, and I want a kiss. It's not unreasonable for a wife to want a kiss from her husband.

"I . . ." He puts a heavy hand on my shoulder and pecks my forehead. "I'll try to be home for dinner."

As dedicated as he is to his job, Nathan almost always leaves at five o'clock. I want to ask what he means by that. Our jobs are equally demanding, but I make a point to cook him dinner each night I know he'll be home.

I step aside. He leaves the room. I want to say more, but I don't know what. Things are a little better, but after last night, we should be more connected.

I go to the entryway, where he's shrugging on his coat. He kisses Ginger on the head, like he just did to me.

There is one thing guaranteed to melt his heart. "Bell would be so mad at me," I say.

He looks up quickly, his eyes big. "Bell? How come?"

Bingo. My coat is hanging by the door. I reach into the pocket and pull out a fun-size Snickers bar from the weekend. "I almost forgot to give you this from her."

He takes it. "Candy? She got it trick-or-treating?"

I nod. "She said it was uncle Nate's favorite. I tried to tell her you love Twix, but—"

"I hate Twix."

I cock my head at him. The hostility in his tone is disarming. "I know that, Nathan. I'm teasing you."

"Oh. Yeah. Thanks." He fixes his tie. "See you tonight."

"You messed it up. Now it's crooked." I go to him.

"It's okay," he says, stepping back. "I'll redo it on the train."

He leaves, and I stand there a few more moments by myself. My heart pulses under skin Nathan didn't touch—the forearm he didn't pull to bring me close. My unkissed mouth.

Ginger whines at the door Nathan just walked through. Every day she wants go with us. Every day she's disappointed.

Later, while I'm tucking in my blouse, I remember Nate's pile of clothes from the night before. I pick it up and separate each piece into an already brimming bag of dry cleaning. His gray, checked Prada tie was my Christmas gift to him years ago, purchased with my first bonus check. He knows what it cost, which is why I'm surprised to find it wrinkled at the bottom of the heap. I uncurl it, sliding the silk through my fingers. There's a smeared red mark near the edge.

My heart stops before I register any real thought. I hold the fabric up to my face and examine it. The stain is small. I could've easily missed it. I rub it with my thumb, but it's already set. *Lipstick?*

A lump forms in my throat. No. My Nathan would never, ever let another woman rub lipstick on his tie. *My* Nathan respects what we have. Respects me. We've shared enough conversations over the years about friends' infidelity to know where the other stands. Urges are natural. Temptation can't be avoided. I don't care if Nathan flirts, even though it isn't in his nature. When we're out together, he doesn't even look at other women. But he's supposed to come to me if it ever gets to the point that he'd act on it. This is the smart, sensible decision we've come to—together.

Ginger's wet nose against my pant leg is a reminder that she needs to go out. I'll be late for work if I dawdle anymore. I shove the tie in the bag, but shove and bury as I do, I don't think I'll be able to put it out of my mind. Even though I know in my core—my Nathan would never cheat on me.

But I haven't seen *my* Nathan in months.

FIVE

As I predicted, the lipstick stain on Nathan's tie sits like a nugget in my brain all day, uncomfortable enough that I can't forget it for very long. As a result, I find myself standing over the laundry bag as soon as I get home from work, trying to decide how to proceed.

Trust isn't really an issue in my marriage. After five years, though, Nate's behavior has become less predictable—practically overnight. He's distant—physically and emotionally. He's made subtle changes in his appearance, styling his hair differently, spending more time at the gym. And, as much as I want to pretend like our marriage is perfect, I may have one flaw so great, I couldn't blame him for withdrawing.

Nathan gives me everything and asks for very little. The one thing he *does* want, though, he hasn't been quiet about. While I once wanted it as badly as he did, the weight of both our disappointment on my shoulders has become too much. After seven months of trying to get pregnant—seven months of heartbreak every time I got my period—I went back on birth control. It was Nathan's suggestion. Watching me go through it was too hard for him. He thinks it's temporary. "We'll try again later," he told me. "There's no reason it has to be now." But the more I think about it, the less I'm able to see myself walk that painful path again. Children might not be in our future because of decisions I made in my past. If I force myself to, I can accept that. Can Nathan, though?

Maybe not. Maybe the last couple months, he's been preparing himself for the possibility that I can't give him what he really wants.

I reach into the laundry bag and pull out his tie. The stain is small—almost nothing. There are two possible outcomes to asking Nathan about it.

One—he's innocent, and I've just broadened the gap between us by making an unfounded accusation. Is this really enough evidence to draw such a drastic conclusion?

Two—Nathan had sex with another woman. The thought knots my stomach, and I have to breathe through the discomfort. It's too unexpected. Too sudden. No husband can go from doting to heartless in so little time.

I'm almost angry. The whole thing is just too stupidly cliché. If Nate were going to cheat, he'd be

54

more creative about it. He'd make at least this small effort to hide it.

I sling the bag over my shoulder. I can't see any benefit from bringing it up. My faith in him is stronger than a tiny blemish. Ginger follows me to the front door, where I leash her and put on my coat. With Ginger and the laundry bag in tow, I head down the hall to elevator.

Just as I step inside, I hear, "Hold it, please."

I catch the doors, stopping them just as they're about to meet. His voice shouldn't be so familiar after a day of living here, but I know it's 6A.

Finn boards the elevator. Ginger greets him with a wagging tail. He ruffles the fur on her head.

"Hi," I say.

"Hello again."

It reminds me of when we met, when he said the same thing. "Keys?" I ask.

He pats his pocket and nods. "Those auto-lock doors will take some getting used to."

"Fight it as you might, you will lock yourself out at some point."

"Good thing I have a cool neighbor." He grins. "What're you two pretty ladies up to?"

I shrug and try not to blush at his sugary words. "Just the usual stuff," I say. "Public defecation, sniffing butts, things like that."

He chuckles. "I hope you're talking about Ginger."

"She has all the fun." I show him the sack over my shoulder. "I got stuck with the errands."

"Dry cleaning?"

"Yep."

"The place by Home Depot?" he asks. "That's where I'm going. I'll walk you."

With a ding, the elevator doors open. "Thanks."

"Did your husband mind about the beer?" he asks as we head outside. "What's his name again?"

"Nathan. And no, not a bit. He was happy to share." Nathan didn't question me, and isn't having a man alone in the apartment worse than a potential lipstick stain? Is it? If so, why *didn't* Nathan care? He seemed more concerned about missing out on the leftovers.

"Sounds like a good guy."

The bulky bag is like a barrier between us. *A good guy.* That's one accurate way to describe my husband. For some reason, I'm tempted to pull out the tie and show Finn. Get a man's opinion. Ask how a cool wife would handle this without making it worse. I don't know why, but Finn also seems like a good guy, and a good guy would be appalled by his friendly neighbor's philandering husband.

"How could anyone cheat on someone like *you?*" he'd respond. "I'd kill to have someone make me a homemade meal each night. Especially if that someone were *you.*"

I'm getting ahead of myself in a million different ways. Why would Finn care if Nate were unfaithful?

Unfaithful. The thought rings ridiculous. Nathan is the gold standard of husbands.

"I've been wondering," Finn says as we cross a street, Ginger trotting alongside me, "if you can recommend a gym within walking distance?"

"We go to New York Sports Club." Nathan got a trainer who tries to get me to sign up whenever I tag along, which isn't often, and much less lately. "It's on Twenty-Third."

"Cool," he says excitedly. "I had a membership there when I was younger. With everything going on, gym time was the first thing I cut out. Need to get back to it."

I look sidelong at him. He hasn't shaven since I last saw him, and he wears scruff well. Emboldened by the fact that I'm carrying Nathan's marked tie, I drop my eyes to where I really want to look. His sculptured shoulders. Biceps that stretch his sweatshirt. His sleeves are pushed up, displaying brawny forearms. Normally, I'd bite my tongue, but now I wonder if Nate bothers to bite his anymore. "Well, it doesn't look like you've missed even a day," I say.

My face warms. I look at the sidewalk. Unless it's my imagination, Ginger shakes her head at me. I can't believe I said that. I've admired other men before, but once I hear what I said to Finn out loud, it doesn't sound like meaningless flirting. And I don't really want to take it back.

"Thank you." Finn rubs his stomach. I can't dream up anything less than a six-pack under his hand. "But I'm normally in better shape."

He's in excellent shape. "Could've fooled me," I say.

"Well, maybe moving has helped."

"Do you need help?" I ask. I have a hard time picturing a man like him decorating. "With the little things, I mean. Making it into a home. I'm good at that kind of stuff."

"Sure. Maybe."

I wonder if I've overstepped some male-female friend boundary. I'm new at this. The only males I socialize with anymore are either my friends' husbands or my husband's friends. None of them rank even close to Finn—or Nathan—in the looks department. Does that mean we shouldn't be friends?

I need something to ease the weird tension, so I choose a safe topic. "So, what kind of job did you have on Wall Street?"

Before he can answer, Ginger bolts after a squirrel and yanks the leash out my hand. "Ginge—"

Finn takes off. Within seconds, he chases her down and gets ahold of her leash. With a hearty laugh, he squats and scratches her behind the ears. She's still on full alert with the squirrel in her sights, but then she sits back and licks his cheek.

"That squirrel owes me," he calls.

"I'm impressed," I say, smiling. "Maybe you're in better shape than you claim."

He gets up and brings her back. "That, or I'm an undercover superhero of the speeding-bullet sort."

"Sounds plausible," I tease. I go to take Ginger's leash, but he keeps it. I readjust the laundry bag and we continue on our way. The sidewalk is littered with leaves in various stages of death. Green, orange, brown. Against the mottled, gray concrete, they're beautiful.

"So," I say. "We were talking about—"

He looks over quickly, as if he'd forgotten I was there. "Yes," he says. "My job. I did investment banking type stuff. It's boring." He scuffs his shoe on the ground. "That part of my life is over. I want to get into something new. Something meaningful."

"Any ideas?" I ask.

"I've always loved photography. That's the dream. I can do basic graphic design for things like websites or logos. I'd need more training, but you get the idea."

"Not really," I say. "I'm not a creative person."

"Everyone's creative, Sadie."

"Not me. I've failed at ceramics, piano, painting—you name it. Even those dance classes where you just mimic the teacher. I look like a fish out of water, no offense to fish."

He crooks the corner of his mouth, and one deep dimple smiles at me. "You said you're good at decorating. And you cook."

"Thanks to Pinterest boards and recipes."

"Always?" he asks. "You follow them exactly?"

"I did in the beginning, but . . ." I shrug. I realize I haven't actually followed a recipe in a while. "I guess you're right. The more I learn, the more experimental I get."

"Well, that's something. I like to cook about as much as I like math. But I still consider them both expressions of creativity."

"Even math?"

"Sure."

We approach a corner and turn together, continuing in the direction of the hardware store and drycleaner. "Do you ever stop and wonder?" he asks. "About your life?"

I look up at him. "That's a bit random."

"It's not, really. Go with me."

"Can you be more specific?"

"Like, do you ask yourself—how did I get here?"

I don't have to think very hard to find my answer. Other people wonder about those things. Even Nathan might ask something like that. Not me. I believe in taking responsibility for yourself.

"Not really," I say. "For instance, my job pays well, but I leave it at the office each night. That's my choice. Nathan doesn't—he wants work to challenge him. Sometimes he brings it home."

"But is it what you envisioned yourself doing?"

"I guess. I was just happy to get my degree. It would've been easy to skip college—my brother did. My parents didn't have the money." Or they might have, if they hadn't gambled it away over my

60

childhood. "But I took control and made it happen for myself."

He furrows his eyebrows. "You don't think there was anything else at play? Luck? Fate?"

"I don't believe in fate," I say, "but, sure, a little luck goes a long way."

He nods slowly. "I like to have a little faith in the universe, personally. It's nice to think there's some outside force looking out for me."

"There isn't, though," I say, and quickly add when he looks surprised, "for me. I wouldn't tell anyone else what to believe."

"And you apply that morose outlook to everything in your life?"

I give in to a small laugh. "I'm just realistic. I mean, when I met Nathan, there was practically an audible click, like popping two batteries into a remote control." I smirk. "Two *sexy* batteries, that is. But the thing is, we had similar backgrounds and interests, so we also made sense together."

"I see." He nods. "So that's that, then?"

"Pretty much. I'm the master of my own fate. If I don't like something about my life, I change it."

"Hmm." He scratches his jaw as he considers this. "Does that make marriage difficult?"

"How so?"

"What if you don't like something about your life together, but he does? What if your views don't align?"

"We don't have that problem," I say. In the back of my head, I know that isn't entirely true. It's impossible to see eye to eye on everything and big life decisions aren't exempt. I continue, pushing that thought back where it belongs. "And before you say I'm lucky, because other people have said that, don't. I married a man whose personality works well with mine. It was a decision like anything else." Because I can imagine Nathan, a true romantic, cringing, I add, "The lucky part was our great chemistry."

"Was?" he asks.

There's the tiniest hint of hope in his voice. I squash it. "*Is*. Our chemistry's still great."

"Well," he says with a light sigh, "sounds perfect."

I smile, even as I glance at the ground. It isn't the first time I've heard that about our relationship, and it always makes me giddy. Since I grew up watching my parents not just fall out of love, but eventually come to hate each other, having the perfect marriage is no small victory.

"Okay, I'll take the bait," I say. "Somehow, I get the feeling this conversation isn't about me. Do you ever wonder how you got here, Finn?"

His offers me a sly grin. "Sometimes," he says. "When I was younger, I wanted to be a *National Geographic* photographer and in my off time, I thought I'd do stuff like weddings and family portraits. For *fun*." He laughs. "I was going to balance the hard edges of nature with tea candles and white lace."

"That's not impossible."

"Trust me, I've done a wedding. It was anything but fun."

"I meant, it's not too late to make a career out of it if you're committed. What do you like taking pictures of?"

Absentmindedly, he wraps Ginger's leash around his wrist. "Anything. Strangers interest me. Landscapes and nature can be good. They can also be pretty boring."

"I think so too. At least, most of the ones I see."

"If I finish moving in, this would be a good week to get out and shoot some stuff on my own," he says, almost to himself. "I had a hard time finding subjects in Connecticut. The wedding I mentioned? The people there either paid a lot to erase their own expressions or they ran from the camera. After a while, I stopped trying so hard."

"You won't have that trouble in the city," I say.

"Nope. Like I said, work is the reason I moved back." He glances over at me, his eyes lingering. "Already, I'm feeling more inspired."

Immediately, I look forward. He's definitely flirting. I slide my hand under my coat and rub my collarbone. "Can I—um, see some of your work?"

"I'd like that." He stops suddenly.

I glance back at him. "What's wrong? You didn't forget your wallet again, did you? Because then I might get a little suspicious."

He grins, showing me all his teeth. "Isn't this the dry cleaner?"

I look up. "Oh. Can you stay with Ginger? I'll only be a minute."

He nods, showing me the leash. "I got her."

Inside, there's one person ahead of me. The buzzing fluorescent lights are made for examining suspicious stains. I look back through the glass door. Finn and Ginger sharpen into focus. I have the sudden, jarring feeling that we've been here before. As if Finn and I stood in this same spot in some alternate universe. Déjà vu comes on quickly, but it lingers. As I try to put my finger on it, my phone rings. I answer Nathan's call.

"Hi," he says.

"What's up?"

He pauses. "Nothing. What're you doing?"

I take my bottom lip between my teeth. Even though he used to do it all the time, it's been a while since Nathan called for no reason. "At the dry cleaner. You?"

"Still at work for a little longer. I just . . . thought I'd check in."

I smile. "I'm glad you did." The bells on the door jingle as other customer leaves.

"Hello?" Chin-Mae asks. I'm being called to the counter. "Name?"

"It's my turn," I tell Nathan.

"Okay. Bye."

He hangs up so quickly, I check the screen, taken aback.

"Name?" Chin-Mae demands. She's been doing my dry cleaning since I was in college, but she always asks for my name.

"Hunt." I step up and slump the bag between us. As I remove the tie, my glow over receiving Nathan's call dims. I show it to her, pointing to the stain. "What is it?" I ask.

She nods and marks it with red tape. "Okay."

"Do you know what it is?" I point to my mouth. "Lipstick?"

She squints, picking at it with her fingernail. "Okay. No problem."

I frown. We don't normally converse beyond this kind of thing. She seems to understand what dog slobber is. Is she agreeing that it's lipstick? I check her face for judgment. She clearly doesn't grasp the gravity of the stain.

I leave our clothing and fold up the bag. Finn waits with Ginger, like they're my new family. So far, our conversation has been easy. Maybe too easy. It should be harder for me to imagine stepping through the doors and slipping an arm around Finn's waist. I shake the thought out of my head.

"Let's cross here," he says when I come out.

"But Home Depot's on this side."

He nods down the block. "I know, but there's a good coffee place over there. My treat."

"I'm good. I try not to drink caffeine this late."

"Dessert? Tea? This spot, Quench Coffee, is my favorite."

"I've only been there about a hundred times," I say. "They have the best pastries. Especially the—"

"Dark chocolate pistachio croissant?"

"Oh my God," I say, standing up straighter. "Isn't is to die for?"

"Absolutely. I'd go to my grave right now, as long as I could get a bite on the way."

I laugh at his serious expression. "Most mornings, I go out of my way for their coffee. They know us there."

"Sure you don't want anything?"

I shake my head. "I can wait here with Ginger if you want to grab something."

"It's okay," he says, looking forward with a hint of a frown. "Let's keep going."

Ginger and I stay on the sidewalk in front of Home Depot while Finn runs in. During the five minutes he's gone, my emotions run the gamut. This has been a strangely intimate experience with a man who isn't my husband. But any guilt vanishes when I remember the tie—the one *I* bought him. I want to confront Nate. Not just about this, but about his distance the last couple months. Is it someone at work? Is he thinking about her when he's with me? Has he crossed any lines? My stomach churns. I don't want to nag him. If it's a simple crush or flirtation, I don't begrudge him that.

It's no worse than me being here with Finn.

What *am* I even doing here?

I search through the display window for Finn, but I don't see him. My hair feels windblown, and I wish I had a comb to run through it. The door to Home Depot opens. My heart skips a beat. It isn't Finn.

I think I have a crush.

SIX

As Finn and I leisurely head toward our apartment building, I convince myself this is as far as our friendship can go. We're neighbors, and neighbors don't need to spend this much time together. I have no reason to see him beyond today, other than an occasional "hello again" in the hallway. But when Finn stops at his door and turns to me, with his disheveled, golden hair, I can't bring myself to say goodnight first.

He shifts his Home Depot bag to the other hand. "So . . ."

"So."

"About the unpacking. It might actually be nice to have a little help with the kitchen."

I glance at the metal 6A nailed to his door. "Now?"

"Whenever you're free, but before

Thanksgiving."

"Big plans?"

"Kind of." He looks away, at the ground. "The thing is . . ."

I wait. He shifts feet and bobbles his keys in his palm. "Yes?" I ask.

"As I mentioned, I moved to Greenwich for a reason."

"Work," I say. "A lot of finance guys do that."

"Yes, but also—I mean, there were other reasons. So, well, let me back up a little."

Now, he's fidgeting with the key ring, pulling it open with his nail. His face is flushed. Is he nervous? Before Nate proposed, he wiped his palms on his pants so many times, I fell into a fit of giggles. Instantly, he calmed, got on one knee, and asked me to marry him. My laughter is better than Xanax, he always says.

But Finn is a stranger. I don't know his quirks, his telltale signs, his habits. Whatever Finn's trying to say, it's personal. We're just neighbors, though. I need to remember that. And based on the fact that I'm curious about what he can't get out, I have to stop him.

"It's okay," I tell him. "You don't need to explain anything."

"But I want—"

I hold up my hands. "I don't. I don't want. Nate is probably waiting."

"Of course." He glances at his hands, his

expression fallen. It makes me wonder if he wishes someone were waiting for him too.

"I'm sorry," I say. "I didn't mean to rub that in."

He raises his head a little. His melancholy look morphs to curious. "Rub what in?"

"That someone's waiting for me, and you're—" I stop before I put my foot in my mouth.

"What?" he prompts.

Alone. It's my turn to look sheepish. I want to tell him good luck with his apartment. Moving is one way to learn who your real friends are, but decorating is a whole other beast. I hope he has someone he can call. Instead I say, "Never mind. Goodnight."

"Night." He unlocks his door and goes inside.

I take Ginger into my dark apartment. It's past six, and Nathan isn't home. I lean back against the door. After a warm, easy evening with Finn, I can't help acutely feeling the cold distance Nathan has put between us.

Finn may be alone in a new apartment, but right now, I'm alone in my marriage. It's a first for me. I recognized the loneliness on Finn's face just now because I feel it too.

Was Finn flirting? Or was he just looking for company, a friendly neighbor to borrow sugar from? Hunky, athletic, kitchen-averse Finn—baking. The image makes me smile. I wonder how far he's gotten unpacking the kitchen he says he doesn't use.

I feed Ginger and check my phone. There's nothing from Nathan. Remembering he might not be home for dinner doesn't help the emptiness in my chest. I need a distraction, and Finn needs a hand. When we moved into this apartment, Nathan had no problem with the heavy lifting. It was the little things that got to him—getting books on shelves, setting up the printer, organizing the hall closet. That was when I took over. Some light manual labor might get my mind off things.

I leave Nathan a note.

Across the hall. Come get me when you're home. 6A.

I scribble a heart and stick the Post-It on the refrigerator. Nate will tell me if he's uncomfortable with me spending time at Finn's. He's up front about those things.

I run a brush through my hair. Keys, cell phone, and a portable speaker in hand—music is a lifesaver during the moving process—I walk back to Finn's place. When I reach his door, I pause. The elevator beeps, on its way up from the lobby. I wait to see if it's Nate, but it passes our floor, so I knock.

Finn doesn't answer right away. He takes so long that I wonder if he's gone back out. I rap a little harder. A third time feels desperate. I'm about to leave when he yanks the door open. I catch a flash of his abs right before his t-shirt falls over his stomach. He tugs the hem into place and scrubs a hand through his messy hair.

"Bad time?" I ask. He was clearly shirtless, and he's wearing lounge pants now instead of the jeans he had on earlier.

"No." He's out of breath. He gestures behind him. "I was just lifting."

I arch an eyebrow. "What happened to unpacking?"

"That too. Between reps."

"Should I come back . . .?"

"No." He opens the door wider. "Please."

The dim apartment is warm and smells like Pumpkin Spice. The opposite of friendly. Romantic.

"I'm sorry about the lighting," he says. "I only have one lamp that I've been moving from room to room. I'm waiting on a furniture delivery with the rest."

Several lit candles in the main room explain why it smells like fall. "It's cozy."

It's an odd feeling, walking into an apartment identical to mine, but with hardly any furniture and a new carpet. His white walls make it seem bigger than ours, but also harsher. Nathan and I painted the living room grayish-blue in April on a day when I got my period. We'd discussed buying a two-bedroom apartment in this neighborhood. Nathan had been up for a promotion, and we knew we'd need a nursery eventually. But the idea hasn't come up in months, not since it became clear pregnancy wasn't going to come easily.

"You should paint," I say. "The white is very . . ."

"White," he says.

"Yes."

73

"Maybe, if I have the time." He nods at the speaker. "What's that?"

"Changed my mind about helping you out. I brought music in case you don't have anything set up."

"Best idea I've heard all day. One of them, anyway." He glances at a box next to us and slides it with his foot behind the door. "Let's go in the kitchen."

I follow him. His place has a hallway with four doors, all of them closed except for a bathroom. A three-bedroom apartment seems excessive for a single man. Then again, maybe he's planning ahead.

The kitchen has no candles, but there's an overhead light Finn doesn't switch on. He's unwrapping something in a plastic bag. I wait in the doorway as my eyes adjust.

"Light bulb," Finn says, holding one up. "From Home Depot." He's tall enough that he doesn't need a chair to reach the ceiling.

"Do you have a flashlight?" I ask.

"I'll grab it." He sets the bulb on a table and comes toward the doorway. He's mostly a silhouette, barely lit by the glare of candles in the other room. The hollows of his cheeks are shadowed. He stops. It could be the low ceiling, but he seems twice my size.

Adrenaline jolts me. This place is unfamiliar. Dark. Private. The air between us changes, growing heavy, uncertain.

He lays a warm hand on my shoulder. "Excuse

SLIP OF THE TONGUE

me."

Goose bumps rise over my skin. I'm blocking the doorway. I step aside so he can pass. My brain recovers slowly, unwrapping a thought piece by piece like a package. I like the easy way he moves. His unassuming charm. The way his bottom lip seems stuck in a perpetual pout. I'm attracted to him.

"Do you mind?" he asks.

I nearly jump out of my skin. "What?"

He holds out a flashlight. "So I can change the bulb."

"Oh." I take it. "Yes. Okay."

He gets into position. I turn the light on and shine it at him.

He waves his arms in front of his face. "Jesus. I need to see the lamp—it doesn't need to see me," he says.

I giggle and shift the glare to the ceiling. "Sorry."

"You will be if you blind me. Then you'd be forced to take care of me."

I mock gasp. "How do you figure?"

"Out of guilt," he says simply.

"Guilt?" I tease. "What's that?"

"Ha. How much time do you have?" He screws the light bulb in and brushes his hands on his pants. "That should do it."

I flip the light on. Nothing happens. "Is it in all the way?"

"Yes. Are you sure that's the right switch?"

"It is in our kitchen."

I aim the flashlight along the walls, searching for any others. Finn removes the bulb and blows on it.

"I think we're screwed," I say. "That's a little light bulb humor for you."

"Very funny." He tosses the bulb in a full garbage can near the sink. "Thanks a lot, Home Depot. Now what?"

I get two candles from the living room and set them on the kitchen counter. "We forge ahead. There's a job to do."

He tilts his head. "Are you sure?"

"The show must go on."

He chuckles. "I should invite you over more often. You're like a human inspirational poster."

"Hmm." I try to think of something uplifting that relates to switching on a light bulb. A familiar quote comes to me. "I will love you the same in the dark as I do in the light," I murmur, though I probably should've kept it to myself.

"Now you just sound like a Pinterest board."

"It's from Nathan's vows." I force a smile. "He wrote that."

"Oh." Finn leaves the room and returns with a box in his arms. "Pots and pans."

I peek inside. "A lot here for someone who doesn't cook."

"How about under the stove?" he asks, as if this is our apartment.

"Makes sense. Where's the rest?"

"Outside the doorway, to the left."

I find a box labeled *Silverware*. Finn's handwriting is unusually neat. I take the one underneath it too, since it has other drawer items, including a utensil organizer. The first two of its three labels have been crossed out with black marker: Marissa. Donate. Kitchen.

Marissa? An ex-girlfriend? Is that the real reason Finn moved?

I don't ask. It isn't my business, and I tell myself I'm better off not knowing. I return to the kitchen and get to work unpacking the boxes in a way that seems right to me. The sterling tings each time I drop silverware into the organizer. I have to squint to make sure each one goes in the right slot. Finn's making a lot of noise trying to get all the pans to fit.

"By any chance, was your kitchen in Connecticut a little bigger?" I ask.

"What gave it away?" He sighs, pulling out a solid black pan. "What the hell is this thing? Can I get rid of it?"

"Cast iron skillet," I say. "Why on Earth do you own it if you don't know what it's for?"

He does a bicep curl and sets it on the counter. "Hell, I don't even need a gym membership while I have one of these."

"Skillets make frittatas, not muscles." I say *muscles* flirtatiously. It's a good word for that.

"A fri-whatta?"

I squeeze my eyes shut as I laugh. His furrowed brow alone has me doubling over.

"I'm serious," he says.

"I know." I gasp for breath. "That's why it's so funny." I point behind me, into the other room. "There's a box that says *donate* if you want to put it in there."

He glances over but leaves the skillet where it is. "Thanks, but since you interrupted my workout, I think I'll squeeze in a few reps as we go."

I smile, and in the silence that follows, I think about Finn's arms. How they might feel around a woman. How they might feel around me. It's nice to be held. I wish Nathan would knock on the door. Drag me home. Put his own arms around me. Make love to me. Remembering his vows has made me feel warm inside, fuzzy. And maybe even a little guilty? Which is odd for me. I've never been a big believer in guilt or regret.

I remember a recent discussion Nathan and I had over the summer. A friend of mine admitted over drinks to having second thoughts about her fiancé. I came home, turned on a bedside lamp, and told Nathan.

"Will she marry him anyway?" he asked.

"I think so. Out of guilt if nothing else."

"You wouldn't have gone through with our wedding if you'd had any doubts," Nate stated.

I agreed. "And I hope you wouldn't have either."

"Probably not. I have no way of knowing, though. I never had any." He sat up against the headboard, his eyes sleepy but engaged. "But she's staying with her fiancé out of guilt and

nothing more. How sick is that?" he asked. "Imagine if no one felt guilt. We'd be free of our own demons."

"Without guilt, there'd be no remorse," I said. "Sure, we'd all be happier if we could forgive ourselves for this or that. But imagine the world we'd live in if people had no reason to think twice about how they treated others."

"All right, but hypothetically speaking—if we could learn as a society to deal with our guilt in a healthier manner, we'd function better. Don't you think?"

"Give me an example."

He thought a moment. "Take your friend. If she didn't feel guilty about calling off the wedding the week before the ceremony, she'd save herself a lot of misery. Yeah, it would suck. People have flights and hotel reservations and both parties have put a lot of money into it. But now, what'll happen is— they'll get back from their honeymoon, and reality will settle in. Maybe they won't realize it at first. Maybe they even have a kid or two. Ten years down the line, they're divorcing, tearing the family apart, fighting each other tooth and nail, taking years off their lives from the stress."

I nodded along with everything he said. Nathan's not only smart, but emotionally intelligent. I love that about him. "Or stay together and set a bad example for the kids," I said, thinking of my own parents. "But I think what you're talking about is shame. She'd be ashamed to call it off because of how it would look and what it would cost everyone. She wouldn't necessarily be remorseful."

"What about you?" he asked. "You claim that you never feel guilty."

I waggled my eyebrows at him. "And imagine if the rest of

79

the population were like me?"

"The horror." He reached out and pulled me flat on the bed for a kiss. "Terrifying, really."

I touched his cheek. "I want to be more like you."

"How am I?" he whispered.

"I don't know. But you always get it right. You always know what I need, even if it's space."

"Space," he mused. "That's something I'll never give you too much of. Promise me the same?"

I promised, of course. Was I breaking that promise now by not pushing him harder to tell me what was bothering him? Each day I've thought about bringing it up, something has stopped me. *I'll wait until the weekend in case it's a big deal*, I'll think, or, *After the holidays*. Or, *Maybe tomorrow he'll be different*. Then there's the fact that he's already hurting over the sudden decline of his dad's health. I don't want to needle him.

But this tiny, red-stain of a clue—I'm more worried now than I was.

"You're quiet over there," Finn says.

Sweating, I shrug my cardigan off my shoulders and place it on the back of a chair. My tank top sticks to my stomach.

"Hot?" Finn asks.

"Kind of." There's another box at my feet, though I don't remember it being there before. It looks heavy, so I open it on the ground. Carefully, I lift a set of dinner plates onto the counter. "I was thinking about what you said earlier."

"I'm sorry about the Pinterest joke. I'm not even really sure what that website is . . ."

"Not that," I say. "I'm not that sensitive. I meant the guilt thing, when you asked how much time I had. What do you feel guilty about?"

He clears his throat. "Oh. You mean . . . right now?"

"In general. What are you holding on to?"

He blows out a sigh that ends in a laugh. "That's a tough question. If you want to see an American panic, ask them what they did wrong today. Sometimes I'm surprised we aren't all curled into balls by breakfast time."

"Interesting. You make it sound like an epidemic."

"It kind of is, but I'm guilty of it too." We both laugh. "Guilty of feeling guilt."

"I don't feel guilt," I declare as if I'm on trial. As if I'm trying to convince him. "I don't have regrets."

"About anything?" he asks, surprised.

"Pretty much. Most things, I can't control. And those I can, I always try to make good decisions with the information I have. At least, decisions that work best for me."

"And your husband."

I stop rinsing out a bowl. "Well, yes. I mean, what's best for me is almost always best for Nathan."

"And if it isn't?"

I dry the dish and place it on the shelf with the others. Once, a long time ago, I made a decision for

81

Nathan. It hadn't been easy. Many people would even say it was bad. Wrong. But my life with Nathan is better for it, so how can I feel guilty about that?

I try to think of a choice I've made that wasn't best for Nathan, but I did it anyway. Nathan is the most important thing in my life. Do I know, though, without a shadow of a doubt, that I can and will put him before myself? In an ideal world, the answer is yes. And most of the time I do.

But then, I think about our trouble getting pregnant. Nathan may have been okay with me going back on birth control for now, but that won't last. He's prepared to exhaust every option. I know better, though—some people don't get everything they want. And there has to be a point, when the heartbreak becomes too much, where someone says—enough is enough. A hard decision to make, but one that's in both our best interests.

"Compromise," I say. It's a canned answer, but the alternative is the truth, which is that I don't know what I'd do if faced with a choice between what's best for me and what's best for Nathan.

"Where is he?" Finn asks after a moment.

"Who?" I pick up a heavy serving dish, blow on it, and designate a musty corner cupboard with extra space to be the party platter home.

"Your husband." He clears his throat. "Where is he?"

"Oh." With some effort, I slide the large plate into its spot, close the cabinet, and take a breath. "I don't know. We have a very relaxed—"

"So you've said," he says. "You don't care where he is?"

I look down at my hands. Finn continues to press an issue I don't want to think about. I came here to distract myself, not confront demons. I could try and guess where Nathan is, but the point isn't that he's not here. It's why. What's keeping him away lately? Another woman? Or, worse—me? Except for bowling nights, it takes a lot for him to miss dinner.

"Of course I care," I say. "But I trust him."

"I didn't realize we were talking about trust."

Neither did I.

"Something wrong?" Finn asks.

I keep my back to him. "No." I take out another dish in a floral pattern. Where the hell did he get this—a flea market? *Men.*

Finn wipes his hands on a rag, takes the plate from me, and sets it aside. "I know we don't know each other very well—"

"We don't know each other at all." I turn to face him. "We're half a step up from strangers."

He winces, almost imperceptibly. "Okay . . . well, then, think of me as a stranger. Sometimes it's easier to confide in someone you don't know."

My chest is tight. Actually, Finn *doesn't* feel like a stranger, but more like we've known each other a long time. Longer than Nathan and I, even, which makes no sense. Meeting Nathan felt fresh, like a beginning, as if he'd just been born and walked right into my life. Finn could be an old friend, though, a t-shirt I've worn a thousand times.

"I found something." The words tumble out.

"What did you find?"

"It's stupid. And cliché. It's dumb to even mention it." I roll my eyes and lean my back against the counter. "I found a lipstick stain."

"When?" His expression closes. "Where?"

"Last night, on his tie."

"Jesus, Sadie." Finn runs both hands through his hair as if I've just told him something about his own spouse. He makes a face. "I'm sorry."

"You are?" My heart skips. "Why? You think it means something?"

"Oh. I—" He scratches under his collar. "Probably not."

"You're lying."

He exhales a nervous laugh. "I just—I mean, how would I know? I've never met the guy. But every time I see you, you're alone."

"I told you, last night he was bowling."

He raises both palms. "I'm not saying anything. Are there women at the bowling alley?"

"I don't know." I haven't been to a game. Maybe I should, though.

Finn reaches out and hesitantly rubs my bare shoulder. There's a sheen of sweat at the base of his neck, and my scalp grows hot. I move my hair over one shoulder as he slides his hand a little higher and presses his thumb along my collarbone.

I part my lips, and when he does it again, I close my eyes. "That's nice."

He isn't gentle. I can feel the strength of his hands as he massages my shoulder, then my neck.

"The thing is," I say in the dark, "I haven't always been the best wife, but he's been a flawless husband. That's why it doesn't make sense."

"Have you asked him about it?"

"No. It seems ridiculous to even bring it up. Anyone who knows us . . ." I pause, unable to think of how to explain it. "He wouldn't."

We stand quietly for a minute. Finn slips his fingers under the strap of my tank top. It slides down my shoulder. "Sorry," he mutters.

I don't fix it.

He continues to work the tension out of my neck. "When you say you haven't been the best wife . . ."

"That's not what I mean." I shake my head. "I've never been unfaithful. It's just, when one half of the relationship is perfect, the other half is bound to be a let down, any way you cut it. I don't always say and do the right thing."

"And he does?"

"Always," I whisper. "Until these last two months."

"What happened two months ago?"

I bite my bottom lip hard. It's what I've been asking myself over and over. One day, he was himself.

The next day . . . off. "He found out his father is dying."

"I'm sorry."

"He turned down a promotion at work so he could stay available for his dad. But a few months ago, I *took* a promotion, and now I'm making a tiny bit more money than him."

"Would that upset him enough to ice you out?"

"I don't think so. The difference is negligible, really." The Nathan I know wouldn't be so petty, but lately, I've been learning quite a bit about the man I married. "He seemed happy for me."

"So, you think maybe . . .?"

"What?" I ask.

"I'm not stupid," he says. "I'm not going to say it first."

"That he met someone? No. I don't think so. There must be another explanation." I open my eyes, and Finn seems closer than he was a few seconds ago.

"Hi," he says, "again."

"Hi." My voice is creaky. "What's the diagnosis?"

He slides a finger up the back of my neck. Goose bumps light up my skin. "Some tightness, but relatively knot-free."

"That's good."

"Yes, it is." He inhales deeply and stares at me. "I have to tell you something."

My hairline prickles. I can sense it'll be heavy, and I'm not sure I want to hear it. I force a crooked smile that probably looks as awkward as I feel. "I smell like dog food?"

"I want to kiss you," he says without missing a beat. "I won't, but I just thought you should know."

My stomach drops as if I'm in free fall. I bite my lip involuntarily, then release it, afraid it'll look like an invitation. Can he really come out and say that? Without prompting, without wavering? You can want to kiss someone and not say it. Should I be angry he confessed that? I'm not. I'm curious. Stirred, even. Since we're being honest, I ask what I want to ask. "Why?"

"Why do I want to kiss you? Or why did I tell you?"

My heart rate picks up. I lose my nerve. "The second one. That's not the kind of thing you just come out and say to a stranger. A *married* stranger."

"Because I like you." He absentmindedly caresses the nape of my neck with his fingertip. "So I want to be honest."

I put my hand over his wrist, and he stops. Now, and for the last hour, it's as if we're the only two people on the planet. The Bad Wife and the Stranger. If I let him kiss me, nobody would ever know. *He* doesn't wear lipstick. Neither do I.

"You're leaving, aren't you?" he asks.

I nod. I don't have to pull his hand away. He takes it back willingly.

"It's probably best." He hands me my sweater and the speaker. We forgot to turn the music on. "I can finish up here."

87

Already, before I can get a word out, he's walking me through the apartment.

I say the only thing left to say. "Goodnight."

"See you around." He pulls the door open, then shuts it again. He sighs. "Talk to him. If you want to know what's wrong, just ask him."

I pull my sweater around me, even though hair sticks to the back of my neck. My feet sweat in my boots. "Thanks."

"Sure." He lets me out.

I walk across the hall, unlock the door to my apartment, and find the lights on. I set my keys down as Ginger comes in, wagging her tail. "Nate?"

"In here," he calls from the living room.

I remove my shoes and socks, put them on the rack in the entryway, and find him on the couch in his sweats. "Why didn't you come get me?" I ask.

He pauses whatever sports channel he's watching. "I didn't know where you were."

"I left you a note."

"You did?" He hits play on the remote and returns his attention to the TV.

I go into the kitchen. The Post-It is still on the fridge, but it's been moved a few inches to the left. He just lied to me. I pull it off and go back to the living room. "You didn't see this?" I ask.

He shuts off the TV, stands, and stretches. He's so tall, his fingertips graze the ceiling. "I figured you were out shopping or something."

"You should've called me. What about dinner?"

"I made a grilled cheese."

I don't know what to say. If he's home, I make him dinner. Period. I want to tell him that. To tell him I know he moved the Post-It. I'm fairly positive he did. Though, I could be mistaken. Do I really remember where I stuck it? I'd sound hysterical if I were wrong.

"Where were you tonight?" I ask.

"I went to see my dad."

"Without me?" I ask. "I would've met you at the hospital."

"I wasn't planning to. I just decided to stop by on my way home from work."

I crumple the Post-It in one hand. Nathan's dad's health has declined quickly since they discovered his lung cancer. When we found out he'd been sick a while, Nathan blamed himself for not making his stubborn dad see a doctor sooner.

"He's better, by the way." He sniffs. "Radiation just hit him a little harder than usual. They're keeping him there."

"Did you call your mom?"

"Yeah. She's sending 'healing energy from California.'" He tosses the remote on the couch. "I'm done with the TV if you want it."

"Maybe we can watch something together?"

There are shows Nathan and I watch together, and there are ones we watch when we're apart. I can't stand medical primetime drama. He'll leave the room if he sees Tim Gunn. But when we find a show we

89

both love, we always watch it the same way—gasping simultaneously. Laughing at the same things, even those that aren't meant to be funny. Yelling at idiot characters.

"I'm going to read," he says. "I'm finally starting that Erik Larson book I ordered forever ago."

Historical nonfiction. Not my thing. I know he's been looking forward to it, though. "All right."

He turns to walk away.

"I was at the neighbor's," I say. "That's what the Post-It said. He asked me to help him unpack the kitchen."

"That was nice of you," he says. "Moving on your own is a bitch."

"I think you'd like him." I hesitate. Maybe if they knew each other, the temptation of Finn would disappear. The funny thing is, I think they'd get along. "You should go over and say hello sometime. I don't think he has a lot of friends."

Nathan turns his head halfway over his shoulder. "His heater still busted?"

"Yes." I run my hand over the back of my clammy neck and remember Finn's fingers there. "I'm sweating like a pig."

Nathan takes a long look at me and opens his mouth like he's going to speak. After a brief pause, he asks, "What's his name?"

"Finn." I wait. "He worked in banking or something."

Nathan shifts on his feet, watching me. "I'll try

to get over there to take a look, but no promises."

He goes into the bedroom. I make myself something to eat and watch TV, but I'm not paying attention. Nothing has really happened today, and yet, my mind is spinning—from Nathan's lipstick stain and his dismissal just now. From Finn's strong hands and his confession. What is a kiss, really? Two body parts touching, like one hand to another. The thought of Finn's unsolicited, forbidden kiss shouldn't stir something deep inside me.

I'm still sticky, so I leave the dishes for the morning and decide to take a shower. Nathan doesn't look up from his book. I undress in the closet and slip on my robe. As I'm taking my birth control, I notice the dry cleaning bag has new things in it. I drop to my knees and rifle through until I find his tie. I pull it out quickly, straightening and smoothing it over the carpet. It's crumpled, but clean. I sigh, a mix of relief and embarrassment, as I hunch over the bag. Then, I smell it. Cigarette smoke.

I set my jaw. Nathan quit years ago and hasn't slipped up once. This isn't his stink stuck to his suit. It's someone else's. Or it's from a bar. Either way, it is *not* from a hospital. How desperate must he be to lie about seeing his sick father?

My cheeks warm. I can barely form a thought that doesn't involve me hurling curse words. I leave the pile where it is and charge to the foot of the bed. "Where were you tonight?"

He turns a page. "I told you. The hospital."

The smell is trapped in my nostrils. I swipe my nose hard. "Where else?"

He glances up. "I went there from work, then I came home. I was watching TV for a while before you got here." He cocks his head. "Why?"

I try to calm my breathing by inhaling deeply. He's turning me into someone I don't recognize—a suspicious wife. My friends and co-workers have their husbands on short leashes, and I've never understood why. Is this what happens if you don't watch them closely? "I've had a weird day," I say.

This is the part where he puts down his book and asks why. Then takes me in his arms and assures me I'm the only girl for him—now, and always.

"Well . . ." His eyes drift to the floor at my feet while he furrows his brows, as if he's thinking much too hard about his next move. He hesitates so long, the silence between us becomes awkward. "This is a weird city," he finally says and looks back at the page.

It must be an interesting book. I'm tempted to ask what it's about that it's worth more of his attention than his own wife. Or just skip the whole passive-aggressive route and accuse him of fucking around behind my back. What would he say to that?

This paranoia is new to me, just like his attitude. I don't like it. I want things to go back to the way they were. "I already took the dry cleaning," I say evenly.

"I know."

"Your clothes from last night were pretty dirty.

And now there's more."

"I get a few passes, don't I? I'm always picking up your stuff."

I narrow my eyes. It's only half true. He likes things tidy. It's not as though I leave a mess everywhere I go, though. I'd rather leave messes for the morning, but by morning, the messes are already gone. "I didn't mean it like that," I say.

Somehow, he still seems to be reading.

"Nathan."

He looks up again and makes a move like he's going to put his book down. But he doesn't. I see a flash of indecision, and then his expression clears. "What?"

My stomach fills with butterflies. We promised each other, I want to say. If you were tempted to act on something, you were supposed to tell me. And now, I'm the one who's tempted. If Finn had just kissed me and not said it aloud—would I have stopped him? I don't know. Which means I need to tell Nathan about it. That was our deal. It's not so easy, though. How do I tell the person I love most in the world that he's failing me? And that another man is making it better? Maybe Nathan tried to come to me and couldn't. We'd made it sound so easy.

"What is it?" he asks. "There's a ton of detail in this book. I need to concentrate."

"Never mind." I turn away and slam the bathroom door shut behind me. In the shower, my body shakes. Not because of what Nathan said, but because he said it at all. He doesn't shut me out, snap at me, or leave the room when I enter.

I'm scared.

I wait for him to come in and apologize, but he doesn't. When I get out, he's already asleep, an hour earlier than usual. I climb into bed, but I might as well be somewhere else for all he notices.

Maybe even in the next apartment.

SEVEN

I'm calmer when I wake. Having gone to bed so early, Nathan left before I was even out of bed, which is uncommon. I take Ginger downstairs and find myself in a winter wonderland. Everything is freshly powdered. It's the season's first snowfall, and the air is alive. It used to excite me, but a couple years ago, I slipped and twisted my ankle on an ice patch. Now I wear rain boots to and from work. Carrying an extra pair of shoes annoys me. The snow only stays white for a day anyway. Then it turns putrid and asphalt-gray.

Ginger sniffs a shrub with extraordinary fascination. She stops, looks around the street, and then returns to investigating. I should hire her out to the police department. *Or have her trail Nathan*, I think, pulling my coat closer around me. It's only the third time that morning I've thought of the lipstick stain and the smoky suit.

"Come on, girl," I say. "Hurry up."

She marks the bush, but that's all. Nathan must've taken her out already.

I pull her back toward the building, where I spot a woman and young girl at the entrance. They both wear matching pink caps and have long, blond curls. With her free one, the woman is punching a number on the entry keypad over and over. "What the hell is wrong with this thing?"

"Hello?" I ask.

She turns around. Her smile is so big, I could count all of her teeth. "Hi," she says. "Do you live here?"

The girl, in a huge puffy coat, looks at me. "What's your dog's name?"

"Ginger." Ginger, waiting patiently, hears her name and begins to wag her tail. "You can pet her."

Her hand looks white and small in Ginger's red fur.

"Would you mind letting us in?" the woman asks. "We live here, but they keypad doesn't seem to work."

"It probably froze last night." I pull out my key and let them in. Warmth welcomes us like a hug. "At least the common spaces are heated."

"It's a beautiful building."

"Thank you." I don't know why I said that. It's not like I have any more claim over the place than she does. I pull Ginger to the elevator and when it arrives, I select the sixth floor. They get on a second after.

"Can I push the button?" the girl asks, and then frowns at the panel. "Never mind. She already did."

"Just pick another one above six," the woman says, winking at me. "Live outside the law, baby."

"You live on six?" I ask. I'm not on a first-name basis with all my neighbors, but I don't recognize them.

"Just moved in. I told my husband, if we're moving to the city, you damn well better believe we're getting a nice place. I could do the starving artist thing in my twenties, but I'm a thirty-two year old mother now. I refuse to wrestle rats for food."

"*Mom*?" the girl asks, her voice high-pitched.

"I'm kidding, sweetheart," she enthuses. "There are no rats."

"Well—" I start.

The woman cuts a finger across her throat and shakes her head. She knows. Rats generally stick to the underground, but I've seen a mouse or two in my time at the apartment. Or three. We share a smile as the doors open.

The woman heads down the hallway with her child as I pull Ginger along. She stops at 6A. I look between the door and her. She's knocking.

I draw my eyebrows in. She's knocking? The hallway no longer feels warm. My fingers are like little icicles, so I stick one hand under an armpit, keeping Ginger close with the other. Should I keep walking or

97

say something? How do I ask her if she's confused about where she lives without offending her?

"Should we hide?" the girl asks.

"Yes, let's." They both move out of the way of the peephole, so it's just me standing there, stuck to the spot.

Why we're all here in front of Finn's apartment, I can't fathom. Before I make any decisions or come to a single conclusion, Finn opens the door. He's sweating, and his hair is in complete disarray, but he smiles at me as if I'm holding an oversized check with his name on it. "Hey," he says softly, affectionately. "You must be looking for—"

"Boo," the girl screams, popping out from behind the wall.

He jumps, bracing himself against the doorframe. His entire body locks up. "Ma-Marissa?"

My blood runs as cold as my hands. *Marissa*—the name from one of the boxes in Finn's apartment.

She leaps, and he lifts her up without a thought. The woman peeks out from the other side of the wall, grinning. "Surprise!"

Finn's mouth drops open. "Kendra? What're you doing here?"

The woman—Kendra—moves in front of the door and rolls her eyes at me. "We drive an hour from Connecticut to see this new apartment, and that's the greeting I get. Men."

If I look as horrified as I feel, she doesn't seem to notice. My stomach cramps, as if it's going to bottom right out. Just last night, Finn said he wanted to kiss me. And now I'm standing in the middle of his . . . family?

"Babe," Kendra says, "you're sweating like a whore in church. You still haven't fixed the furnace thingie you told me about?"

"I—"

A familiar silhouette—*my* familiar silhouette— comes into view behind Finn. Nathan saunters into the doorway with a wrench in his hand. "Nathan Hunt, at your service."

What's going on? I give Nate an inquisitive look, but he's smiling at Kendra. Finn and I exchange a glance. We haven't done anything beyond walk, talk, and unpack. But our friendship suddenly feels like a dirty secret for which we're about to get busted.

"Oh, my," Kendra says to Nathan, dumbstruck. "*You're* the landlord?"

It's not an unusual response for Nathan to receive from women. In a suit, he looks as though he stepped out of a GQ spread—but this? He's slick with sweat. His flannel is open to the neck. His chocolate-smooth brown hair is mussed. If possible, he's even more fuckable.

Nathan wipes his hand on his jeans and holds out his hand. "Your neighbor, 6B. Sadie's husband."

Kendra takes his hand and blinks. "Who's Sadie?"

"I am," I say quietly, as if I'm ashamed by the name.

"Oh." She smiles warmly at me. "So you've met my husband."

I look from her to Finn, confused. Are they separated? Divorcing? I don't like being in this position—dazed, and feeling weird about something I haven't even done. It's Finn's fault I feel this way, so I look to him, a film of red creeping over my vision.

Finn rubs the back of his neck, appropriately sheepish. "We met the day I moved in," he says, gesturing at Ginger, "the dog ran off after a squirrel, and I chased her down."

"Then he came over for a beer," Nathan says, grinning. "Or so the story goes. I wasn't around." He's friendly by nature, and his smile is authentic, so I don't think he means anything by it.

"Really?" Kendra asks. Her smile wavers a little, as if that concerns her. Then again, I'd be concerned too if my husband had moved out of my house to get his own place. Except she isn't acting as though they are. "How nice to have a young couple next door," she adds.

"I agree." Nathan bends over to the girl. "And who's this?"

She glances up at her mom before she says, "Marissa."

"Nice to meet you, Marissa." He smiles. "How old are you? Seventeen?"

She laughs. "I'm seven!"

"Oh yeah. I should've known." Finally, Nate glances up at me. Under his bright, happy veneer, I recognize something darker. "I have a niece your age."

My throat dries, and I swallow. I wonder what he's trying to tell me with that look. *And a niece is all I'll ever have?*

"Does she live in the city?" Kendra asks. "Maybe we can get them together."

"No," I answer for him. I don't want this to continue. To me, Bell is sacred, and she doesn't belong in this conversation. "I thought you went to work," I say to Nate.

"Not yet." He straightens up and comes out of the apartment to stand by me. "You didn't mention Finn had a family," he says, looking dotingly on Marissa. "I would've tried to get to the heater sooner."

Everyone turns to me. "I . . ." I pause. "I guess I didn't think of it."

"I figured. Anyway, I can't fix the radiator right now. I need a part from the hardware store." He looks at Finn. "If you can pick it up, I should be able to finish later. If that doesn't work, though, it might need to be replaced."

Kendra makes a face. "So it's going to stay this hot? Can't the landlord do something?"

"He'll give you the runaround for weeks," Nathan says. "I'd remove it, but you can bet your," he glances at Marissa, "*you-know-what* the cold's going to be worse."

"It's fine. She's heard worse," Finn says about Marissa. "Mom here's got the mouth of a sailor."

"And you fucking love it," Kendra says, slipping her arm around his waist. Finn glances briefly at me and then away. In my experience, this isn't how separated couples act. I swallow at the subtle display of affection, and ashamedly, feel the slightest tinge of jealousy. "At the altar," Kendra continues, "when the priest asked if I took Finn to be my husband—"

"She said 'Of course I fucking do,'" Finn rushes out, slurring the words together. "Not only have I lived the story, but I've heard it over and over."

"They haven't, honey." She rises up to kiss his cheek, then runs her hand over the stubble on his chin. "This is new."

His jaw tenses. "It's Movember. Mustache November. I'm growing it out."

"Great," she says cheerily. "Maybe I'll grow my hair out too."

A stiff giggle escapes me before I can stop it. She isn't talking about the hair on her head. When Nathan understands, he also laughs.

Finn doesn't look amused. He moves away from her. "Let them go. They have to get to work."

"I do," Nathan agrees, "and I need a shower."

The men shake hands. "Thanks again," Finn says. "I owe you."

"Not yet," Nathan says. "But once I fix it, I expect a six-pack. And none of that generic bull. The expensive, craft beer."

"Nathan," I scold, shaking my head.

"What?"

Finn smiles. "You got it."

Nathan flashes Kendra his panty-dropper smile. I know it well, but not from this angle. Does he smile like that often when I'm not around? "Nice to meet you ladies." His eyes linger on Marissa. He started looking at babies that way last year. At least, that's when I started noticing it. Is it wrong for me to be jealous of a little girl?

I follow Nathan inside our apartment, my mind spinning. I feel like a fool in a number of ways. I want to know what Nathan and Finn talked about. Why Finn didn't mention a family.

As soon as the door closes, Nate's smile is gone. He unbuttons his flannel as he walks away.

"You didn't have to go over there," I say. My tone is unintentionally accusatory.

He disappears into the bedroom.

My blouse sticks under my armpits. I'm hot one minute and cold the next—it's starting to annoy me, and winter hasn't even technically begun. I remain where I am. Finn claimed honesty was his reason for telling me he wanted to kiss me, but not mentioning a family was a lie. I don't know why I care. It's not my business. I don't like being blindsided, though.

I remove Ginger's leash. Belated embarrassment over my behavior sets in. I'd thought Finn was flirting with me. And it was as if everyone in that hallway just now was in on the joke, waiting for my reaction to finding out Finn was married. Even Nathan.

What do I care anyway? I hang up my coat. I've got something pretty good right here in my own apartment. Our hot sex from a couple nights ago hasn't been far from my mind. I find Nathan in our bathroom, steam curling over the top of the shower rod. I pull the curtain open.

His eyes are squeezed shut as he scrubs shampoo into his hair. "What are you doing?" he asks.

"Joining you," I say, unbuttoning my collar.

He doesn't respond right away, doesn't look at me. "Didn't you already shower?" he asks.

"I don't care."

"You were leaving for work."

"I, don't, care," I intone. I pull my blouse out of the waistband of my skirt. "You know how I get when I'm in the mood."

His cock twitches. My insides clench. *Yes.* This is what I want. Seeing his desire with my own eyes will always get me warm between the legs.

Nathan runs his hands over his face and rinses. "I'm already late."

"So what?" I slide my hand down his bicep, elbow, forearm. I reach for him. "I want you."

He catches my wrist. "I said no."

I withdraw. Shower water drips from my hand to the toe of my boot. "What?"

"No."

"Why not?"

"I told you. I'm late."

"That's never stopped you before."

"And I don't want to."

My heart cracks, and it must be audible. Nathan drops his eyes from my face to my chest. He can switch off his attraction to me, just like that? Or have I been blind, in denial? Maybe he's been feeling this way for some time. "You mean me. You don't want *me.*"

He looks away, and after a brief hesitation, picks up a loofah. He squirts body wash onto it but doesn't move, as if he's forgotten its purpose. "No. Not right now."

It dawns on me that maybe he didn't want me the other night, either. Maybe he wanted a slut, not a wife, and that's what I gave him. But it's a lot harder to pretend you're fucking someone else when it's daytime. "Then when?" I ask.

"I don't know. I'm not having this conversation in the shower."

"Are you kidding me? You can't just drop this on me and end the conversation."

He turns his back to me and puts his palms against the wall. "Maybe not. But right now, I think it's best if you leave me alone."

My jaw tingles. My blouse hangs open. It didn't really occur to me, over the past couple months, that he might not want me. If he's angry, if he's sad, if he's screwing someone else—that, I can find a way to deal with. But if he feels nothing for me? That's as deadly to our relationship as a bullet in the heart. My hand hovers over his back. "Why?"

He slaps the tile with one hand. "For fuck's sake, Sadie. I said I don't want to talk about it."

I step back, almost tripping over the bathmat. My urges jump from ripping the shower curtain off its rings to begging him to stop this. I don't know which of the two will make things worse and which will make things better. Is it even that black and white? Stumped, I leave the bathroom, leave the apartment, leave his bullshit. In the elevator, my hands shake as I close my blouse, tuck it back into my skirt, and get my coat on.

Before all this, Nathan had never denied me so much as a kiss. I'm the one who pulls my hand out of his first, who has to be called back to the doorway for a goodbye peck when I'm running off to work. I love his affection. Sometimes I forget to show mine, but he doesn't.

He takes care of me—not because he has to, but because he wants to. That's the fundamental difference between him and other husbands I know. A few years back, my girlfriends and I went to Atlantic City for a weekend. I drank one or six too many dirty martinis, got sick, and according to my friends, wouldn't calm down without talking to Nathan. He picked me up that night, a three-hour drive to the casino and another three back home. I fell asleep with my head in his lap as he stroked my hair with one hand and steered with the other. In the morning, anyone else would've lectured me. But he made me bacon and eggs while we laughed.

Outside, the sun shines, but it's blustery. The wind freezes my ears, nose, fingers. Somehow, it gets inside me and ices over my heart. The heart that's unprotected and defenseless because Nathan broke down the walls around it.

Because Nathan once loved me hard enough to make me feel safe in his care.

"Space. That's something I'll never give you too much of. Promise me the same?"

EIGHT

Amelia Van Ecken gives me a dirty look across the conference table. I don't know how long I've been on the receiving end of my boss's stink eye—black-framed glasses tipped to the end of her nose and everything—but I know why. We've been in this meeting forty-five minutes, and I haven't contributed a word.

When she dismisses everyone from the conference room, she tells me to wait. "Let's go to my office."

I shut my laptop and follow her out. Amelia Van Ecken Communications, or *avec*, takes up the seventh floor of an office building near Bryant Park. The open, partition-less space is bright with sunlight from the floor-to-ceiling windows. There's a chandelier in the center and plush, blue velvet club chairs near the elevator. She never reveals her real age, but for her early-thirties, she's done more than almost anyone I know personally.

"Howie," Amelia calls. Her long, blond bob moves as a unit, like it belongs on a Lego instead of a human. "We'll take two lattes from that place I like. You know the one."

Howie slowly rises from between the rows of desks where my colleagues tap and click furiously. His mouth is thinned into a line. "Do I look like your assistant, Amelia?"

"All you boys under thirty look the same to me. I don't know where Jack is. He must be cleaning up the meeting." She stares him down. "It's on Sixth Ave."

Howie scowls at me. I shrug. He knew what he was getting in to when he was hired.

"Bring them straight here," she adds. "A cold latte will put me in a bad mood."

"What do you call this?" he mutters.

She hears him, but to her, it's likely a compliment. Amelia employs male underlings so she can get back at her ex-husband by ordering them around. Nobody says it, but we're all thinking it.

"Shut the door and sit." She flops into her white leather chair and checks a gold-rimmed, Kate Spade desk calendar while speaking to me. "What was that today?"

"Which part?" I take a seat across from her and cross my legs.

"Don't bullshit me. I expect more. That's why I promoted you instead of Howie." She points a black and white polka dot pen at me like a command. "You were distracted."

I was. If only it'd been the other way around, and work had been enough to distract me from my life. Too much has happened in just a few days. Before Nathan turned down my advances, I'd suspected this was just a phase. Now I have information I can't ignore. Somewhere along the way, Nathan and I have gone from a team to opposite sides.

"I'm sorry," I say. "I have a lot on my mind."

She nods, and her leather seat creaks. "Divorce the asshole. Believe me, you'll be better off."

My cheeks crack when I smile, as if they've been out of use for a while. "You loved Nathan when you met him at last year's holiday party."

Her eyebrows gather, but magically, no wrinkles appear. "Did I? Oh, yes. I forgot. It's coming back to me." She waves a manicured hand. "Honey, he's too handsome to be a good husband. You can't have both."

I can't help but laugh. "As logical as that sounds, it couldn't be further from the truth. Nathan is . . ." Again, I'm having trouble describing his character. I could tell her how he puts others before himself, and that he loves and trusts blindly—too blindly sometimes. But words don't seem like enough.

Amelia sighs. Her veneer clears a little, like wiping steam from a mirror. "I remember, Sadie. I kept thinking how obvious it was that he just adores you. He always made sure you were enjoying yourself."

I straighten my back a little as warmth seeps through me. Even *she* sees how perfect we are, and considering her views on marriage nowadays, that's a feat.

"I remember that we were deep in conversation with some clients," she continues, "and your husband brought over a round of drinks without prompting. The clients loved it."

"That's Nathan," I say. My smile wavers. Or, that *was* Nathan. This year's party is in a month. I don't think he'll want to come. If he does, though—how long can we fake it? Will Amelia and my colleagues see right through us? "This isn't about me, though," I tell her. "Nathan and I are great. I'm worried about a friend, actually."

She pops her lips open. "Sure."

"Honestly." Amelia talks about her personal shit all the time, so I know what she's been through. I'm not comfortable bringing my problems into the office, but I need to talk to someone who might understand. "A very close friend. She's not doing well."

There's a knock on the door. "Come in," Amelia says.

Howie enters with our coffee.

"Now, was that so hard?" she asks.

SLIP OF THE TONGUE

"Not at all." He sets them on the desk. "Just don't expect me to get the IncrediBlast Mascara launch proposal done tonight like originally planned."

"Oh, but I do expect it tonight," she says casually. "Wait." She takes a tentative sip of the latte. "Good. You're dismissed."

He leaves us alone again, and I pick up my drink.

"So this friend," Amelia says. "What's wrong with her?"

I try not to look affronted. "It's not *her*, I don't think. I mean, who's really to blame in these situations?"

Amelia waits me out, tapping the end of her pen on the word *November*.

I scratch my wrist, then under my nose. Not even the intricate terrarium hanging by the window is enough to keep my attention today. "How long was Reggie having his affair before you found out?"

Amelia stops drumming her pen. She talks about Reggie frequently enough that I'm not uncomfortable bringing him up. "About a year. And that's only the affair I know about."

"What were the signs? Looking back—what was different during that time?"

She purses her red lips. "The smallest thing would set him off," she says. "He'd get angry with me for no reason at all."

"Really?" I cough, my throat dry. "Don't most marriages kind of go through that?" Mine hasn't really, not until recently. But I've seen whispered

113

arguments between my friends and their husbands over things that just don't bother Nathan or me—whose turn it is to pick a movie or who last used the bicycle and let the tire go flat.

"I'm guessing by the look on your face that your friend's husband displays this behavior."

I school my expression so I look just the right amount of concerned. "He seems to be, I don't know, fed up with her? Annoyed."

"That's typical. My psychologist will tell you he's not really angry with you—sorry, *her*. He's mad at himself, and he's taking it out on you."

"Her," I correct.

"Right. Sorry."

I raise my eyebrows at her. "It's *not* me."

She shows me a palm. "I know," she says defensively.

"Is there anything else you can think of?"

"Oh, that's only half of it," she said. "Here's an example. Once, I'd made a drink and dropped ice on the floor without realizing it. He slipped—just a little mind you, he didn't even fall—and he exploded at me. I was so upset, I cried. Later, he came into the bedroom as sorry as could be. Said he'd take me anywhere I wanted for dinner to make it up to me. He felt terrible."

"I don't understand."

"Everything was extreme," she says. "Extreme anger became extreme remorse. He'd withhold love for days and then drop an insane amount of money on a bottle of wine or Louboutins to make it up to me."

Ever since this began, Nathan hasn't given me a genuine *sorry* that I can remember. He hasn't made any attempts to smooth things over or comfort me. He withholds, then withholds more, to the point that I'm beginning to get desperate. "He felt guilty?" I deduce. "About the affair."

"Exactly," she says. "You could be a therapist."

"It's not a difficult conclusion to come to."

She makes a thoughtful sound. "So, does that sound like your friend's husband?"

"I haven't seen him apologize . . ."

"He'd do that in private. His temper happens in the heat of the moment. The apology has better timing." She shakes her head "Sick, isn't it? Reggie was a manipulative asshole."

"And if he doesn't? Apologize?"

She takes a sip of her latte, studying me over the rim. Her lipstick leaves a splotchy red mark on the white lid. "I don't know, honey. Doesn't mean he isn't having an affair. Doesn't mean he is. Guilt manifests in a lot of ways. A lot of women get a Jekyll and Hyde on their hands when he's stepping out. Everyone is different, though."

I spin the cardboard holder around my cup. Amelia is open. I'm not sure where the line is with her, but my question burns hot. I need to get it out before it sets my insides on fire. "A year is a long time to be sleeping with someone who isn't your wife . . ."

"Yes, it is." She looks directly at me. "You want to know if Reggie and I were intimate during that time?"

I lift the coffee to my face, as if the cup will hide my embarrassed nod. I sip, and liquid warmth travels down my throat.

"We were for the first few months. Then it got to be less and less. He'd make up excuses. And then it just stopped. He showed no interest in me."

My stomach somersaults. *It just stopped.* I can't imagine never feeling Nathan's weight on top of me again. Never climaxing under his skilled fingers and firm thrusts. I love the face he makes a few seconds before he comes, like he's trying to catch something I can't see. This tune is too familiar to ignore, though. The lipstick stain, the telltale cigarette stench, his defensiveness and unwarranted anger—Nathan's behavior is a textbook example of a cheating husband. But if what Amelia says is true, it's fresh salt in my growing wound. Just because Nathan's unusual behavior started two months ago doesn't mean the affair did. How long has this been going on?

Oh, God. Nathan's as vital to me as my own heart, as the blood in my veins. If he's planning to leave me for another woman, he might as well slice me open and leave me to bleed out. Amelia's expression is sympathetic, but not surprised. In her world, this kind of thing happens. It happened to her. It happened to many of her friends. I wouldn't be surprised if she's had this same conversation with others.

I return to my office. Throughout the day, I wonder what the right reaction is. Anger? Sadness? Confusion? The thought of bringing it up gives me cramps. I'd rather hide under my bed and ride out the storm. I don't have real evidence. Not even a gut instinct. My heart says it can't be. My head knows it can. People cheat. I'm not immune to it. The potential consequences of an affair turn my blood cold. Would I have to leave him? Would I want to? Would he leave me first?

My heart doesn't beat—it throbs like an open wound no bandage could hold together. Who could possibly have Nathan's attention? Finn's wife was beautiful and funny—why would he want to kiss me when he has her?

Even if I could stomach the thought of confronting Nathan tonight, I can't. It's his night out, and he'll be at Brooklyn Bowl. Still, I can't help hoping, as I make my way home from work, that he's waiting there for me. That he regrets turning me away this morning.

I'm steps away from my apartment when the door to 6A opens behind me. "Sadie." Finn's urgency echoes in the hall. I stop. Nathan hasn't said my name with that much emotion in a while. "I've been waiting for you," he says.

It may be the wrong man. It may be the wrong apartment. But I got my wish. There is someone waiting for me after all.

NINE

"Let me explain," Finn says.

I don't turn around. I can think more clearly if I don't see him. "You have a family."

"Yes, but—"

"You lied."

"No," he says. "I tried to tell you after our walk to the dry cleaners, but you shut me down. You knew I had something important to say, and you didn't want to hear it."

I keep my eyes forward, unsure who's at fault. A few more steps, and I'd be home. Ginger is most likely waiting in the entryway. Sometimes, I think she hears me coming from the elevator. "You should've told me anyway," I say, but I hear the waver in my own voice.

Finn's door closes and latches shut. He comes up behind me. "Let's not do this out here."

"Why not?" I ask.

"You know why."

I ball my fists. If I press him, whatever's between us will no longer be unspoken. Deny it as I might, the fact remains that Finn's here and Nathan isn't.

Finn takes my elbow.

I glance back at him, startled by the warmth of his hand, the way it melds with my skin. "Where are they?" I ask.

"Not here."

"Where?"

"Home."

I shouldn't have turned. Now I don't want to look away. I'm reminded of how nice it is just to be near him. "You locked yourself out," I say.

His green eyes mellow. He digs into his pocket, opens his fist, and shows me a key. He leads me to his door, keeping his free hand on me as he unlocks it. His hold is authoritative. Strong. I let him pull me into his apartment.

He slides my handbag over my shoulder and puts it on the ground. He goes for my coat, but I stop him.

"You'll overheat," he says simply.

After a moment, my shoulders ease. I let him take it off. Entering his apartment is like nearing the equator.

"Can I get you a drink?"

I don't know why I'm here. I've never been very good at denying myself, and I'd rather be here than in my empty apartment right now. I walk farther inside.

Sunlight is dying, streaming reddish-orange rays through the open window. A draft flaps the cover of a paperback on the ledge. In the center of the room, propped on a sideways wooden crate, is a record player.

"Kendra never let me get one," he says from behind me. "If it's not the latest thing, it's better left in the past. Everything in New York is old to her."

The record sleeve has grayed, worn edges. *Janis Joplin's Greatest Hits.*

I turn and look at him across the room. I think he's keeping his distance. "So what is it?" I ask.

"What?"

"You're separated? Getting a divorce?" I cross my arms. "Mid-life crisis?"

"Worse."

It's getting darker. A car horn blares in the street.

"None of the above," he says. "We're fine."

Instantly, I understand how that's worse. Finn and I both have other places we should go and try to be happy. "You're not separated?"

He shakes his head. "Like anyone else, we have our issues. But once things are wrapped up at the house, she and Marissa move in. I came early to set up the place, and, to be honest," he pauses, "to get some alone time."

"When?"

"End of the month. After Thanksgiving."

My nails bite into my palms. "But you wanted to kiss me."

121

"You didn't want me to?"

Though I'm not always up front, I've never been much for lying. "I did," I admit.

"You're not separated, either. You're not having doubts about Nathan." He pins me with a look. "Are you?"

"No," I say too emphatically.

"So why am I the bad guy? This isn't one-way. We're attracted to each other."

I open my mouth to deny it, but we both know it's true. I'll only sound defensive. Adults should be able to talk about these things. "Fine," I agree. "But you should've told me about them. You weren't wearing a wedding ring."

He shows me his hand, where there's still no evidence of his commitment. "I don't wear it while I unpack. I'm alone in my apartment. I wasn't trying to trick you."

I rake my hands through my hair. "It doesn't matter. You have a child."

"Would that have changed how you feel?"

"Yes," I say. "I wouldn't have—"

"What?"

I didn't come over here last night with any intention other than helping a new friend. Would I have told him, days ago, he couldn't walk me to the dry cleaner because he has a family? No. It was innocent. Now I know the truth, and I'm still here.

Sweat drips down my temple, and I swipe it away. "What now?"

He crosses the room and stands in front of me. His presence is palpable, like a stroke against my arm or a hand around my neck.

He reaches out. I struggle with my protest, but he just picks up the record and slides it out of the sleeve. "It's been a while since I did this," he says.

I study his face, but he's focused on getting the vinyl on the player. The song warbles a little before it plays. He shuts his eyes and moves closer to me, as if it doesn't count if he can't see. "Nice, isn't it? 'Ball and Chain.'"

He's referring to the song, but his smug irony isn't lost on me. I don't respond. The wrinkles around his eyes deepen as he smiles. His beard is darkening to dirty blond as it grows in. Suddenly, I can't remember the exact shade of his irises, if they're pine trees or emeralds.

"Finn."

He opens his eyes. They're a rich forest green, but his pupils expand, turning them dark. Looking down his nose at me, he sticks his hands in his pockets. He's close enough to nudge me with his elbow. "I bought this at a thrift store tonight. After Kendra left."

"Will she be mad?"

"She's already mad. Where's Nathan?"

"None of your business."

"I answered your questions."

"I didn't hold a gun to your head."

"Is he home?" he asks.

123

I frown. Not answering isn't any better than lying, but I can't peel a *yes* from my mouth. It's not true.

"Stay," he says. "Have a drink."

"It's a million degrees in here."

"You don't mind."

My huff comes out a sultry exhale. "I don't?"

He shakes his head slowly. "No."

He's even closer now. Close enough that it really does feel like it might be a hundred or more degrees in here. He presses the tip of his shoe into mine like a kiss. I could easily move away. I have half the living room behind me. "Are they coming back?" I ask.

"Not tonight. They couldn't take the heat."

The heat is intense, but not enough to keep a family apart. "That isn't the reason."

"Marissa has to go back to school tomorrow. Kendra hates the city. I don't have space for a second car. Our beds haven't arrived yet. Take your pick."

My chest rises and falls. Neither of us even blink. "Where do you sleep then?"

"Mattress on the floor," he says. "It's enough."

My throat is raw. I realize it has been since I left the bathroom this morning. It's thick with unshed tears and bottled accusations. With lust, served neat, undiluted and strong. "Do you get hot?"

"Unbearably."

The record sticks. With his hands still shoved in his pockets, he leans forward and plants his lips on mine. We each go stiff, breathing through our noses.

Here's a man who wants me. I can sense it in his every movement, no matter how restrained. I don't think there was ever a moment he didn't want me. And what about me? Haven't I wondered about those pillowy lips of his? He touches my cheek. Keeping my eyes closed, I lean into his balmy palm.

He pulls away but leaves his hand. Our eyes meet. He slides his thumb firmly over my mouth, so my teeth slice against the inside of my bottom lip.

"Sadie." He treats my name like it's some kind of command. He doesn't care that it doesn't belong to him. He doesn't ask my permission.

The music continues to skip. The last light disappears fast, as if turning a blind eye—let the dusk deal with cheaters and liars.

Finn lowers his head. I should stop him. He's risking even more than I am—and yet, that's part of why I don't want to. There's nothing headier than being wanted that badly. My stomach is all rocks and butterflies. I'm back in ninth grade, in a stranger's garden, strangling a red plastic cup in my hand as I receive my first kiss. How can it feel the same, when back then, there were no stakes?

He wraps his other arm around my neck and draws me in like he can't wait another second. His lips on mine are a thousand times better than my first kiss. I've had years of practice since then. Finn's mouth is soft but greedy. I try to keep up.

He tightens his hold on me, and his groan tastes sweet like candy. I can't resist hugging him back, fisting the fabric of his t-shirt. Hard, alive, he presses against my stomach, and the butterflies go wild.

I haven't seen another man's cock in seven years.

Panic smacks me in the chest. My excitement incinerates into a puff of smoke, searing me. I push Finn away, but I'm the one who stumbles. I bump the crate, and the record player clatters to the ground. The music stops.

I cover my mouth. "I'm sorry."

He's breathing hard, staring at me. "Why?"

"I . . . didn't mean to . . . your record—"

"No. Why did you stop?"

It should be obvious, but even I can't get the words out. I'm afraid of going any further. What if I hate it? What if I don't? "I'm scared."

He stares blankly at me. I can't tell if he's mad or relieved. Finally, he runs both hands over his face. "Thanks for being honest."

I step back. "I have to leave."

He pushes some sweat-stuck hair off his forehead. "I don't want you to."

"I know."

"Wait." He pulls me forward by my bicep, so I'm directly in front of him. He brushes his palm over my hairline and runs his fingers through the strands. I'm damp under my breasts and arms. He thumbs my slick upper lip, but I don't think it's helping.

"He'll think you ran home from work," he says.

I wrap my hand around his wrist, and he stops. "Bye," I say.

He lets me go. I gather my coat and handbag and walk out. The hallway, though heated, is refreshing against my sticky skin. I go home.

The entryway lights are on. Ginger doesn't greet me right away, which can only mean one thing. "Nathan?" I call.

"Yeah."

I cover my mouth, turn to the nearest wall, and put my forehead to it. He's *not* here. He *can't* have been this close. Just across the hall as I let Finn put his hands, his mouth, and his claim on me. Feet away as I crossed a line I never thought I'd see, much less step over. But in my heart I know the truth. Even while Nathan is in the next room, he and I have never felt farther apart.

TEN

"Busy tonight?" Nathan asks from the passenger seat as we cross the Williamsburg Bridge in a cab.

The driver shrugs. "Meh."

The chilly New York night has cooled my sweat, and now I'm bundled into my coat. I wish I'd had time to grab gloves. *Or a scarf*, I think, as Nathan unwraps his from around his neck.

I look out a window at the black East River. I'm not sure what I was thinking volunteering to come watch Nathan bowl. He was on his way out the door when I returned from Finn's apartment. I panicked, afraid he'd see the evidence of Finn's kiss on my face—my rosy lips from his scruff or the guilt in my eyes. He didn't mention it.

Bowling alleys aren't my thing. The campy eighties songs in the background and bad fluorescent lighting. The processed food. Stale, yellowing pretzels.

Day-old nachos. But in the year he's been playing, I haven't come to watch. My reckless moment with Finn had me worried about the growing distance between Nathan and me, so I invited myself along. He was in a hurry, but he didn't protest.

One thing I hadn't thought much about until now was the commute to Brooklyn. He's been spending a lot of time there.

"Don't you usually take the subway?" When I look away from the window, I catch Nathan glancing over his shoulder at me.

He turns forward again. "Yes, but I'm late." After a brief hesitation, he passes his scarf back.

I coil it around my neck, already warmer. It smells like him. The gesture wouldn't have made me think twice months ago, but tonight, his scarf is better than a bouquet of roses. "How much is a taxi?"

"Don't bust my balls, Sadie."

I reel back slightly. "I'm not." The driver narrows his eyes at me in the rearview mirror, quick to team up against a nagging wife. When I shift in my seat, the leather creaks. "You think I'd rather be on the subway? I was just curious."

"It's a lot more than a subway pass."

The driver grunts, "It's Brooklyn."

They exchange a look and shrug as if they're old pals. Great. Nathan is chummier with the cabbie than he is with me.

"How was work?" I ask, inviting a more neutral topic.

"Busy." He rests his head against the seat with a sigh. "You know how it is around the holidays."

The Family-kind locations get overcrowded this time of year, especially now that it's started to snow. He raises money in an upstairs office and doesn't see half of what goes on in the shelters, but he internalizes their strife anyway. I admire his commitment, even if I don't always understand it.

"I've been thinking," I say, then pause. Whenever I say this, Nathan feels the need to tease me with something like "uh oh" or "God forbid." Usually, it annoys me to no end. "I've been thinking," I repeat, in case he didn't hear, "we should skip Thanksgiving this year and serve dinner at the kitchen."

He lifts his head a little. "Really?"

"Yeah."

He turns in his seat, and this time, he stays. "I've been trying to get you to do that for years."

"I know. But I've decided this year, we're not dealing with my parents' manipulative bullshit."

He's about to smile, but he stops himself. I don't know why he won't, but I can see I've made him happy. I'll take what I can get. After my conversation with my boss earlier, I thought long and hard about doing something special for Nathan. There were no shortage of ideas, but it was harder coming up with one specifically for Nathan that didn't also directly benefit me, or even us as a couple. Every year, Nathan asks me to serve at Family-kind with him, and every year I say no. My mom gives good guilt-trip, and my brother piles on so he and my niece don't get stuck alone with our parents. Nathan never tells me no. He just volunteers the night before instead of Thanksgiving Day.

Nathan looks back through the windshield. "We'll see."

"I already called my mom."

He stares forward. He has a striking profile, as strong and silent as he is. At first, it's just another nose, mouth, set of eyes. And then, when you look closer, an art and symmetry so beautiful, it takes my breath away. "You did?" he asks. "You told her no?"

There's hope in his voice. It's as if I've been sitting in the dark, and a small light has finally turned on. "She tried to talk me out of it, but I held my ground. Andrew and Bell are coming over Wednesday night for an early Thanksgiving dinner, and the next morning, the three of us are going to the Family-kind soup kitchen—with or without you."

I watch his Adam's apple bob as he swallows. Almost imperceptibly, his shoulders ease back into the seat. "Thanks."

I allow myself a small smile. His approval feels like finding a small oasis during a long trek across the desert. I wonder how much farther I have to go until I reach the other side.

Brooklyn Bowl is nothing like I expected. From the

outside, it looks like a warehouse. But from the moment we step inside, it's dark and crowded. The music is turned up loud. In an area opposite the entrance, lasered lanes and multi-colored bowling balls create a neon playground. Everything glows black-light blue and hot magenta, and after each clatter, opaque mouths swallow up straight, white, bowling-pin teeth.

"Just another Wednesday night," Connor Vicks, Nathan's college buddy, tells me.

This is not the sad, empty bowling alley I'd pictured. The music is fresh and reminds me how out of touch I am with what's underground-cool. Here, Nathan isn't one half of a stuffy married couple. He's the popular, fun, drinks-on-me Nathan I met seven years ago.

I rise onto the balls of my feet, tracking Nathan. Thankfully, since he left me here while my back was turned, his height makes him hard to lose in a crowd.

"Have you said hi to Donna?" Connor asks.

"She's here?"

"Sure. It's Wifey Wednesday after all."

I tear my eyes from Nathan. Connor has the kind of face that becomes attractive over time. He's best when he smiles. Nathan says he only got Donna's attention because he plays guitar. "What's 'Wifey Wednesday'?"

"You know. When the wives come out. Sometimes they even get their own lane. To be honest, I've probably seen Donna roll one ball. Of course, she got a strike. I think they mostly just drink wine and gossip."

I can only imagine the look on my face, but to Connor's credit, he's unruffled. He doesn't let his slip show. In the year Nathan's been part of the team, he's never mentioned wives' nights.

Connor's wife, Donna, waves at us. She beckons me over to a two-top bar table. Donna looks the same, even though I can't remember when I last saw her—black hair, straightened within an inch of its life and, heavy eye makeup. She always has something animal print on. Of all Nathan's college friends, Donna and I are the least alike. She's also the friendliest.

"Oh my God—you came!" She hugs me tightly when I'm close enough. "I've been bugging Nathan for months to get you here."

I'm too embarrassed to tell her the truth— Nathan didn't want me here then, and he doesn't want me here now. "I've been busy," I say.

"I know, but it's been almost a year since the alumni dinner."

I think back to the night we'd seen Donna and Connor at an NYU-sponsored dinner. Nathan and I had drunk too much, and he'd put his hand up my dress during the dean's plea for money. Donna had busted us. After a giggling fit, Nathan overspent on a hotel room, and we slept in the next day.

"This is Nathan's wife Sadie," Donna tells two other women at the table.

They both groan. "Nathan is such a sweetheart," says a blond woman in a black halter-top. "He talks about you all the time." I wouldn't normally be surprised to hear that, but now, it catches me off guard. I'm sure he's spoken fondly of me—in the past. We shake hands. "I'm Alyssa," the woman says, "and this is Joan."

Joan could be Donna's sister, with the same dark features and tan skin. She has a warm smile. "Nice to finally meet you."

"I'm sorry," I say, looking around the three of them. They're my age, maybe a little younger. "I didn't realize this was a thing. Nathan didn't really give me all the details."

"Don't worry." Joan waves her colorful acrylic nails. "Nathan says you do this on purpose."

I lean in to hear her better over the music. "Do what?"

"Spend a couple nights apart. Keep the marriage fresh. He says you love your alone time."

"I do, but if I'd realized—"

"You're lucky he agrees to it," Alyssa chimes in. "Tried that once with Bob—'alone time.' He threw a fit. We drive each other crazy, but I guess he likes that." She lowers her voice. "Wives only come Wednesdays. Monday night, Bob thinks I'm at home pouting. Really, I'm sprawled in front of the TV, pigging out the way I can only do when he's not around. It's my special night."

The women laugh. That's more or less what I do

when Nathan's gone, so I smile along with them.

"If I didn't live in Brooklyn, I probably wouldn't come half as much as I do," Joan says, checking her cleavage is on full display. I'm in the same blouse that stuck to my back in Finn's apartment as he pressed his mouth to mine. Joan's pink lips spread into a sugary smile. I wonder if she wears red lipstick too.

"Which one's your husband?" I ask her.

"Fiancé, actually." She points to one of the men with Nathan. "That's my Mikey."

Mikey, balding with a beer belly, stands next to Nathan, who's easily the most handsome man of the group. And at the precise moment Nate throws back his head and laughs, I wonder if I should've been more worried about that over the years.

"You said you live in Brooklyn?" I ask.

Joan nods. "Park Slope."

"We're all there," Donna says. I must look confused, because she continues, "You knew that. We moved from Hoboken recently."

I vaguely recall Nathan mentioning it. Except for my brother in New Jersey, my attention wanes when people mention anything outside of Manhattan. "Of course."

"Park Slope is where it's at, especially if you're, you know—*thinking ahead*." Donna winks, her eyes sparkling with the reflection of the laser lights. I try not to look scared by her unsubtle suggestion. "You should come over sometime. I'll make sangria."

"All right," I say with some excitement, as if

sangria is a good reason to go anywhere. In reality, suggesting that we have dinner with his friends seems like a good way to get Nathan's attention. "I'll talk to Nate."

Joan sips something red and fizzy through a tiny black straw. "I told Mikey, if our marriage is half as good as Nathan and Sadie's, we'll be so lucky. So, so lucky."

Her words sound almost mocking, but her tone isn't. I'm confused, and a little mad that Nathan abandoned me with these women. Does Joan, with her sweet drink and sweet smile, know something I don't?

"Thanks," I say. "But it's all him. He's a great husband." Two months ago, I would've accepted her compliment easily—maybe even a little smugly. Does it make me a fraud, playing into the image they have of us? Nathan and I have held our place as an enviable couple so long, I'm not ready to give it up.

I touch my unfaithful lips, as if they might give me away somehow. "Excuse me."

I fight the crowd to get back to Nathan, who's involved in a conversation with Mikey, Connor and some men I don't recognize.

"Hey," I say.

He looks down at me. "What's up?" His tone is light, but his smile falters.

"I just met Joan." I look for a spark in his eyes— fear, excitement, anger—anything.

He just stands there, then glances at his friends,

137

who are ignoring us. "Okay?"

"She seems nice."

"I don't really interact with them too much."

"Oh." I study his face. He's a bad liar. At least, I think he is. He hasn't done much of it to my knowledge. "She made it sound like you're all best friends."

"She's exaggerating." He turns away.

"Why didn't you ever invite me to *Wifey* Wednesday?"

Nathan sets his jaw without looking at me. He says something right as the music crescendos.

"What?" I ask.

He turns and shouts, "I invited you *lots* of times." The music cuts out, and a few people look over at us. He lowers his voice. "You insisted on spending time apart."

"I *insisted*?" I reel back at the accusation. "We agreed it was good for us to have separate interests."

Connor leans over. "Anyone need a drink?"

Nathan gives Connor an easy smile. "I'll take another IPA."

When Connor's gone, Nathan speaks to me from the side of his mouth. "We'll talk about this later."

"I want to talk about it now."

He takes my arm firmly, steps out of the circle, and walks us a few feet from the men. His forearm between us is like a bridge I want to cross, but he removes his hand from me too fast. "I've invited you," he says calmly. "The first time, you said no. The second time, you said no. The third, fourth, and fifth time—no. Eventually, I stopped asking."

"Because when we come out together, you're always checking to make sure I'm having a good time. And I wanted this to be your time to relax."

"You wanted that time for yourself," he says.

"That's not fair," I say. He makes it sound as though I kicked him out two nights a week, but I only thought it would be good for us to try something new. "Time alone is nice for both of us. We came up with that plan together."

"No, we didn't. You brought it up at dinner one night. Said you heard it's good for couples to miss each other. What was I supposed to say to that? You want to spend time away from me, I'm not going to force myself on you."

I gape at him. He'd grumbled over the idea, I remember that, but he didn't refuse it. I thought he enjoyed coming here. "Is this what you've been mad about?"

"Don't come here, to my night out, and pick a fight. I won't do this here."

"Nathan, answer the question. Is this why you're pissed at me?"

"I don't know." He rubs his eye with the heel of his hand. "I've been stressed about my dad. Work's crazy this time of year. I'm here to chill, Sadie. Why are you trying to put more on my plate?"

My heart beats in my throat. I can't tell if this conversation is making things better or worse. I touch his forearm. "Babe."

"I need to get my shoes on. The game's starting." He walks back to his friends.

I recoil, grinding my teeth. "Sorry to disrupt your 'game,'" I yell after him. Either he doesn't hear me or ignores me. "Looks to me like it's just a bunch of grown men drinking beer and showing off their balls."

Joan laughs beside me. I have no idea where the hell she came from. "How long have you been there?" I ask.

"Just for the part about the balls. It's dead on, but kind of cute how much they love their team."

Cute? I look at Nathan's back. It's just a stupid hobby, isn't it? Or is this where Nathan comes to have fun, flirt, and possibly even forget about me?

"I'm so glad you came," Joan says. "Donna told me you were funny. It's nice to have another chick here."

There isn't an ounce of malice in Joan's voice. I don't know what to believe. If I ask Donna whether she's heard anything about Nathan, she'll see the crack that's begun to form in my marriage, and I don't ever want people to doubt us. It reminds me of the way I feel about my parents, which is that they'd be better off apart. They hate each other but refuse to divorce. Nathan's parents, on the other hand, loved each other but couldn't keep their marriage from crumbling.

Nathan glances back at me. He's too far to hear,

but he can damn well see. I sling an arm around Joan, pleased with the way Nathan lowers his eyebrows. "Let's get a drink," I say. "And not those girly beers the guys drink. I want the hard stuff."

She jumps up and down. "I just knew I'd like you."

Nathan watches us for as long as I can see him, and then we turn our backs to slide onto two fortuitously open barstools.

I flag down the bartender and order an Old-Fashioned for each of us. I generally try to avoid following in the footsteps of my alcoholic father, but my world is upside down tonight, so I go with it. Joan's never had one, and she makes a scene with every sip. "It's so strong," she cries. Then, "Jesus, woman. You have a pair." I clink my glass with hers.

The men crowd around a scoring machine and take turns rolling their big dumb balls down the narrow alley. The pins smile at me until Nathan scatters them with a strike. I applaud from my barstool. He glances in our direction. Maybe he's right, and it was a bad idea to suggest spending this time apart. Does it make me a bad wife? It never occurred to me he'd want me here as much as the women seem to think.

Lasers cut across the darkness. My stool has a bum leg, and it rocks when I sway. The bourbon hits me all at once.

I *am* a bad wife. I can still feel Finn's thumb on my bottom lip. Sweat trickles down the back of my neck where his arm was curled around me. I can hear the clunky thud of the record player as it hit the ground. I'll buy him a new one, a better one, to make up for breaking his small declaration of freedom.

I billow the neckline of my blouse. Finn's apartment is stifling, and I miss the warmth. His hot breath, his hot body. I shut my eyes and wonder about his mattress on the floor, if he sleeps there naked, sheets shoved aside. My clammy skin sliding against his. I bite my lip.

"We never drink this much." Alyssa flops over Joan's lap to get to me. She also had an Old-Fashioned or two. "You're a bad influence."

I smile wickedly. "I try."

"Will you come every Wednesday?" Joan asks. She's pouting as if I've already said no.

"And ruin playtime for Nathan?" I ask. "Hell yeah."

They don't seem to understand my insinuation that he's been flirting with them—Joan, specifically. They laugh and laugh. I join them. I can feel the mascara-black circles under my eyes from a long day. I lick my thumb and scrub them off.

"You're making it worse," Joan says. "Let me try."

She wets her finger. I flinch each time her nail gets too close to my eyeball. "I think it's permanent."

"Damn it," I say too loudly. Her lashes are thick and long. "Your makeup is perfect. How do you do that?"

She launches into a lesson on smudge-proof eyeliner. So she can apply fucking mascara—who cares? I have a communications degree and the attention of *two* godlike men. Would Finn find Joan attractive? I try to be subjective. The only thing we have in common is our dark hair. She's curvier than me and wears it well. Neither of us looks anything like blond, petite Kendra. I close my eyes briefly. Bile rises up my throat, and I have to push the image of Kendra and her daughter away.

I get out my phone and call my brother to ask him what his type is these days. "I'm sleeping," he answers.

"It's not even midnight," I exclaim.

"Call me when you have a kid, you drunk." He hangs up.

I giggle. Andrew doesn't like to be woken up. I love him because he knows Nathan and I were trying to get pregnant, and he doesn't treat me like glass because of it.

I'm not sure how much time has passed when Nathan finds me. "We're leaving."

"Five more minutes," Donna pleads with him.

"Fine." He nods down at me. "I'll meet you out front."

I grip the bar to keep steady. "Nate, wait, stop—"

He hasn't moved an inch. His eyebrows are drawn together. "What?"

"I'm ready. I'll come with you." I lean over to get

143

my purse from under the bar. I swipe for the strap, miscalculate, and slide off the stool.

Before I fall over, Nathan catches me by the waist and hoists me back into place. "You're drunk, Sadie."

"No, I'm not."

A chorus of giggles erupts, including my own.

"Come on." Nathan heaves a chest-expanding sigh. Maybe it's the alcohol coursing through my system, but I think he might be a little amused. "Let's go home."

"I just need to say bye." I turn to Donna and Alyssa and promise, as loudly as I can, "I'll see you next week. For wivesies night."

"I need your number," Donna says.

Alyssa claps her hands. "Me too."

I look back at Nathan, who rolls his eyes. "I'll be out front."

"You won't leave me?" I ask.

"I doubt you'd even make it home." He leans in a little. "Go straight to the front. Don't wander off somewhere."

His breath tickles the outside of my ear. Was alcohol the route back to him all along?

I give Donna and Alyssa my number. I don't ask for theirs. They can get in touch if they want. "Where's Joan?" I ask, realizing I haven't seen her for a few minutes.

"Probably fighting with Mike," Alyssa says.

"Oh." I put my phone away. "Tell her I'll see her

next week."

I go looking for Nathan. Connor calls me over. "Glad you made it. Donna's loving that you're here."

I look around distractedly as I say, "Me too."

Mikey appears and introduces himself. "Joan's boyfriend," he tells me in a thick New York accent.

My attention catches on his introduction. "She said you were engaged."

"Oh, yeah. Yeah, we are." He grins. "Keeps slipping my mind, but don't mention that to her. She gets pissed."

I can't remember if Nathan said to meet him in the front of the building or on the sidewalk. Once again, I search the crowd for him, and then for Joan, who is not here fighting with Mikey as Alyssa said she'd be. She's nowhere to be seen. And neither, for that matter, is Nathan.

ELEVEN

Nathan definitely told me to meet him out front of Brooklyn Bowl. I think. I squint at the bouncers, who lean against barstools and chat. A group of guys spills out of the building, making enough noise to echo down the street. A stocky man throws his arm around me. "Where we going?" he asks.

"I'm not with you."

He looks down, and his thick-rimmed glasses fall forward. He pushes them back into place. "You are now, sexy. Come on."

He leans his weight on me. My world is already off kilter, so we stumble forward a few steps. His friends cheer us on.

"Okay, fine," I say. "Let me just get my husband."

"No shit?" He releases me as if I'm contagious, then speed walks away to catch up with his friends. I fix my blouse and wander down to the corner to look for Nathan. The area is deserted. When I turn around and start back, I spot Nathan talking to the bouncers.

"Christ, Sadie," he says when he notices me. "I told you to wait here for me."

"I couldn't find you . . ."

"I was in the bathroom." He holds out my coat, which I'd forgotten since the alcohol is keeping me warm. His arm sags, as if it weighs a hundred pounds. "You're drunk, you don't listen, and you're out in the freezing-ass dark. What's the matter with you?"

"I don't know." It's a bad time to hiccup, but that's what I do. He rolls his eyes as he walks away. Still, I don't think he's as annoyed as he pretends. "What were you doing in the bathroom?" I ask, struggling to get my coat on and keep up with his long strides.

He looks at me, his confused expression almost cartoon-like. "What kind of a question is that?"

So he disappeared at the same time as Joan. It doesn't mean anything. Or it could mean a million different things.

I trip over uneven sidewalk and drop my purse. I'm one arm in my coat and one out. The world is slightly spinning, so it takes me a minute to pull myself together. "Will you hold my purse while I put on my coat?" I ask, straightening up. He doesn't answer. He's halfway down the sidewalk. "Nathan. Hello?"

He stops and sticks his hands in his pockets but

doesn't turn around. When I finally get my coat on and my purse back on my shoulder, I catch up with him. "Sorry if I'm inconveniencing you," I say dryly.

He doesn't answer, but takes my elbow as we cross the street.

"Can we just get a car home? I've been in the same boots all day, and the subway is still blocks away."

"I need the fresh air." He takes out his cell. "Want me to get you a car? Who knows what the subway'll be like at this hour."

"No." I yank on his arm, and he drops his phone.

"Sadie," he groans.

"I'm sorry." I pick it up, brush it off, and hold it out to him. "It's fine, babe. Not a scratch."

He glances at me sidelong as he sticks it back in his pocket. "What were you drinking?"

I grin. "Old-Fashioned."

His raises his eyebrows. "Thought you hated those."

"I figured they'd do the trick if they're potent enough for my dad."

"Potent, huh?"

I hope he'll ask what I'm trying to accomplish by choosing my alcohol by that criteria. At least it would start a conversation. He leads me across another street. I glance at his hand on my arm. I'm not even sure he realizes he's doing it. "You'd save yourself some trouble if you just held my hand."

149

"It's no trouble," he says and lets go of me when we're back on the sidewalk.

"Oh." I nearly trot just to keep up with him. "Did you win tonight?"

"We were just screwing around."

"But you kept score. I saw. I saw three of your strikes."

He rubs his nose. "I guess, technically, I won. But it wasn't really—"

"I knew it," I say, clasping my hands. We're nearing the subway, where it's more crowded, so I'm not the only loud girl. "You're the VIP."

"VIP?" he asks. "You mean MVP."

"You're my VIP *and* my MVP." I slur the last part because of my goofy grin. I think I'll make those girls at the bar my new friends. Assuming none of them are sleeping with my husband, that is. The thought makes me snort. "Hey," I cry, suddenly remembering my talk with Donna. "Donna invited us to Park Slope for dinner and sangria. I think we should go."

Nathan nods at me. I swear he's holding back a smile. "Yeah? You'd leave the city for once?"

"I'm here, aren't I?" I ask. I'd prefer we were in Manhattan, where a cab ride home would take five minutes, but I keep that to myself.

"I guess," he concedes. "Thanks for coming."

It takes me a moment to register his unexpected gratitude. Maybe all Nathan wants is for me to take a little more interest in his life. If that's the case, I'll definitely show up for the next Wifey Wednesday. "I really like the girls," I say and mean it. Riding the Brooklyn wave that got us into safer waters, I continue, "They made Park Slope sound great."

Instantly, he tenses, and I watch his almost-good mood extinguish. "Really?" he asks, pursing his lips. "Is that what *the girls* said?"

I frown. There's no missing the sudden irritation in his voice. What set him off, though? Does he not like me hanging around them? Joan, specifically? "What's wrong?" I ask. "You don't like them?"

"I have no problem with them." He kicks a beer can on the sidewalk. It flies into a brick wall with some Banksy-style graffiti. He sighs. "Awesome. We'll go to Park Slope if that's what you want."

I furrow my brows at his sarcasm. "I thought you'd like the idea."

"Whatever."

My smile fades. "Whatever," I mimic. "So grumpy all the time."

He glances at the ground but quickly looks back up. "Are you really coming next week?"

"Yes," I say. "One-hundred percent. I will be there."

He scratches his jaw and squints ahead of us. Bedford station is in sight now. People of all sorts are gathered around it, loitering by storefronts, smoking, playing music. Others are just trying to get through. "I don't think you should."

His words sting, transporting me right back to

this morning's rejection in the shower. I felt like we were making progress just now. I keep coming back for more, though, and I struggle to get words out. "You don't want me there?"

"I don't know. I think I need these nights to myself right now."

Without warning, tears scald my eyes. Maybe it's the bourbon. Maybe it's the ache of my feet, swollen from a long day in heels. It's hard to swallow the truth—but in a way, these little jabs, like his earlier dismissal in the shower, are breakthroughs. Before now, he hasn't really admitted anything is wrong. At least we're no longer on different planets.

"Don't cry." He mutters too softly for me to determine if he's annoyed or concerned. I don't know how he can tell. He didn't even look at me.

Our footsteps are hollow on the sidewalk. I wait until I'm sure the threat of tears has passed to ask, "Why don't you want me to come?"

"It's complicated."

"I have time."

He shrugs. "I don't want to talk about it. For one, you're wasted."

"I'm sobering up fast."

He swallows, focused on the subway stop ahead. "You won't even remember this tomorrow."

"You know that isn't true," I argue. "You just want an excuse not to talk. It's really unfair to shut me out like this." He picks up his pace, and I pick up mine. My boots are getting tighter and tighter, the balls of my feet screaming. I avoid making eye contact with people I pass. "Nathan," I say. "Hello?"

He turns on me. "It's unfair, is it?" he asks. "Is it fair that I've told you a hundred times about Park Slope, yet you act like you've never heard of it until *Donna* mentions it?"

Between his pace and all the people around, I have to concentrate to catch each of his words. I'm shocked. It's entirely possible he's mentioned Park Slope before, but I usually wave it off when he talks about moving. Gramercy Park is perfect for us. Growing up so close to Manhattan, it was the only place I ever wanted to be, and it has everything we need. "I'm sorry," I say. "It's just that Brooklyn—"

"Is it fair that every other wife shows up for her husband but mine?" he continues. "And when you do, you have the gall to accuse me of not wanting you there. No, it's not fair, but that's how it is in Sadie world."

My mouth falls open. *Sadie world?* I have no response. If I live in my own world, it's not news to Nathan. He used to love doting on me. I've always made sure he knows what an important part of that world he is.

I'm a few paces behind him, and my feet start to cramp. They hurt. I hurt. "How long have you been feeling this way?" I ask.

He gets out his subway card and wipes his forehead on his sleeve. "Can we talk about this tomorrow?"

"No," I say.

He heads down the stairs, and I hobble after him, rifling through my purse for my wallet.

Nathan waits at the platform entrance for me. "Midnight in a subway station is not the time to have this discussion," he says.

"Fine." I swipe my subway card and go through. "Go sulk by yourself. When you're ready to talk, find me."

"Come on, Sadie," he says. The turnstile beeps at him when he tries to pass. "Wait. My month is expired."

"I don't care," I call behind my shoulder and storm away. An overhead marquee tells me the subway is five minutes away. It should be enough time for Nathan to buy a new monthly pass, but still, I glance over my shoulder for him. I have to stop at a bench to take off my bootie and massage my foot.

Nathan walks in my direction, putting his new pass away and sliding his wallet into his back pocket. "I don't like when you run off like that," he says as he approaches.

"Tough shit."

He nods at my feet. "Cramp?"

"It's fine." I look up at him and then away. "Are you going to tell me what your problem is?"

"Not tonight," he says. "I wish you would respect when I tell you I'm not ready."

I shake my head, done with this. "And I wish you would respect when I tell you not to talk to me until

154

you're ready to work this out."

He puts his hands in his pockets and hesitates. "Look—"

"That was a nice way of saying leave me alone."

I stare at his feet until he finally walks away. He goes to the next bench and sits.

Nathan and I suck at this. Maybe we should've fought more over the years—maybe it would've prevented things from getting this far. The worst part is the fresh, sharp memory of how we used to be. How he used to know me. It wasn't long ago that Nathan brought home *the* coffee table of my dreams because he'd spent months stopping by flea markets to find it. He listened to me. He sensed what I needed. He always knew how to make me happy.

It's been seven years since he walked into my line of sight and flipped my world right-side up. What hurts the most is that I remember that happy moment like it was yesterday.

TWELVE

Nathan and I met at a summertime barbeque in the Hamptons. It was an engagement party for Jill, my closest friend, and Victor, the man I'd introduced her to. They'd rented a house for the weekend. Victor and his friends were short players for a beach football game, so they invited some guys from the house next to theirs.

Jill and I came onto the deck wearing skimpy bikinis and sipping strawberry margaritas. The tall, muscular quarterback was getting rushed when our eyes met. He dropped the ball immediately and jogged toward us. Since he looked as though he had something to say, I leaned over the railing to hear better.

"What's your name?" he asked.

The glass was sweating in my hand. He had large, cappuccino-colored eyes and a suntan to match. Jill nudged me to prompt my answer.

"Oh." I looked up from his broad chest, which was slick

with sweat and sand. "Sadie," I replied, wary of his question but smiling. It's hard not to smile when a man like him pays you attention.

"Have you been here before, Sadie?" he asked.

"To the Hamptons? Yes—"

"No, here." He pointed down at the sand under his feet. "Have you stood here?"

Jill put her ice-cold hand on my forearm and squeezed. She told me later the sparks between us were flying.

I giggled nervously. Having seen my reflection in the sliding glass door earlier, I knew my mouth was red from the drink. "Yes. We had a bonfire on the beach last night."

"Okay." The handsome quarterback dropped to his knees and looked up to the sky. "Thank you, God. If I ever doubted you—"

"Hunt, what the fuck're you doing?" called one of the players from the beach.

The man met my gaze again and responded only to me. "I'm worshipping the ground she walks on. Literally. It calls for at least that."

I blushed profusely while Jill clapped. "Are you all watching?" she yelled at the gawking men. "That's how it's done." She winked at him. "Bravo."

It was too much, but it worked. I would've swooned if he'd only offered to refill my drink.

"Stay and watch the game," he said. "Will you, Sadie?"

My cheeks ached from smiling. "Yes."

"Don't skip out on me. Okay? I'm coming back for you."

And he did. His name was Nathan. When

football ended, and they'd cleaned up, Nathan and his friends came over for dinner. Later that night, he and I shared stories and a blanket on the beach. We made wishes on shooting stars. I was twenty-four.

From that day on, Nathan adored me. And I let myself be adored. That didn't mean I loved Nathan any less than he loved me, though. It was just how we were. How we used to be.

A bottle shatters on the ground. My sunny Hamptons afternoon is swallowed up by a frigid, starless subway station in Brooklyn. I'm shivering, my shoe in my hand. Nathan, on his bench a few yards away, doesn't look over at me. Maybe he can't worship my ground anymore, because he's found a new place to kneel.

The subway was supposed to arrive three minutes ago. My body sags. I just want to be home in bed.

"Hey," I hear. "You. You lied to me."

It takes me a moment to realize I'm being addressed. I look at the group walking toward me— the bespectacled man and his friends from outside of Brooklyn Bowl.

He plops his ass next to me on the seat. "You told me you were married," he teases.

I spare him a sideways glance, but I'm hardly in the mood. "I am."

"Liar." He makes a face like he's constipated. His glasses slide a millimeter down his red nose. "You hurt my feelings."

I wedge my bootie back onto my bloated foot. "You'll survive."

"I won't. I need a kiss to make it better."

His friends laugh. A woman nearby looks up from her book then back down.

I stand up and walk away. He yanks my elbow, pulling me back. With a flutter of his eyelashes, he shuts his eyes, puckers, and breathes beer fumes on my face. "Just one. Please?"

"Let go, asshole." I pull too hard and stumble back into a wall of a body. My heart leaps as two hands land on my shoulders, trapping me.

"It's me," Nathan says above my head.

I exhale as the tension in my body eases. I turn to thank him, but he steps around me. Spectacle's eyes are still shut when Nathan shoves him backward. He stumbles across the platform, and his glasses clatter to the ground. "Hey, what the—"

"That's my wife." Nathan's shoulders are nearly at his ears as he stalks toward the guy, who's probably half a foot shorter and starting to look more like a kid.

"Are you crazy, dude?" he asks when he's regained his footing. "You could've killed me. You don't push someone in the subway."

Nathan leans down and nabs the glasses. "Don't forget your hipster crap. Who do you think you are, Clark Kent?" He throws them at the guy, who catches them at his stomach like a line drive.

Some people snicker. The group he's with

collectively *oohs*.

"Fuck you. I'm not the one pushing people around like some stupid superhero."

"I'm teaching you some respect," Nathan says. He's outnumbered, but he doesn't seem to care. "She told you she was married."

"Twice," I add.

"She doesn't *look* married." The kid puffs his chest out triumphantly, as if he's insulted us.

His friends begin to disperse one by one, apparently bored with the confrontation. "Come on, dude," one of them says. "Back off."

He follows them, scowling as he inspects his lenses.

I've had my fair share of drunken admirers. Nathan usually lets me handle them unless I need back up. Tonight, I'm glad he was here. I look up at him. "Thank you."

The platform trembles as the L train approaches. Nathan just nods and pulls me by my bicep up to the yellow line. We wait in tense silence until the doors open. There are plenty of open seats, but I take a middle one so Nathan can have the end. He stays standing. Once we've crossed back into Manhattan, I get up to be next to him. The late-night train moves fast, rattling us around. I let my shoulder bump his.

"You're quiet," I say.

Predictably, he doesn't respond.

I grab the lapel of his coat and run it through my hand. "That was sexy," I say.

He arches an eyebrow. "Getting hit on by a drunk hipster?"

"You know what I mean." I pull him a little closer. "The way you defended me."

"I would've done it for anyone."

For some reason, he wants his words to sting. They don't. He might do it for anyone, but he'd never *not* do it for me. I keep my hold on the soft wool. There's one thing that can obliterate my anger from earlier, and it's arousal. I lean into Nathan. It becomes clear to me that I don't truly believe he's been with Joan. If I did, I wouldn't be able to stomach having sex with him. And right now, I definitely can.

I slip my hand into his coat. "You're getting so hard."

His nostrils flare as he glances down at me. "Hard?"

"Your muscles." I rub his flat, ridged stomach. "Don't think I haven't noticed. And your hair. It's different, but I like it—"

He grabs my wrist, stopping me. "Don't."

Don't. The other night, during sex, he covered my mouth when I said his name. He still doesn't want me, his wife. It's okay, though. I'm turned on enough by the way he claimed me in front of those guys to play along. "I don't normally do this," I say, glancing around the car. "But I was wondering if you'd like to come home with me tonight."

"What're you doing, Sadie?"

"Sadie? Who's that? Your wife?" I shrug. "I don't

162

mind. I can keep a secret."

"This is ridiculous."

The subway stops. Someone gets off, someone else gets on. I blink up at Nathan a few times and slide my hand through his, back to my side. "You're a faithful husband," I say. "I get it. But we don't have to touch to have fun."

"What do you mean?" he asks.

"Haven't you ever talked dirty?" I ask. "Or doesn't your wife like that?"

He hesitates, but responds, "She does."

The subway jostles us, throwing me against him. He catches me, and I'm hit with the smell of cigarettes. "Have you been smoking?" I ask, surprised enough to break character.

He pinches his eyebrows together, but then his expression eases. "Don't tell my wife."

I bite my lower lip. *Bingo*. He's interested. I rise onto the balls of my feet. When he doesn't move, I motion for him to bend down. He does. I whisper in his ear, "You're making my knees weak. Not sure I can stand much longer."

"What . . . what do you suggest?" he asks.

"How about I kneel? Right here. Take you in my mouth."

His breathing deepens. "We're not alone."

"Who, them?" I ask, nodding to the other passengers. "They can fuck off. Or watch. If you don't mind, that is."

His hand tightens around my bicep. "Christ,

Sadie . . ."

The train comes to a grinding halt. If he weren't holding me, I'd fly forward. The doors open. We're at our stop. He and I stare at each other a moment. "Go ahead," I dare him. "You've been trying to get rid of me all night, haven't you?"

He hesitates, but releases me and leaves the car. I give him a head start. When he's halfway up the stairs, I catch him checking over his shoulder for me. I'm not there, but he doesn't stop.

Right before the subway doors close, I hop out. By the time I'm on ground level, he's gone.

My phone rings. I answer it with, "You left something on the train."

"Yeah?" Nathan asks. "What?"

"Me." I swallow, checking left and right. There are people around, but fuck it. This is New York City. Nothing shocks anyone. "Do you normally walk away from a woman who's ready and willing to suck your cock?"

The man walking ahead of me looks back, but I avert my eyes.

"Fuck, Sadie," Nathan says. "You aren't playing fair—"

"I bet it's huge. A tall, strong man like you." Nathan and I can talk it up in bed, but I'm not used to being this candid. Especially in public. I can't let him distract me, though. As long as Nathan wants me, I haven't lost him. As long he reacts, even if it's with anger, then there's still a chance. I can't seem to connect with him emotionally lately, but sex can bring him back to me, even if it's only for a little while.

I press on. "Does she let you come in her mouth, your wife?"

"No—" The word comes out strangled.

This is supposed to be for him, but it's working on me too. I'm getting wet. "I would. Like a good fucking slut."

The line goes dead. I check the screen. He hung up. *Shit*. Why? If he wants a slut, I can be that. He doesn't need to find a Joan, or anyone else, to satisfy him. But what else can I do to show him I care? He rejects my touch. My words. My love. All that I have. I'm at a loss.

By the time I reach our apartment building, my self-doubt has become a hurricane inside me. It shouldn't be so much work to get my husband to notice me.

But when I get off the elevator, Nathan's there, leaning against the door of our apartment. His arms are folded over his chest, his eyes dark. I can't read his mood. I don't speak as I approach, afraid to say the wrong thing.

"How'd you find me?" he asks.

My heart skips. He still wants to play. I don't miss a beat. "I followed you."

"Why?"

"Because, I . . ." I glance at the door. "I . . . want to come in."

"My wife is home."

My thighs tremble. My panties are sticky, already damp from earlier. This is having a swift effect on me. "Are you suggesting—"

He whirls me around and pushes me up against the front door. "This what you want?" he asks. "Is this why you won't leave me the fuck alone?"

I'm not sure if we're still role-playing. My breasts are mashed, but I like this new side to Nathan. The shock alone is enough to get me going. "Yes," I say. "I want this."

He pulses his hips into my backside, and I have my answer. There's no question he still wants me, even if I am his unexciting wife. With my cheek against the door, I can see Finn's apartment. My mind flashes to earlier, Finn's hot, his hungry lips. "Here?" I ask.

"We can't go inside," he taunts. "You want this, don't you?"

There's no chance I'd stop him now. Anything I get from him feels like a small victory.

He yanks up my skirt and runs a hand up the silky inside of my tights. "All these goddamn layers."

"Rip them."

He doesn't waste a second. He stretches the fabric from my leg and uses his other hand to pierce it. Once my tights puncture, they give easily. He rubs me, dominating my senses, drowning out anything that isn't his touch. When I'm whimpering, he slides his fingers inside me. He knows me well. Within seconds, I can't catch my breath, and the door rattles against my chest. He takes his hand away, and I know what's coming.

He gets his keys out and unlocks the door, hurrying me inside.

"What about your wife?" I whisper.

"We'll have to be quiet."

I turn on the lights. He turns them back out and pulls me against him by my waist. He starts to gather my skirt in his hands when Ginger pushes her nose between us.

"Ginger, no," he says.

Her tail whacks his leg. She jumps up on us, wanting to play.

Nathan takes her collar. "I said *no*. Down." He pulls her away and leaves me standing there. I wait, breathing hard, my knees nearly knocking together. A door slams.

Nathan returns. The apartment is still completely dark. "On your knees."

I drop down to the cold, hard tile. I'm salivating, ready to take every inch of him. Fucking in the doorway, we've done, but I don't remember ever blowing him here.

I push his hands away from his pants. He's too slow. I take him out, the long, hard cock that belongs to me, the one I know better than my own pussy. I run the tip of my tongue around the underside of his crown. He fists my hair. I lick his shaft. Suck his balls. Bite the inside of his thigh, the way he likes. I know I'm golden when his cum beads on my tongue.

I blow him to get him off—slow, then fast, then slow again. I take him deep for as long as I can manage, then suckle his tip. With a groan, he falls onto his outstretched arms against the wall. He thrusts lightly, working himself deeper into my mouth. He shudders, close to the edge.

Spreading his hand over my scalp, he threads his fingers in my hair. "Fuck me, you're too good. I'm going to come."

I bob my head faster. He hasn't finished in my mouth since before I can remember, but not because I won't let him. He likes to fuck me at the end, come inside me.

Not tonight. My only warning is a hoarse shout before he floods my mouth. I'm even more turned on now, knowing he was so excited he couldn't wait any longer. I've done and been exactly what he needed.

He pulls out, panting.

"I swallowed it all," I say. "Like a good slut."

He stares at me, his mouth open as he labors for breath. He tucks himself back into his pants. "Are you mocking me?"

"No." I bite my bottom lip and slide my hand between my legs. "I loved it. I want more."

"When it's convenient for you."

I scoff. "What's that supposed to mean?"

He walks away. After a moment, Ginger comes bounding out, nearly tackling me to the ground. I get up and take off my boots. I leave my tights, holding onto the small hope he'll want to rip them more. In the bedroom, I find him shirtless in his underwear. He pulls on his sweatpants.

"That's it?" I ask.

"I told you in the shower this morning, Sadie. I don't want this right now, but you keep pushing me. I can't keep a clear head when we're fucking."

"What do you need a clear head for?" I ask, crossing my arms. "Tell me, so I can help."

"I will," he looks pointedly at me, "once my head is clear, and I know what I want to say."

I scowl, my cheeks heating. I'm tempted to seduce him again just so I can show him how it feels to be rejected. "You know what? Just get the hell out."

"What?"

I grab his pillow, carry it into the living room, and toss it on the couch. Next, I go to the linen closet and get a clean set of sheets.

"What're you doing?" he asks.

I unceremoniously drop them next to the pillow. "Have fun sleeping on the couch."

He blocks me as I try to reenter our bedroom. "I'm not trying to hurt you." He runs his free hand through his hair and pulls it. The pain in his face makes me pause. "I just need this. I need to figure my stuff out."

"What stuff?" I plead. I'm tired of fighting—with him, with myself.

"I'll come to you when I'm ready. I promise. Until then, I'm asking for this one thing. Back off."

"You say that like it's no big deal. You live in my apartment."

"*Our* apartment."

"You know what I fucking mean. Don't twist my words. We live together. How am I supposed to ignore you?"

"Not ignore," he says. "Just a little space."

"You told me never to give you space."

That makes *him* pause. He looks me over, my ripped tights and hiked up skirt. "I know. I did say that, but . . ."

I shake my head and push past him. I get into bed, buzzed, aroused, and dejected. Ginger pads between the couch and the bed, confused. In the dark silence, I'm defenseless against the onslaught of emotions. The tears come. He doesn't want me on the most basic level, and it's something I never thought I'd have to deal with. What do I do with that? Where can we possibly go from here?

I sob with my fist in my mouth so he won't hear. Nathan's getting further away, but he's still in the next room—and somehow, that makes it worse.

THIRTEEN

When Finn spots me coming up the sidewalk toward our apartment building, he holds the door. "Hi," he says as I duck inside. I try not to look at him, but it's hard. He smells earthy, like he's been sitting around a fire on a winter night, draped in blankets. "How've you been?"

"Okay." I stop to get the mail.

He waits as I sort through it. Perhaps sensing my mood, he says, "Hey. What's Mickey Mouse's favorite book?"

I glance up finally. His bright green eyes make me self-conscious about the bags under mine. I toss everything but a bill in the recycle bin. "I give up."

"*The Great Ratsby.*" He grins. "Marissa came up with that. She has a sudden fascination with rodents."

It feels good to smile. "Smart girl."

He hits the elevator call button. The doors open,

and we get on. "It's late," he says. "Just getting home from work?"

I nod. "We had an event in SoHo. How's unpacking?"

"Hot." We stand there a moment. As if the word itself is a heater, the space warms. He licks his lips. They look dry from the cold, but still rust-colored and inviting. My hands twitch as I remember how I lost control last week and grabbed onto him while he kissed me.

He laughs. "We forgot to hit the button."

My cheeks flush. Or maybe I was already blushing from my memory. Either way, the tension eases, and I relax. "Is the apartment almost done?" I ask once we're ascending.

He shrugs. "Not really. I got distracted."

"With what?"

"Finally got some of my equipment out. I took my camera for a spin or two."

"That's great," I say, smiling. "Get anything good?"

"I'm a little rusty," he admits. "But there's a lot to work with in this city. In fact, I even scored my first gig."

"Wow." I pick up on his excitement. "Congratulations."

"Thanks. She's a small business owner, so I'm cutting her a deal. Hopefully, she'll refer me to others." We arrive at the sixth floor, and he touches his hand to the small of my back as we get off.

"Your beard's growing in," I note on the short walk to his door.

He scratches it. "It itches."

"You could shave it."

We stop at his apartment. "You don't like it?"

I've never been much for facial hair. Nathan has a blade-like, square jawline, and it'd be a shame to hide it. On Finn, though, it works. Very well. "No, I do."

He nods. "Then I'll keep it."

I go to leave, but being near his apartment makes me think of how it feels inside. The warmth. The slight buzz from breaking the rules. I can almost hear the skip of the vinyl. He has his key in the door when he notices I'm still standing there.

"I'm sorry about your record player," I say. "I'll replace it."

"It's fine, actually," he says. "Vintage. Well made."

"Oh. Okay. Good."

Slowly, he curves his mouth into a smile, as though I've been caught confessing a secret. I'm not sure I have a secret. If I did, it would probably be that after almost a week of near silence in my own apartment, I kind of want to go to Finn's, listen to some music, and chill. "Night, Sadie," he says on his way inside.

At work the next day, everyone in the office gathers

in the conference room for a meeting. As Amelia discusses updates to our website, she points at me. "Headshots," she says. "Don't let me forget."

"Headshots?" I ask. "Why?"

"We need to update your blurb on the site. Now that you're dealing with clients more in your new position, I want your face out there. It's not enough just to list your accomplishments."

I sit forward. The last week, I've had a lot on my mind. Mostly work, Thanksgiving plans, and the fact that Nathan is still sleeping on the couch. But since I saw Finn last night, I haven't thought of much else. As Amelia starts in on the next item of business, I speak up. "Can I hire my own photographer?"

"Fine by me," she says. "Just try to have fun with it. Make sure it reflects what we do here—incorporate a hobby or something. Send me the bill."

A hobby, I think to myself later, when I'm riding the subway home from work. Being silly with Nathan is my definition of fun. The nosebleed section of a Yankees game, my feet in his lap as I scarf down a relish-laden hotdog—the only reason I put up with baseball.

Fun is racing against the clock at the Union Square farmer's market, trying to come up with a more creative dinner than Nathan in ten minutes. Even when his ideas are better, he declares me the winner.

Cooking for Nathan. Being with Nathan. That's my hobby.

Tonight, he's bowling. Even though it's Wednesday again, we didn't need to discuss whether or not I'd come along. As much as I'd like to be there, I'm respecting his wants and needs. He doesn't want me there. Doesn't need me bringing him down.

After taking Ginger out, I'm not in the mood to sit still. I pour myself a glass of wine as I prepare a steak salad, garlic potato wedges, and broccolini. I eat alone at the counter, stabbing at romaine lettuce, feeding Ginger table scraps. There's enough for two, but this meal won't be any good tomorrow.

I wonder about Finn. If he's been eating well. How often he goes back to Connecticut. What he does all day. One gig won't be enough to pay the rent in this building. Make that two gigs, if he accepts the job to do my headshots. His excitement last night over finding work he's passionate about has stuck with me. When I tell him about the job, I'll be the reason for his enthusiasm.

After my second glass of wine, the silence in the apartment is deafening. I put leftovers in a Tupperware and grab my keys. I knock on Finn's door, rocking in my Minnetonka moccasins. He probably isn't home. Out for dinner. Visiting Connecticut. At a movie. I've convinced myself he isn't here when he answers in a t-shirt and basketball shorts.

He leans his shoulder against the doorframe, an absurdly pleased smile on his face. "Hello again."

"Hello." I glance into the apartment. The lights

175

are on, but I don't hear anything—or anyone. I should've thought this through more.

"I'm alone," he says.

"Oh." I look up into his eyes. "Me too."

He nods as if he understands. How could he possibly know how painful it is for me to be alone tonight while Nathan is cavorting with his friends and their wives?

"Come in," he says.

I don't even hesitate. Tonight, the gray cloud over my head can take a break. "I brought you something."

He shuts the door behind me. "Is that what I think it is?"

"It's dinner."

"God in heaven," he groans, "you are an angel."

I grin. "That might be a stretch."

"You wouldn't say that if you were me. I haven't had vegetables in a week."

It's supposed to make me laugh, but instead it makes me a little sad. He has more furniture since I was here last, but the couch is covered with a sheet. The TV is still in its box. There's an entertainment center in the corner, but it's not lined up right with the walls. I bury my hands in my sweater sleeves, even though his heater clearly still isn't fixed.

"Are you doing okay?" I ask.

"What?" He follows my gaze around the room. An Ikea coffee table is in pieces by the sofa, the instructions spread out. "I'm having a blast. It's the first time in years I get to live like a bachelor. And it's just as good as I remember."

I don't point out that bachelorhood can have as many ups and downs as married life. Last time I was here, I found the apartment refreshing, a clean slate. The mess makes me second-guess myself. TV dinners and living out of boxes? First dates and awkward conversation? I don't recall my single days fondly.

I hand him the Tupperware. "Sorry to spoil the party, but there is broccolini in there."

He raises his eyebrows. "Good thing broccolini's my favorite."

I laugh. "Try again. That wasn't convincing."

"No, really." He motions for me to follow him into the kitchen. "I like how small it is. Better than broccoli, those big-ass motherfuckers."

I'm full on giggling into my hand now. Five minutes here, and I'm no longer a villain—or a victim. I'm not ruining someone's day just by being around.

"Will you eat with me?" he asks.

I gesture in the general direction of my apartment. My hand is still sleeved like a five-year-old. "I already ate."

"But you'll sit?" he asks, pulling out a chair for me. "Just for a few?"

He goes to a cupboard without waiting for my answer. I tuck some hair behind my ear and take a seat at the table. At the moment, I'm more comfortable in a stranger's crowded, unorganized kitchen than I am in my own bedroom.

He puts all the food onto a plate, even though I suspect if I weren't here, he'd eat straight out of the container.

"So," we say at the same time. Both of us smile politely.

"Go ahead," he says.

"It's nothing. Just . . ." I push up my sleeves. I want to relax tonight, and I can't do that while there's an elephant in the room. It's best we fess up to our mistake and move on. "Last week."

"Right. That's what I was going to say."

I nod. Kissing Finn was wrong. I repeat that sentence in my head to avoid remembering how it felt. "I'm sorry."

"I'm not."

I blanch. My next sentence was going to be, *It won't happen again.*

"I mean, I *am* sorry," he says, bringing his plate to the table. "Kind of. Not that it happened, but that it's happening like this." He gestures between us. "I wish things were, you know . . . different."

I cinch my eyebrows. "You do?"

"Yeah." He forks some broccolini into his mouth. "I do."

Well. I don't know what to do other than watch him chew. Am I supposed to agree? Sure, Finn is jaw-droppingly attractive. Just being around him makes me feel warm. Welcome, even. Light. Happy? He likes me. My mood has improved since walking in the door. But the truth remains beneath the surface. It won't last. Just because I feel better now doesn't mean I'd trade the life I have to kiss Finn. That is, if I still even have that life. Nathan can, and might, take it all away. Maybe he already has, and he's just trying to figure out how to tell me.

"You're sad," Finn says.

I look up from staring at his wood table. "I'm fine."

"No," he says as if he has a direct line to my thoughts. "You're *sad*. I can tell."

With my hands in my lap, I spin my wedding ring around my finger. Finn looks at me intently. If he wants me to say Nathan has made me sad, I can't. Not to him. An admission like that to another man would be more intimate than a kiss.

"I came over here to ask you a favor," I say brightly, remembering how excited I am to be able to give him work. "A photography thing."

He frowns. "You need coaching in the art of changing the subject."

"That could be," I admit, smoothing my hands over my thighs.

"I'll allow it. For now. What's the favor?"

"Headshots." I roll my eyes. "It's stupid, really. My boss wants them for the website. Now that I've been promoted, I have my own *About Me* section and everything."

"Your own section, huh?" He takes a bite and nods at me. "So what's your picture now? A question mark?"

"A silhouette with a bowl haircut," I say, deadpan. "No wonder business is slow."

He smiles as he chews. "Sadie?"

"Yes?"

"You make a mean steak."

I grin. "Thanks."

"I'm happy to take your photo. Honored, really."

"You'll get paid, obviously." I smack my forehead like a sitcom character. "Duh. I should've led with that."

"Don't worry about it. I could use the practice. How's this weekend?"

"Are you sure? It's so soon."

"Absolutely. Let's do it."

"Great," I say with relief. Amelia won't be on my ass about it. "Where?"

"I get to choose?"

"She said to 'have fun with it.' I have no idea what—"

"I'll take care of it. Come over Saturday morning. I'll look at your company's website and get a feel for things."

I get a business card from the pouch on my key ring and slide it across the table. "Here's the info."

"Amelia Van Ecken Communications." He studies it, flips it over. "We'll get a picture for your card too."

I wave my hand. "Our marketing girl handles that stuff."

"Insist on a picture. It helps for clients to see a face." He swallows some food and takes a swig of beer. "Especially yours. I'd buy anything you were selling."

I try not to smile. "I'm not really selling anything."

"Then I'd believe anything you said."

I scrunch my nose. "If that's true, you need lessons in the art of the poker face. Your cards are showing."

"Sorry, Sadie," he says. "I don't play games. Not with something this serious."

His comment hugs the line of flirtatiousness. Is he referring to my work? Or us? Either way, I've been down this path with him. I know where it leads. A suggestive comment becomes an inside joke becomes a kind of intimacy that opens the door for more. My conscience has enough to deal with. Not only did I kiss another man, but now I'm back in his apartment, planning to spend more time with him. "I should get home," I say.

Finn sits back in his chair. He keeps ahold of his beer by the neck. "Isn't it bowling night?"

"You remembered."

"Of course."

I don't move. Just because I should doesn't mean I want to.

He rolls the base of his bottle over the wood a few times, and then stands. He puts his dish in the sink, and on the way back, opens the fridge and shows me a Heineken. "Have one. It will help."

He could be referring to the heat, but I think he means my problems with Nathan. Staying in this chair isn't as bad if Finn doesn't technically ask. I'm comfortable in our own little world. Nathan doesn't even know I'm here—and would he care? What do I have to go home to?

He pops the cap and gives it to me over the table. I take a longer drink than I intend. And he's right. It does cool me down.

"What did he say about the lipstick stain?"

I put the bottle down too hard, and he flinches. The fact that Nathan and I aren't speaking makes the topic a bit difficult to broach. Finn is the only person I've told. I'm beginning to regret that I did if he means to hold me accountable. I'd rather forget the stain ever existed. After all, Chin-Mae returned the tie good as new.

"Sadie," Finn prompts.

I read the Heineken label. It's a product of Holland. Interesting. I'd thought it was a German beer, yet it's right there on the front. Shows how little I pay attention. I look for that number, the one that tells you how much alcohol is in the beer.

"The alcohol by volume is five-point-two percent," Finn says. I don't hide my shock over his mind-reading skills. He takes the bottle out of my hands and puts it on the table. "I asked you a question."

I don't look at him when I answer. "I haven't

brought it up."

"Why not?"

"Because I trust him," I say. "And I don't want to set him off."

Finn cranes his neck to get me to look at him. "Does he have a temper?"

"No," I respond immediately when I realize what Finn must think. "Not at all. Just a lot on his mind."

"Have you found anything else that indicates . . .?"

I almost wish he'd finish his sentence so I'm not forced to fill in the blanks. Anything to indicate Nathan's cheating on me? He's fallen out of love with me? He's unhappier than he's ever been? I pinch my eyebrow between my nails until my eyes water. I pick up my beer with a look that dares Finn to take it away again.

"I don't know," I say. "A couple times he's come home smelling like smoke when he shouldn't. Like he stopped by a bar after work, or during lunch." I wait for Finn to tell me I'm paranoid. He stays silent. "I met this girl," I continue, "at the bowling alley. This woman. She's a girlfriend of one of the players. Wednesday nights, wives are invited to the games."

Finn's forehead creases. "It's Wednesday now. He never told you?"

"He did. I turned him down to watch TV, and because I think he's more relaxed when I'm not around."

"Why?"

"He doesn't have to worry that I'm having a good time. It's just the way he is."

"Oh." He taps his index finger idly on the table. "So who's the girl?"

"I don't know. I just got a feeling, you know? She's not his type, I don't think. I just . . . wonder. When I try to ask him what's wrong, he doesn't want to talk. He gets defensive."

"Huh."

"Huh?"

"That's not a good sign."

"I know it isn't," I say immediately. As upset as I am with him for his silence, I also worry about him. "He wants time to figure stuff out. I don't know what exactly—" I stop, suddenly aware of my surroundings. Normally, the only person I confide in about my relationship with Nathan is Nathan. Sometimes my brother. Finn and I have crossed a line. I'm not sure how he'll interpret my concerns over Nathan. "I shouldn't be talking about this with you."

"Why not?"

He knows why not. It's best I don't say it aloud. Then again, maybe I don't know what's best anymore. Nathan's in Brooklyn right now, and so is Joan. But I'm here. "Because you kissed me. And I want you to do it again." I slouch further into my chair, even though he doesn't move an inch. "That's not an invitation."

"I know. Believe me, if it were, there wouldn't be

a table between us."

I swallow. The picture he paints is clear. "You make it sound like you want something to happen between us. What about Kendra?"

It's his turn to fidget with his beer. Without looking away from me, he picks at the corner of the label. "What do you want to know?"

"Anything."

"Kendra?" He works his jaw from side to side before swigging his beer. "I can tell you why I married her. Marissa. It was an unplanned pregnancy. I wanted to do right by them. Kendra didn't stop me."

His candidness catches me off guard. "Oh. You mean you weren't . . . you don't . . .?"

He shrugs. "Yeah, I love her. We were together over a year when I ended things. I thought I was too young to be tied down. Then I made the unoriginal mistake of having breakup sex." He's not looking at me anymore. "Not that Marissa's a mistake."

I'm glad he doesn't catch my grimace. "That's when Kendra got pregnant. Breakup sex?"

He rolls his lips inward and nods. "It's just not how I pictured things, you know?"

I tilt my head. I know all too well what he means. I, too, thought myself invincible at that age. I wasn't. Our situations aren't so different. But it seems that while Finn's decision set him on a path for life, mine cleared the way for me to choose my life.

"How did you picture things?" I ask.

He squints at me but looks lost in thought. "Kendra teases me for being an idealist. Secretly, I think it bothers her. There's no romance in staying with someone out of obligation." He flexes his hands around his beer. "I guess I'm weird for thinking I'd marry for love."

"It's not weird." The resentment in his words is clear. "But I hear it's nearly impossible for a woman to get pregnant on her own." I wink. "Just what I've heard."

He smirks. "She lied about birth control, Sadie. You can't tell me that's not fucked up."

"Still," I say, "it's not fair to put all the blame on her."

He scoffs, opening his hands to the table. "I literally could not accept more blame. I married her. For years, I did everything for them."

His face reddens as I wait for him to continue. When he doesn't, I ask, "You don't anymore?"

He spins his bottle on the table, and I wonder how much he's had. He keeps eye contact with me, though, and looks sober. "Kendra's family is in Connecticut. Affluent people live in Connecticut—which, by the way, is not something I aspired to be. I was happy to try and make it as an artist, but I couldn't support a family on hopes and dreams. It was safer to raise Marissa there. Quieter. In other words, boring as fuck." He sniffs. "Back then, I was the only man under thirty on our block."

It's an explosion of information, but I take it all

in, piece by piece. I think that's what he needs—someone who isn't Kendra to listen. "That's why you're here and they're not?" I ask.

"I want Marissa to grow up in the city, where there's diversity, adversity, culture," he says. "Not fucking Greenwich. Kendra grew up in Greenwich, and she's always gotten what she wanted. If not from me, then from her wealthy parents. That's more dangerous than a few homeless people on your doorstep." He stands and gets another beer. I've barely asked, and he's burbling and spilling over like an active volcano. After Nathan's silence, I hang on to every one of Finn's words. "So I told her—Kendra—I said, 'I'm moving back to the city. You can do what you want.'" He sits down again.

"And?"

"And she wants to stay together, so we're selling the house, and they're coming. Soon." He shakes his head. "Her family is up in arms."

"How come?"

"It's not appropriate. They didn't want Kendra to marry me in the first place. Her dad pulled some strings and got me into an MBA program without even asking if it was what I wanted. Their princess wasn't going to marry an unsuccessful artist."

"They made you give up photography?"

"No. I did it to give Marissa a stable home. I'd already been out of school and trying to turn photography into a career for a while when Kendra got pregnant. I submitted to Kendra and her parents thinking it was best for Marissa, but . . ." He takes a drink.

I bite my lower lip. I'm sitting in another woman's kitchen, about to advise another woman's husband on their relationship. Is there someone out there doing the same with Nathan?

I shoo the thought away. "Finn, you need to talk to Kendra even more than I need to ask Nathan what's going on. You should be saying all this to her. She's uprooting her life—and Marissa's—for you. You owe her the truth."

"That's the thing." He leans over the table onto his forearms. "I do talk to her. She knows how I feel. She knew I'd never abandon my own child or shirk my responsibility. We didn't have to get married. It's as if she knows how much I wanted something different, and she refuses to let me have it."

"Different . . . how?"

"I used to be a romantic guy. I did the grand gestures. I was the secret admirer and the kid under a girl's window with a stereo over my head. I once brought a girl flowers in front of the whole cafeteria to cheer her up. I want to be in love. I want to grow *with* my partner, not against her." I shift in my seat at the intense longing in his eyes. "I've never said that out loud," he admits. "I've been hanging on to this shred of hope, thinking either things with her would change, or . . . or she'd fucking see that she deserves a man who loves her more than I do."

Finn sighs, weary from his speech. As I watch his

body deflate, I think about another man who can woo a woman as if his life depends on it. Who made me feel so special, my way of thinking changed. Nathan made me believe in romance and in the healing powers of true love. What happened to that man? Did I crush it out of him, the way Kendra has with Finn? If so, how? I've never forced Nathan to stay with me. I've told him more than once I love him too much to trap him in a bad marriage. I'm one of the few people who believe divorce can be a good thing. My mom would've stayed sober and done an all right job with my brother and me, but she made the mistake of loving my dad. Eventually he dragged her down to his level.

"I'm sorry," I say. "It sounds hard. But maybe you need to say more."

He studies me closely. "Meaning . . .?"

"If you don't want to be in the marriage, you don't have to be. I know you think she's forcing you, but she's not."

"It's complicated." He sits back and rests his ankle over his knee. "There's Marissa. And Kendra— I do love her. I know how I sound, but I do. It's just that lately, I've been wondering . . ." He looks at me as if I'm supposed to finish his sentence.

"Wondering what?"

"About life. How we get to be certain people. The paths we choose. Whether fate has my back or is just playing a cruel joke."

"Fate," I repeat.

"A pebble can change the course of your life. You can run it over, get a flat, and never get back on track. Or you can swerve around it and end up on a different road."

I pinch my lip and look away. It's no pebble of a thing, me sitting here. Nathan with Joan. I should be there, lest Joan's fate overtake mine. Not that I believe in it. Nathan does. If he thinks our romance is dead, he might go looking for it somewhere else and blame it on fate like Finn is attempting to do.

I yawn. My beer is almost empty. I wonder if continuing this discussion is smart. Finn might get the wrong idea, thinking somehow fate brought me into his kitchen tonight. When really, I think I just didn't want to be alone. What would happen if Nathan came home early and didn't find me there? I stand. "I'm going to take off. It's been a long week, and it's only Wednesday."

He also gets up. "Get some sleep. Drink lots of water. For the photo shoot, I mean."

No doubt he's noticed the shadows on my face. "I will."

He walks me to the front door. "I don't know how you can stand it in here," I say.

"Me neither. Tell Nate thanks for trying."

I look up at him. "You got the part?"

"He didn't tell you? He came by to fix it, but it still doesn't work. I have to replace the whole thing. I'm waiting for a new one."

"He didn't mention it." I shift feet. "When he's

here . . . what do you talk about?"

"Typical stuff. Tools. Mechanics." He lifts a shoulder, looking past me. "I asked him about the beer I had at your place. We figured out we're both Yanks fans." He returns his eyes to me. "Don't worry. You didn't come up."

I'm not worried. Nathan is too trusting to suspect anything.

"Oh. Well." I glance around the apartment. It's not as bad as I thought earlier. A white sheet, folded up in one corner, covers a Victorian-style couch. The button-tufted bench is deep green velvet with carved wooden legs. It's not something a man would pick out—more like a woman's version of pissing on a fire hydrant. I suspect it's as uncomfortable as it looks, and I pity Finn and his situation a little more.

I look back just as Finn leans in to, what? Hug me? Kiss me? I flinch, and he ducks left at the last second to get the door. "See you Saturday morning."

I step back. "See you then."

In my apartment, I move Nathan's bedding and sit on the couch. I turn on the TV and change channel after channel, but I'm not paying attention. I replay my conversation with Finn. He's a hearts-and-flowers guy. So is Nathan. I wouldn't be surprised if Nathan had his own version of cheering a girl up in high school. They're just a couple of starry-eyed, doting Yankees fans. I'm not sure what to make of the fact that they're alike in some ways.

I switch to a sitcom rerun and hug Nathan's

pillow to my chest. After a minute, I write him a text.

I miss our romance.

I erase it.

FOURTEEN

Nathan walks into our bathroom as I apply my third coat of mascara. In the reflection, I catch him scan my outfit, lingering on my backside. "Client meeting on a Saturday?" he asks.

"Nope."

"Really?" He reaches past me for his toothbrush. "That's the dress you wear to close deals."

I check my lipstick for the fourth, fifth time? I've lost count. "Yep."

He loads up on toothpaste, sticks the brush in his mouth, and leaves the bathroom. It's the abrupt end of another conversation. But then, he stomps back in and pulls the toothbrush from his mouth. "Where are you going?"

For the last week and a half, we've been sidestepping each other, averting our gazes. He's still sleeping on the couch. Neither of us has made a move to change that. There's been no invitation on my end, no request to come back from him. Progress is at a halt. Why not give him a taste of his own medicine? A giddy current travels up my insides as I ask, "Since when do you care?"

He looms behind me. "Come on."

"'Come on' what?" I lean closer to the mirror and pretend to focus on my eyeliner. The deep indigo of my dress turns my irises almost purple. "I won't bother you with my plans."

He spits in the sink, tosses the brush on the counter, and walks out. He isn't the only one who can keep a secret. Not that it's anything exciting—seeing Finn today is a work obligation. He doesn't know that, though.

I select nude YSL patent leather pumps. I don't normally waste them on work, but they lengthen my legs, and I have a feeling the camera will love them. My dress, fitted with a scoop neck, doesn't offer much coverage. I select a wool coat and scarf and head for the front door.

Nathan looks up from the couch while he laces his tennis shoes. Judging by his Adidas athletic pants and long-sleeve t-shirt, he's got another pick-up game in Brooklyn. It's his second this month. "I'm your husband," he says. "I have a right to know where you're going."

I stop in my tracks. It's oddly intuitive of him to choose this moment, when I'm off to spend the day with another man, to remember I exist. It's also infuriating of him. He's given me nothing since the night I sucked him off five feet from where I'm standing. "I see," I say, turning to him. "*Now* you're my husband. I didn't realize we got to pick and choose when our vows apply."

He pulls back. "Our vows always apply—period. Don't question that because of a few rough weeks."

"Try months," I say.

"When have I ever left you in the dark?" he asks.

If nothing else, Nathan has been better about keeping me in the loop this week. A text or scribbled note lets me know where he is or where he's been. The question is whether or not I can believe him. "Where are you going?" I challenge.

He points to his sneakers. "Basketball game."

"Where?" The game is in Brooklyn. I know it, but I watch his face closely as he answers.

"Same as usual." He says it as if he goes there every weekend. "Park Slope. There's a court between Michael and Connor's apartments."

We stare at each other, him on the sofa, me across the room near the door. He's always spent time with his friends in Brooklyn. I swear it's been happening more lately, though. "I'm getting headshots taken for work."

"Oh." He goes back to tying his shoes.

"By Finn," I add.

He stops. "Finn. Across the hall?"

"Yes."

"Why?"

"He's a photographer."

"You told me he was an investment banker."

"He was." I wrap my scarf around my neck. "Now, he's a photographer."

"That's convenient."

"Yes," I agree. "It is."

Nathan leans his elbows on his knees and gives me another once over. This time, he narrows his eyes. "It's a little sexy."

I shrug. "It's for the website. I want to look good."

"You'll freeze."

"Oh, well. What's that saying? Beauty hurts."

"I don't think that's it." He stands. "Beauty is pain. Or the other way around."

He makes no move to leave. My neck begins to sweat. The scarf quivers when my heart beats. "Why doesn't his wife live here?" Nathan asks. "What's her name again?"

"Kendra. They're moving." I swallow. "She will . . . live here."

"When?"

"Soon."

He flaps the hem of his shirt as if he's hot. We still haven't switched on the heater, though. "Are you doing this in his apartment?"

"No. We'll be outside." I lean back against the wall. "Do you want to come? You're better at this creative stuff than me."

He looks past me into the entryway. "I have the game. I'm sure Finn's plenty creative." He snorts. "*Finn*. What kind of a name is that? Is he an appendage?"

I cross my arms, unimpressed with his attempt at an insult. But at least he's taking an interest. It could mean giving up alone time with Finn, which I've come to enjoy, but it'd be worth it. "I'd like for you to come, Nathan. Can you reschedule the game?"

"Can you reschedule the shoot?"

My question annoys him. I see it in his eyes. As if it took *him* two hours to get ready for some stupid basketball game. I brace myself against the wall and keep my voice mellow. "It's just that my hair and make up are done. And Finn's already set his day aside."

"I was making a point."

"What point?" I ask.

"Never mind."

"No, what?"

I can tell he's about to brush me off again, but he stops. He blinks to the side, gnawing his bottom lip. "I don't ask you for a lot," he says. "Do I?"

I don't really need to think about it. It's no secret Nathan goes out of his way for me time and time again. My girlfriends tease me about it—with envy. I show my love in a different way, but does he not see it? Have I failed him there? I give myself over to him in the kitchen and the bedroom. There, in my most intimate places, he's my king. I'll make whatever food he wants, and I'll fuck however he wants. Every time. "No, you don't ask me for much," I agree.

"It would be nice to . . . get a little bit more back. I wish you knew what was important to me the way I know what's important to you. I'd never really expect you to give up your photo shoot to spend the day with me. But why should I always have to skip my plans?"

I feel a pang in my heart, equal parts guilt and sadness, over the implication that I don't care as much as he does. But I can't quite swallow it all down without pointing out the obvious. "Because you made me this way," I say. "If I'm selfish, it's because you nurtured that in me. You practically forced me to be adored all these years."

He frowns, and I see the struggle on his face. I think he wants to let go of what's bothering him, but he won't allow himself to—maybe out of principle. Maybe there's still a point he has to prove. "I want you to feel adored," he says. "I guess I just . . . want to feel some of that back."

I glance over my shoulder at the front door and back. Finn and I didn't set a time, so maybe we can push the headshots back. "I'll come with you to Brooklyn," I say. "Would that help?"

"I'm not trying to guilt you into it," he says. "You were right. It doesn't make sense to cancel for a basketball game you won't even enjoy."

198

I slouch my shoulders. "I don't get it. If you didn't think I'd enjoy it, why'd you make a point to bring it up?"

We look at each other a few moments, and I think we're both trying to understand the other person. The problem is, Nathan's held my hand through much of this marriage. I've never been good at these things, but he has. Now, I feel lost without his guidance, as if I'm being tested but haven't learned as much as I should've. When he sighs, I feel like I could do the same.

"I'm not doing a good job of explaining." He checks his watch. "And I should head out, or they'll cut me from the game."

"What about Ginge?"

"I'll take her quick." He whistles, and Ginger gets up.

"All right. If you're sure." I take the door handle and look over at him as if there should be more to say. He concentrates on getting Ginger's in her leash. "Have fun. Bye."

I walk out. Finn's place seems farther than usual, the hallway narrower, as if I'm moving in slow motion. I knock. Finn opens right away with an eager smile, and I'm inside before Nathan even leaves our apartment.

I accidentally kick over a large camera bag near the door. When I put it upright again, Finn steals a glance at my bare legs.

"We should go now," he says. "There's a chance of rain later."

I think I hear footsteps in the hallway, the jingle of Ginger's tags. "I might need a drink first. To loosen up."

"No time. I don't want to lose the light."

I'd rather lose the light than run into Nathan with Finn. "Yes," I tease him, "that would be a shame."

He half-smiles at me. "I got that from the *Photography 101 Manual*. It's under the chapter titled 'Douche-y Things Photographers Say.' Forgive me?"

"Sure." I stall, in case Nathan is waiting for the elevator. Finn has his camera bag over his shoulder and his hand on the doorknob, but I'm peering into the living room. A box labeled *Equipment* is open on the floor. "Is this an old camera?"

"From college. I have a newer one, but I'm more comfortable with this one. Don't worry, it still takes great photos."

"I'm not worried." He could tell me he's using his cell phone. I wouldn't know any better. "Did you study photography, or was it something you just kind of picked up?"

"I majored in it at NYU."

I turn back to him. "Really?"

"I was serious about it. But like I told you, life got in the way." Finn's cheerful disposition is beginning to dim. "We should go," he says.

In the hall, Finn double checks his front door is secure. Nathan did the same thing the first few months after we moved in. He didn't trust the automatic lock.

"Where are we going?" I ask when we're on the elevator.

"Williamsburg."

"Brooklyn," I mutter under my breath. Another convert. "Great."

"You look nice, by the way," he says. "Stunning, really."

The doors open. I shield my eyes against the light spilling into the small lobby. "Thank you." My lipstick feels as thick as my wool coat. "I know you're supposed to overdo it for the camera."

"They'll turn out nicely." He holds the door open. "After you."

We exit onto the sidewalk. Nathan and Ginger are on a small patch of grass in front of the building. Ginger whines when she sees me, pulling on her leash until Nathan introduces her to a tree trunk. She forgets all about me. They might as well be strangers. I can't think of anything new to say to him. I'd invite him again because I want him there, but he might think I'm expecting him to drop everything for me.

"We'll get a cab to save time," Finn says from the curb. I can't tell if he's pretending not to notice Nathan.

Nathan squints at me, at Finn, and a chill runs up my shins to my shoulders. He sticks his hand in his coat pocket. The collar is pulled up around his neck and makes his hair look almost black. If anyone's going to speak up, it should be him. I already went out on a limb by inviting him and offering to change my plans. He made me promise to back off, to let him come to me.

He looks away.

"Sadie?" I blink my gaze back to Finn. He's holding a taxi door open for me. "Coming?"

I tighten the sash of my coat and get in the car.

FIFTEEN

The cab's backseat TV blares a weather update. Finn was right—they're predicting rain. I turn it off, and we ride to Brooklyn in silence. I insist on paying for the trip, but he won't let me.

"I'll add it to the bill," he finally says the third time I shove cash at him. The taxi leaves us on a corner between two industrial buildings.

Finn slumps his camera bag on the sidewalk and unpacks it.

"We're doing it here?" I ask. There's a street sign, an overflowing garbage can, and a lot of chain-link fence.

"Around the corner," he says. "This block is pretty quiet on the weekend, at least by New York standards. Not bad for a city with over eight million people."

I wander down the sidewalk a little. There aren't many people here for a reason. It's ugly, gray slabs and bare trees. "I thought maybe we were going to a park or something," I say.

"Maybe if this were an engagement shoot." He's right behind me, and I jump. "*Avec* is edgy. Modern. A park would be too traditional."

I sidestep a rotted Styrofoam container. "This is modern?"

He aims the camera at me but doesn't take a picture. "Let me do my job. If you don't like the pictures, we'll go to a park."

I sigh. "Deal."

"Come." He walks over to a pitted concrete wall tagged with graffiti. I edge toward him, making no secret of my hesitation. He takes my shoulders and positions me in front of it, facing the street. With a knuckle under my chin, he lifts my head, angling it an inch right, a millimeter left. His eyebrows are drawn with concentration. There's nothing romantic about his touch, but no matter where my head goes, I can't take my eyes off his face.

"Beautiful," he murmurs.

"We haven't done anything yet."

He steps back. "Take off your coat."

I slip it off, but there's nowhere to put it. "I—"

"Ground. Toss it. Come on."

Reluctantly, trying not to move my head, I heave it a few feet away so it's out of the shot. I send my scarf along with it. That's what dry cleaners are for, I suppose.

He's already shooting, and I'm not even positioned yet. "Wait. Stop. What do you want me to do?"

"Just stand there. Don't smile."

Not smiling for a photo is harder than I realize. My face muscles twitch the more I try to keep still. I don't know what the hell to do with my hands.

He lowers the camera. "Forget about the photo. Just look at me."

I do. The sun is on top of us, and his eyes are stunningly green. "Good," he says. "Just keep looking at me like that. Think about me."

"Just a second." I close my eyes and picture Finn the first time I saw him in the hallway, his white shirt, his sweat-dampened hair. I open my eyes again. Instead of modeling, I pretend I'm there to study him. To watch Finn in his element. He takes a picture and adjusts a few dials. I'm lost. I went years without a camera until I got a smartphone. Nathan'd cocked his head when I'd mentioned that on our third date, perplexed. Or was it our fourth? We'd been at a Mexican restaurant in Hell's Kitchen, two margaritas deep.

"Freeze," Nathan said out of nowhere from across the small, intimate table.

"What—"

"Un-uh. Don't move an inch. Just stay as you are." He took my picture. "I want one to show my dad. He doesn't believe you're the most beautiful girl in Manhattan."

"Nathan." I rolled my eyes, secretly hoping he believed all the compliments he gave me. I would learn, over time, that he did. Every one.

I didn't find out until months later I had a guacamole smear on my cheek. When I'm being snobby about something like thread counts or coffee beans, Nathan whips out that picture, and we double over with laughter.

"What were you just thinking about?" Finn asks.

"What?" I blink and beat my eyelids like a strobe. Reality creeps back in. "I don't know," I lie. "Nothing in particular. Why?"

"Try to go back to that place. You weren't smiling, but you looked . . . happy. It was perfect."

It's too late. The moment has passed. *Perfect.* Is there such a thing? I never believed there was until I met Nathan. My childhood was definitely flawed. My parents missed my fifteenth birthday because they lost track of time at a casino. As I blew out the candle on the cupcake my brother brought over, I wished for new parents. Perfect ones. It wasn't the only time I made that wish.

"I'm just following your direction," I tell Finn.

"Then you're a natural." He comes up and hands me the camera. On the playback screen, my eyes are slightly narrowed, my lips slack. I'm rosy-cheeked from the cold. He picks up my coat and pulls it around my shoulders. "Let's move. This shade of gray is washing you out a little."

I follow him, carefully cradling his machinery.

I'm not sure if I like the photo. There's too much emotion for it to be professional. I decide not to point that out just yet.

He stops in front of a red-brick wall. "This'll work," he says. "How do you feel?"

My breath fogs, but I'm not shivering. "Good."

He rubs his hands up and down my biceps before kneading my shoulders. The strength in his long fingers is undeniable, even through the wool of my coat. Again, there's nothing sexual about it, but my body warms, and not just from his hands. It's nice to be worried about. Taken care of, even if it only lasts a couple seconds.

"Ready?" Finn slips my coat off and puts it down. "Lean against the wall."

He takes the camera back and retreats without watching where he's going. A couple in matching puffy coats almost mow him down. He doesn't notice, snapping a picture, studying it, then coming back to me. He motions me off the wall and pulls my hair forward over my shoulders. He runs a few strands through his fingers, lays them against my dress. My scalp tingles, and the feel of him spreads down my neck, leaves my fingertips buzzing. A sensation between my legs makes me suck in a breath.

At that, he looks up. The wrinkles between his brows are deep. For a split second, he looks as though he's forgotten we're here to work. He wets his bottom lip. There's heat in his eyes. I've seen it before, this intensity, the almost-pained frown on his face, though I can't place exactly when he's looked at me this way.

"Hello again," I whisper.

His expression eases. "Hi."

"You said that when we met. Why?"

"I told you," he says. "I thought you were another neighbor."

"Someone else in the building looks like me?"

He lifts my chin until the back of my head touches the brick. My throat is exposed. He leaves me there to take a picture that can't be anywhere near professional. I right myself, and he doesn't stop me, just studies my face. "Your eyes are mesmerizing right now. It's like you're wearing color contacts."

"How do you know I'm not?"

He tilts his head. "You can smile now."

During the next ten minutes, he's all business. He gets close, squats, backs up, stands. He says things like "bend that leg" and "cross your arms" and "let's try it without lipstick."

It takes me a good few minutes to remove the grease from my lips.

He watches, laughing. "You look like you made out with a clown." He asks for my cosmetic bag and dabs liquid foundation around my mouth with a sponge, his touch alone keeping me warm. I have nowhere to look but at him. His lips are bright pink like the tip of his nose. They're parted, the bottom one begging to be nibbled. I wonder how cold his face and hands must be.

Finn leaves me there and moves to the middle of the street. He wants my coat on, then off, then over my shoulders. He's visibly perturbed when he has to move for cars and takes it all very seriously. I like watching him work, knowing he's studying me through his lens.

With a strike of lightning, he lowers his camera. We both look at the sky. A heavy, gray mass has gathered in the distance. "Shit. Let's go back," he says finally, packing up his things.

I quickly dress in my coat and scarf before requesting an Uber. Now that the session is over, I shudder a few times in a row, as if my body's been holding it off. My cheeks ache. I roll my neck.

"You were great," he says. "We definitely got something."

I'm not so sure. I worry the pictures are too out there for the workplace. "Maybe we can try a few normal shots to be safe."

He laughs from where he's crouched. "You don't trust me one bit, do you?"

"No, I do. I do," I say too fast. "I so appreciate you doing this."

The Uber arrives at the curb. Finn hoists his camera bag over his shoulder and gets the door. "Weather permitting, we can take a few simple photos by the plants near our building," he says. "Just to ease your doubts about me."

We slide into the backseat and say hello to the driver.

209

"It's not that I doubt—"

"I'm teasing you." He puts an arm around my shoulders and pulls me in. "Cold?"

I should back away. Once I have it, though, his warmth is impossible to reject and feels as necessary as taking a breath. "A little."

He squeezes me to him. Moves his hand up and down my bicep. "You're shivering."

The driver looks at us in the rearview mirror. "You guys are a cute couple."

"Thanks," I say.

Finn arches an eyebrow, pleased—because she thinks we're together, or because I didn't correct her? I don't even want to correct her. I've missed the look she's giving us, the one a woman makes when she's more envious than jealous. I get it all the time with Nathan. That feeling, coupled with the heater blasting from the front seat, leaves me slightly woozy.

We're just like actors in a movie, I tell myself. After a few minutes, the urgency to get warm lessens, and the door opens to another less pressing, but still basic need. Because that's how my arousal feels— essential. The more it's ignored, the fiercer it grows. I snuggle into his side. All it takes is his hand on my upper thigh to invite an assault of graphic fantasies. Finn shoving me down on the backseat because he can't control himself anymore. Thrusting his fingers under the hem of my dress to find me ready for him. The lower half of my body aches with sudden demands.

"Some of those photos were for me," he whispers into my ear. He couldn't have chosen a worse moment to tease me. My legs are jelly-like. "Does that make you mad?"

I check to see if the driver is paying attention. She must know I'm married. How can something so vital and concrete in my life be hidden? "What if I say yes?" I ask.

"I'll delete them. If you're sure it doesn't . . . turn you on."

I try not to pant. "Why would it?"

"Imagining me looking at them later."

I turn my head. Our mouths are a breath apart. One more inch and they'll touch. Again. Those lips are the color of sunburnt rock but whisper soft. I can't stop the image of him looking at me, my exposed, white throat on his computer, his dick in a firm fist. It should disgust me. It makes my panties damp instead.

"No response necessary," he says as the car pulls up to the curb. "I can read it on your face."

He gets out like nothing's changed, taking my elbow to help me from the seat. "Let's try over there," Finn suggests. A pair of trees in front of our building create a golden-brown canopy.

The chill in the air is electric. He can't miss the threat of rain, but he gets his camera out anyway. This time, he doesn't position or touch me. He just takes a few close-ups.

"We didn't even need to leave the premises," I

joke.

Hiding behind the lens, he says, "Stop trying to destroy my creative vision."

"Does that help you—*you know*? When you're looking at them later, by yourself in the dark—are you thinking, 'Oh, God, this one is so *artistic*?'"

He scolds me with a lifted brow. "Are you teasing me?"

The smile on my face is forced for the camera, so he can't tell by my expression. "I—"

"I'm a grown man, not a teenager in my parents' basement," he says. *Click.* "I don't get myself off in the dark unless I'm in bed." More concerned with his work, he doesn't make eye contact. "And the answer is no. I couldn't give a fuck about the composition so long as I'm looking at you."

I flush hot. He's not being subtle. I'm not exactly discreet, either. Flirting with him feels good, though, like salve on a burn. "Let me at least put on some lipstick, then."

"No. I like you without it."

I'm about to say this isn't about what he likes, lipstick is more professional, but I'm cut off by a rumble of thunder. Without warning, raindrops drum the top of my head. "I think that's our cue."

He doesn't move. "Stay there."

"My hair—"

"So what?" he asks. "We got what we needed. Don't smile."

The rain falls harder, skipping right from

drizzling to pouring. One minute it's on top of me, and the next it's sideways. He takes more pictures.

"Your camera's going to get ruined—"

"Try not to react to the rain." He gets close to my face. Moves some strands of hair that've stuck to my cheek. "I know it's hard. Just let it happen to you."

I stand very still, my hands awkwardly stuck at my sides. I could never do something like this for a living. Not modeling, and not the photography side of it. I feel ridiculous, but Finn's snapping away as though he's struck gold.

"You look—Jesus, Sadie. Fucking gorgeous." The adoration in his eyes soothes the chill in my bones. I forget that I'm wearing expensive-as-fuck shoes in a mess of wet leaves and that my Chloé handbag is on the ground, getting soaked.

"Really?" I ask.

He looks affronted. "Are you kidding? You're confident. Sexy. I wish you could see yourself through my lens."

I am confident. It's only these last few months that've made me forget it. Finn doesn't hide what he wants. He doesn't play games. With him, I remember how it feels to be seen. Worshipped. I close my eyes and tilt my head up to the rain.

"You're killing me," he mutters. "Always killing me. Turn around."

I trust Finn more now that my skin feels like my own again, so I do as he says and face the street.

"Now look back at me."

I turn my head, touching my chin to my shoulder. My mascara must be smeared. Rain trickles under the neckline of my dress, gathering in the underwire of my bra. "Like this?"

"This one look is enough to make a man come undone. To make a man forget his own name." He shakes his head. "You're telling me that's not art? That doesn't make you feel something?"

I pinch my bottom lip between my teeth. Finn's attention makes me feel a great deal of things. His craving is written on his face. It gives me back the power I lost months ago when Nathan stopped looking at me the way Finn is right now.

Thunder cracks between us like a whip. We both jump. "We should go in," he says, as if it's just occurred to him.

I gather my things as he snatches his camera bag off the ground, then holds the building door open and motions me to move faster. My heels sink into the soil, slowing me down.

He laughs loud enough for me to hear over the storm. "Just take them off," he calls.

I remove my nude pumps, cradle them in my arms, and run with bare feet through the grass to him. Inside, a man exits the elevator with an umbrella in hand. Finn sprints ahead to catch the doors.

Finn scrubs his hands in his hair. "You must be freezing," he says as we ride up to the sixth floor.

I scrunch my nose. "I am."

"It'll be worth it. You won't even recognize yourself."

"I'm sure my boss will love that," I say sardonically.

His laugh is deep and throaty. "I'm talking about those last few. They're not suitable for work."

My dress sticks to me everywhere. Until the doors open, the small space holds a noticeable charge, even though we're out of the storm's grasp. We walk briskly down the hall, dripping onto the threadbare carpet. He jingles his keys in his pocket until we reach his apartment. "This is the first time I'm grateful for my busted heater." He unlocks the door, and we hurry inside. Warmth envelops us. I dump my purse and shoes in the entryway by his camera bag, and he hangs up my coat and scarf. "They should dry quickly," he says as he disappears down the hall.

It isn't until I'm halfway into the living room that I stop and realize where I'm standing. Why did I come in here? There's a heater, a shower, and a change of clothes waiting for me across the hall—but not much else.

Finn returns and holds out a towel. I use it to squeeze excess water from my hair. "Finn—"

He whips the sheet off the couch. A cloud of dust motes twinkles in the yellowed-gray afternoon light. "Sit," he says. "We'll take a look at what we got."

My body is loosening with the heat. I dry my collarbone and chest with the towel. "I should probably go home," I say. "Get out of these clothes."

"Probably." Neither of us makes a move. He removes his camera from around his neck and sets it carefully on his new coffee table. "I'll make us a warm drink."

SIXTEEN

Locked in the hallway bathroom of Finn's apartment, I stare at the screen of my phone. There's nothing there worth looking at. The coffee aroma drifting my way makes me simultaneously shiver and salivate. Though my clothes are getting dry, I'm chilled from the inside, as if my bloodstream carries chunks of ice. Stay here, where it's warm and inviting? Or go home to an empty apartment? I send Nathan a text.

Coming home soon?

As I wait, I inspect my reflection. My straightened hair is curling. My scrubbed-off lipstick has left my mouth pink. I find body lotion in a cabinet under the sink and use it to remove my smudged mascara, wondering if it belongs to Finn or Kendra.

My phone vibrates on the sink counter. I pick it

up and read Nathan's reply.

Not yet. Basketball game was cut short because of the rain. We're having a beer.

Sitting in a pub on a rainy afternoon sounds about right for my mood. I did tell Donna I'd try to make it out to Park Slope soon, and I should probably be anywhere but here. I invite myself.

Which bar? I can meet you.

He's typing. I wait. I could shower, change, and be on the train within an hour. If only Brooklyn were closer. My phone alerts me to his answer.

At Mikey's place. Poker.

I look back into the mirror. If Joan mentioned living with Mikey, I don't recall. Suddenly, I regret drinking as much as I did that night. They're engaged—I remember that. Generally, engaged people live together. She could be there right now with Nathan, who knows I won't show up because I have a real thing about gambling. My dad and mom are casino rats. They came home many nights reeking of cigarettes and cheap liquor. They lost money they didn't have and cash they'd promised me. First, it was for little things—a ticket to my high school prom, lunch money. Then it was college applications, and finally college itself. They did one thing right, though—maintaining a level of poverty scholarship funds smiled upon. That was when I recognized I was the only one who could shape my life into what I wanted it to be.

I'm about to exit the bathroom when another

text comes through from Nathan.

The game will go late. Don't feel like fighting the storm. I might crash here.

That's what you think, is my first thought. I type rapidly and end up having to fix several mistakes.

You're a grownup not a kid at a sleepover. I want you to come home.

I don't think an actual confession would shock me more than his next response.

If I'm not in our bed, what difference does it make where I sleep? I'll be home when you wake up.

I narrow my eyes at the screen and wonder who this man is. He isn't my Nathan, who used to call me randomly at work just to say he was thinking of me. This man doesn't even think spending the night elsewhere merits a conversation.

After I leave the bathroom, I grandly dump my phone back in my purse. Nathan has plenty of reasons to come home, but he's given me none to do the same. In the living room, I close my eyes and appreciate the rich smell of coffee brewing. I lay the towel Finn gave me on Kendra's green velvet couch. My dress is slightly damp. It's my undergarments, though, that're wet enough from the rain to make me uncomfortable.

Finn returns barefoot with two mugs. Steam curls over the rims. "You didn't need to do that," he says.

"It's a lovely couch."

"It's an eyesore."

It is a beautiful and well-made piece of furniture. It belongs in a store window or a historical movie set in an English castle. It doesn't fit Finn, though, who is more bull-in-a-china-shop than monarch. He still hasn't done anything with the apartment. I wonder if his reason for not liking it extends beyond personal taste. I don't decorate the apartment with anything I think Nathan wouldn't like.

The coffee warms my hands and cheeks. It smells of going home for the holidays, even though those aren't particularly favorable memories for me. Trips to the Beckwith family home generally boil down to Andrew, Nathan and I trying to survive my parents' bickering.

Finn and I each take a sip. "This is good," I say. Already, it's eased my tension. "Did you spike it or something?"

"No, but I can." He grins. "The beans are from Quench Coffee."

"That's why I like it."

"I've been going there since college," he volunteers. "Minus the Connecticut years."

I look away. *Connecticut* is a dirty word. It's a side of Finn I don't want to think about. It's a side of myself I don't want to acknowledge. Rain beats against the window. "Can you seriously spike this?"

He leaves the room and returns with Kahlúa. "Try that," he says with a conservative pour.

I taste it, looking up at him. "More."

He tops my drink off, then his own. "Cheers."

"What to?" I ask.

He sets the mug on the table without drinking any and picks up his camera. "Bad decisions?"

Mid-sip, I flit my eyes up to him. He isn't dense enough to believe we're doing nothing wrong, but there's no reason to acknowledge it. I gulp down some coffee and ask, "Are you trying to get me to leave?"

"Not quite." He glances at me from under his lashes as he plays with the camera. "I was talking about gray as a background for your headshot. Not the best decision on my part."

I purse my lips. "That's what you want to cheers to?"

One cheek dimples with his smile. Each time he hits a button, the camera beeps. He hums. "I can definitely work with most of these, though."

I lean forward. "Can I see?"

"Let me find a good one." He shuffles toward me, distracted by his task, until our naked feet touch. My knee ghosts against the fine hairs on his shin, and my skin prickles. He holds the screen in front of my face. "Here. How's that?"

In the photo, my arms are crossed, my smile confident. It's good, although the graffiti on the wall behind me gives me pause. I'd prefer a less aggressive backdrop. "It's an option . . ."

"Not my favorite." He flips through a few more shots and chooses one taken seconds before the rain started. My squinted gaze holds the secret to my next client's success. New York City fall is my backdrop, with multi-colored foliage against a graying sky. I'm not as poised.

"What else?" I ask.

"What about this one?" He shows me another. My head is twisted over one shoulder, my expression playful, my hair plastered to my cheeks. I don't remember biting my lip, but the evidence is there on the screen. I'm not looking at the camera, though. I'm looking above it. At Finn. My insides tighten.

Finn touches something, and the screen goes black. He holds the viewfinder over his eye. *Snap.*

"Finn . . ."

He brushes his knuckles softly down my cheek and clears some hair off my neck. He takes another, but the graze of his touch remains.

"I took my makeup off." My attempt to thwart him sounds as lame as it is.

"Hmm." He adjusts a dial before taking the next photo. "I noticed. Funny how I . . . I mean, the camera . . . likes you anyway."

This time, when I say his name, it's a warning. "Finn."

"I can't help myself."

"You can't?" I ask. "Or you don't want to?"

I see the edges of his smile from behind the camera. He lowers it. I'm likely wearing the same expression I was in that last photo. I'm not a model, and I'm no actress. That lusty look in my eyes was the real thing, and it's not going away.

Finn reaches out and traces my neckline. Just the feel of his hand through the fabric sends my heartbeat racing. Lights up my skin with goose bumps. He pushes a fingertip into my dress, against my skin. It's not enough. That simple, barely-there touch puts me more on edge than if he'd just gone and grabbed me. He tugs until I sit forward.

"Can't help myself," he answers my last question. "Don't want to. Won't." Slowly, deliberately, with ample time for me to protest, he lifts my hair off my neck and slides my zipper down the length of my spine. He peels the dress over one shoulder, exposing the curve of it.

And he takes my picture.

He angles my jaw a little to the side. The room is darkening from the storm. The only sounds are raindrops against glass, my body-swaying breath, the slice and click of the camera.

"Fix your hair," he says quietly.

"How?"

"However feels right."

I rake a hand through my roots. I gather it in a loose, damp ponytail.

"Pull it."

The little I've already given in makes my restraint slippery. He's not asking, so I don't have to decide for myself. I curl my hair around my hand and make my scalp tingle. I wait for his next command, my ass melding to the couch cushions. My dress is stiff. He pushes it down by the neckline, over my bra, to my

223

waist.

"You're made for the camera. For this lighting." His voice scrapes like a dull knife on my skin. "For me."

Despite the heat, a series of tremors run through me. I try to keep them inside, try not to move, as if my participation is ambiguous. There are things I want to feel—Finn's tongue in my mouth. His hands on my breasts. The rock hardness of him pressed to my thigh. I don't know if all that means I want to do this, though.

"It's okay to move," he says.

I hug myself to stave off any more trembling and run my hands over my biceps. I drink more coffee and Kahlúa. The heat coats my throat and chest like a syrupy waterfall.

"You asked what I like to take pictures of," he says from behind the safety of his black box.

I look at him. His one exposed eye is squeezed shut. "Strangers," I say.

"The opposite. I prefer someone I know. I get to see a new side of them."

"What are you seeing now?"

"You have a lot of levels, Sadie. You don't show them easily. Maybe you don't even realize they're there." He can see all of me, yet I'm missing most of his face. I'm not sure if that's making this descent into moral gray area easier or harder. His words are physical, hands on me, several of them all at once.

I suppose Finn is right—people are just layers

upon layers, some permeable, some impenetrable. I'm no exception.

"You wear nude, lacy bras," he adds. "I didn't know that."

My laugh dies before it ever leaves my mouth. Instead, I exhale softly. My panties match my bra, and he must be wondering about them. I shouldn't encourage him, but his attentiveness feels like a warm lamp in a cold room. "What else?" I ask.

"You take direction well."

"There's one I haven't heard before . . ."

"Lie back. Feet on the couch." His voice has taken on a new tone, one not to be argued with. I move lengthwise on the couch and rest my shoulder blades against the arm.

"Let me see you. All of you."

The pulsing swell of arousal between my legs is the only thing driving me now. I've barely slid my dress over my hips when Finn comes around the table and grabs the hem. He yanks it down, down, down, over my thighs, calves, ankles, to the floor. When was I last undressed in front of someone other than Nathan? I cross my ankles and cover my bra.

"How can I see when you do that?" he asks.

"You can't," I say. "That's the point."

"You don't want me to?"

I hesitate. I'm not worried he won't like what he sees—I'm worried he will. That he'll want to do more than look. That I won't stop him, even though I should. Shouldn't I? It's not as if Nathan has made any effort to stop *me*. He watched me walk away this morning. He ignored my requests for him to participate in the shoot, to come home, to let me come to him. He's turned down sex, intimacy, conversation. After a quick glance over the past few months, I'd be stupid to think he wants me to chase after him anymore.

I unfold my arms first.

"I've never seen anything like you," Finn says, capturing my every move. "Now your legs."

I uncross them, bending one knee, scraping the velvet over the ball of my foot. It's more coarse than comfortable. "Have you done this before? Photographed someone like this, I mean."

"Haven't taken things this far, no." He pauses. "I guess I never had the right subject."

"Not even—"

"No. She doesn't inspire me."

I keep my eyes on the lens. To him, I'm the right subject. The only subject. How can so much have blossomed in so little time? Yet, I understand it. I'm wrapped up in him enough that I want the camera gone, but not enough that I'm bold enough to do something about it. I want to pause time. For this not to count. In the steely gray early evening, in a warm place that seems as if it could only be my imagination, I think, maybe for tonight, this could be a private space between realities. Somewhere only we exist.

A bolt of lightning reminds us how dark it's gotten. Finn switches on the lamp at the foot of the couch. I look down the white-dune hills and curves of my body at him.

He takes my ankle and lengthens one leg. His touch on such a private part of me is foreign at first, and then it liquefies, melding with my skin. My silence is a form of trust. I'm not stopping him.

Keeping a firm grip on me, he puts a knee between my feet. "Are you shaking because you're scared?"

Since I first saw Finn in the hallway, we've been engaged in this drawn-out, fucked-up dance of innuendo and lingering glances. Foreplay with him is the space between us: the things we haven't said; the admissions we haven't made. If I'm scared, I can't feel it, and if I'm shaking, it's surpassed by my anticipation. "I'm not scared."

"Good." He leans forward so the camera looks directly down on me. "Show me."

"What do you want to see?"

"Whatever you want me to see."

His attention is heady, addicting. I won't know how far I'm willing to go until I get there. When I do, I'll stop. It won't ever be too late to walk away. And if I don't walk away at all? I'll have my answer—I can't stop.

My hands are unsteady as I reach under myself, arching my back. I unclasp the single hook-and-eye of my bra and remove it with the delicacy it demands. My nipples pebble with their freedom, with Finn's eyes on them.

Finn watches my every movement, unwrapping his present with captivated eyes. His gaze devours this private part of me. "What fucking tits," he says, and my body trills. It's crass and unlike him, as if he just had to say it. I'm getting wetter, too swollen for my panties.

"Finn," I say like a prod in the arm, because he's not taking pictures.

"Sorry." He aims the lens right at me, but nothing happens. He sets the camera on the table with a thud. His hands are on my waist. Large. Warm. He slides me down the couch until my head falls from the arm to the cushion, and my crotch is pressed up against his knee.

For an electric moment we stay that way. Only my chest moves, and his hair, which lags behind his sudden movements, falls sluggishly over his face. He lowers his head.

When he's an inch away, I slap my palms against his chest, halting him. "Finn." His name comes out like a moan. "God. We can't."

His hair is liquid gold, tickling my forehead. "I can."

I open my mouth to say "It's wrong" but it comes out as a hoarse whisper.

"Aren't you curious?"

"Yes, but—"

"So let me satisfy it." He cups his hand under the hem of my dress, right over the core of me. I hiss through my clenched teeth. "Your curiosity, that is."

I should leave. I should be outraged. I should not, however, be surprised it's come to this. As if I didn't know it might.

"I want you, Sadie." I can practically taste the coffee on his breath. Lightly, over my lace thong, he strokes my opening with his fingertips, presses his palm to my clit. "I think about nothing else. Just you. Your eyes. Your lips. Your wet cunt."

I groan. A flush overtakes my entire body— embarrassment. Arousal. He's only touching me enough to tease my pleasure to the surface, just to where it overtakes my protests.

"We can do it this way if you want," he goads. "If it makes you feel less guilty. It'll take longer, but I don't have anywhere to be."

I'm trying not to squirm. His gentle, fluttering touch is infuriating. My panties are wetter now than they were even seconds ago. Knowing one word will get me what I want destroys my control.

"I think about you too," I say.

He stabs a finger into the fabric, almost piercing the lace, nearly inside me. My hips buck. I put my palms on his cheeks. I don't know if it's to stop him or bring him closer. The thought of another man terrifies me. The reality, though, excites me. That he wants me this badly. That he can't keep his hands off what doesn't belong to him. My mind is wondrously wrapped up in him, and we've barely touched.

With his other hand, he grabs my hair by the roots. "If you can't do this, I will," he says. "I'll make this decision for us. When you hurt tomorrow, physically or emotionally . . . when you question what we did . . . when you ache to do it again—I'll take the blame for all of it, Sadie."

He assaults my mouth with his kiss. My heart seizes up with surprise and fear. His tongue dominates mine, his lips hard and bruising, and the burn of desire scorches my final reservations. I catch up with his greedy lips, sweeping my tongue in broad strokes, searching for purchase with my teeth. I nab his pouty bottom lip, as I've wanted to for weeks, and he growls into my mouth.

He's stopped touching me, but I bury my hands under his clothing. He's fiery hot, shuddering when I spread my fingers across his abs. I pull at his shirt, and he props himself on one arm to remove it by the collar.

As I thought, my blond, bearded lover has the physique of a Greek god. I run my hands over the planes of his pecs, the grid of his stomach. He doesn't let me adulate long. He pinches my chin between his fingers and turns my head toward the room, the front door. "I saw you in the hallway with him the other night," he says into my ear. "I was crazy over it."

I curl my fingers into the scratchy velvet. It's infuriating—Finn watching us, thinking he has any right to be crazy over me, bringing it up now. Any emotion I have is fuel on the fire, though. It just makes me twist under him, desperate for some measure of relief.

He jams my underwear to one side, and my groan is guttural. He smiles. "There she is," he says. "I've been waiting for that."

I turn my head back to him. "What?"

He kisses me once, much more gently. "I saw it through the lens. It's hard for you to open yourself up, but you want to. You want to be explored." He drags his hand from my throat to my chest and spreads his fingers between my breasts. "Open for me."

My exhale stutters from my mouth. I try not to hear his words. My body is asking for this—not my mind, not my heart. We're connected, but not bound. If anything's going to open, it'll be my legs. "Are you going to fuck me or not?"

His eyes twinkle as he narrows them. He takes both my wrists, clasps them in one hand, and pins them by my head. The angle of my right arm blocks part of my vision.

"That what you want?" he asks. "Me to stick it in without any fun first?"

A mischievous thrill shoots up my spine like an arrow. "Fun?" I breathe.

He slides his free hand under my ass and squeezes. His fingers roam, tracing the elastic of my panties. My stomach dips and swells with each breath. I haven't shaken this hard since high school, since the night my dad caught me trying to sneak his car out of the garage.

"Fun. You know, F . . ." Finn nips my stomach.

"U . . ." He dips his hand between my legs. "N."

He snaps the elastic of my panties against my skin. I gasp loudly. The sting makes me writhe, my wrists still secured by his hands. He breaches my opening and without ceremony, his fingers are inside me. I don't stop his sudden, searching thrusts. I'm in trouble, and I can't seem to put the brakes on. My compliance is easier won than I thought. All I can say is "God, oh, God" over and over. No other words seem to fit.

"How's it feel to be this wet for so long?" he asks. "To finally be this close?" He releases my wrists before I can answer and sits back on his calves. My hands tingle as blood flows back to my fingers.

He undoes his pants with focus, his lips parted, the bottom one exposed to me. How would that plush mouth, that scratchy beard, feel eating me out?

He looks up as he takes out his cock, huge and hard in his fist. His fingers glisten with my juices. "I just want to taste—" He gets a condom from his back pocket and rolls it on. "Just for a second—" He pulls my hips up his thighs, fits himself to my opening, and slides inside me. His eyes go to the ceiling like he's in prayer, and he clenches his teeth.

My vision doubles. I was expecting the *fun* first, but the surprise of him, stiff as stone, tilts my center. He takes me by the waist and pumps into me a few times. We both grunt.

After weeks of foreplay, I think I'm going to come already, but he pulls out and drops me back onto the couch.

I lift my head, breathless. "What're you doing?"

Removing the rest of his clothes, he says, "Warming you up."

SEVENTEEN

Finn wants to make art of his fucking. His prize-worthy lips are on my pubic bone. A few licks, a chaste peck on my nethermost lips. He sucks my clit, kisses me right on the pussy, dips his tongue in me like I'm ice cream melting over a cone. He's warming me up.

I arch my back, moan at the ceiling, rake a hand into his hair. The strands are soft, but I pull them hard. He eats me more furiously. I slap my other hand over my mouth, as if screaming will give us away. I can't take it. My thighs quiver around his head. He stops and looks up at me. "How do I make you come?"

"For one," I pant, "don't stop to ask questions. I was almost there."

He grins lazily at me, his eyes hooded. "Flip over."

"But—"

He lifts me with a hand under my ass, urging me onto my stomach. I do as I'm told. He covers me completely with his body, somehow both comforting me and sending me to the edge of madness. He knows what I need before I do. We're both sweating, our bodies suctioning together. "Here's a tip," he says, pushing my hair aside. "Don't make it easy for me. You tell me how to make you come, I'll find another way. I want you on the brink for as long as I want to keep you there. Until I decide to push you off."

"You don't have to push me at all."

"Is that right? You're the type who comes at the drop of a pin?"

"Right now I am," I say.

He kisses his way down my spine. Bumps tingle over my back with the scrape and scuff of his beard. He pinches the meat of my ass between his teeth, then tongues my slit from behind. With each lick, I mash my face harder into the couch. He pushes my thighs apart and kisses the insides, massages them, his hands dangerously close to my core. He loves every inch of my legs with his mouth, then the bridges of my feet and the paper-thin skin around my ankles.

"This is what happens to a man consumed by a woman he can't have," he says from somewhere I can't see. "I get carried away. I want to see and touch as much of you as I can, while I can."

I'm still thrumming from how heavy his cock felt

inside me for that brief moment. I want it there again. "Fuck me now," I plead. "Get carried away another time."

He chuckles, low and deep, and climbs back up the couch. He puts his mouth in my hair, nuzzles me. "Do I have to fuck you?" he asks. "Can I make love to you? Can I do a little of both?"

I am, almost literally, jelly underneath him. There isn't much I'd protest to at the moment. "Whatever you want."

"That's what I like to hear. But the first time, I want you on your back so I can see you."

I turn over. I admit, I couldn't give a damn how he takes me as long as it's without mercy. I don't deserve mercy tonight, and I don't want it. He settles himself over me. I lock his big body up in my thighs, calves, and ankles.

Looking between us, he takes himself in his hand. He tests me with just his tip and checks my expression.

"Let me watch," I say. I want more, even just a little bit.

I loosen my grip, but stay wrapped around him. He lifts his body so I can see. He's only inside of me enough to tease. The rest of him is poised to enter. His size might scare me if I weren't used to Nathan.

"Am I hurting you?" Finn asks, stilling completely. "I know it's big. I haven't even started, though."

I realize I'm squeezing my eyes shut. My

shoulders are hunched around my neck, my fingers dug into the cushion. Why did I have to think of Nathan right now?

I open my eyes. "All at once," I say.

He clenches his jaw, desire flickering in his eyes. "It might hurt."

"I want it to."

He inches inside me a little deeper. I can't take my eyes off the way we look together. He's staring at my face. "I don't want to hurt you."

"Yes, you do. Think of how good it'll feel to finally—"

He thrusts hard, boring into me with an unrestrained groan of pleasure. Pain rips through me. I bite down on my lower lip until the throb turns good. He stops, breathing hard. Sweat drips from his chest to mine.

"Go," I say.

He pulls away and eases back in. We both watch my pussy take every inch. "Harder," I say.

He looks down at me. "Tell me you want me."

"Tell me I'm a slut," I shoot back. I don't know where it comes from. We're each hot enough that Finn won't catch the flush of my face. I'm not embarrassed that I want to be called that. I'm embarrassed it's so important to me, I couldn't keep it to myself.

"If it's because of what we're doing," he says, moving in and out of me slowly. Even though it's good, I need more. "I'm not going to call you that.

You aren't that."

I grab his face. I love that he cares, that he wants me to feel comfortable, and I want to repay him for it. "I want you, Finn. Ever since you looked at me that way—"

"In the hall," he finishes my sentence. "Like you *knew* me." He understands. "Sadie, you looked at me like I was . . . I was someone you'd loved and lost— and then found." He buries one hand in my hair and kisses me, his lips both firm and reverent. Apparently, sweet pillow talk is the way to Finn's cock, because he finally fucks me how I want. His thrusts come harder, deliberate, almost violent. The couch rocks, its oak frame grating against the wall. I'm going to come, not just because it feels so good, but because it feels so wrong. Finn reminds me of Nathan in a lot of ways. He's also different. New. Rough. *Wrong.*

Finn grips my chin. "Look me in the eye."

I thought I was. Finn looks at me, is looking at me, the way Nathan does—or did. As if I'm the sun in his universe.

My chest tightens. Panic comes easier than my orgasm, and it builds fast.

Finn releases my face and smacks the side of my ass cheek hard. I'm startled back to the moment.

"You need this, don't you?" he asks.

I mouth the word "please."

He gets up on both forearms and drives into me. Relentlessly. Powerfully. He holds nothing back. He doesn't worry about breaking me. He lets go. I let go, slithering under him. Nothing is more important than reaching the top of this hill.

I come, grasping his shoulders to keep from losing myself. He grimaces as I make deep imprints in his skin with my nails. Either he likes it, or he's in pain.

He seizes my face in one hand and forces my head still. "Are you on birth control?" he demands, his eyes like the white-hot center of a fire.

"Yes," I gasp, "but you're wearing a condom."

His face contorts. With his thumb, he applies pressure to my lips until I open them. I suck, taking in his tormented expression. "Jesus," he says. "Shit." The top of my head squishes into the arm of the couch as he loses himself in me. With his ragged, out of control pace, I can't do anything more than lie there until he barks out "fuck!" and comes.

He collapses, spent and sticky. His thrusts lengthen, slow. I run my hand over his sweat-slickened back and massage his scalp, trying to calm him down.

He kisses the outer shell of my ear as if he's aiming with his eyes closed. "You're here," I think he says. His voice is muffled by my hair.

"Are you?" I ask. Compared to the violent way he just came, the silence is deafening.

"I'm here. Give me a minute."

He slides his arms under me and holds on like I'm trying to escape. I'm not. I have nowhere to go. The realization hurts like a punch in the stomach.

Maybe I lied just now. Physically, I'm here, but part of me isn't and may never be.

It takes Finn some time to recover from the way he devoured me. He mutters, raw and raspy. "Jesus, Sadie. I feel like I just came for the first time in years." He sighs. "Too much of that could kill a man."

My laugh is breathless—his heavy body is crushing my lungs. I can't imagine sex taking down a man of his size.

He lifts his head. His hair is damp and smooth, like polished honey-oak floors. Some strands fall around his face in slow motion. "I'm sorry about that last thing."

"I understand." Between my ringing ears and fuzzy head, our conversation earlier this week isn't entirely clear. Still, I remember the important details. "Kend—she lied to you about birth control."

"You can say her name. Kendra." He clears his throat. "I haven't been with anyone since I met her. I guess I got a little scared at the last minute."

"I don't want that either, Finn. Believe me. It's the absolute last thing I want."

He thumbs the hollow of my cheek. "Why? Kendra begs me for another baby."

"Perhaps Nathan and Kendra should get together, then." I wince before I've even finished the sentence. Finn stares at me. "I'm sorry. I shouldn't have said that."

"It's fine. Is it so far outside the realm of

241

possibility at this point?"

I look away so he doesn't see it in my eyes. The truth—I'd kill Kendra before she could have Nathan. He's too good for all of us. Is he, though? Is he the man I married? I never thought I had it in me to cheat on him, but I'm not as surprised at myself as I should be. I'm not the angel he is, or was.

Finn pulls out of me, discards the condom, and fits himself into the tight space between my body and the back of the sofa.

As I move onto my side to get comfortable, he grabs me. "Don't," he says. "Don't go yet."

"I'm not. I'm here for now." I stare at the apartment, weirdly familiar, like my own, and utterly different. The record player is squarely in one corner, partially hidden by bubble-wrap cascading off the entertainment center. The radiator kicks and sputters but keeps blowing. "Did he sit on this couch when he came to fix the heater?" I ask.

Finn kisses me behind the ear. "Let's not go down that path."

The image of Nathan in this room spasms and fades to black, like turning off an old television set. I don't notice the sickness in my gut until it disappears. "Yeah. You're right."

"And you're calm," he says. "Not that I'm complaining, but I was worried you'd be more . . . not calm."

I'm not sure what he wants me to say. A post-orgasmic stupor will only last so long, and then who knows? Right now I feel like a butterfly with damaged wings and a rare opportunity to return to my cocoon for a few hours. "I'm content," I say. "It's been a while since I was anything other than confused. I don't see the point in fighting it."

Finn nuzzles my hair. "That means a lot to me."

I glance back at him. He sounds sincere, and though we've become close, there's much we don't know about each other. "Why? Why does this mean anything to you?"

He squints at me. If he's attempting to peer into my soul, he might not find anything left after what we just did. "It feels right, doesn't it? Like this is supposed to be. I question everything in my life, all the time. Kendra. Work. Whether I should've stayed in Connecticut. The only sure thing is Marissa. And then you come along, and it's like things fall into place. Suddenly, taking this risk, moving back to the city—it was the right decision."

"But what about Kendra?"

"She's always driven the conversation of *us*, and I let her. Being back in the city revitalizes me, though. You're part of that."

I face forward again. "I'm not sure I understand what you're saying."

"I'm saying I finally have a reason to be firm with Kendra." He pauses. "You."

I tense in his grip, and I don't try to hide it. Several questions hit me at once. He would tell her? Why now, and why me? What did the last hour mean to him, and is it the same as what it means to me? Do I even know how I feel? "Me—?" I ask hesitantly.

"I feel something for you. Something strong." He squeezes me close. "Now more than ever, I could see us together."

I can't help my small scoff. Any woman would be lucky to have him, myself included. It's been less than two weeks, though. "Together?" I ask, because I can't seem to stop repeating him.

"I know it's soon. And maybe it's impractical. But it's like I was going through the motions until I found you."

I'm silent. It's the same romantic, lofty bullshit Nathan loves. It's always been hard for me to understand why he's that way. He might've said something similar a couple weeks after we met. I wouldn't have believed him, but Nathan's been proving the truth behind his words for years. Up until recently, I've had no reason to doubt him. I don't know if I buy into fate, but before Nate, I would've laughed in Finn's face just for suggesting it.

"I don't expect you to answer," he says after a minute. "That's just me. Your situation might be different." He swallows. "Is it?"

"I don't even know." I close my eyes. My voice is robotic. "I can't trust how I feel, because I'm lonely at the moment."

"No," he whispers hotly into my hair, drawing out the word. "No, no, no. I don't want you to feel lonely, not ever. Especially not in my arms."

"I'm sorry. I didn't mean this actual moment. Just in general." I move against him to show I don't regret being here. He kisses my cheek, caresses the skin under my breast. I'm still alone, but Finn chases that feeling away. "I had a wonderful time today," I say.

"You mean it?"

"Yes. You pushed me outside my comfort zone." I think of Finn looking through the photos later, after I leave. "The pictures came out beautifully."

"A photographer is only as good as his subject."

"I don't believe that," I say with a small smile. "You are really talented, Finn."

His heart beats against my back. "Thank you, Sadie."

"As for in the bedroom . . . well, you could use some practice there."

He grunt-laughs, then tweaks my nipple without warning. I suck in a breath. "Careful," he says. "I might want to practice with you again. Soon."

I roll my lips together. I know he's playing around, but it does bring up questions. "Is that what you want?" I ask. "To do it again?"

"Would it make me a shit person if I said fuck yeah?" He rubs his scratchy jawline against my cheek. "You're just as beautiful as I thought you'd be when you come."

I snort. I'm sure I look a lot of things when I come, but beautiful? The moments before climax are savage. My body will contort any ugly way to reach ecstasy. My mind will go anywhere. There's no black too opaque, no light too blinding. Nothing is off limits. It's raw, and raw is ugly, but it's the truth. "Bullshit. You don't really think that."

"I do," he says. "I physically can't stay away from you now that I've seen it."

"And you sound pretty worried about it," I say wryly.

"I probably am, somewhere inside. I'll deal with it later."

"So, you want to do it again." I'm still processing all of this. Once could be argued as a crime of passion. But twice? "Two times . . ."

"Three, four, a hundred. I'm not asking much." He takes my earlobe between his teeth. "What'd you expect? Honey on my tongue. Warm around my cock. Silk in my fingers. How can I stay away?"

I lie very still, except my breasts, which heave in his embrace. I like when he talks dirty. I'm turned on again, and I'm sure he can sniff me out. "And if I say you have to?"

"Don't."

"Let go of me," I say.

He hesitates and then opens his arms. I flip over so we're chest to chest. I thread one leg through both of his and rest my head on his bicep.

He strokes my back. "I want you as my own," he says.

I'm getting that. This isn't a heat-of-the-moment kind of mistake for him. "Try to stay in this moment."

"You feel guilty."

Do I? Aroused as I was, my head was clear when I decided to go through with this. I pride myself on owning my decisions, no matter the results. "Guilt isn't something that occurs to me the way it does others," I explain. "I told you that."

"I don't believe you. You wanted me to hurt you earlier. That was your guilt."

I study his chest like it's a treasure map. There isn't much hair, but it's darker than it is on his head. I know he's right. Nobody is devoid of guilt. I'm good at controlling it, though, and why is that so bad? It doesn't serve me to dwell on it. "I'm not usually like that," I say. "I don't usually say those things."

"You asked me to call you a slut."

I exhale through my nose. When Nathan called me that, my orgasm ripped through me with unforgiving intensity. Maybe it was guilt that drove me to try and recapture that sense of worthlessness. After being revered in the bedroom for years, it was shocking and explosively hot to be someone else for once. "Yeah . . ."

"How come?" He tugs on a strand of my hair to get me to look up. "Hey. I'm not judging. I thought it was hot. But I won't call you that without knowing why you need it."

"If I'm a slut for being here," I say, "it's not the right kind."

"What the hell does that mean?"

Nathan obviously craves something I'm not. Who knows why? He's held me in his palm so long, maybe he's tired of trying not to crush me. I wanted to show him the other night that I can be what he wants, whatever that is. He doesn't need to find red-lipstick girls. "I think Nathan wants someone he can treat like shit," I say, sounding as confused as I am. "I don't know why. Some men just want that, I guess. But why all of a sudden?"

"If he treats you like that—"

"He doesn't. That's what I'm saying. He's incredibly good to me—and maybe he's sick of it." I start to look away but stop. Finn's watching me closely. Listening. I owe him my attention. "So, here I am being what Nathan wants, just not with him. Something forbidden and bad. Wrong." I blink. "Call me a slut because it's what I deserve. And," I admit, "because it turns me on."

Finn sighs deeply, heavily, as if he carries the weight of the world on his shoulders. He kisses my nose, my eyelids. "I wish—so many things, Sadie. I'd erase all this for you."

I don't want it erased, though. Is a scar bad if everything that led to it was good?

It doesn't matter. This is real life. Things can't be erased. Mistakes can't be undone. I've made a choice that has found me in another man's apartment, another man's arms. And I feel something here, something surprisingly solid. The timing, our connection and proximity—Finn has a point. It *is* as if something greater is bringing us together. Could it really be fate? He wants me—he told me as much to my face. Nathan has said he doesn't. How far are they each willing to go? How far am I?

EIGHTEEN

Ginger isn't at the foot of the bed when I wake up the next morning. I wonder how Nathan would feel to know she waited for him all night on the tiled entryway instead of her normal spot on the bedroom carpet.

But when I get out of bed and head into the living room, I stop. Ginger's tail is sticking out from behind the couch. Nathan is sprawled out underneath a blanket, his feet sticking out the bottom. I grip one foot like it's a raft and I'm stranded in the middle of the ocean. His skin is ice. Our no-heat tradition seems more stupid than adorable.

"Nathan, honey." I shake him. "Honey."

He squints and groans, "Sa-die."

"Go get in bed. It's freezing out here."

He shuts his eyes again, stretches one arm to Ginger's head, and ruffles her fur. "*Extreme Hangover*," he mumbles. "*Home Edition.*"

I smile. His hair is pointing in every direction. I can smell alcohol from where I stand. "The hard stuff?" I guess.

He nods.

"When'd you get home?"

"Said I'd be here when you woke up."

It would've taken no small effort to get here by this time while wrecked. I'm still mad he spent the night out, but that gesture helps his case. "Come to bed."

"Can't move."

"Then I'll bring the bed to you." I get our huge, fluffy comforter from the bedroom and cover him with it. I tuck in all the corners. Not a single appendage on his body should be cold.

His eyes are shut. He's still petting Ginger, his long fingers sifting through her fur.

"Need anything?" I ask.

He swallows audibly, smacking his tongue in a battle with dry mouth. He feels for my hand. I stare in disbelief for only a second before I give it to him. My heart rate kicks up a notch. He pulls gently. Before he can change his mind, I untuck and burrow underneath the covers. He brings me close to his body. For all his muscle, Nathan has the most comforting arms in the world. I hope he can't feel my racing heart.

I rest my cheek on his pec. His feet may be cold, but his chest is hot. It's my home. He cocoons me with the comforter from head to toe under a white cloud. I can't see his face, but he's here. I feel him. Safe in his arms, I wonder if I could say anything to him right now. I wonder if I should.

His breathing evens out. I think he's fallen asleep, but he slips his hand into my sweatshirt. He rubs my back. I've needed this simple touch, and I want to be content with it. But my imagination has other ideas. The thought of him and Joan in this same position hits me hard. I don't even know if it's Joan I'm picturing—it could be any woman. Donna. Kendra. Cindy Crawford, who Nathan has a thing for. Last night, I lost my right to care about that, but I do. Intensely. Even though I was the bad wife, even though I let another man inside me and I haven't even showered yet, I'm terrified that Nathan has even so much as looked in another woman's direction.

I unearth myself from the comforter, sit up, and look back at him. "Where were you last night?"

"I told you." Nathan sighs, drowsy. "Mikey's."

"Who else was there?"

"All the guys. I lost money. Not a lot, but—"

"And the wives?"

He pauses and, infuriatingly, chuckles softly. "What, you think they had their own table going or something?"

"So Joan wasn't there?"

He wrinkles his nose and opens one eye. "Joan? Mike's fiancée?"

"Do you know another Joan?"

He closes his eye again. "She lives there. She made us food."

I fume. Cooking for Nathan belongs to me and me alone. "Why didn't you order out?"

"Uh. She offered, so we let her." He shrugs. "She stayed in the bedroom the rest of the time. Why?"

I shake my head. My thoughts tumble around like dice. Can Nathan lie this easily? If so, since when? I'm not sure how to interpret him, as if he's speaking a foreign language. On a night five years ago, Nathan called me twenty minutes before he was supposed to pick me up for the theater. He'd lost the tickets to a Broadway show we'd been looking forward to for months. He said, since I was already dressed up, he was sending a car for me. We'd have dinner instead. It was a lie. I knew before I hung up that he was going to propose, and he did. During a sunset helicopter tour of New York City. We were over the Empire State Building, where we'd spent half of our first date.

Now, I'm wading in uncertainty. What he says is convincing, but it's also convenient. He can say he was with Joan, and it wouldn't be a lie. I'll only know if I ask him specifically whether or not he's slept with her. But at the moment, he's not doing everything in his power to keep me at a distance, and for that reason, I don't want to bring it up. "Never mind."

"Can I go back to sleep now?"

I nod, even though he doesn't see. He's already drifting off again. "Do you want me to stay?" I ask.

He breathes through his mouth for a few

seconds. "Hmm? No. Take Ginger out." For being barely cognizant, he says it with edge, as if I've angered him.

I get out from under the blanket—my touch, my love, spurned once again. Ginger looks up. "Walk," I say, and she leaps to her feet.

"Sadie . . ." Nate says. "Favor?"

I turn back. He's like a little boy, puffy-eyed and bundled in his blankets. *Come back*, I want him to say. Or, *I'm sorry*. At this point, I'd even take a confession. *I slept with Joan, it meant nothing, I love you.* "Anything," I say, and I mean it.

"Make coffee."

How can two meaningless words feel like the tip of a blade pressing into my chest? Not sharp enough to pierce the skin, but a reminder that he could if he wanted. I take a deep breath and realize I'm wrong. It's not what he says that stings. It's what he doesn't. "Sure, babe."

I could put on a pot to brew while I'm downstairs, but I have some things to make up for myself. After making myself presentable to the public, I swap my slippers for Chucks and Nathan's ratty sweatshirt for my coat.

I walk Ginger in the direction of Quench. It's Nathan's favorite coffee by a mile. Despite his hand on me a few minutes earlier, I can't help feeling chilled to the bone. As if a freeze rises from the storm's leftover puddles. Nate's momentary lapse can more likely be credited to a hangover than a change of heart, and it hurts. "Take Ginger out," he said, and, "Make coffee." His orders were as empty as the neighborhood on this Sunday morning.

Since there are no patrons at Quench, I bring Ginger inside. They know her here. Gisele, the chipper culinary student who works mornings and weekends, comes out from behind the counter to greet us.

"How's my favorite pup?" she asks. She sets a paper cup with water in front of Ginger.

Gisele treats Ginger better than some customers, and I don't blame her. New Yorkers are heinous before caffeine. "How's school?"

"I'm the only one in my class not hanging on by a thread because Thanksgiving break is on the horizon. In other words, I love it." She brightens as she goes back to her place behind the register. "By the way, I might take International Cuisine next semester. Maybe you and Nathan can be my guinea pigs."

"We're always up for that."

She grins. "Where is he this morning?"

"Asleep," I say. "He hit the booze a little hard last night."

With a laugh, she shakes her head. "It must take an entire brewery to bring down a guy his size."

"Don't let his height fool you. If there's hard liquor involved, he's the tallest lightweight around."

We exchange a smile. "Two coffees?" she asks.

I glance at the pastry window. "We need

256

sustenance too. What's Nathan order these days?"

"He hasn't been by in a while." She has her back to me as she pours our drinks. "I was going to ask if he got a new job or something. I don't see you guys walk by anymore."

"We've been out of sync lately," I say. "We used to try to leave around the same time, but because of my promotion, our schedules are different."

She puts our drinks in a tray. "Cool."

"I guess we'll take two dark chocolate pistachio croissants."

She picks up tongs but only puts one pastry in a bag. "He doesn't like those. I'm not supposed to tell you because he knows you love them."

I raise my eyebrows. "Why should I care if he doesn't like them?"

She shrugs. "Maybe he doesn't want to hurt your feelings."

I roll my eyes. "Nathan thinks everyone is as sensitive as he is."

"Croissant for you, glazed donut for him. I think he's ordered that a few times." She passes two pastry bags across the counter. "Donut's on the house. Tell him to feel better."

"Thanks, Gisele. I will." I pay for mine with a smile.

At the condiment station, I pop the lid off my drink to pour half and half in my coffee. I've been to Quench a hundred times, but this morning, an old memory nags me. I haven't thought of it in years, but

I've never quite been able to shake it.

When I was in college, in this exact same spot, I bumped hands with someone while reaching for creamer. Between his soulful green eyes and shoulder-length, dirty blond hair, he was, up to that point, the most beautiful boy I'd ever seen. The sun came through the window, turning the amber strands in his hair gold.

"Sorry," he said. "After you."

"Thanks." I poured half and half, sneaked a glance at his pink, ripe-looking mouth, and then passed the container. He smiled as if he knew exactly what effect his protruding, full lips were having on me. I could sleep on the bottom one for fuck's sake. I nearly lost my balance.

"Pistachio?" he asked. He was talking. I had no idea what about. Who knows how long I'd been on the planet of dumbstruck women.

"Excuse me?"

"Is that the pistachio croissant?" he asked. "I was going to try it . . ."

"Oh. It's the best." We both looked at it. "Do you want some?"

He was surprised. "Okay."

I tore off a piece. "Hope you don't mind my germs."

"Not one bit." He took it from my fingers. I watched him chew and lick a dark-chocolate glob from the corner of his mouth. "Delicious."

"Told you."

We smiled at each other a little too long. I couldn't think of one normal thing to say. I just wanted to tell him how something *he was—cute, sexy, unexpected. I looked good, hair straightened and makeup done, dressed up for a class presentation I had later that morning.*

Finally, he said, "I'm waiting for someone. Can I sit with you for a minute?"

I hadn't planned on staying. I was going to class early to rehearse my PowerPoint slides. My feet wouldn't move, though. "Sure."

He picked up his coffee, chose a table by a window, and pulled out a seat for me. "You go to NYU?"

"How can you tell?" I asked as I sat.

"Your bag looks heavy. Textbooks?"

"And a laptop." I set my oversized tote on the ground. "Back problem waiting to happen."

He smiled. I almost missed the dimple that creased his cheek because of my fascination with his lips. "I'm a photography major. I want to take beautiful photos. Or, photos of beautiful things." He tucked some loose strands behind his ear.

"I should've guessed."

"How come?"

"You look like an artist," I said shyly, but it was the truth. I could see him in a paint-splattered smock or easily commanding a room full of models. "Maybe it's the hair."

His eyes brightened. "All right, then. I've been debating a haircut, but if you like it, that's a solid argument against one."

I blushed and glanced at the table. It wasn't every day a man this good-looking noticed me, much less deferred to my judgment. There was a lot I wanted to ask him. When would he graduate? Had he moved here from somewhere? I wasn't sure where to begin.

Before I could figure it out, banging against the window startled us both. A plump redhead pressed her breasts and palms against the glass. "I overslept," she shrieked with huge eyes. It took a moment for me to recognize my classmate out in the wild.

"Becky?" I asked.

She bolted toward the door and blew inside the coffee shop like a hurricane. "I was supposed to get up early to finish my slides but I drank too much last night. I overslept. Please help me. Please, please—" She grabbed my arm and pleaded with the man across the table from me. "I'm sorry to steal her, but both of our grades are on the line." She returned to me. "I need help finishing them before class starts. Bring your coffee. I need it."

I didn't know why I was already halfway out of my chair. Becky and I were presenting to our Ethics and Media class, but we'd decided to be responsible for our own parts. Her desperation, her I need, I need, sent peals of urgency through me, though, and it was true. My grade on this project was tied to her. "I'm sorry—" I didn't know his name.

"Ah—" He looked between Becky and me. "You have to go? You're sure?"

"Class starts in an hour," Becky said. "We have to go. Now."

"I'm sorry," I said again, picking up my bag.

He handed me his coffee cup. "Take it. For her."

I shot him a grateful glance as Becky hurried me out the door. I went back the next day around the same time. For months, I mistook other tall, honey-blond men around the East Village for him. I'd checked his coffee cup for a scribbled name with no luck. I thought of him often. But I never saw him again—until now.

I look back at Gisele, as if she has some magical answer to the storm brewing inside me. She's restocking the pastries. She wasn't even old enough to work here ten years ago.

"Hello again."

We shared sips of coffee, flirtatious glances, and a dark chocolate pistachio croissant. Finn and I have met before . . . and he's known it all along.

NINETEEN

In one hand, I balance a drink tray and Ginger's leash. Between glances down the hall at my apartment, I quietly knock at Finn's door.

He opens it shirtless. Mussed. His hair is one unruly wave over his head. He smiles widely. "Morning, beautiful."

It's been ten years. Now, he has crow's feet that remain even after he's stopped smiling. His shorter hair is darker, closer to the color of the beard he didn't used to have. But his honeyed-green artist's eyes, and his expressive lips—those are the same.

"Hello *again*," I say.

He opens the door a little wider. "Come in."

"I can't. That's not why I'm here."

"Ah," he says with a slight nod. He crosses his arms over his chest. His sweats, missing the drawstring, slip a little. "You're feeling guilty about yesterday."

"No." I scratch under my chin. Because of the hair fringing his waistband, and the unmistakably long, ridged outline of his crotch, I don't think he's wearing underwear. I probably caught him naked in bed. "I mean, I don't know."

He follows my gaze down and adjusts himself. "Sorry. Morning wood."

I'm suddenly hot in my coat and scarf. I look anywhere but at him. "Sorry."

"Want to tell me why you're here?"

"Right. Yes." I straighten my shoulders, remembering myself. Finn has kept yet another crucial piece of information from me. Our conversation at Quench a lifetime ago was short but promising. Electric. I know he felt what I did that day. "Why didn't you tell me about Quench?"

He looks from my face to the coffee and back. "You remember? Since when?"

"Just now." Ginger sighs loudly and lies down next to us. "You should've said something, Finn."

"Why?"

"Because—" My feet in socks and shoes, my neck wrapped in cashmere, I sweat. "You lied."

"When? How?"

"You made me think we were strangers."

"We were." His cheek dents with one dimple. "I wanted you to remember on your own."

"Why? What difference does it make?"

264

He takes the tray from me. "Come inside."

"I can't. That's for Nathan."

"Sadie—" He sets it on the ground next to Ginger. "Do you believe in fate?"

"Not really."

"No? Not even a possibility it could exist?" With his tilted head and small smile, it's as if he knows something I don't. "Maybe we have to go through certain experiences in order to get where we're supposed to be."

"And that place we're supposed to be is predetermined? By who?"

"I don't really think fate has to mean we have no control. Our decisions lead us along a path, and that's a kind of fate. Isn't it?"

I look down. His bare feet are inches from the toes of my sneakers. I can't tell if he means what he says, or if he's justifying what we did.

"Why did I choose Quench that morning when I could've gone to Starbucks by my place?" he asks. "I don't know. But I did. Why'd you let me sit with you?"

I shift feet. "You know why."

"You were attracted to me?" he asks, and then answers himself, "Yes. As was I to you." He nudges his toe against the sliver of exposed ankle between my sock and jeans. It tickles in a hair-raising way that makes me want to peel his sweatpants off. "Were you with him back then?"

I raise my eyes to his. "Not yet."

"I wasn't with Kendra. You and I—we met first."

We share a moment of quiet while I let myself get caught up the same eyes and lips that mesmerized me back then. Finn and I, we did meet first. If we hadn't been interrupted, where would we be today? "I went back the next day to find you."

"So did I." He shrugs. "I guess our timing was off back then. But now . . ."

He has me on his hook. I want to know what happens next. He's had two weeks to think this over to my twenty minutes. "Now?"

"Now, we get to make things right. I know it seems like I've been pushing, but it's because that moment in the hallway struck me like lightning. I wanted you to experience that on your own."

I frown. "Is getting struck by lightning good?"

He adjusts his stance and gestures between us. "Isn't it possible that Kendra and," he looks past me, "Nathan were simply instruments to bring us together? That we're supposed to be having this conversation?"

Do I believe an otherworldly force has led Finn and me to each other at the expense of Nate and Kendra? No. I can almost see, though, the poetry of how we got here, standing in front of each other, when we have good reason to be elsewhere. I'm afraid to think I could've loved him the way I do Nathan if only Becky hadn't overslept and botched our presentation.

I take a step backward. "I have to go."

"Come back later?" he asks hopefully.

"I can't."

He blinks directly to the pastry bags sticking out of my purse, as if he's been trying not to look. "Pistachio?"

I hesitate and nod. "My favorite."

"I know," he says softly. He takes a strand of my hair in his thumb and forefinger. "Come back here."

It's hard to say no. Because I'd like to snuggle into his warmth. Because his built body is divine-like. I want to learn to sculpt so I can put him on my dresser. Heat billows from behind him. I get closer. He slips a crinkled bag out, reaches inside, and holds up the croissant. "Open for me."

I've heard those words before, in this same apartment. He's so sure I'm opening more than my mouth to him. He feeds me some of the pastry, then takes his own bite. We lock eyes and chew. With an "*mmm*" he kisses my cheek. I should pull away. I can feel each of his beard hairs on my cheek, stiff but soft, tickling but sharp. And last night's musk sticks to him. And his pants are tented. I put my hand on his chest and push. He's immovable.

"Your hair's still curly," he notices.

"I haven't . . ." I sigh, frustrated that words don't come out like I want. That my hands and feet don't act how they should. "Last night, I didn't—and this morning, I just ran out for a minute . . ."

He slips an arm around my waist and hides me in the doorway. He brushes his lips over my temple. Ginger's sleeping, but it feels like she knows everything.

"I'm still everywhere on you then," he says, grazing the tip of his nose along my jaw, under my ear. "I haven't showered, either. I want you in my bed. I want my sheets to smell like us."

I'm overheating. I push for real this time. "Nathan's waiting."

He backs off, his body noticeably tense. "*I'm* waiting, Sadie. Ten years I've been hoping to turn a corner and run into you."

"You don't mean that."

He puts the heel of one hand to his forehead. "I'm not trying to come off as a creep. It's not like I thought I'd ever see you again." He massages his temples with long, strong fingers. "But I kept my eyes open whenever I was in this neighborhood. I've spent more money at Quench than one person should. I hoped. I watched. For you."

"Me?" I ask. "Or anyone who isn't Kendra?"

He sets his jaw. "What kind of a question is that? Kendra and I have our own shit. It has nothing to do with you."

"Fine." I don't want to get into it with him. If I know Nathan, he's still dead to the world. His hangover remedy is to sleep the next day away. I want to be there when he wakes up. I want to be there if he reaches for me again. "I'll see you, Finn."

"When?"

"Whenever I see you. I can't make any promises."

He's hurt. I'm going to walk away. I am. But ten years ago, I would've dropped Ethics and Media for another chance with the golden boy I'd let get away. For an irresistibly sexy, shirtless Finn, asking me to stay. When I'd thought of him after that day, it was with regret. I'd walked out on something special. The way Finn believes we're meant to be, I'd believed myself a fool to go with Becky.

My heart softens a little. "You really looked for me after that day?"

He takes my hand and kisses my palm. "I did. You are not just anyone to me. You're the one who got away."

He begins wrapping up my croissant. I sigh, not with longing, but with a sinking feeling in my stomach. "Keep it. I don't think I'll be around today," I say, as though a pastry is a consolation prize. The truth is, I could stay here. It scares me that I want to just as much as I want Nathan to pull me back under the covers. It scares me that I don't know if Nathan would care beyond missing his coffee fix. Finn looks like he's going to be as sick as Nathan, but at least he'd accept my comfort. I glance down the hall. "I'll walk Ginger before work tomorrow," I tell Finn.

He frowns. "I'll be there."

I pick up the coffee, wake Ginger, and enter my apartment with as little noise as possible, slipping off

my tennies. Ginger wraps me in her leash trying to get
to Nathan. Her tail goes a mile a minute.

"Hush," I whisper when she whines. "Daddy's
sleeping."

We've been gone less than an hour, but when I
let her go, she bounds into the other room.

It doesn't matter that I tried not to wake him,
though. Nathan's not on the couch anymore.

I look around the quiet apartment. Has he left?
When? I swallow thickly. It's disarming to think he
was somewhere out there while I canoodled Finn, and
not fast asleep as I'd blindly assumed. "Nate?"

"Got coffee?" he answers from our bedroom.

I breathe out, relieved that he's still here. After
this morning's breakthrough, I have a shred of hope
this could be a good day for us. I find him in front of
our closet, freshly showered with a towel around his
waist.

I lean against the doorway and take in the scene
before me. "Are you going somewhere?"

He avoids eye contact as he takes his coffee from
the tray and tastes it. "It's almost cold."

"Blame it on Ginger," I say. "She wants to smell
everything. It's not easy walking her while balancing
two coffees."

He turns back to surveying the closet. When he
takes another sip from his cup, his towel loosens. He
catches it with lightning speed. Nathan hasn't
undressed in front of me since I sucked him off in the
doorway. I think about Finn's morning wood. Did

Nathan jerk off in the shower? It's been almost two weeks. It seems ridiculous to hope for a glimpse of my husband's cock.

For a brief second, he has the decency to look sheepish about it. It passes. "Is there food?" he asks.

"I'll get it." I push off the doorway and go get the pastry from my purse. It's the least I can do, considering the real reason his coffee is cold.

In the ten seconds I was gone, Nathan has changed into his underwear and hung the towel in the bathroom. I can see the push and pull of his muscles when he moves. He's chiseled, but lean, thanks to his six-foot-three frame.

Nate takes the bag from me, looks inside, and groans. "How'd you know exactly what I wanted?"

I warm with pride. "Gisele picked it out."

He cuts his gaze to me, sharp as a knife, as if I just admitted to tossing his laptop out the window. "Gisele," he says, deadpan.

"Yeah." I scrunch my eyebrows. "From Quench."

His jaw is clenched like he's trying to snap it. Her name has set him off. Why? She's been a friend since she started at Quench last Christmas. She's young. And beautiful—there's no denying that. Nathan once defended her from a handsy businessman. It was sweet. She kissed him on the cheek. I hugged his waist and did the same.

I tilt my head. *Gisele.* Is it her? I blanch. Gisele makes more sense than Joan. She's younger than me,

271

and prettier too. Nathan and I have joked that her French boss is in love with her, and that's why she basically does what she wants during her shifts. Like give my husband free pastries.

"Why are you pissed now?" I ask him.

He relaxes his expression and moves on to the donut, unperturbed. He takes a large bite. "I'm not. I just think it's funny."

I taste bile in the form of chocolate and pistachio. The man thinks it's fucking funny to jerk me around. "What is?"

"Forget it." He swallows the food in his mouth. "I'm going to volunteer."

"Again? You just did that."

He plucks a t-shirt from a shelf. "You say that like it's a strip club. It's a soup kitchen."

I hold my coffee to my chest and feel nothing. I wish it were hot. I'm losing this conversation, and I don't know if the way to get answers is to rage or submit. His nonchalance makes me think the conversation is over.

"I know, and I love that you're so generous, but . . . I miss having you around here," I say gently, trying for kindness. "I thought maybe we could chill today. Sleep off that hangover."

He looks puzzled as he pulls on his shirt. "Are you hungover?"

It'd be easy to blame last night on the Kahlúa, but it only loosened me up. "No."

"How'd it go yesterday with the photos?"

I'm surprised by the question. It's maybe the only topic I don't want to discuss, yet that's what he finally decides to ask about. "Fine . . ." I glance away. "I think we got what we needed."

"Good. Are we paying for it?"

I shake my head. "Amelia is."

"Even better." He stands in his shirt and boxer briefs, watching me. I wonder, since he makes no move to put pants on—is he debating staying in?

"We can watch whatever you want," I tempt him. I meant what I said. I miss him. "I'll make sandwiches. With bacon."

"I know you don't get the volunteering thing," he says, "but to me, it's worthwhile."

I don't know how to take that. Spending time with me isn't worthwhile? I've wondered before, even when things were good, if it ever bothers Nathan that I don't give back the way he does.

During one of our first dates, he told me he believes all people are inherently good. I'd thought it was really sweet—and possibly an embellishment. It wasn't. Since then, Nathan has turned down a promotion to help a father who's never been quite present in his life. Nathan over-tips for bad service, especially around the holidays. He's gotten Ginger into a dogfight because he was too polite to ask a woman on the sidewalk to put her poodle on a leash. And now more than ever, he gives up personal time with me to help at the shelter. Generosity is important to him in a way it isn't to me. I believe

273

people earn what they earn. Like how Nathan and I each worked hard enough to move into better positions at better pay. Unlike a sulky waitress who'd rather be at a New Year's Eve party than serving us champagne. I'm generous with him. With Andrew and Bell. It's not something I just give freely.

"I'm trying here," I tell him. "If you don't want to stay here, I'll go with you."

He smiles wryly, but not at me. At a heap of jeans. He pulls a pair out. "You hate the soup kitchen."

"I don't hate it. I'm just not one of those people who loves it. I don't get the satisfaction you do from—"

"Being selfless?"

A lump forms in my throat. It makes it hard to swallow. Nathan insinuating I'm shallow bothers me, because compared to him, I am. I don't cross the street to give a homeless man my boxed leftovers. I've never spent a Sunday morning calling friends to find a home for a stray dog. That's Nathan, not me.

Am I selfish? I look around the room. My nightstand is piled with books and magazines I've been meaning to start. My drawer is a collection of displaced things—coins, paperclips, pens, birth control, receipts, lip balm, an old watch, and more. On his side sits *The Martian* with a bookmark in it. I thought he was reading Erik Larson, but it turns out he's burning through his stack. His drawer holds a flashlight, an extra phone charger, and no clutter. He's been watching less TV.

I swallow any shame and raise my chin. Maybe I don't often put others first. Maybe I don't notice the small things like he does. Does it make me a bad person? Do I deserve to be shut out? No. He isn't being fair. I'd rather spend my Sunday taking care of him instead of others—that's how I'm selfless. It was my idea to get Ginger from a shelter instead of a store. I'm messy sometimes, because doing dishes or laundry can wait and sated, post-meal cuddling on the couch shouldn't. I've always been this way, and he knew it when he married me.

"I'm not as good as you," I say. "That's what you're trying to say?"

With his back to me, he pulls on his jeans. "No . . ."

"What then?"

He sighs, muttering. "I don't think I even know."

I latch onto the hint of concession in his words and his puzzled tone. "I *am* making an effort, Nathan," I say. "I've been taking Ginger out more to help you. I'm coming to the shelter with you on Thanksgiving like you always wanted. I came to your bowling game."

"Yeah," he says, turning back to me. He puts his hands on his hips. "That is pretty selfless, trudging down to Brooklyn like that."

I can't tell if he's teasing me. "Well, it *is* Brooklyn," I joke.

275

He shakes his head almost imperceptibly. He's not playing.

"Come on," I say, exasperated. "You're defending that place to the death. It's the home of skinny jeans and vegan booze. What happened to the guy who once moved a 'stroller parking' sign in Williamsburg from a restaurant to a trashcan?"

He walks around me. "We're overstaffed as it is," he says, both ignoring me and shutting down my offer in one sentence. "Apparently, everyone's in the holiday spirit."

I follow him through the living room, and Ginger follows me. "Then why do you have to go?"

"Because it's part of my job."

"No one else in your office does it as often as you."

"And because I like doing it, Sadie." He picks his hoodie off a hook by the front door. "It reminds me why I do what I do. I don't have a religion. Serving others is how I get clarity—you know that. Is that a crime?"

"No," I say immediately. "I love that my husband is such a good person. Even if he can be a real fucking jerk."

He freezes in the middle of zipping up his hoodie. Even Ginger sits back and stops panting.

"Nathan," I say to his profile when he doesn't respond.

"What."

"We need to talk."

He runs a hand through his damp hair and scratches his scalp. "I know."

I chew the inside of my lip. I can't feel him here, and it scares me. I want to touch him, but if he recoils, I don't know what it would do to the fight building inside me. And I can't lose that now that I'm starting to find it. "I'm ready. Now."

"Not now."

"Why not? Work can wait."

"I need time to gather my thoughts."

"What thoughts?" My stomach aches. This is real. Whatever's happening, we can't ignore it anymore. "I'm afraid."

He closes his eyes. His jawline is sharp, not with anger, but as if he's holding in tears. He doesn't cry, though. Not ever. I know my Nathan—he shows his love by hiding his pain from me, and sometimes I forget it's even there. "I don't think I know what I want yet," he says, "and I'm afraid if we talk now, I'll get even more confused." He swallows. "I need to come in with a clear head."

I almost don't speak, because just the threat of his tears stuns me. He really is hurting, and that means he still cares on some level. It's not enough for me, though. I need him to care enough to turn to me. "I can't keep going like this, Nathan. You won't even look at me."

He meets my eyes. "Helping others always puts things into perspective for me. So I'm going to go do that. When I'm ready, I'll come to you."

"This isn't fair. You can't shut me out indefinitely. We fix this by talking, not by each trying to do it on our own."

"You don't think I know that?" he asks. "Who's the one that concedes in every argument we have? Who goes the extra mile to fix problems in our marriage before they even reach you? Me. I do." He stabs a finger in my direction. His face is red now, and any pain has cleared. "And you just float along, never paying attention to anything other than yourself. I've held your hand through this entire marriage. Maybe, for *once*, one goddamn time, you could be the one who—" His face falls when he realizes he's yelling.

My heart pounds as my face heats. I can't remember Nathan ever raising his voice at me. How long must this have been bottling up for him to explode? Does he mean what he says, or is he just trying to hurt me? I can't decide if I want to scream back at him or burst into tears, but the look on his face stops me. Finally, I see the awareness and compassion that disappeared two and a half months ago. I think he might even close the distance between us, wrap me in his arms, tell me everything is fine. Everything will be okay. It's all I've wanted for months—for him to lower his shield and show me the path back to him.

"What?" I ask. "Keep going. I can take it if it means we end this horrible silence."

He picks his keys up from the bureau. "I'm too amped right now, and outbursts like that're exactly what I'm trying to avoid. I already told you, I'm not trying to hurt you, and—just . . . I'll see you later."

"Think you'll be sleeping here tonight?" I ask, letting the sarcasm drip. At some point, I curled my hands into fists. If I thought I could get it out without my heart stopping on the spot, I'd throw Gisele and Joan in his face. Even though an affair is unlikely, at least it would shake him up. "Or will you find somewhere better? Maybe *Family-kind* has an extra bed."

He says nothing and sticks his feet in his tennis shoes, not bothering with the laces.

I don't want *nothing*. I'd rather he told me to fuck off than remain mute. I'd take the worst thing he could think of over nothing. "I'm sick of this asshole bit, Nathan," I warn. "I want my husband back."

He opens the door.

"I'm going to check on you. I'll call all the soup kitchens in the city." I know he wouldn't lie about volunteering, but at this point, I'll say anything to get a reaction. "You better be there. If you're not, I won't even give you a chance to explain."

He glances back at me, a look of pure confusion on his face. Then, his furrowed eyebrows draw inward. His expression sours. He shakes his head at me like I'm begging for a second chance I won't get. I'm not begging, though, so why does it make me feel pathetic?

279

I wait through the few seconds it takes him to decide how to proceed. I wait for him to tell me I'm insane. I want him to. I want him to lose control and call me names if it means we'll finally have it out.

When he leaves, he doesn't even care enough to slam the door.

TWENTY

Each step beyond the entryway where Nathan left me feels like a great distance. The mysterious gulf in our relationship is murky and flooding over. Will the gap get even bigger? I don't know if I'd be able to build a bridge over an ocean. Or if Nathan even wants to.

His silence echoes louder in our apartment than his words. Ginger is sprawled on the floor as if it's just another day. On the TV console, Nathan's watch, hastily left behind, ticks loudly from under some discarded receipts. Movies line the shelf beneath it. I've never purchased a DVD in my life, but all my favorites are there.

A few winters ago, Nate brought home groceries and a movie. While I made popcorn in the microwave, he came up behind me, wrapped me in a blanket, and kissed my cheek. I never wondered how he knew when I was cold. I didn't remember mentioning *The Princess Bride*. Nathan just knew these things. I thought it was normal. I was happy without realizing it was because of those small details. I thought they made him as happy as they made me.

I inhale a deep breath. Why does that small, insignificant memory hurt this much? There are so many to choose from. Our wedding day. The first time Nathan kissed me. The night, early in our relationship, when he let me stain his dress shirt with mascara and never made me tell him why. But no, it's a random night in front of a microwave.

I pick up a receipt for fifty-seven dollars worth of Subway sandwiches. Once a month, he treats his office, even though I've asked him not to. It's not his job to be a hero. I crumple it up, my small act of rebellion.

His open laptop stares at me from our desk in the corner. I go over and tap the space bar until the screen flickers alive. There isn't a single thing on his desktop. Mine is cluttered with folders, photos, files.

I'm not sure what I'm looking for. I don't sit down, but I lean over and open his browser. His inbox is his homepage, and his account loads. I read the first couple subject lines. Despite being organized, he's not good about separating his work and personal life. I close the window. The truth is, I have no desire to snoop through his things. If Nathan is hiding something from me, it's killing him. He'd struggle lying to his worst enemy. I don't need, and I don't want, to see it in an e-mail or on a receipt.

Being in this apartment is like putting a plastic bag over my face. I go through the motions of cleaning up. I am, by nature, a messy person. Aside from washing dishes after a homemade meal, I don't like housework, not laundry, not cleaning. I do my best to pick up after myself. Maybe it's not enough, though. I throw out my half-drunk coffee cup and return our comforter to the bed. Nathan must've been in a hurry, since he normally folds his blanket and puts it with his pillows to one side of the couch. It's been a while, so I bleach the kitchen sink, the bathroom and toilet. In the shower, I scrub myself— my hair, under my arms, between my thighs. I shave my legs. Erasing Finn from my body means ridding myself of Nathan's momentary affections too.

Nathan needs time to sort out his thoughts. What does that mean? Based on his tirade, I wonder if he feels our marriage is one-sided. That I don't give as good as I get. How can I prove him wrong if he has several years' worth of small details against me?

I unscrew the caps off the shampoo, conditioner, and body wash to clean out gunk and switch out the blade of my razor for a fresh one. I could go to Family-kind and show him I meant what I said—I *am* trying. Even if he doesn't want me there, at least my effort would be noted.

I get out of the shower, towel off, and start with my hair. He loves it sleek and my makeup natural. I choose ass-hugging jeans that drive him crazy and a pink angora sweater that makes my boobs look a size bigger than they are. Not that Nathan's ever complained about them. From a dusty bin, I pick out a pair of boots with stacked, four-inch heels. They hurt my feet, but sometimes it's worth it. Sometimes it's welcome.

I go out to the elevator. Passing 6A is like walking through a ray of sunshine on a cold day. And it's not because Finn's heater is strong enough to warm the hallway. My body just knows what it's like in there. Softly lit, inviting, safe. His apartment set up is similar to ours. It's not hard for me to envision his home as my own. Sleeping in an empty bed doesn't exactly help. I'm the one who told Nathan to go, but I wouldn't have expected him to stay away.

I've been standing at the elevator for minutes when I realize the call button isn't lit up. I never hit it. I can't go to Family-kind. Nathan doesn't have the heart to turn me away in front of all those people. He'd grit his teeth and tolerate me. I don't want to get rejected, hurt, shocked yet again today.

I walk back toward my apartment feeling as clean and shiny as a new penny—on the outside. I have to pass Finn's door again, but this time I stop. I shouldn't feed into his lofty notions, but I shouldn't do a lot of things, like knock on his door. He doesn't open it at first. Eventually, though, I can sense him on the other side, debating. It's not the enthusiastic welcome I expected.

He unlocks the door. His lips are thinned into a line. "Every time you knock, I have to get dressed.

Soon, I'm not going to bother."

My cheeks warm like he's the sun, and he's only looking down on me. Despite being back in his revealing sweats, his hair and skin are damp. He's no longer musky, but as fresh and soapy as I am. "Sorry," I say and mean it. I don't know what I want, but it isn't to jerk him around. "I just thought . . . I—"

He sighs, overpowered by something I can't see, and opens the door wider. "You don't have to explain. I'm glad you're here." Black Sabbath plays in the background. There's a new shoe rack and umbrella holder near the entrance. I nod to a pile of broken-down boxes. "You're making progress."

"Yeah. I need somewhere to channel all this . . . you know," he pauses on a shrug, "nervous energy."

I bite the inside of my bottom lip. "Do I make you nervous?"

"Nervous? No. That's not what you make me."

I put my hands in my back pockets. "What then?"

He idly looks me over. "Pink's a good color on you. That sweater looks . . ." His lazy gaze stops at my breasts. "Soft."

I try not to show my amusement. I didn't pick this for him, but I'm glad he likes it. "Thanks."

He lifts his chin, his eyes back on mine. "So? You coming in?"

Minutes ago, if someone'd bumped into me, I'd have cracked down the middle. Now, my insides jiggle like jelly at the thought of being near him again. I have a greater urge, though, and it's to get out of this stuffy apartment building. "I want to be alone," I say.

"Okay . . ." He shifts from one bare foot to the other. Another sigh, this one deeper but shorter. "Then why'd you knock on my door?"

"Will you come with me?"

"You want to be alone—with me?"

I look down. He needs a welcome mat. The carpet here is noticeably wearing. "Yes."

"Give me a sec to change," he says. "Come in."

I might not come out until nightfall if I do. "I'll wait out here."

Finn looks both ways down the hall. "All right. Don't disappear on me."

"I won't." Nothing can move me from this spot now that I've decided I want to be with Finn today. I'm lighter just being in his presence. Nathan's harsh words melt off my shoulders.

He comes back in jeans, a button-down and boots within moments of leaving me there. In the hallway, he shrugs his jacket on. "Ready," he says.

He runs a fine-tooth comb through his hair while we ride the elevator down.

"I told you I'd wait," I say with a half-smile.

"I wasn't taking any chances." He winks at me. "Everything okay?"

I nod. "Better now."

We exit the building and stop on the sidewalk. I look toward Lexington Avenue and then in the opposite direction. Finn is expecting me to take him somewhere, but I hadn't thought this far ahead.

Finn's big, paw-like hand scoops up mine. "Come," he says, and we go right, deeper into the city. Our tree-lined street is an explosion of peaking, reddish-brown foliage and a smattering of summer green.

Finn squeezes my hand before he releases it. I'm grateful he doesn't make me say it aloud—we can't touch outside of four walls. "Why'd you change your mind about seeing me today?"

I tunnel into my coat, a futile attempt to recreate the warmth he just took away. "I don't want to get into it."

"That's fine. You don't have to." He scratches his beard. "Not right now. Eventually, though."

"Eventually what?" I ask, gawking up at him. "I have to get into it?"

"Yeah." He sniffs, shooting me a sidelong glance. "I'm not going to come running every time you get into a fight with him. I want to be there for you, but not like that."

"What makes you think we got into a fight?"

"Am I wrong?"

I stop abruptly. This is the opposite of what I had in mind for us. I need my brain bleached like my bathroom tile, not another argument. "If you're just going to yell at me, then we can part ways now."

"Yell at you? Have I raised my voice?" he asks. "I'm just saying, I don't want to be here with you just

287

because he can't be."

"I don't know why I want you here," I say. "Accept that or go. I'll understand."

He looks at the ground a second. "Just tell me I'm not a substitution for him."

I think Finn means more to me than that, but it's hard to know when my heart doesn't know what or who to beat for. I'm only sure that I'm not sure of anything. "My feelings are complicated," I say.

"We can make this work, Sadie. But I don't want to be second place."

"Finn, he's my *husband*. There is no place behind his."

He shakes his head. "Maybe it feels that way now, but it won't always." He engulfs both my hands, cupping them in his. "Jesus. Did you bring gloves?"

I shake my head, but I'm warmer already. Despite any reservations either of us might have, there's real hope in his eyes. It's infectious.

He brings our hands to his mouth and breathes hot air on them. "I'm not pushing you. I just need to know when you're with me, you're *with* me. You aren't wishing you were—somewhere else."

That isn't a promise I can make, but I don't want to hurt Finn, and I definitely don't want him to leave. The need to have him here runs deep after this morning's game of back-and-forth. "I want to be here," I say, "with you."

He kisses my knuckles, the pads of my palms. "I can see you're sad. You don't have to be sad. If you let me, I'll take your pain away, sew you up, heal you. It has to get worse before it gets better, but I can do it."

I watch him with awe. He truly is happy to be with me in this moment. "How can you be so sure about me after so little time?"

He gets lover-close and sticks my hands into their respective pockets. For a few private seconds, he laces his fingers between mine. "Honestly . . . I've probably lost it."

It feels good to break into genuine laughter, and to have him join in. I realize I've come to expect his intense responses, so poking fun at ourselves is welcome. "Please tell me you understand we can't leave our spouses of years for each other. You've known me two weeks."

"In my mind, I've known you much longer." He smiles down at me before we start walking again. "And, we can do whatever we damn well want."

"We can . . . but should we? It isn't fair to them."

"No, it isn't. It also isn't fair that he's had you for so long when it should've been me." Without missing a beat, he adds, "Should we go to Quench? Finish the conversation we started ten years ago?"

"Definitely not," I say. "They know me and Nathan there—" Gisele's sweet, unassuming smile comes to mind, and my mood darkens. Her young teeth are too white for a coffee shop. "They know us as a couple."

Finn grunts. I sense his irritation when he says,

"I've always thought of that as our spot, Sadie."

"What about Marissa?" I ask, steering the conversation back on topic.

His back goes straight. "Marissa?"

"If there's any reason to stop this, it's her."

"Marissa will always be my priority," he says. "That doesn't mean I have to be unhappy, does it?"

"No." I can't help but think of my brother. Andrew is stubbornly unhappy. He'd rather that than risk getting hurt again, even if he won't admit it. I worry about the message he's sending his daughter. "I guess not."

"I'm a good dad. Falling for someone else doesn't mean I have to lose my little girl."

His matter-of-factness stubs out any argument I could come up with. The man knows what he wants. He wants Marissa. He wants me. I, on the other hand, can't possibly think that far ahead yet. "I don't know, Finn."

He shrugs. His shoes scuff the concrete. Even in my highest heels, I only come up to his chin. "I don't expect you to. It's not exactly something we can work out overnight. But it's important to me that you know everything I'm thinking."

It's a refreshing change, someone letting me in, even if it isn't Nathan. But my true relief is that Finn doesn't need anything from me at this moment.

We wind through the streets, going nowhere until we come to a natural stop in front of a vintage clothing shop with artwork in the window and heavy metal on the speakers. Finn seems drawn by the music. Inside, we gravitate to the same watercolor nude hanging over a rack of clothing. The woman is hunched forward on the floor, her legs spread under her. She's shades of pink with reddish nipples and an opaquely black bellybutton. Even though she covers her crotch with a hand, her fingers are cracked, as if we're being spied on. The same black hair on her head sprouts around her slender fingers.

"Help you with something?" the clerk asks.

"No," we say loudly and in unison.

Finn stares up at it. Quietly, he says, "I can't get it out of my head—fucking you. Not last night or this morning or even now. Your perfect tits. An ass I can get a handful of."

"Don't talk like that." It's too much. His words make me dizzy, unsure of my self-control.

"You have the body of an angel," he continues. "Or a devil. I haven't decided."

I shift my eyes from the painting to his profile. "Is that a compliment?"

"No," he says, looking back at me. "It's trouble."

TWENTY-ONE

On Nineteenth Street, Finn wants to know what the next showing is. The theater clerk barely looks up from her computer, either tweeting or looking up movie times. "There's one starting in five minutes," she says.

"Is it good?" he asks.

"Of course. It's great."

"Honestly," he says. "What's the truth?"

She checks over her shoulder before she says, "Total crap. It's a box office bust."

"Perfect." Finn takes out his wallet. "Two adults for the box office bust."

Minutes ago, Finn had me hot and bothered in the middle of a vintage shop. I'm not sure I can sit still for the next two hours. "Finn—"

"Yes, sweetheart?"

Warmth surges through me. He's caught me off

guard. I can't be his sweetheart, but this woman doesn't know that. Finn looks about as delighted to call me that as I am to hear it. I decide to shut up. "Nothing."

He grins. "Good."

But as soon as we enter the popcorn-scented lobby, my loose muscles pull as taut as guitar strings. Finn asks me if I want something. I tell him I hate popcorn, and he looks pleased with each piece of information he gets. I don't hate popcorn. I hate the way it stirs my memory and my guilt, both of which are better off buried.

We walk side by side into the dark theater. His knuckles brush my wrist, and I get an actual electric shock from the carpet. My hairs stand on end. I realize he's going to touch me when we sit down. That's why we're here. To do more of what we did yesterday.

Him, flipping me over on the couch—first, onto my stomach to explore me from behind, then onto my back when he was ready to fuck.

His teeth, grazing the arches of my feet.

His hands, spreading me apart for his mouth.

"You all right?" he asks.

I'm hobbling. "Yes."

We stop at the top of the aisle. A trailer for an action movie shakes the theater like an earthquake. My eyes adjust. The *empty* theater. Finn leads me to the middle of the very back row. He seats me on the inside, closest to the wall. As soon as I'm there, he whips off his jacket and huddles over me. He runs the tip of his nose along the shell of my ear, breathes hotly on my skin. "I couldn't wait any longer," he says, pushing my coat off my shoulders. I wiggle out of it. "You have no idea."

The memory of him inside me stings fresh— hurts, even, but in a good way. I put my hand directly on him and feel how hard he is. "I have some idea."

He says my name through gritted teeth, as if the smallest thing will make him explode, then pushes me flush against the back of the seat. He kisses me hard, but I'm in the middle of my own feverish storm. I give it right back to him. I scrape my hand against the bulk in his pants.

He mirrors my movements and massages the seam of my jeans up against my clit. His fingers work fast from the start. I see stars right away. The stiff fabric and his urgency annihilate my control. I lose my breath, unable to continue kissing him.

He chuckles. "Already?"

"You can tell?" I ask.

"You freeze up before you climax."

My hand is splayed across his crotch. My shoulders are nearly at my ears. My thighs shake from the pressure. I whisper, even though we're alone, "You're going to make me come here, in public?"

"Eventually. We still have a couple hours." He covers my mouth with his again. We make out like we're both starving and the other person is food. He pops open my jeans but doesn't touch me where I want. His hand is under my sweater, skipping up my stomach, yanking at the underwire of my bra.

I pull him closer by his shirt. He's nearly in my seat, hungrily exploring every inch of me, when voices startle us apart. I bang my spine against the armrest. An elderly man and woman shuffle into view, and then down the aisle. A group of girls enters behind them and sits a few rows in front of us.

"What the *fuck*," Finn hisses.

I'm also panting, but somehow I manage a laugh. "Did you honestly think we could be alone in the middle of Manhattan?"

"I have a hard-on the size of fucking Manhattan." He throws his head back against the cushion and looks up at the ceiling.

"I'm sorry, baby."

"Not as sorry as I am. I've got to sit through a shitty movie with the goddamn Empire State Building in my pants."

I giggle a little harder, but my glee fades quickly. Now I'm thinking of the way he plowed into me last night with his building of a cock, gave me all of it, even though he knew it could hurt. "How big *are* you?"

He looks sidelong at me. "I don't know."

"Liar. Every guy knows."

"Not me."

I don't believe him. Nathan is equally shy about being well endowed. He'll joke with me, whispering about his cock in public to make me blush. But when

I tease him about his size, he shuts up.

Finn and I get comfortable. He pulls my leg over his and throughout the movie, absentmindedly rubs his hand on my thigh. I have no idea what's happening in front of my eyes. I'm turned on and confused, a dangerous combination. I think I could justify anything right now, including getting arrested for indecent exposure.

Images flash across the screen the way my memory replays my short history with Finn. I start at the beginning, in the coffee shop, looking up at him in the sunlight that poured through the window. Perhaps it's a more pivotal moment in my life than I realized. Perhaps my love story actually began then instead of on a beach years later. I can't say this is love. Whatever it is, it's coated in lust—I know that. My judgment is unreliable. But I can't deny that this could easily become more.

I fast forward to yesterday. The way he lovingly fixed my hair for our photo shoot. Kahlúa and coffee under the gray cover of storm clouds. My dress pushed down one shoulder for his camera, for his eyes. The way he pinched my skin in his teeth and refused to let me come at first. Him, above me, muscled arms, kissing his way down my torso, blond hair tickling my skin.

My pants are still unbuttoned. I slide my hand down the front. It's a few seconds before Finn straightens up next to me. "What are you doing?"

I bite my bottom lip and breathe through my

nose. My fingers know this song by heart, but even if they didn't, I don't think it would take me long. Remembering all the ways Finn touched me has me riding the tallest waves, singing at the highest pitch.

Finn doesn't take his eyes off me.

"I can't wait until the end," I say.

He grabs my wrist to still me. "But I want you to. I want you sitting there for the next couple hours, aching to have me inside you. Wondering how I'm going to make it happen when we have nowhere to go fuck."

He removes my hand and kisses each of my fingertips before nipping the pad of my pinkie. I gasp silently. My chest rises and falls. I slide down in my seat, buck my hips, try to rub my clit against the rigid seam of my jeans. I may be able to do this without hands.

"Stop squirming," he says, his voice deep and low. "You really can't handle it, can you? You want my cock."

Cock. My vision blurs. I need it. I think I'll die without it. I bend over his lap. He doesn't stop me from undoing his fly. He also doesn't help me. I get frustrated fumbling in the dark and start pulling at the denim like a junkie who needs a fix. Finally, I get into his underwear and take him out and into my slobbering mouth. With a groan, he shoves me down until he hits the back of my throat. He tests my limits. My eyes water, and I fight for air. He lets me up. I immediately go back for more. When my side cramps from the angle, I get on the floor, contorting my body into the small space. My knees protest against the ground, but I don't care. Finn moves his hands to my shoulders. There's tension in every part of him as he digs his fingers into my skin, his thigh muscles going taut. I can feel his effort to stay quiet through his entire body.

I'm prolonging my own orgasm, but this satisfies me in a way nothing else can, not even sex. His pleasure before mine. I want him to use my mouth how he needs. He isn't gentle.

He pulls my head back by my hair, and we look at each other. I gape inelegantly, my mouth wide and wet. He grabs my biceps and drags me up. My knees, stuck to the floor, come up with a pinch.

Finn turns me toward the screen and sits me on his lap, between his thighs. "Close your legs," he says.

When I do, he yanks my jeans and thong halfway down. "Finn—" I don't recognize my own guttural voice. With the crinkling of a condom wrapper, one of the girls shifts like she's going to turn around, but she doesn't. "We can't. Not here."

He lifts me up just enough to spread only my lips for him. "You sure?" he taunts. He leaves me suspended and trembling on the blunt tip of his cock. The film has gone quiet for a solemn scene. I brace myself against the seatback in front of me as he guides me down by my hips. My closed legs resist, but he pushes through it, splitting me up the middle. My teeth hurt from clenching them. The onscreen actress cries silently. I'm sure everyone can hear me breathing through my nose. Finn fills me completely so I'm seated in his lap. My muscles contract around him and release. I loosen my grip. This is what I need. I'm too stunned to move, so he urges me up and down by my waist. I can't tell if the sparks in my eyes are from Finn hitting me in all the right places, or if they're part of the movie.

Finn's mouth is in my hair, hot on the back of my neck. "Ride me, Sadie."

I swivel my hips in circles, chasing my orgasm. He puts his hands under my sweater and pulls on the cups of my bra. I suck in a moan as he grasps my breasts. I ride him, possessing his cock. The actors go about their business. Every few seconds, his fingertips tighten on my nipples. I make a small noise, and his tugging becomes tweaks and pinches. He wants me to scream. Cries of pleasure travel up my throat. I squirm more frantically on his lap trying to hold them in. When the intensity overtakes me, I let out a groan. He lets go, and we still. More than one moviegoer looks back. Our bodies tremble together. We wait. When they turn forward, Finn massages the sting away as he takes over and begins bucking up into me.

When I'm close, he pushes my upper back until my face is level with the seat in front of us. He grips my hips and fucks me straight into an orgasm. We talk to each other—*oh, God, fuck me, yes!* My pussy constricts around him, sucking him deeper. My climax lasts longer than I'm used to, intensified by the angle, the friction, the thrill of being in public, my impossible struggle to contain myself.

A silhouette rises in front of us, blocking the screen. I reach back and hit Finn's arm, trying to get his attention. He grabs my elbow and pulls me onto him harder, faster.

"Finn—" He slaps a hand over my mouth.

A girl looks right at us as she passes the last row. My ears ring. I miss whatever she mutters. Finn fucks me at lightning speed, grits out, "Hol-y—*Sadie*," and pulls my hair as he comes. For a few seconds, he shudders uncontrollably, muttering words I can't decipher.

I'm immovable. Unable to function. *Holy Sadie.* I can't imagine ever getting up from this spot, but almost immediately, Finn springs into action. He lifts me off his lap. I'm disoriented. I let him move me around. He puts me in my seat, turns to block me from the aisle, and does up my pants. My nipples are still out of their bra, pressed against the softness of my sweater. He fixes that too.

When the door opens, light slices through the theater. Finn's zipper hisses. A man whisper-yells at us from the end of the row. "Excuse me. Hello?"

"Fuck," Finn mutters, running his hand through his hair and beard.

I look over his shoulder. The theater attendant waves a glowing, orange wand. "Sir? I have to ask you both to leave."

Finn takes my arm and pulls me up so fast, the

301

room spins. I'm throbbing in my jeans. We inch toward the man with the vest. The girl who ratted us out stands behind him, her arms crossed.

I trip. Finn slips his arm around my waist. "Did you get everything?" he asks me. "Purse?"

I nod, even though he isn't looking at me.

"Sir," the man starts, "you're not—this behavior isn't permit—"

"We're going," Finn says irritably. He moves his hand from my waist to the back of my neck and doesn't take it off me. I can barely keep up with his purposeful strides.

The attendant trails us. "We ask that you not return."

Finn doesn't even look back. "We won't."

We're back in the well-lit lobby. I keep my head down, letting my hair curtain my face. I feel the employees looking at us anyway. I don't want Finn to let go of me, but we're in public now. I duck out from under his hand, and he lets me.

Outside, the cold November air is a slap in the face. It shocks me all the way into my lungs. Finn takes my coat from my hands and wraps it around my shoulders, even though he's still holding his jacket.

"Fuck this," he says as we walk. "All I want to do right now is lie down—with you. My heart's going a mile a minute."

Mine's also pounding, but not like his, I'm sure. He came mere seconds before we were interrupted. "Are you all right?" I ask.

"Aside from the fact that I'm still wearing the condom?" I giggle as he wraps his arm around my neck and tilts my head back by my chin. "On top of the world. You?"

"Good," is all I can think to say, even though I'm soaring. My insides are gelatin. The intensity of my orgasm has left me glowing from the inside.

"Those people got a little more show than they bargained for, didn't they?"

I smile. Somehow, he's able to guide us through the crowd while looking down at me. "That girl saw us," I say.

"Yeah, she did. Kind of hot, though, isn't it?"

My insides pull deliciously. It does turn me on. It's more than that, though. "She knows our secret."

He pulses his eyebrows. "Are you worried about running into someone you know?"

"A little," I say. "I don't know if Nathan would even care anymore, though."

Finn looks forward again. "I'm sorry to hear that. I mean, I'm not, but I am. I'm sure that doesn't feel good."

It doesn't. My mind flashes to the pathetic look he gave me earlier before he walked out the door. I'm less important to him than stepping in a pile of shit— at least *that* would be irritating enough to elicit a reaction. I push Finn's arm off.

"I hate that I can't show you how I feel," he says.

"I'm pretty sure you just did," I tease him.

"Which neighborhood is he in today? So I know

where to avoid," he adds.

He's frustrated. Any honest thing I could say would only make things worse, though. "Most likely, he's not far from here," I say. "He usually volunteers at the kitchen near Sixth Avenue."

Finn leaps off the curb and hails the first cab he sees.

"Where are we going?" I ask as he ushers me in.

"Anywhere but here."

As we pile into the cab, I don't tell Finn it doesn't matter where we go or how far we get. The day has to end at some point. And when it does, I'll go home to Nathan. That's a reality he can't escape.

TWENTY-TWO

Anywhere turns out to be Times Square. On a Sunday, even in the cold, the blocked-off area is a disaster. The crowd is thick, made even denser by puffy coats and thick-soled boots. A trashcan overflows onto the sidewalk. The cabbie drops Finn and me off as close to the center as he can get.

"Why are we here?" I ask. Billboards flash over us. I've spent every year since I moved here avoiding these tourist-infested blocks.

"Do you know anyone who'd come here on a Sunday?" Finn asks.

"No. Not a single person. Not during the week unless it was work-related and definitely not on a weekend."

"Exactly."

People walk around us in multiple directions. A toddler face plants between a stranger's legs and cries.

Finn's plan dawns on me, and I look up at him. "We're alone here."

He taps me on the nose. "Beautiful *and* smart." I can't help my smile. "What's your maiden name?"

"Beckwith."

"Beautiful and smart Sadie Beckwith."

I clamp my teeth together. It's been a while since anyone called me that, and I don't even know that woman anymore. I'm Sadie Hunt through and through. "Do you have any siblings?" I ask, changing the subject.

"No. You?"

"An older brother. Andrew. You'd like him."

He perks up. "Yeah? Why?"

"If there were an artist in our family, it'd be him. He runs a garage, but he also loves tattoos. Giving and receiving. And he's a dad to a daughter, like you."

Finn smiles crookedly. "I'd love to meet him." Before I can protest, which I'm about to do, he adds, "One day. Not now, obviously."

I'm already picturing it, though, what it would be like to introduce them. I may have spoken too soon. Andrew is all kinds of fucked up when it comes to the opposite sex, but he wouldn't approve of what I'm doing. In fact, I think if Andrew found out about Finn, he'd take pleasure in wringing his neck.

"What'd I say?" Finn asks. "I meant down the road, Sadie."

"It's nothing."

"It's something," he says. "I'm sorry. I just get

excited when I think about a future. For us."

I can't even hear the words without panic rising up my throat. In an attempt to stop the direction of the conversation, I wave my hands and say, "No. It wasn't that."

"What then? Something about your brother?"

I've backed myself into a corner. "It's just that Andrew, well—he really likes Nathan. I mean, he loves him. They're brothers. Andrew doesn't like many people."

Finn's eyebrows sit low. He flits his green eyes over my face. "So you were wrong just now. He *wouldn't* like me."

"You have some things in common. Art, fatherhood. Stuff like that. You know?" I swallow dryly. "Andrew's protective of me. Of Nathan too. I'm sure if the circumstances were different—"

He looks away. "We're getting ahead of ourselves."

"Yes." My relief comes out in a long sigh. "Let's take a step back."

"All right." He shifts on his feet and scans the faceless crowd. "Can I kiss you?"

I blink up at him, surprised. I shouldn't even be considering it, but I feel bad about our awkward conversation. And it's true—I can't imagine a single person I know coming here. "Okay."

He tilts his head. "Thank you. It's just that in the theater, things got a little intense."

"No." I shake my head. "It was just what I

needed."

"Well, I feel like I need to kiss you now. So that you know, even when it's like that, it means something to me."

He looks nervous. And adorable. The tip of his nose is red from the cold. His hair messy from our romping. I slip into him—my arms underneath his coat, my body against his.

He bends his head and brushes his lips over mine. He whispers into my mouth. "In so little time, you've lit up my world like the sun. And you've warmed me just the same."

His words melt like butter on my tongue. He kisses me thoughtfully, like the way I read my favorite books, fearful of missing even one word. This thing with Finn isn't just sex. Something else will bloom if I nourish it. He feeds my newly hungry soul, but he isn't afraid to show me his fear. It's obvious in the way he grips me.

We part to look at one another. Times Square suddenly sparkles. The neon signs are reflected in his eyes. I'm grateful for the cold that keeps us close. I touch my mouth, burnt by the small shrub on his face.

He catches my hand and thumbs my lower lip. "I'll shave."

"No. Don't." I smile and repeat what I said to him years ago about his long hair, "You look like an artist."

He studies me a moment and smiles. "Are you

hungry?"

"I guess."

"Your stomach grumbled."

"No, it didn't." I laugh. "Did it?"

"I felt it. You're pressed up against me, after all."
He kisses my palm. "Come."

He takes me to a chain restaurant with burgers
and beer. It's dim inside, night or day. Each table has
its own yellow lamp. At this odd time of afternoon,
the bar and restaurant areas are crowded, but not full.
The hostess hugs two menus and shows us to a table.

Finn stops her. "Can we get a—"

"Booth? No problem," she says. She's been at
this a while.

A minute later, we're nestled into one corner on
the same side of a squeaky, springy bench. Our
waitress wears a black polo and a nametag that says
Ashley! Albuquerque, New Mexico. Finn orders us some
greasy food and two hot chocolates with whipped
cream.

"If you're going for romance . . ." I start.
Families populate the tables around us. A crayon flies
by our booth. "You nailed it."

He winks. "Romance isn't really about
atmosphere, is it? Maybe for some people."

"Not us?" I ask.

He shakes his head. "For us, romance is these
stolen moments to ourselves. It's taking you in a
theater full of people because I can't survive another
second without being inside you."

He looks as though he expects a response, but he's robbed the breath right out of my lungs. Breath I need to live, let alone speak. He's right. Our time together is always charged by what we can't say or do.

"The pictures turned out exquisitely, by the way," he says. "I'm going to hang them in my living room like art."

I wiggle against him. "You can't."

He slips his hand between my denim-clad thighs and rubs. "My bedroom then?"

"I don't think Kendra would go for it."

He stops touching me.

"Sorry," I say and close my mouth to keep any other stupid comments inside.

"It's fine," he says calmly. "We should be able to talk about them."

"Should we?" My stomach gets queasy, which doesn't bode well for the heavy food he ordered. "I'm not sure."

"Yeah. We should. Especially if this might get serious. And it could. Is there anything you want to know?"

Sex is the first thing that comes to mind. Now that I've been irreversibly intimate with Finn, curiosity about Kendra and him needles me. "Are you this insatiable with her?"

"No."

"Were you ever?"

"Not really. We've never lost control in a public place, for example." His expression softens. "I've never risked everything just to be inside her."

I look at my hands in my lap. It's the truth. He's putting his whole life on the line for sex. I am too, of course, but I don't have as much as I once did. Nathan might've already gone there with another woman. If I thought Nathan weren't about to drop a bomb on me, I'm sure I'd do better at resisting Finn.

"What about you?" he asks.

"Our sex life?" I bite my bottom lip. Nathan could fuck with the best of them, and he only got better with time. He isn't as adventurous as Finn—up until the whole slut thing, that is—but my body is his well-worn map. He knows every curve of every road.

If I were that candid, though, Finn would probably get up and leave. "I have no complaints," I say, not wanting to lie. I look up at him from under my lashes. "I hope that doesn't hurt your feelings."

When he swallows, his throat ripples. "No. I want you to be honest."

"We've done it in public, but not with other people in the room."

"You liked that, though?" he asks hesitantly. "It seemed like you did."

"Yes. You have rough edges. Nathan doesn't take things to that level very often."

He strokes my hair away from my face. "It's just because you make me crazy."

I smile so Finn doesn't see the hurt on my face. Does he think I don't make Nathan crazy? Is that why Nathan needs a slut? Is Nathan going to someone else looking for what I can't give him? There are, after all, things I might be incapable of giving. Things he deserves. Things that sleep deep inside me, a black, empty pit in my stomach. Nobody can fill that void, probably not even Nathan at this point. If he isn't planning on leaving me, if he still cares at all, he still couldn't fix this feeling that I've failed him as a wife.

"There you go, looking sad again," Finn says. "You're thinking about him."

"I'm sorry. I can't help it. We're going through so much, and I can't even pinpoint what's wrong. I'm lost."

"If he isn't talking to you, he's talking to someone else. I hate to say that, but more than likely it's true. Look at us."

Yes, look at us, where we aren't supposed to be. Or do I have that all wrong? Am I finally where I belong? I don't know anymore. "Do you think Kendra's talking to someone else?"

"No. She doesn't want anyone else. Normally, we're pretty candid."

"But, you haven't mentioned—"

"Of course not. I might, if I weren't worried about her family trying to keep me from Marissa."

I take his hand. Of course, I've considered Marissa. She's nearly old enough to understand our affair. I haven't thought about her in terms of divorce and custody, though. "I'm sorry. I didn't realize . . ."

"It just means we have to be a little more careful.

And if we decide to—"

Our waitress whistles and sings, "Yoohoo, love birds. Hope you're hungry." Ashley wears an enormous grin as she delivers spinach-and-artichoke dip, fries, and a basket of chicken tenders. "First time in New York? It's romantic, isn't it?" She clucks her tongue. We're both looking up at her. "Just wait 'til it snows. Hope you get a chance to see it during your visit. Your hot chocolate'll be right up."

Finn turns back to me and laughs. "When people think we're together, I swear, it turns me into a teenage girl. I love it."

He kisses the tip of my nose when I wrinkle it. "It is fun," I say. "Like acting."

"Yeah." He feeds me a fry and then eats one himself. "As I was saying, an affair wouldn't look good in a custody battle. If it were anyone else, I'd stay away, but it's not. It's you, my coffee girl."

His coffee girl. I'd smile, but my mouth is full.

"If it were to come to that, though," he continues, "I mean, let's be frank. We're adults here. How do you feel about kids? Why don't you and Nathan have any?"

My angora sweater is already itchy, but the neckline starts to burn against my skin. I scratch my throat. His question is simple, but I don't even know where to begin. I swallow my food. "Kids?" I repeat.

"Yeah. How do you feel about being a stepmom? Hypothetically. Or not. I'm sorry. I don't want to scare you off, but I can't not ask."

The restaurant is suddenly bright. I pull on my neckline. Maybe Marissa is a blessing I hadn't considered. An answer to the lonely part of me not even Nathan can touch. "I don't know if I can talk about this."

"Why not?"

I scrunch my eyebrows. Kids? How do I feel about them? It's complicated. I don't even understand my feelings, and I'm sure any way I try to express them will come out wrong. It's been months since Nathan and I talked about having a baby, and since then, so much has changed. "I just can't."

He stops chewing and tips his head to one side. "Sadie. Babe. You're in pain."

"Aren't we all?"

He sighs. "I guess. I know I am. Kendra is."

"Nathan is," I say.

"You make me happy, though," he says. His smile is forced, but I really do appreciate the effort. "If he's cheating on you, I'll kill him. I will."

"Finn. That's not really fair."

"Maybe not. But if I were a fair man, I wouldn't be here right now."

I frown. Whatever Finn says about himself is also true of me. There's no getting around that. I've let Nathan down, and it isn't the first time. I used to make him happy, though. Now, I don't even have that to fall back on.

The truth is, cheating on Nathan isn't even the worst thing I've ever done to him.

Finn puts down a chip he's already dipped. His eyebrows are drawn. "What is it?" he asks.

I just say it. "I had an abortion when I was younger."

The skin at the base of Finn's neck pulses with his quickening heartbeat. "I see," he says. "And you regret it."

I look up at him. "I didn't say that."

"Oh. No—I'm not saying you should, I just thought—" Finn looks as uncomfortable he sounds. "I'm sorry. That was a stupid thing to assume."

"I get it, though. A normal person would regret it. I, on the other hand, was relieved."

He taps a finger on the laminate table. "I don't think there's any 'normal' in that kind of situation," he says slowly, as if his thoughts are forming at the pace of his words. "Whatever you felt, someone else has felt that too."

I shrug one shoulder. "I guess. It was the right decision at the time." I swallow. "Except that, well," my heart rate picks up, "now, Nathan and I can't get pregnant."

A look of fear flashes over his face before he schools it. "You're trying?"

"We were," I slice my way through the thicket of words in my way, "for seven months. It was awful, so we stopped. I went back on birth control. He thinks we still have a chance, but I think I fucked that chance up." Once they're out there, words I haven't even said to my husband, a realization hits me. All

315

this time, I've been waiting for Nathan to recognize the significance of my profound flaw. And then what? Leave?

"Jesus. I'm sorry."

"I had my chance to be a mother," I say, "and I passed it up. I made the best choice I could at that time."

"It doesn't work like that, and you know it," he says, almost incredulously. "You, who doesn't even believe in fate, think you have an allotted number of tries to conceive?"

"Maybe it's crazy, but I can't get pregnant. There's the proof." My hands are curled in my lap, all bloodless white knuckles and engorged red fingertips. I try not to want it. Most days, it works, but Finn has forced open a door I usually keep closed.

"Is there evidence linking abortions to future pregnancy problems?"

"Not really," I admit.

"So? There you go."

"We were so excited when we started trying. But then it didn't happen, and I felt responsible. The more we talked about it, the further away it felt. I don't want to put him through the disappointment anymore."

Finn isn't as close as he was a minute ago, but we're still huddled in a corner. When he breathes hard, I feel it on my face.

I scoot toward him. "I need to use the restroom."

"Sadie—"

"I'm fine." I nearly force him out of the booth, feeling light-headed. "Really. I'll just be a minute."

I feel Finn's eyes on me as I hurry away, and all I can wonder is what exactly he sees.

TWENTY-THREE

I can't breathe. I'm on a toilet in a restaurant in Times Square, and I can't breathe. I'm having an affair in a restaurant in Times Square and my throat won't open. Back at the table, there's an untouched hot chocolate and a man who isn't my husband.

Nathan always wanted a baby, but we didn't start trying until a year ago. Every month I bled, my heart broke more. For myself. For Nathan. I tried to be strong for him, but it's hard to hide from someone who knows me better than I know myself. When Nathan caught me on the bathroom floor clutching a tampon, he made an appointment to put me back on birth control. *We have all the time in the world*, he said. *We'll talk to a doctor. We'll try again later.*

I told him I could keep going. I knew he already loved this child that hadn't even been conceived. But he refused to put me through the disappointment month after month until we had more information.

I get up from the toilet. The mirror above the sink is splattered with water spots. It reflects a pallid picture. Behind me, the word *go* is carved into the stall door. I'm hot to the point that I could vomit if I set my mind to it. I wet a paper towel and dab it along my hairline, down my neck.

My beautiful, pink angora sweater suddenly seems stupid, like dressing up a Barbie only to leave her out for the dog to chew. I turn around and lean back against the sink. I was wrong about the door. There's more in fainter letters, as if the vandal got tired partway through. *Goodbye.*

That's easy for you to say, I think. Just go. Just walk away. Is leaving Finn the right thing to do? Or would Nathan and I be better off apart? I wash my hands and flick a paper towel into the trash. I'm halfway back to Finn when I'm nearly accosted.

"Sadie Hunt!" I'm pulled into an enormous hug and engulfed by a cloud of perfume. Jill pushes me back by my shoulders. I'm looking at a face so familiar, it makes my heart stop knowing Finn is half a restaurant away. "What the hell are you doing here?" she asks.

Jill has been a close friend of mine for at least a decade. Since Nathan and I started having problems, my friendship with her has been put on the backburner. She knows us better than most people, especially since Jill and I were together when Nathan and I met.

"I was about to ask you the same thing," I say, still stunned. I could list a thousand places I might run into Jill—Lord & Taylor, ABC Kitchen, hot yoga. A bar and grill in tourist central wouldn't be on there.

She leans in to whisper. "I have family in from Minnesota. Of course they want to come to fucking Times Square on a weekend. The little shits need to piss every hour. We just came in to use the bathroom." Her husband, Victor, stands off to the side with another man, their hands stuffed in their jacket pockets. She waves wildly at Victor. "Did you see? Nathan and Sadie are here."

Vic and I smile at each other. We've known each other longer than he's known Jill or I've known Nathan. We bonded in a college writing course when we were paired together and discovered we'd both fabricated our personal nonfiction essays.

A woman in running shoes heads toward us, trailed by two young kids. "We'll be quick," she calls as she passes us.

"That would be a miracle." Jill rolls her eyes. "Are you *eating* here? Should we go to the table? Maybe Nate can snap Vic out of his shitty mood. He hates entertaining my sister's husband."

It feels like there's an elephant on my chest. I don't want to lie to Jill. I can't tell the truth. "I'm alone," I say. Apparently, I'm still not much for creative writing. I can't think of anything to say except, "I also came in to use the bathroom."

She looks surprised. "What're you doing in

midtown?"

I wipe my brow. "Christmas shopping." My voice is unnaturally loud, but I can't seem to control it. "I know it's early. I hate the December crowds."

"I'm impressed," Jill says. "Nobody can deny you're a real New Yorker, running around Manhattan in November in only a sweater."

She purses her lips. I think. Is she on to me? Did she see something? I can't abandon the lie now, or she'll ask questions. "My coat's at a table. I-I decided to get a coffee. Need my strength."

"You're braver than me, leaving your handbag unattended in this tourist trap."

Jesus—is she normally this suspicious? I can't tell if I'm reading into her tone, her looks. It's taking all my strength not to glance in the direction of our table. To check if we can even see Finn from here. Jill might recognize my coat. My purse. Has she seen them before? Probably. I can't remember.

"Let's do something soon. Maybe over Thanksgiving?"

"Can't." My throat is dry as a desert. "Nathan and I are going to the shelter."

"Oh, boy. How'd that happen? Did you say the wrong name in bed?" She cackles. I laugh, because it's what I would normally do. "I'm kidding," she says. "He must be over the moon."

Victor comes toward us, rolling his neck. "Hey, Sadie."

"Nathan isn't here," Jill says.

He snorts. "Did I ask?"

"No, but I know you're looking for an excuse to ditch Gary."

"Not at all. I love Gary." Victor and I exchange knowing grins. "Where is Mr. Perfect, anyway? Haven't heard from him in a while."

"He's out being charitable." I rub my hairline. "Actually, if you could not mention running into me—I'm shopping for his Christmas present today."

"Don't expect that kind of dedication from me," Jill declares loudly, competing with the din of the crowd. "Christmas shopping in New York, when the Internet exists? You can send me a link to what you want, Victor. If I approve, maybe it'll end up under the tree."

"Of course, dear." He raises his eyebrows at me. "Have I thanked you lately?"

We laugh. Jill shoves his arm. I introduced Victor and Jill. They're complete opposites, and Jill is always lamenting how much better my relationship is than hers, but she fits Victor like a lid on a cup. Even though she has a tendency to pop off now and then.

There's a special bond between the four of us, since it was at Victor and Jill's engagement weekend in the Hamptons that I met Nathan. Vic and I fancy ourselves matchmakers, even though it annoys Jill and Nathan when we brag about it.

Jill's sister returns, kids in tow. "All set," she exclaims. "We should be good until we get back to the hotel. Right, boys?"

Jill gives me a look before air-kissing both my cheeks. "It's been too long. We have a lot of catching up to do. Talk soon?"

I nod, say goodbye to Victor, and watch them go. Even long after they're out the door, I stand there. Jill knows me well. She doesn't judge. But telling her about Finn would mean admitting my problems with Nathan. Even if she is my closest friend, I don't want her seeing the cracks in my marriage. I'm not ready to give up the best-couple title she uses to introduce us at parties.

I take the long way back to the table. I'm going to be on edge now, knowing they're in the area.

Finn stands to let me in the booth. "I was beginning to think you took off."

"Sorry. I ran into some friends."

"Friends?" He repeats, freezing as his eyes dart around the restaurant. "They're here?"

"They just left." I exhale. "But they didn't see anything."

"Should we go?" His angular face is tense and lined. I love that he's concerned for me. I think most men in this situation would say not to worry, they're gone, drink your hot chocolate, when can we fuck again?

I pull Finn down by his jacket. "Let's stay. As much as I hate that it has to be this way, I kind of don't hate it here."

He settles in next to me and cups my cheek. "You sure you're all right?"

I nod. I actually am. My heart rate has calmed. Finn's big body blocks me from view, like we're in our own little world.

"Tell me about your friends," he says.

What could be more harmful than what I've already divulged to him? I lean into his palm. "Jill and her husband, Victor, who I know from college. We normally get together a couple times a month."

Finn smiles. "That's nice."

I leave out the part about Vic and Jill being the reason Nathan and I met.

"And how do you know Jill?" he asks.

I have to think for a moment. With Victor, the memory is clear, but it's as if Jill was just kind of there one day. "I'm not sure. We just got to be friends over time since we have similar taste—and distastes. She's bossier, and I'm more introverted." She and I bonded over a love of designer clothing, good-looking men, and strong cocktails.

"Oh," I say, remembering. Of course. We met *because* of fashion. "I met her at the dry cleaners of all places." I smile. "The one on Twenty-Second you and I went to, actually."

"No shit?" Finn twirls my hair around his finger. He's glowing. "Tell me the story."

"Well, I had this beautiful Burberry coat that I'd spilled coffee all over. Jill was waiting in line behind me when I picked it up. The dry cleaner had mostly gotten it out, but there was still a faint stain. Jill was horrified. Before she and I had even exchanged a word, she was demanding the cleaner try again. She said something like, 'You're killing Burberry. What gives you the right to kill a fashion icon?'"

Finn laughs, though I'm not sure he grasps the gravity of such a situation. "Then what?" he asks.

"We got to talking. I liked her. She invited me for coffee if I promised not to spill it on her, and then we exchanged numbers. We'd been friends for a few months when I took her to a dive near campus where we ran into Victor, and they hit it off."

"I'll bet they're pretty thankful you were clumsy with your coffee," Finn says.

I grin. "They like to pretend I ruined their lives. But they love each other."

I take a sip of my hot chocolate, which is lukewarm now. Finn thumbs the corner of my mouth. "Whipped cream."

We sit quietly for a few moments. The stain never completely came out. I donated the coat when Nathan started at the Family-kind Association. It was an expensive cup of coffee. From Quench, of course.

I sit up straighter when the connection between meeting Jill and Quench Coffee occurs to me.

Finn goes rigid next to me. "What's wrong?"

"It's weird . . ." I stare straight ahead of us and try to nail down the memory. I wasn't the one who spilled the coffee.

Finn follows my gaze, trying to figure out what I'm looking at. "Are your friends back?"

"No. It's about the coat."

"Oh." He relaxes a little.

"Remember when you and I met—"

"Of course."

"I was on my way out, but you asked me to sit down with you. Then we were interrupted by that girl in my class. Becky. She hadn't finished her half of the presentation we were giving that day."

"It's burned in my memory. What grade did you get, anyway?"

"I don't remember. She and I crossed the street," I continue, "and as we were passing the dry cleaners, Becky's heel got stuck in a grate. She grabbed my elbow, and I dumped coffee all over myself."

"So it was Becky's fault." He raises his eyebrows. "Sounds like she owes you a coat."

"It was my first big purchase as an adult, that coat. I ate noodles for a month to save for it. I was devastated. Since we were by the cleaners, I dropped it off, and we went on to class."

"You're adorable when you're animated," he says.

I demonstrate by tracing my finger across the table like I'm drawing a treasure map. "Listen. If you hadn't kept me at Quench, Becky wouldn't have found me there."

He laughs with disbelief. "So you're saying *I* owe you a coat?" He leans in and nuzzles my cheek. "Let's go right now. I want to get you one."

"Hang on." I push him off. He reluctantly lets me. "I'm not done."

I'm piecing everything together in my mind. Details rush back to me, fitting together like puzzle pieces. "I picked up the coat at the dry cleaners a few days later, and that's when I met Jill. Follow me?"

He's watching me closer now, his interest piqued. "I follow."

"I didn't mention this earlier, but Jill and Victor hosted their engagement celebration weekend in the Hamptons."

"They needed a whole weekend for that?" Finn's wry smile tells me he finds this whole thing cute, but in about two seconds, he won't. After all, he's the one who believes in fate.

I search his eyes. "Victor invited some guys from next door for beach football since they were short a few players. Nate was one of them."

Finn's smile droops and then vanishes. "What are you saying?" he asks.

I exhale a breath I didn't realize I was holding. "Nathan and I met because of you."

TWENTY-FOUR

At first glance, it seems farfetched, but the truth is actually cut and dry—one fateful moment with Finn in a coffee shop years ago led me to Nathan. If Becky hadn't ruined my coat, I wouldn't have met Jill at the dry cleaners and introduced her to Victor. But does the story stop there? Was marrying Nathan a stepping-stone on the path back to Finn? If there is such a thing as fate, at what point is it finished?

"I'm the reason you married another man." Finn isn't pondering fate the same way I am. He just looks irritated. "*Me*? Is that a joke?"

I shake my head. "You're the reason."

He drops the palm of his hand heavily on the table. The chicken tenders jump in their basket. "That's all sorts of fucked up."

I can't read his mood. I know he, like Nathan, wants to believe in things like soul mates and destiny.

Where does that leave each one of us, though? It was a silly chain of events to follow, but a pit forms in my stomach. If I'm the master of my own fate, then I'm responsible for the outcome. I got myself here with Finn. I let Nathan slip away.

Finn rubs his forehead as he stares toward the restaurant bar. "You and I—we were supposed to end up together. It got twisted." He glances back at me. "I let you walk out of that coffee shop and into another man's arms."

Finn's conviction is written plainly on his face. He thinks he's to blame for this. I want to tell him how ridiculous that is, but he's taken on a lot today, and I want to comfort him. He's had reason enough to walk away. It says something that he hasn't. "Maybe it's all part of a greater plan, Finn. And if that's true, no decision is the wrong decision."

When he nods, some of his golden strands fall into his eyes. He pushes them back. "Maybe. But I hate that it had to happen this way. I wish you hadn't left in such a hurry that day, and I'd thought fast enough to get your number. Maybe all this could've been avoided."

He's getting closer to me as we talk. I, on the other hand, wedged myself into the corner at some point.

"You're skeptical," he says, reading my expression.

"I love Nathan," I say. "I don't wish my marriage away."

"I know." He leans in still. "You can love him and understand he might not be right for you."

"How do you know that, though?"

"I don't. But if I had your love, I wouldn't waste it like he does. He's playing a game with you. He'll regret pushing you away, though, when he realizes I'm here, waiting to catch you."

Would Nate really regret it? When will he wake up and see what he's doing? If he hasn't yet, he won't. So why would I keep waiting for him to? If Finn weren't here, I wouldn't have a choice. I do, though. At least, I think that's what Finn is saying. "It sounds like you've made up your mind about us," I say. "Which means you've made up your mind about Kendra."

Without looking away, he laces our fingers together. "I don't want to scare you off. I feel like I've known you all this time, though. Even if it's in a vague sense. To me, none of this feels accidental or rushed."

Our hands fit well together. This could be a normal, natural Sunday afternoon for us. "But we barely know each other." My go-to argument is becoming less solid the more time we spend together. Hours seem to pass slowly with Finn. Time expands between us as we fill it getting to know each other.

"Yeah." I hear the smile in his voice before I see it. "Still so much to discover."

It *is* a strange thing to know so little about Finn. I haven't learned his quirks. I haven't experienced the evolution of his habits from cute to annoying to missing them when they stop. I don't know what angers him nor why. Could I take this journey all over again with Finn?

"What's your favorite color?" I ask.

He smirks. "Why's that the first question people ask when getting to know someone?"

"Because 'what's your credit score' might put some people off."

"At least that would tell you something," he says, chuckling. "What would my favorite color honestly say about me?"

"Well, if I were to go shopping for you, it would help me pick something out."

"But my favorite color to wear isn't the same as the color I'd want on my walls. And neither of those colors are what I'd choose for a car."

I don't know why I giggle. It's the same for me. I like to wear black, but that doesn't mean I want to sleep in a black bedroom. "So, you're not going to answer on principle?"

"Nope."

"All right. What book are you reading?"

"*Zen and the Art of Motorcycle Maintenance.*"

"That's inspirational, right?"

"Something like that." He touches my cheek. "Soul searching when I should've been soul *mate* searching."

My cheeks flush like a schoolgirl's.

"What're you reading?" he asks.

"Nothing at the moment. I don't read as much as I should. I keep meaning to."

"Then why'd you ask?"

"Well, wouldn't that give me some insight to you?" I ask.

"A little. A better one would be *when* I read."

"Why?"

"I read before bed," he says. "That's when my mind is most active, and for me, that isn't necessarily a good thing. So, I read to calm myself, about three or four times a week. That's just fiction. I research my craft in the mornings. It gets my juices flowing."

My eyebrows are halfway up my forehead. I forget sometimes that Finn is dealing with a move, a new job, and the women in his life. "Okay, then. I feel like I just learned some stuff."

"You said you think you *should* read, but you don't. That gives me some insight into you that I'll probably sit and think about later."

This statement alone shows me even more about who Finn is. He listens to little things I say and thinks about them when I'm not around.

"When do you eat?" he asks next.

I tilt my head with a smile. "That's pretty standard across the board, isn't it? Morning, noon, and night . . ."

"Touché. What's something you consider a special treat?"

"I don't know. Hot chocolate?" I tease, glancing at the half-drunken mug. He waits, unconvinced. I can see he's determined to get somewhere, so I go with it. "I love smoothies."

"When was the last time you had one?"

"Um." I pick at nothing on my jeans. "This summer. August twentieth, actually."

"I see."

I look up. He *sees*. Obviously, he's intrigued by the fact that I know the date. "It was a comfort smoothie," I say.

"How come?"

I think back. "I got a prescription for birth control."

"And you were sad, so you got it to cheer yourself up."

"Nathan did," I say. "He took me there after, six blocks out of his way. We were both late getting back to work."

To Finn's credit, he doesn't pull away when I reminisce.

"Maybe I should've been treating him, though," I say, "now that I think about it."

Finn squeezes my hand. "It's okay to not want children, Sadie. It doesn't make you a criminal."

"Nathan definitely wants a baby." I lower my eyes to the table. I did too, up until I went back on birth control. Now, if we choose that path again, all I see is a future of disappointment, shame, and sadness. And I let myself remember, just a little, that my whole marriage hasn't been perfect. There's been pain this last year. But at least I had Nathan to lean on then.

The more I think about the likelihood of infertility, the more fear beats down my maternal urges. "What if we can't figure it out?" I ask, more to myself. "What if we just want different things?"

Finn slides his thumb over the nook of my thumb and index finger. "I'm fine with not having more children."

The comment catches me off guard. I look at him for what feels like the first time in a while, as if I've been off in another world. His eyes are somber, but it's hard to feel any darkness in their honey-flecked green. "Really?"

"Really. I have Marissa. She's all I need."

It's the first time children have actually been taken off the table for me. I've considered not having a baby a lot over the last year. Especially these last few months. Part of me can't envision a life without one. The other part sees the sacrifice and heartbreak that children can be, even when they don't exist. Finn is offering me an out. "You don't want kids?" I ask. "Definitely?"

He cocks his head. "I said I'd be fine with not having them. I'd also be open to it, if that's what . . . the other person wanted."

"You and Kendra don't talk about it?"

"We do. She wants another one. I don't—not with her."

He says it so definitively that my heart aches a little for her. And just as suddenly, I'm embarrassed. Not in a bad way, necessarily—it just makes me more aware of what we're doing. Finn would consider having a baby with me.

"I know that sounds harsh," he continues. "She's just so hard to deal with sometimes. I learned years ago that if I'm not explicit, she'll twist my words into something else. To her, maybe means yes. For instance, she said she wanted to get Marissa a dog. I said I'd think about it. I come home from work that same day, and guess what I find? 'But you said yes,' was her defense."

"You have a dog?" I ask.

It's his turn to look uncomfortable. He takes his hand out of mine and wipes it on his jeans. "If she got pregnant, I'd just feel more hopeless than I do now. I think it's supposed to be the other way around."

As much as what he's saying puts me off, because as a woman, I can relate better to Kendra, I also admire him. It isn't always easy to tell your partner what you *don't* want. "It'd be easier for you to just give in to her."

"You have no idea. We have to have the discussion every few months, and it's never pretty."

"So you don't have sex?" My tongue gets looser the more time I spend with Finn. I think that means I'm comfortable, but I'm not sure. I'm not this way with many people. "You don't have to answer that."

"Why not? Don't you think you have a right to know?"

"I don't know that I have any rights . . ."

336

"You and I are sleeping together, so, yes, you do."

"And Kendra and Nathan don't have a right to know?"

He frowns. "I can't exactly just tell Kendra about you. I'd have to divorce her first."

He says *divorce* casually, as if it'd take no more than a phone call. I wonder how long he's been thinking about leaving her. It might not have as much to do with me as I think, and that gives me some comfort. "Is that what you want?" I ask.

"I . . ." When he moves, the gummy bench grunts like some kind of sea mammal. "We've talked about a lot today. I don't want to overwhelm you."

"Overwhelm me."

We're both surprised by my challenge. We've been circling this topic all afternoon, though. I don't think it'll help anything to go home tonight with more questions than answers.

"All right," he accepts. "If you told me you were ready, I'd have the first of many difficult conversations with Kendra. My ideal situation would be to end things with her, share custody of Marissa, and be with you."

He moves back a little. I'm grateful for the space. I asked to be overwhelmed, and I think I might be. I can't tell if I'm feeling butterflies or barbed wire in my stomach. He's serious about me. Is that a surprise, though? This has never been a fling. We aren't take-it-or-leave-it fucking. I might, on some level, use Finn to escape my situation with Nathan, but when Finn's inside me, I'm not thinking of anything else.

"You want me to love you," I state.

"I do. I don't expect it now, and maybe I shouldn't expect it at all. I want it, though."

This must be what it feels like to free-fall without a net. We're moving fast, but it might be up or down, left or right, right or wrong. I don't know. I can see myself with Finn. I'm not sure I can see myself without Nathan.

Finn blows out a breath. "Heavy, huh?"

"A little."

"I think you get it, though. What we could be. I see it in your eyes."

What do I really know about Finn? I take stock. First, the green couch would have to go. The record player could stay. I don't have any vinyl, but I like music. I can make him dinner with his cast iron skillet. Marissa would have her own bedroom that I could help decorate. Ginger has claimed nooks and crannies in our apartment, but Finn has the same ones. They're just on the other side of the hall. What becomes of Ginger, though? What becomes of Nathan?

"I just need some time to adjust to the idea," I say. I don't want to hurt his feelings, but I feel I need to be explicit. "More time than this."

"Believe me, Sadie, I get it." He looks earnest, almost happy. Not like I expected. "We're not seriously talking about this. You know that, right?"

338

He covers my hand again. "I just have a hard time keeping my feelings inside. And I can't stand to see you living like a zombie, doing your best not to set him off."

I raise my eyebrows. My marriage has been a drain lately, but my heart still beats strongly. For Nathan, and now, for Finn too. "Do I seem like a zombie to you?"

"Not right *now*," he teases, smiling warmly. "Right now, you're alive. You're radiant." He chuckles. "And now, you're blushing. You don't know what that does to me, seeing you get shy." He kisses my cheek, my temple. "See? I know you so much better, just from one simple, not-so-simple question."

I can barely remember what the question was, especially with Finn's lips on me. It wouldn't be such a bad life, fucking in movie theaters, warming each other up with hot chocolate, kisses, and dreams. What girl wouldn't want to be told she's radiant, to have a handsome photographer make her feel undeniably sexy, to have had a romantic moment in her past so powerful, it remapped her life? It wouldn't be such a bad life.

But, I can't help feeling it would never move above second place.

Finn pays the bill, and I realize he never answered my question about sex. From what he's told me about Kendra, I don't think of them as intimate. They must be, though, after so many years together.

Even if it's occasional. And what if it's not? What if the next time he goes to Connecticut, he does to her what he did to me?

The thought makes me uneasy. I'm not sure if it's jealousy, or something else, but my timing is off. It doesn't feel right to bring it up now that we're leaving. I put my coat on, pick up my purse, and follow him out.

Ashley is chipper as ever. "Enjoy your stay!" she calls after us. I wonder just how new she is to the city.

When we're on the sidewalk, Finn says without looking at me, "I want to get you that Burberry coat."

I balk. "No, Finn. Absolutely not."

"I insist. Let's just pretend it really is my fault your coat was ruined. I like to think it played a part in our love story."

"Finn, really. I can afford my own coat."

"I know. But I'm offering. How can you say no?"

Admittedly, it's hard to turn down Burberry. Since I got a raise and Nate turned his down, I haven't wanted to spend too much on myself. We're in a better place financially than we've ever been, but it still feels a little like rubbing it in his face. "I can't just show up at home with Burberry," I point out.

"Would he notice?"

His question physically pierces, like a little knife. Nathan knows the contents of our closet. He would notice if he cared enough to look. All my pulse points throb at once for what seems to be slipping through my hands more every day.

"I'm sorry," Finn says. "That was insensitive. Please don't frown."

"It's okay."

"Why don't you keep it at my place?" he suggests. "At least for a little bit." Without waiting for my answer, he takes my hand. We cross the street. When we're on the other side, he ducks into a cramped doorway of an apartment building. He pulls my front flush against his, drapes me back over his forearm, and ghosts his mouth over mine. His whiskers tickle my upper lip. "By the way, it's blue," he says. "My favorite color."

I try unsuccessfully to suppress a smile. "So what does the color blue say about you?"

He studies all the parts of my face—mouth, nose, ears, chin—as if he's memorizing it for an exam. Then his eyes return to mine. "It says I never had a favorite color until I met this girl in a coffee shop with eyes so blue, they're almost purple, like the absolute final moments before sunrise. This girl stayed on my mind. When I saw things like a cluster of irises or a peacock at the zoo, I would think of her and say to myself, that is my favorite color."

TWENTY-FIVE

Amelia pays the cab fare and meets me on the busy curb outside of Chelsea Market. Without even a glance, she swipes away the one wrinkle in her loud DVF wrap dress. "As I was saying," she continues our conversation from the car, "Misty Burroughs is not a woman we want to disappoint."

"Who *do* we want to disappoint?" I ask.

She narrows her eyes at me. "Watch it. As much as I like you, I'm still your boss."

"Oh," my tone and movements are flowery as I pull on the marketplace's heavy door, "let me get that for you, Miss Van Ecken."

She grins smugly. "That's more like it, minion."

Once indoors, I pluck my gloves off by the fingers and stick them in my pocket. Amelia unfurls her scarf. I automatically fix the static flyaways that stick to her collar.

"The coat was a good choice," Amelia says, eyeing me. "Misty can probably pick out Burberry blindfolded."

I unbutton the collar. It's funny how quickly a person can go from freezing cold to burning up in this city. When Amelia called me this morning to say we had an impromptu lunch meeting with the on-fire online entrepreneur, I'd waited until Nathan had left for work to knock on Finn's door.

"You wore me out Sunday," he teased, still half asleep. Two days later, my body was also still stiff. He passed me my brand new, navy Burberry coat, then kissed me. "Sorry for my morning breath," he said, and I sighed, "I wish I cared."

"That's why I picked you for this meeting," Amelia is saying. "I don't know when or where you got that coat, I've never seen it before, but you're good at pulling things out of your ass right when we need them."

"I assure you, this did not come from my ass," I say. We cross the indoor, warehouse-style food hall packed with gourmet eateries, curated gift shops, and bookstores. "Where are we meeting her?"

"Friedman's."

The rustic restaurant is small, with glass windows and a door that opens to the market. "There's not a lot of space," I say.

"I know, but she insisted. She swears by their Reuben."

I'm quite sure Amelia hasn't looked at bread in years, but I'm a regular consumer. "I'm surprised I haven't been here," I say. "I'm always on the lookout for good sandwich spots."

"I would've taken her to Cipriani, but word on the street is that she's leaving her current firm because they're too stuffy. So, this is me, going with the flow." She looks around. We avoid the community tables and pick a four-top near the front. "Let's set up. We have about ten minutes before she arrives."

We clear off empty cartons and balled up napkins. Thanks to the lunch crowd, it's noisy and warm. Amelia pulls out a file. I'm about to sit when I do a double take at the counter. Nathan is in line waiting to order. He throws his head back and laughs. Bumping into my own husband is strange enough, so it takes me a moment to notice he isn't alone.

I shift my eyes to the woman next to him and recognize her immediately, even without her Quench Coffee apron and nametag. There's no mistaking Gisele's petite frame and long, black curls. Her youthful glow.

Heat races from my chest to my neck and ears. The din of the crowd becomes excruciatingly loud, the overhead lights searing.

"Sadie?" Amelia asks. "What's wrong?"

My hand is clenched around the back of the chair. Nathan is hard to miss. He's tall, lean, with a full head of beautiful, brown hair. But this can't be him. He hasn't laughed like that in weeks.

I tried to make him lunch this morning—I used to do it a few times a week before I was promoted—

but his distracted "no thanks" felt like a slap in the face. Now, I understand. Why would he want his wife's boring lunch when he could have the city's best Reuben with adorable, perky Gisele?

I'd convinced myself I was paranoid. But am I really one of those wives who chose denial over reality? It hits me that I never *truly* believed Nathan could cheat on me. It's too out of character, even with his recent distance. But here's my proof, right in front of my eyes. And I can't ignore it anymore.

"Excuse me a second," I tell Amelia as I walk away from the table.

"I thought we'd wait for Misty to order—" The ringing in my ears drowns her out. My eyes are lasered on Nathan's back. He sticks his hands in his pockets like a smug bastard.

"What are you doing here?" I ask as I approach.

Nathan pauses a second, then looks back. His face brightens, but he shuts it down immediately. "Sadie."

Gisele turns around too. "Hey, Sadie. I didn't know you were coming."

"I asked what you're doing here," I say to Nathan.

He thins his lips, gesturing toward the register. "Getting lunch. What are you doing here?"

"Meeting a client." I wait. For what, I don't know. A bumbling excuse? A confession? An outburst? This is new to me, but I know one thing— Nathan is a shit liar. It won't be long before he breaks down. "You just randomly walked all the way here from work?" I accuse.

"It's only a few avenues. I come here all the time."

"That's news to me," I say.

"I've told you about this place lots of times, Sadie," he says. "I've tried to lure you to meet me here with sandwiches, remember?"

"Bullshit." The word *sandwiches* jumps out at me, but whether he's actually mentioned this place before isn't important. I turn on Gisele. "What about you?"

She shifts her doe-brown eyes up to Nathan. "I'm sorry. Did I do something wrong?"

"No—"

"Wrong?" I ask. I've known her almost a year. That's almost a year she's looked me in the eye each morning and smiled as if we were friends. "Answer my question. Why are you here?"

"Sadie," Nathan scolds, shocked.

"Well, I'm not really supposed to tell," Gisele says, hedging. As if she recognizes I'm about to explode, she talks faster. "They're trying to keep it a secret until we know more, but we're looking to open a second location here in Chelsea Market. You wouldn't believe the foot traffic this place gets."

I purse my lips. Convenient. She's made that up on the spot and has the audacity to stare up at Nate as if he's going to come to her rescue. As if he has all the answers. My blood boils at the way she innocently draws her eyebrows. I should win a medal for not

347

wringing her neck. "How opportune. So you just happen to be here, walking around?"

"Kind of." By her hesitation, she's choosing her words carefully. "I mean, the owner and I just met with the property manager about a space a few doors down. I decided to stay for lunch and ran into Nathan. He let me cut in line."

"That's true," gruffs an old man behind them. "She cut."

I return my glare to Nathan, who's looking at me like I'm a science project he can't figure out, and shake my head. "Liar."

The area immediately around us gets quiet. Slowly, he narrows his eyes. "Excuse me?"

We stare each other down. Neither of us speaks. My heart beats everywhere—in my ears, my throat, my stomach. "You heard me," I say, "you fucking liar. I've been tiptoeing around, trying to play nice for you, giving you the benefit of the doubt. But all this time—*months*—" My throat locks up, strangling my words. I can barely get them out. "I was right."

"Right about what?" he asks.

"You're having an affair—"

"Oh, *no*!" Gisele gasps as her chin wobbles. "No, no, no. Sadie, you have it all wrong. I swear."

Nathan's mouth is as wide open as his brown eyes. He doesn't even blink.

"You must think I'm an idiot," I say, not bothering to hide the anger in my voice. "That I had no clue what was going on. Well, I've been onto you for weeks, Nate. At first, I thought it was Joan—"

Nathan takes my arm roughly. I go immediately silent, surprised by his grip. "Excuse us, Gisele," he says. "And I have to apologize for my wife. I am so sorry about this." He pulls me out of the line, over to a corner that's marginally more private, and loosens his hand but continues to hold me. "What is the matter with you?" he asks. "*Joan?*"

"I thought she was the one," I say, shaking my head. "Maybe she is. Is she? Is there more than one woman?"

He barks out a short, surprised laugh. "You need to calm down. You're making a scene for no reason."

"No reason?" I try to wiggle loose, but he won't let me. Gisele rushes by us in a flurry of black ringlets, her head down. "This explains so much about the past few months," I say loudly enough for her to hear. "Why even put me through this? Why not just cut me loose?"

Nathan's eyes go round, and he turns sheet-white—as, likely, do I, because blood drains from my face. This is it. I can see his realization that he's been caught. This is really happening. "Wait," he says. "You seriously think I'm having an affair? Like seriously?"

"How many?" I ask quietly.

"How many . . .?" He closes his mouth and swallows hard. "There's only you, Sadie. How could you possibly think I would . . . that I could even touch another . . .?"

I close my eyes. Even if he deserves it, I don't like the pain in his face. "I know about the lipstick on your tie."

He releases me, and I look at him again. "What lipstick?" he asks, pinching his eyebrows together.

"After bowling practice a couple weeks ago." I can't help picturing the deep red smear, and it spurs me forward. "I was going through the laundry, and I saw it."

"Saw what? Lipstick? On my tie?"

I'm growing tired of this back-and-forth, of feeling like I have to watch where I step and plan my maneuvers. Finn was right. Nathan *is* playing games, and it has to end here. If he doesn't stop, he'll push me right into Finn's arms. "This isn't a game, Nate," I say, steadying my voice. "I don't deserve this."

"*Game?* You think all this has been a game?"

"Whose lipstick was it?"

He slow-blinks. "I don't know—it was probably ketchup. I eat a lot of fries when we play. Nine times out of ten, I spill on myself."

"Ketchup," I repeat without inflection. Red and sticky, it's a handy excuse, but I'm not buying it. "What about the other night when you came back from the hospital smelling like a bar?"

He scoffs. His unfamiliar disdain makes me feel even further from him. "You're accusing me of lying about visiting my sick dad?"

When he says it out loud, it sounds so unlike something Nathan would do, I have to pause. I put the brakes on my rage and think. Nathan would never lie where his dad's health is concerned, and I should know that. But it can't all boil down to something as stupid as ketchup. "Well, I'm right," I say, lowering my voice, "aren't I?"

Nathan gets very still and quiet. There's depth in his eyes I haven't seen since he broke the news to me his dad was dying. With just a glance, he has the power to inspire a wave of doubt in me. My legs, and my resolution, waver. "Aren't I?" I repeat.

"You mean to tell me," he says softly, "for the last few weeks, you thought I was having an affair— and you said and did nothing? You waited, hoping to catch me in a lie?"

I open my mouth and pause. "Well, no," I say. Unlike my palms, which have begun to feel sticky, my throat dries up. "I didn't have actual proof or anything. And I didn't 'do nothing.' I tried talking to you so many times—"

He shakes his head hard. "Not about this you didn't. I wouldn't have ignored an accusation this serious."

"How was I supposed to know you'd listen?" I ask. "Every time I've tried, you shut down."

"It shouldn't even be a question," he says cuttingly. "You should know I would never do that. Ever."

I take a breath and step back. The truth is, if I'd really believed Nathan had betrayed me, I would've said something sooner. I wouldn't have been able to stop myself from finding out the truth, because until recently, we've always had honesty. "I hoped I was wrong—"

"You *are* wrong." I feel people's eyes on us, but I can't look away from him. "Jesus Christ, Sadie," he says, running a hand through his hair and messing it up. "I had no idea our marriage was this weak. So this is where we end up when things get tough?"

"Things haven't just gotten tough—you *disappeared* on me," I shoot back, but my resolve falters. Nathan's no actor. I can tell by his reaction that I'm wrong. Dead wrong. By a thousand miles, ketchup makes more sense to me than Joan. We've been together in Gisele's presence more times than I can count, and never once did I suspect anything. Because it wasn't there. "It's been two-and-a-half months of this. Is it so unreasonable I would jump to this conclusion?"

He frowns. "To me, it is. After seven years, I'd hope you know my character better. What have I not given you during this marriage?" he asks. "I live where you want. I do what you say. It's exhausting, but I do it because I love you more than myself. I'm not saying things haven't been difficult these past few months, but that love doesn't just go away. My character doesn't change."

I look up at him and try to see myself through his eyes. He's always bent over backward for me, and maybe I don't always thank him or return the favor as I should, but I thought it made him happy to treat me that way. I thought *I* made him happy. But if I was self-centered over the years, it was because Nathan's world revolved around me like I was the sun. I didn't ask for that. "I've never made you do anything against your will. I've always told you, if you're unhappy—"

"I'm free to go," he finishes wryly. "Right? I just need to say the word?"

His words resonate with a physical pang in my chest. He thinks I don't care enough to fight for us. And based on my short history with Finn, maybe Nathan's right.

He pinches the bridge of his nose. "I have to get back to the office."

"What about lunch?"

He gives me a look that conveys his lack of appetite and turns away. "I'll see you at home."

Amelia comes to my side. "Sadie. What the hell was that?"

I stick my hands under my armpits to stop their trembling, but instead, it spreads to my shoulders, my torso, my legs. I've made a serious and wrong accusation about something *I'm* guilty of. I hope Nathan understands I was driven to this conclusion by the depth of hurt his distance has caused.

Amelia squeezes my bicep. "That was brutal, but right now, you need to get it together or excuse yourself."

My vision clears. Misty Burroughs is standing at our table with her arms crossed, and her lips thinned into a line.

I swallow down the last few minutes and walk directly to Misty, who's an embarrassingly short distance from me. "Miss Burroughs. I am so, so . . . sorry—and *mortified*."

"What was that?" she asks.

I bite my bottom lip with a belated and unexpected wave of tears. *That* was my marriage bottoming out. I expect a complete reaming out from Amelia later, even though she stands quietly by my side now.

"It was personal business she should've taken somewhere else, right?" Amelia answers for me.

I inhale through my nose and nod, afraid I'll cry if I try to speak. I'm a second from wiping my eye with my sleeve when Misty jumps to catch my wrist. "Honey, no man is worth mascara stains on Burberry."

I pause. The three of us laugh stiffly and awkwardly, but it breaks the tension a little.

"So your husband's cheating," Misty says with a shrug. "Fuck him."

Amelia smiles, relief clear on her face. "He blindsided her just now."

My instinct is to defend Nathan, but I don't. It won't help the situation. "This is very unprofessional," I say and apologize again. "I assure you, this is a first for me—and it shouldn't reflect on the firm."

Misty pulls out a chair and sits. "Look. I'm not married, but my sister's husband did a number on her.

354

When I call and tell her about this, because you bet your ass I will, she'll cheer for the way you confronted him. So, why don't you go compose yourself, and we'll get on with this meeting."

"Of course," I say. "Thank you, Miss Burr—"

"Nope." She stops me with a hand in the air. "It's just Misty."

"Thanks, Misty." I excuse myself and find public bathrooms in the middle of the market. Of course, there's a line. I skip it and go inside to check my mascara, which is really an excuse to stop and take some deep breaths. I can't cry a single tear in this meeting. Misty seems patient, but she's also a businesswoman. She won't put up with this.

In Nathan's face just now, I saw real pain from my accusations. I should've trusted my gut. He wouldn't betray me, but he isn't innocent in all this. He tested my limits, and this is where it's gotten us. The last few weeks, I've lost sight of us—myself, our relationship, and him, the man he really is. I could lock him in a room with Cindy Crawford and give him free reign. He wouldn't touch her. But me—not me. In my blind rage, I put my own sins on Nathan's head. Would Nathan ever understand how desperate I must've been to react that way?

I inhale a few more times and return to the table. Amelia and Misty have ordered food. They're all business, except when Misty turns to me and asks, "Is this the best fucking pastrami you've ever had?" followed by, "And if you think I'm holding an event within a mile of Trump Tower, you've lost your damn minds."

We laugh, talk business, and bullshit back and forth. Misty agrees to give *avec* a try. Once we've shaken hands and Misty shows us her red-bottomed shoes on her way out the door, Amelia and I melt into our seats.

"Fuck," she says.

I nod slowly. "Yeah."

"We pulled it off, though."

"No thanks to me."

"True." We exchange a smile. "I'm kidding," she says. "You did great all things considered. Misty is a known theater buff, and that shit was better than Broadway."

I laugh a little despite myself.

"So what the hell happened?" she asks.

"Remember my friend? The one with the cheating husband?"

"Right. The *friend.*"

"Turns out, her husband wasn't cheating. Turns out, my friend was completely wrong and made an ass of herself in front of a bunch of people."

"Sadie . . ." Amelia studies me. "When I confronted Reggie, same thing happened. He denied it. Made me feel like a complete loon. Turns out, not only was I right, but I didn't even know half of what was going on. Men who cheat are master manipulators. Are you *sure* he isn't lying? Who was that girl?"

"Oh. My. God." I sink in my chair and put my face in my hands. "Gisele. We've known her a long time. My outburst was totally unwarranted. I'll have to send flowers."

"Or the whole flower shop," Amelia suggests.

I grimace. "It was bad."

"Do you need to be excused for the day?"

I give her a pleading look. "Please don't make me. I'll just sit and stew until Nathan gets home."

"Your call," she says, and we stand.

As we head back to the office, I pray for a boatload of work to keep myself occupied. Because each time my mind drifts, I replay my conversation with Nathan. I don't believe in my gut that he's been unfaithful, but in a way, I wish he were. Because the alternative leaves me with a sinking feeling. If he isn't neglecting our relationship because he's found someone else, then it means to him, the only problem is me.

TWENTY-SIX

On the way home, I stop for takeout. Nathan and I may have a long night ahead of us, and I don't know that I'll want to make food once we get started. It's bright as day underground on the subway and dark when I come up the stairs. New York can be stark—a peaceful cluster of trees sandwiched between concrete slabs. A passing stranger's *hello* on a bad day that can feel like a raft in deep waters. Sometimes the sinking sun streaks the sky red, purple, and orange, reflecting off mirrored skyscrapers and blanketing the city. It forces you to stop—walking, driving, hailing, talking—and look, but only for a second, because there's somewhere to be.

I spot Finn outside of a market on our corner. He waves with a plastic bag in his hand. "Hi, beautiful."

I slow down. Finn's the most shameful part of

this—the affair is bad, but the hypocrisy worse—and still, I stop for him. He doesn't *feel* anything other than warm and golden. "Hello again."

"And again and again."

He leans in to kiss my cheek, but I pull away and mumble, "Sorry."

He straightens up. "Can I walk back with you?"

In my pocket, my fingernails bite into my palm. I shouldn't, but I can't tell him no. I want to spend a few minutes numbing myself with him.

"Or should I stay a few feet behind?" He pretends to check out my ass. "I really wouldn't mind."

I crack a smile. "Come on."

It's almost a block to our building, less than five minutes. He doesn't waste any time. "When can I see you again?"

I look at the ground as we walk over brittle leaves and pockmarked concrete. Nighttime in the city is filled with light. I don't even know where it comes from half the time. "You're seeing me now," I say.

"It's not good enough. Hours away from you are beginning to feel too long."

I rub my brow. Between Nathan and work, I've only thought of Finn abstractly today, as one half of the affair. Yet, being around him now, this afternoon already weighs a little lighter on my shoulders. Finn has a calming effect on me. He's adoration, passion, and promise. There are no wounds between us too easy to open. No words flung that would've been better left unsaid. "I had a rough day."

"Did you? Tell me about it."

"No time," I say, looking ahead.

"Then come over." He bumps me with his shoulder. "I have wine. Once you're loose, I'll massage the day right out of you."

"That sounds nice," I admit, but I don't even have to think about it. Nathan will be home by now. As much as I'd like to avoid the aftermath of today's argument, I hold on to the hope that I'll come out of it with a clearer understanding of where his head is. "I can't, though."

"Are you all right?" he asks. "Did something happen with—him?"

"No." For whatever reason, I'm suddenly protective. I've said enough about Nathan to Finn the last couple weeks, and I've had enough spectators for one day. This, whatever's happening, is between Nathan and me. "It's just work stuff."

"Let me guess. Boss problems?"

"A little," I say, because there's some truth to it. She rode me a little harder than usual once we got back from lunch. "She can be tough."

"Amelia, right?"

I glance over at him. Her name out of his mouth surprises me, like it's a word I've never heard before. "How'd you know that?"

He shrugs. "Researching the company for our photo shoot. Work's a big part of your life. I'm interested."

I bite my lip against the urge to warn him he's coming on too strong again. I'm not in the mood to be pried open tonight. But just the thought of an argument tires me. "Oh."

At the entrance to our building, Finn lets us in with his key. When we're alone in the elevator, he touches my chin and lifts my head. "Hey. Sorry for your bad day."

I take a lungful of elevator air and Finn. He smells like a lumberjack tonight, nature-fresh and a bit musky. Soothing. I rise up to kiss him because we're almost at our floor, and I want to, and I think he's trying to be respectful. His lips are more pliant than usual as he lets me take the lead.

We're separated by the ding of the elevator. When I go to leave, he pulls me back by my wrist. He hesitates.

"What?" I ask.

"Remember that I'm just across the hall. Thinking about you. Wishing you were sleeping by my side. If you need me, knock."

I hear him and the sincerity in his words. Being cared for, even for a few moments, is a relief from what I've been going through. I reach up and trace his mouth with my fingertips. "They're the first thing I noticed about you back then," I say. "Your lips make me weak in the knees, always."

"Prove it."

We kiss once more, two unfaithful mouths

362

pressed together, and then walk to our respective apartments without another word.

The apartment is dark when I get home, and I wonder if Nathan is waiting in the bedroom. I'm unpacking the takeout bag onto the kitchen table when I get a text from him.

Stopped downstairs for a beer.

My heart drops. He should be here. There are too many words hanging between us, both said and unsaid. Why doesn't he want to fix this? Does he think it's too late?

He's at a bar that's next to the corner market where I stopped to talk to Finn. We would've walked by it together. Normally, when Nathan goes there alone, he sits at the window to people watch or read a book. There's a chance he saw us walk by. The Nathan I know isn't the jealous type, but he has his limits. He makes his presence known when I encounter overly friendly men—at restaurants, on the train, trolling farmer's markets. An ex-coworker made an inappropriate comment about my skirt once, so Nathan came over on my lunch break and set him straight. He wanted me all to himself then. But does he still?

A tear slides down my cheek. I sniff, wiping it away. I'm more exhausted than sad, tired from an emotional day. I wish I'd never made eye contact with Finn in the hallway while simultaneously craving more of our last kiss. I remember how deep inside me he was this weekend. I've never thought seriously about other men before Finn. Nathan could satisfy me blindfolded with his hands behind his back. He knows my body. He's had me on my stomach, on my back. He's had me half-asleep, outdoors, in my childhood bedroom. In silence, and in chaos. He has not, though, had me recently.

I take Ginger out, but I don't walk her. It's especially cold tonight, and I don't want to run into Nathan on the street like a couple of strangers. Back upstairs, I change out of my work clothes, shuddering as I pull on my flannel pajamas. Even though it's still several days to the twenty-first, I break our tradition and switch on the heater. I've had as much cold as I can take.

I take my soup to the couch and turn on a documentary about Scientology. My mind wanders, though. When he comes home, what will I say? What will he? After the past few months, he doesn't have as much right to be angry as he thinks he does. How do I explain that to him without feeling like a hypocrite? This afternoon's adrenaline from seeing him with another woman has worn off, and the threat of confrontation makes my stomach churn. Growing up, the smallest things turned into the rowdiest fights. My dad tripping over a vacuum cord would end in my mom throwing dishes. Andrew fought that way with Shana, Bell's unpredictable mom, before she left him. Why shouldn't my story be the same? Nathan doesn't raise his voice at me or take his anger out on inanimate objects. Would he, if we really fought? I don't even have to wonder. He's miles from my father.

I hear his key in the door and then his voice. "There's my girl," he coos to Ginger. "Did mama take you out already?"

I change the channel to a sitcom and ignore him. At the heart of it, I'm sad Nathan would rather be alone than here, fixing our marriage. But on the surface, I'm angry. About this afternoon. About tonight. I feel as though I've been chasing him down for weeks. I want him to come to me, but I'm tired of the charade. Since nothing else seems to work on him, I decide to try forcing his hand by acting like a five-year-old.

"Well, unless you were wading in the tub, I guess you've been outside." Ginger's tags clink as he scratches her neck. "Soggy paws," he says to me. "Dead giveaway."

As if on cue, a laugh track sounds on the TV. *Everybody Loves Raymond.* When the grass outside is wet, Ginger tracks mud through the foyer. Nathan's mentioned it before, and he usually gets the mop out. It only seems to happen after I've walked her. It's not like Ginger understands wet grass means a dirty floor, so I guess it's my fault. "Sorry."

He stands there another second petting Ginger. "For what?"

I don't answer, and I don't look at him. I feel

him watching me, though. "New coat?" he asks.

I finally glance over at him. He's in his suit, and his face is flushed, either from the beer or the cold weather.

He nods back into the entryway. "I haven't seen that one before today."

I swallow. I didn't mean to bring the Burberry coat home. I forgot to return it to Finn's. I'm not sure how I can explain a thousand-dollar item of clothing without it showing up on our bank statement. I'm not sure I have to, either.

"I'll take it back," I say, turning to the TV again.

"Why? It's nice."

I change the channel again. I've never been a fan of Raymond.

"You ate?" Nathan asks, noticing my soup container on the coffee table.

"Yours is in the kitchen."

Nathan gets his soup and the sandwich I bought to make up for his missed lunch. He sits in the loveseat by the couch. "Was that *Going Clear* you had on?"

I switch back to the documentary. At least it'll give me something to focus on. I try to listen to the words, but I can't. I don't have to look at Nathan to sense his every move, to know what he's doing. He eats some soup. It's been sitting out, and I should put it on the stove and heat it for him, but fuck it. He takes three more spoonfuls and then has some of his sandwich.

"I had a cigarette on the way home," he says.

The abruptness of his confession is enough to get me to look at him. Nathan used to smoke. Not a lot, but now and then. One of his few flaws. I didn't like it, but I knew it wouldn't last. He was healthy in every other way.

"That's why I smell," he continues. "It's also why my suit smelled after visiting my dad in the hospital. And why I wasn't out front of Brooklyn Bowl when I said I'd be. I went around the corner to take a few drags. It's the stress. I'm sorry."

On the TV, David Miscavige pontificates in grainy footage. I actually open my mouth and attempt to speak. I'd like to tell Nathan it isn't the smell that bothers me. It's his health. It's what it says about his state of mind that he'd smoke while his dad is dying of stage-five lung cancer.

He's that anxious.

Nathan sets his soup on the coffee table and leans his elbows on his knees. "All right. The silent treatment. I get it, and I deserve it. You're pissed."

I shrug, because I sense this plan is working and will lead to what I want—an actual, honest conversation.

"No?" he asks. "Then how come you broke our tradition by turning on the heat?"

"I get cold. At night. By myself."

He has the decency to frown. He scoots over on the loveseat. Our knees brush. "Not much for words tonight, are you?"

I look up at him. He's stifling a smile. When I realize he's teasing me, my façade cracks. It feels like progress. Maybe it's relief, or stress, or anger, but whatever I'm feeling makes my eyes water.

He puts a hand on the curve of my neck and squeezes. "You crying, Pea?"

The old endearment squeezes a tear from me. It wasn't long ago I feared he'd never call me it again. "No."

"Good. You know I turn to mush when you cry."

Something in my chest gives, and I shed a few silent tears. My blubbering has always made him soft, and I'm glad that hasn't changed. "I hate that nickname," I say.

"I know. I won't call you that anymore."

I wipe my face. "Never stop calling me that."

"This has been tough for you, I know. I didn't mean for things to get this far, but the longer I hold my feelings in, the harder they are to get out. And figure out." He rubs my shoulder. "But this afternoon—something broke through. The fact that you've been so confused, you thought I could *cheat . . ."* He shakes his head. "I'm sorry I got so mad, but try to understand where I was coming from—"

I shoot up. His hand catches under the collar of my nightshirt before he jerks it back. It's possible he picked the worst thing to say to me tonight, when I've been attempting to figure out what's going on in his head for months. "Try to understand where *I'm* coming from," I say.

"Okay."

I shut my mouth, startled. I hadn't expected that response, but why shouldn't I? Nathan and I don't typically talk over each other, even in an argument. Standing above him, we're toe to toe, bare feet versus dress shoes. He looks up at me, unbuttoned, his collar open, his tie loose and sagging. "I'm lonely," I tell him. "You've made me feel small. Unimportant. In my own home."

He glances at the ground and back up. "I know. I mean, I don't *really* know, Sadie. I've tried not to think too hard about it."

"Why? Why are you pretending not to care?"

He shakes his head. "Because when I care, it hurts. It hurts me to know I've hurt you. I . . ."

He stops talking. I've lost him. His eyes are fixed on my chest, so I look down. When I stood, my button opened, exposing my breast. Nathan stares as if he hasn't seen more of my own body than I have.

"Nate?"

With one hand, he undoes another button. The hair on my arms prickles as his fingertip grazes the space between my breasts. He stops and looks at me. The heat in his eyes is sudden but raw. He's asking permission. Nothing is resolved. Through it all—my anger, my confusion, my heartbreak—one thing has remained the same. My body craves his touch. Limiting his affection has only made my desire stronger.

I want this. He knows it.

He lifts the hem of my shirt to expose my stomach, but doesn't take it off. My favorite plaid pajama bottoms, which were once technically Nathan's, are several sizes too big and droop to my hipbones. My cotton gray underwear covers more than should be legal. My eyes feel puffy, and I haven't shaved my legs since yesterday, but Nathan sticks one finger in the elastic and slides the flannel over my hips like it's fine lace. My breath snags as his knuckle trails down my upper thigh. He pulls on my pants until they drop to my feet.

He takes my waist, pulls me to him, and presses his face to my stomach. He breathes so hotly on the fabric, I feel it on my skin. "I'm hungry, Sadie."

"I've never denied you."

Pushing my top up under my armpits, he commands, "Take it."

I'm not sure why I can't just remove it, but I don't ask. I hold the shirt up. My body trembles like a teenager's.

"What's this shaking?" He looks up at me, sounding as tense as I feel. "Are you nervous?"

"No." Seven years I've had this. Seven years we've been making love. Yet, I have butterflies, as if I've been waiting to do this my whole life.

He wiggles a finger under the crotch of my panties. "Too bad." He knows I'm lying. "I like the idea that you might be nervous."

He bends his finger to tug the fabric away,

knuckling my folds. I grip the flannel in my hands tightly, melting under his controlled touch.

He stands from his seat and takes a step back. I'm bared to him, my pants and underwear around my ankles, my top pulled up. The TV glare flashes behind him.

I wait, afraid to make the wrong move. He might leave me panting like last time, even though his cock is already straining the fabric of his suit pants. It's that mouthwatering outline that makes me bold. "Why'd you call me a slut?" I ask.

He looks from my tits to my face. If he's surprised, he doesn't show it. "It was the only way I could be with you that night."

It's the answer I expected, but hearing he wanted anyone but me still hurts.

"I thought I could turn you into someone else," he continues, "but I can't. You'll never be that in my bed." He doesn't take his eyes off mine. "It's one of the reasons I haven't been able to be with you since."

I breathe from my stomach. I want to find the meaning in his words, but the tender ache between my legs hurts so much, it's not even pleasant. "Nathan," I plead.

"Sadie." The rough playfulness of his voice makes my skin pebble. His eyes glimmer. He begins unbuttoning his shirt. "Are you sure you want this? After everything we've put each other through?"

Even if I could form a coherent thought against sex, I know what my answer would ultimately be.

"Yes."

"Go get on the bed. Hands and knees."

I shouldn't hesitate. It's not like he hasn't had me in every position possible. I trust him, but it's been weeks, and if I'm this turned on, he must be going crazy.

He pulls his belt through his pant loops and drops it. "Unless you've changed your mind."

"No." I go to pull the top over my head.

He stops me. "I'll do that. Just get into position."

Nathan gets demanding in bed when he's hot. This feels different, though. There's a calm edge to his commands that isn't new, but it's sharper than I'm used to.

I turn and go to the bedroom, feeling his eyes on me. I climb onto the bed, facing the headboard, and do what he says. I display my most intimate places for him. At the same time, my flannel hangs from my torso, covering my upper half like a blanket.

Seconds later, his footsteps cross the living room, and he enters the room. The mattress trembles when he gets on it behind me. I barely register the sound of his zipper before he's teasing me. He slaps the head of his cock against my crack, then drags it up the back of one thigh. His soft skin on mine is maddening, and I drop my head toward the mattress, breathing hard. A trail of pre-cum dries on my skin.

"I'm going to fuck it all out," he says. "I could take my time with you, but I don't want to."

"I'm ready," I say.

"Unless you beg me to," he says, ignoring me. "I can eat your pussy now instead of later. I can tease you to the brink first if you want."

"No," I say, the word hard and imploring. I realize I'm squirming, and I stop moving except for the heave of my chest. "I don't need it. I just need to feel you inside me."

He lines himself up with my throbbing slit, wraps my hair in his hand, and pulls my head back. Kissing me sideways, sloppy but determined, he begins pushing into me. "Like this?" he asks into my mouth. I hear the torment in his voice. I feel it in his touch.

I simultaneously nod and moan. My pussy salivates for him. It's my core, and he's the only one who's truly been there.

He slows down. Takes his time filling me. I'm given each inch with agonizing deliberation, like being fed dessert in tiny bites. I try to push back, but he stops me—*scolds* me—with a firm hand on my ass. We're still kissing. He's never, in seven years, stopped kissing me. Sometimes we fuck quick and hard, other times long and slow. But he doesn't skip the kissing, not ever.

When he's all the way in, he stays there. "I've been dying without this, babe. Fucking you is an addiction I can't kick."

"Really?" I goad him. I just want to be torn apart. "Because you're going easy on me."

"No, I'm not, and you know it."

"This is how you'd fuck a slut?"

373

He growls in my ear, rears back, slams into me. *That's more like it.* "Go on," he says. "Ask for what you want."

This much edge is new for us, but it's just what I want. "Use me. You need this," I say. "You aren't going to break me."

He straightens up and stretches my pussy lips with his fingers until they burn. He thrusts in and out, faster than before, but still with restraint. He holds me in place like that, as if I'm a doll or some kind of toy.

"Quite a view," he says. "Sorry you can't see it."

He's smug. He doesn't realize, though, that the closet door is open. With my head bent and angled, I can see flashes of us in the mirror. Nathan's shirt is off, but his pants are around his knees. His muscled ass cheeks clench and release with each thrust like a well-oiled machine. If he bent over me, his big body would consume mine in one bite. We're in our bed where we belong. It's right. Wonderfully familiar. I'll end my affair tomorrow and put my secrets on the table. All of them. I promise I will. I'll hurt him, but then I'll heal him. When he tries to leave, I'll throw myself in his path. Anything so I don't lose this.

He closes over me again, trailing his lips along my neck, and then bites my shoulder blade. I cry out, and he kisses it. No longer holding back, he shoves my face into the mattress so my lower half is propped up to take more of him. My shirt falls forward around me, but he doesn't fix it. I said I wouldn't break, and I won't. My cheek chafes against the comforter. He leans his weight on my shoulders, angles deep, owns me top to bottom.

I grasp for the bedspread and hang on. He slips one finger and then two over my clit. My control spirals free with his little circles. With a touch honed and perfected from years of practice, he tips me over the edge and into a rippling orgasm. My hips give, and I flatten out onto my stomach. The force of his fucking moves me up the mattress. I slither over the side, catching myself on the floor with my palms. He keeps my bottom half on the bed. My shirttail sticks under my stomach, but I'm still in the dark, facing the belly of the mattress. The way he takes from me is like the first night we dropped the pretense of lovemaking and fucked like animals on a futon in his studio.

"Want me to come in you?" he asks.

"Yes," I beg.

"Wrong answer."

Blood is rushing to my head. "What?"

"You're supposed to tell me I can have whatever I want."

"Whatever you want, Nathan," I repeat. "You know you can have anything."

He holds my hips down, and my attention is reduced to one simple thing—the unrelenting pounding inside me and then the heat of his release.

TWENTY-SEVEN

I'm still half off the bed, waiting for Nathan's cue. We finally fucked again, and two weeks apart made us wild. But the following silence scares me. My locked arms wobble from my weight. Nathan shudders over me, his breathing loud and raspy. After some more languid thrusts of his hips, he stills completely. Seconds tick by. When I think my elbows are going to snap, I move.

"Shh." He runs his hand down my back. "Don't."

I stay where I am, waiting. Darkness creeps on me like an ocean tide. My upside-down face pulses as blood rushes to my head. It's turning painful, but I think he knows. After what feels like forever, he swivels his hips. My stomach drops, my walls clenching around him.

"You're hard again?" I ask.

"Almost."

He pulls out and slides me back up the bed by my hips. My arms tingle. I bend my elbows, but I don't move other than that. This is Nathan's event. He gathers up my shirt and pushes it over my head. Picking up one of my limp hands, he begins to massage it, working his strong fingers into the meat of my palm, around my wrist, and up my arm then down the other. To my shoulders, he applies more pressure. My eyes shut. I don't think I've ever felt more tranquil.

He straddles my outer thighs, elbows the spot where he bit me, and gets a guttural groan. "Keep making noise," he says as his cock twitches against my leg. "I'm almost there."

He moves down my back, and I don't hold anything in. My breathing picks up when he massages my ass cheeks, opens them, and closes in on my anus. I can come again, but Nathan knows it might take more than it did the first time, so he lightly presses against it. As soon as I anticipate it, though, he abandons my anus and slides two fingers into my pussy.

"I came hard," he says. "You're sopping with it."

My arousal springs, a jungle cat waiting in bushes. He knows just how to touch me, just what to say. He pumps into me two, three more times and then slides his hand up my crack. He eases one slick finger in my asshole. I clutch the sheets but relax the cluster of muscles he's currently working. All at once, it's good.

"This will never not get me rock hard," he mutters.

The comforter flutters with my desperate, gaping breaths. "Not even when we're old and gray?"

He grunts and removes his finger. "Turn over. We can make love now."

His cold, robotic tone can't scare me off. He stands and looks at the bed as if he can't decide how to proceed. I get up too and take over, pushing him into a sitting position on the mattress.

We wrap our legs around each other. This time, we're face to face. When I lower myself onto him, he's nice and hard inside me. "Press your tits against me," he nearly groans. "God, you're so fucking hot inside."

He circles me with his arms, urging me into his warm, open chest. He teases my asshole again with the tip of his finger. When he slides it in, my face gets burning hot. He moves it, and I move on him, swiveling my hips to stroke all the right spots. We kiss, and with his tongue searching my mouth, his finger working inside me, and his cock filling me up, I'm possessed by him.

"Watch my face when I come," I rush out, feeding my words into his hungry mouth. "I want you to tell me how I look."

"I already know every detail of how you look." He sounds much calmer than me, although his hairline is damp. Sweat beads on his upper lip.

"What do I look like?" I ask.

"Not yourself . . ."

Instead of distracting me, talking this way is ballooning my arousal. "Is that a polite way of saying ugly?"

"Not ugly, but not pretty. Sexy as fuck, though, like . . ." His breath comes in hot bursts against my nose. He's getting close. "An animal," he grates, "whose prey is just out of reach."

I wrap my arms around his neck and pull myself onto him more furiously. He meets my pace, plunging his finger deeper and faster. His honesty makes me hot. Like my face at the peak of my pleasure, it's not pretty, but it's real. That's more erotic than anything.

He whispers, "You're killing me. Hurry. I'm going to explode. I won't finish before you."

"You can."

"I won't."

He keeps his promise. The balloon pops. When I come, my ribs rattle, my hairs stand on end. He continues to plumb my depths because fingering my asshole turns him on as much as it does me. Inaudible words pass between us. He takes the skin of my neck between his teeth. For a moment, it's as if he's going to rip my head off when he comes.

He doesn't.

When I once again feel my heartbeat independently of his, he detangles from me and steals off into the bathroom. I flop back against the mattress and shut my eyes. Listening to him piss after intense lovemaking is oddly comforting. It's small, but it's ours, and it means something to me.

Our bed is a cloud, and I begin to drift, but then Nathan is back, standing over the bed, looking down at me.

"Everything okay?" I rasp. I remember all of a sudden that his things are on the couch, that we haven't closed this distance yet. He looks torn, as if he can't decide what to do.

But then he says, "Yeah. Let me just get my pillow."

I yawn, watching him pick up his suit, put it in the closet, then walk out of and back into the room. We never finished our conversation, but I slide over in bed to let him in next to me. I turn on my side, facing him. His eyes are closed already, so I study his face, the strong, straight nose, the angular, stubbled chin. I drop my eyes. I haven't had much of a chance to appreciate his body lately. He's been working out harder, and it shows. His arms are sinewy and strong, his pecs firm. When he turns over, the muscles move under his skin. He's always been godly to me, but it bothers him when we eat more and do less. He says he likes to know I still find him sexy. It blows my mind he thinks I might not.

Because I'm content enough to have him back, it takes me a moment to register that he turned *away* from me. After this long sleeping apart, and after the way he just owned me, all I want is to burrow into his arms. He doesn't appear to feel the same way, though, and with that realization, a chill passes through the room.

In the morning, I wake late and to an empty bed. My joints crack when I sit up, my body sore and aching from last night. I warm as the memory oozes over me. The way Nathan lost his thoughts and his control just from seeing my breast. The way he bit and fucked me, then kissed and made love to me.

I pad into the kitchen. I should already be out of the shower, but I can't bring myself to care about being behind schedule. I find my coffee mug waiting and a note from Nathan.

Ginger already fed and walked, sleepyhead.

I smile to myself at the endearment. My chest aches, and for the first time in a while, it's in a good way. Maybe I read too much into his distance last night while we fell asleep. He came back to bed, and that's a start. What's more, the conversation has begun.

In the fridge, there's an unopened quart of milk. Nathan must've gone to the grocery store last night. I forgot to on Sunday . . . because I was screwing Finn instead. Jarred by the thought, I grit my teeth. He's been noticeably absent from my mind the last twenty-four hours. *Screw* isn't really fair to Finn—he cares. He wants me. He doesn't screw. He loves. And as much as his intensity scares me, it also delights me. Will it still if Nathan and I continue down this path to reconciliation?

I put milk in my coffee and take it into the bathroom. I undress and reluctantly shower off last night. I have to forget about Finn and focus on Nathan. As I shave my legs, I decide I want to do something nice for him, something to build on the progress we made last night. I can feel his guard dropping. He just needs a push over the edge. An idea doesn't take long to hit me, and when it does, I know without a doubt, it's the right one. Cook for him. Not just any meal, though. His favorite—barbeque ribs. My imagination blossoms, and I picture him coming home to a candlelight dinner, a sparkling apartment, and a safe, warm environment where we can finally put everything on the table and wipe the slate clean. The more I imagine it, the harder my heart beats.

High on adrenaline, I call in sick to work feeling no guilt as Amelia reams me out. I barely hear her anyway since I'm picturing the shock on Nathan's face when he walks through the door and sees the spread. I hear his laugh when I admit I played hooky from work to get everything perfect. For dramatic effect, I cough into the receiver before I say goodbye to Amelia, hang up the phone, and get started.

TWENTY-EIGHT

Though I've made barbeque ribs countless times throughout our marriage, I stand in the kitchen, reading the recipe over and over. On the counter are bags of groceries from my trip to D'Agostino. They hold ingredients for dinner, a six-pack of craft beer recommended by a young employee, and the best calla lilies in the neighborhood. They're Nathan's favorite flower.

I brush the ribs with seasoning. While I work, I try to mentally prepare for the emotional side of tonight. Nate and I still have a lot of work to do, but I'm confident barbeque ribs will get him to talk. I'm not sure I'm ready to hear what he has to say, but I doubt I ever will be. If we don't fix this now, and it continues to get worse, it'll eventually send one of us over the edge into madness.

Once I've spaced out the ribs on a baking sheet and get them in the oven to roast for the next few hours, I turn and look around the kitchen. Nathan should be home between six and seven, and that gives me plenty of time to scrub the apartment spotless, especially since it's fairly clean to begin with. I unpack the groceries, get the flowers in water, and pick up any mess I've made.

I move into the living room, bundle up Nathan's sheets and blanket from the couch he'll no longer be sleeping on, and add laundry to today's to-do list. As I'm passing the desk, though, I stop. Even though his laptop sits there most days, I notice it now because it's open and dark instead of shut. The urge to snoop is new to me, thanks to the last few months. Nathan doesn't keep secrets. He's terrible at it. But maybe instead of secrets, there are answers there, behind the blackness.

I don't sit down, but I drop the linens on the back of the chair, lean over, and tap the space bar once. After a second, his spotless desktop appears. I open the browser and check over my shoulder, my heart in my throat. I shouldn't be nervous, though. I use Nathan's laptop all the time, and he uses mine. If he were to walk in right now, he wouldn't think anything of it.

Ginger whines, and I jump, forgetting she's even here. I glance over at her, and I swear, she shakes her head, warning me not to proceed.

I start with his search history. It's mostly work

stuff. Nathan helps maintain the Family-kind volunteer site on his own time. His dedication to this organization doesn't surprise me after all these years, but it always awes me. It gives me a sense of pride. And now, it makes me feel dirty for not trusting him. I'm about to click out of the window and shut it down when a folder on his bookmark bar catches my eye.

Brooklyn.

Brooklyn—are you the key to my husband's thoughts? I wonder. *Do you know why he doubts me?* I don't want to know what's in it. Except that I do. I click on it, and a list of bookmarks drops down. Craigslist. Zillow. StreetEasy. My palms sweat. How recently was he looking for apartments in Park Slope, Bay Ridge, Greenpoint, Dumbo? I don't click on any of the links, but I recognize the neighborhoods.

A knot forms in my stomach. I "x" out of the browser quickly, like the computer'll self-destruct if I don't. This is why people shouldn't snoop. You only come away with more questions. Nathan is looking for apartments in Brooklyn, and he knows I don't want to live there. Is he pulling a Finn and leaving, with or without me?

The room seems suddenly bright. In my flurry to prepare for tonight, I haven't had anything but coffee today. I make myself a snack and check on the ribs. All I can do is make tonight the best it can be. Brooklyn might come up at dinner anyway.

In the bathroom, I throw my hair into a bun on

top of my head and scrub the mirror, the toilet, and the tub. I weed through drawers of makeup, lotions, and sample-size toiletries collected over the years. Nathan has been subtly hinting about the clutter for as long as I can remember. I end up with a trashcan full of expired or half-empty junk. I do the same to my nightstand. I am relentless, tossing receipts I might need and moving every last paperclip to the desk organizer in the other room. He'll love this apartment when I'm finished, and the woman I am now.

Once I've gathered our laundry, I take the plastic basket, made heavier by a bag of quarters at the bottom, to the front door. Ginger comes bounding after me, spinning in circles and sniffing out her leash.

"We'll go later," I tell her and grab my keys. "All of us, together."

As I approach the elevator, the doors split open with a ding. My heart skips. For a frenzied moment, I'm sure Nathan will walk out. It's not close to five, but what if he comes home early? I'm not ready. The apartment isn't perfect yet, and I haven't planned out what I want to say.

It isn't Nathan who steps out and stops abruptly, though. My heart rate slows a little, as if I've been presented with a consolation prize. Finn may be second place, but a consolation prize is a prize nonetheless, and I'm glad to see him. In the back of my mind, though, I know the truth. If I want to make things work with Nathan, and I do, I can't lead Finn on.

He wipes his hands on his sweatshirt as he looks at me. He's dirty, his clothing and skin stuck with something gray and tacky. "Just got back from my first pottery class," he says, holding up his spackled palms. "Not as sexy as I thought."

I shift the basket onto my hip. He looks as good in clay as he does in anything else. "Well, I'm not exactly spic-and-span."

He takes in my hair on top of my head and the laundry in my arms. Nathan's boxers are on top of the pile. "I don't know. I think you look pretty hot as a homemaker."

I blush. "I'm a mess."

"We're both a mess," he points out and smiles. "Maybe next time we can be messy together."

The elevator starts to close. I lurch forward. Finn catches it before I do, pushing the door back in place, his bicep flexing. My insides wither remembering those strong, skilled hands around my waist, on my cheeks, between my legs.

It's dangerous. I shouldn't stand here any longer, letting my imagination run wild. "Can we, um, talk?" I ask.

"Of course," he says. "Now?"

"Not now." I wipe my sweaty upper lip on my sleeve. "Maybe tomorrow—"

"I can't wait that long."

We look at each other. The elevator screams.

We've kept the doors open too long. I go inside, and Finn releases the door. "Meet me out front in two hours," I say. "We'll go for a walk."

His forehead wrinkles with his frown. His violet NYU sweatshirt makes his green eyes pop. It's almost hard to look at him. "Why can't we do it here?" he asks.

The doors shut. I'm jittery from consuming almost nothing but coffee all day. His puzzled expression stays in my mind. I deflate against the back wall of the elevator. Chores, dinner, and Brooklyn are momentarily unimportant. What I really want right now is to lose myself in Finn's adoration and warmth, in his big hands, for a few hours. He can help me forget how much hope I'm placing in a basket of dirty clothes.

I can't, though. I don't want to surround myself in him as badly as I want to fight through this with Nathan. I'll tell him we're through. That he has to stay away. He can't really argue—he never had me to begin with. He can't completely own my heart when most of it belongs to someone else. Does he know that it does, though?

I get the laundry going and head back up. When Nathan gets home, the apartment will sparkle, our bed will smell *April Fresh*, and the dining room table will be a spread fit for *bon appétit*. When I picture it, I panic. I can't remember if we have candles, and lighting's vital to set the mood. I tear apart our linen closet until I locate two stubby, jarred soy candles.

Not ideal, but since they're unscented, they won't compete with home-cooked ribs. While I'm there, I unearth and clean placemats and the fine silverware Nathan's mom gave us when she moved to California. Once the table is set, I run down to move the wash into a dryer, then take the stairs back up. My heart pumps. My face is red with exertion. It feels good to move, to use my legs, to feel blood in my veins.

I drag the dining table out of our plain kitchen and into the living room. The loveseat goes against a wall to make room. I vacuum the carpet with special attention to the indents from the chair.

When it's time to get the laundry, I wash my hands of grime and check my watch. I have enough time to bring it upstairs, run a comb through my hair, and meet Finn.

An elderly woman comes up from the basement as I go down. I recognize her from around the building and throw her a cheerful *hello*, even though we've never spoken. The laundry room machines churn, swish, and whir at full capacity, even on a weekday afternoon. My rubber soles screech against the vinyl floor. I toss the basket between the two dryers I'm using. Nathan's clothes are done, but the linens are spinning wildly. I'm bent over, emptying the first dryer's contents into the basket when the door behind me opens.

The air in the room changes. I straighten up. Heavy footsteps cross the floor.

Two hands land on either side of me, trapping me between the dryers. "You wanted to talk?" Finn asks in my ear.

My heart begins to hammer as violently as the dryer shakes. He smells of soap, and my mind goes blank. I can't remember anything I'd planned to say. "Not here."

"Here," he says with finality.

I open my mouth and hesitate. I know the risk of being this close to him. If I don't come out and say what needs to be said, I'll lose this battle. "We're finished," I tell him.

"Finished?" he asks, both softly and gruffly. "Why?"

I shake my head. His warmth spreads through me, and a trickle of sweat drips down my stomach. I could have him. Quick. One last time. Would it make a difference after what we've done? His astute eyes, his generous lips, his big hands and cock. He's so much man, and I love to take him all. I steel myself against the dryer. "I have to . . . I need to . . . make things work with Nathan. He's my husband."

"You don't *need* to," he says simply.

"I *want* to."

He rakes back some strands of hair that've escaped from my bun. Pointless, because he then tugs the rubber band out. He grabs a handful of hair at the back of my head. "You don't want me to fuck you anymore, Sadie?"

I should lie, but I can't. My panties are already

sticking between my lips, my body's demands private but impatient. "I do, but we can't keep doing this." It's obvious he needs convincing, so I continue, "If we end it now, they won't have to know. Nobody gets hurt."

"So that's it then?" He guides my head back, so my eyes are forced to the ceiling. My scalp tingles. The skin at my throat tightens when I swallow. "We're done?"

"Yes." My body gives me away from raw voice to quivering thighs. Finn's effect is immediate. Undeniable. There's no use trying to hide it.

"If they'll never know, then one more time won't matter, will it?" he asks.

"I'll know," I say. "*We'll* know."

He runs his other hand down the front of my stomach and grasps me hard between the legs. He lifts me, moving me a few inches over like I'm his doll. He removes his hand and presses me up against the whirring dryer with his hips.

I groan loudly, surprised. The hot machine is aggressive with my already pulsing clit. My insides tighten into a ball. He's harder than ever, like a tree branch against my crack. "Does it count if I'm not inside you?" he asks.

I gasp, desperate. I try to regain my sense. I try to remember why I'm down here in the first place. For Nathan. "It counts."

He pulls me away from the dryer. Pleasure diffuses through me, lingering but less demanding.

"Sorry, were you close?" he asks, low and mocking. "You can beg. I won't think less of you."

I grit my teeth. Disappointment in myself sears through my arousal. I've made mistakes, and so has Nathan, but every time I succumb to Finn, I make it harder to get back to Nathan. Isn't that what I want? I can't have them both, no matter that I can see a future with Finn. I push off the dryer and turn around.

Finn takes my jaw and kisses me hard. There's ten years' worth of passion in it, and it takes all my resolve to shove him away. He stares at me, panting.

"I can't," I say.

"You don't mean that."

The laundry room door clicks, and the woman from earlier walks in. She buries her head in a washing machine. She doesn't know me. Doesn't know Nathan.

Finn cocks his head at me like we're about to duel.

"Are you done with one of those?" she asks. The dryer I almost just came against finishes. The linens twirl a few times, fall and go still.

"Yes," I say. I finish clearing out both dryers. My clit feels like a cluster of exposed nerves against the hard crotch of my pants. I bite my lip firmly to detract from the sensation. I avoid her eyes as she puts her things in the machine next to me. She slams the dryer door shut, turns it on, and leaves.

"You don't understand," I say. "I'm sorry—"

"What don't I understand? I'm married too."

"But you don't . . ."

"What?" he prompts.

"You don't feel for her what I do for Nathan. You told me as much."

He plunges a hand through his messy, damp hair and looks away. "No. This is all wrong. It's not over."

"It has to be." Because I know I won't be able to convince him of it, and because I have things to do, I pick up the laundry basket.

He steps into my path before I can leave. "This is too good to walk away from," he implores. "You know it is."

I don't know anything anymore. I have to end things with him, even though I can't say for sure if it's the right choice. What if things don't go as planned with Nathan tonight? What if my marriage only gets worse from here? The thought makes my shoulders droop. "I'm married," I say lamely. "You're married."

"I contacted a lawyer," he says evenly, holding my gaze. "This morning, I told Kendra not to come at the end of the month."

My mouth falls open. I shake my head. "You did *what?*"

"She asked why."

My entire body locks up. I slam the basket on the ground. "I didn't ask you to do that."

He thins his lips. "I want a divorce. It's not for you. It just had to be done." He speaks without inflection, as if removing her is a surgical procedure.

"Kendra and I are together for the wrong reasons. You made me realize I have options."

I'm speechless. I didn't expect Finn to fight back, fists flying, making good on his lofty promises. Men aren't supposed to leave their wives for a fling. To Finn, this is more. He can't let go of our first meeting in the coffee shop, and it's equal parts romantic and manic. There *is* something sweet about us finding each other again, I admit, but is it enough to upend our lives for?

I glance at the door to the laundry room, waiting for the next person to walk through. "I need to get back upstairs," I say.

"Don't freak," Finn says. "I'm not asking you to do the same, Sadie."

"Good, because I won't," I say, hoisting the laundry back into my arms. "I want my marriage to work, and because of that, this has to end."

I leave him standing there amongst the machines. My heart pounds. Protests, even, because he's here now and Nathan isn't. Finn's conviction is attractive. Infectious. Dangerous. But at the end of the day, while I can't think of many reasons to walk away from Finn, one truth remains the same—I could fall in love with Finn, but I don't think I could ever truly fall out of love with Nathan.

TWENTY-NINE

It's past six when I run out of things to do. I'd planned to wait for Nathan to arrive before making salad, but I toss all the ingredients in a bowl except dressing, set it aside, and check that the beer is nice and cold. For myself, red wine calms my nerves. I sip slowly to keep my wits about me, since I'm unsure of the direction our conversation will take.

At a quarter to seven, I switch off the oven but leave the food in to keep it warm. I light the half-burned candles and fix the calla lilies I've arranged in the center of the table. They're lovely, but I'll have to move them when we sit so we can see each other. I smile to myself. We can't exactly mend our marriage through a bouquet.

Going through my lingerie earlier, I considered wearing only my sexiest things and an apron. It's gone over well with Nathan in the past, but it isn't the message I want to send tonight. As much fun as I had belonging to him again last night, now I want inside his mind. Since Nathan likes me in white, *"like a doll with indigo eyes"* he says, I picked a drop-shoulder silk blouse just sheer enough to hint at the black bra underneath. Its lace is so fine, it doesn't hide when I'm cold or aroused. My message is serious, but I'm not above stoking his imagination.

Ginger gets hyper after I feed her and chases me through the apartment. I try to save my black pants from her slobber and red hairs, but she thinks we're playing, so I give up and collapse on the couch to let her snuggle with me.

"I know you're impatient," I tell her. "He'll be home soon."

She smile-pants. I rub her snout. Nathan won't mind my furry pants.

I cross my feet under my legs. They're cold, and I need a pedicure. I could get my boots, but I don't want to miss the expression on his face when he comes through the door. Plus, Nathan doesn't like us wearing shoes inside. That's just one of his pet peeves. How can he think I don't know him, like he insinuated in the marketplace? He accused me of not knowing his character. Does he really believe that?

As wonderful as Nathan is, it can be hard to be his partner. The last few months aside, he's so kind, he could make the Pope look bad. Not that I'm a bad person, but with him by my side, I sometimes feel inadequate. During our fourth date, on our way to dinner, we passed a mobile blood bus. Nate asked if we should stop and donate. I wasn't in the mood, so I lied and said I hadn't eaten all day. We kept walking. Concerned, he made me order twice as much food as usual.

Looking around the apartment, I think about how Nathan let me choose and decorate it. I'd coveted Gramercy Park since college. He'd had to ask for a raise from work so we could afford the rent, but it'd been over a year since he'd gotten one. Nathan should've already been making that much. It was a win-win situation.

I pick up *The Shining* from the coffee table, which Nathan reads every few years. I scan a page and swap it for Vogue, the same issue Finn picked up when he came over for dinner.

Finn. Just his name makes me hot under my collar. My mind's still spinning from the way he manhandled me earlier. The ache quickly returns between my legs, as if it were there all along, dormant. I close my eyes and remember. The laundry room— there's a place Nathan and I have never fucked. Now, it belongs to Finn, him pressing me up against a machine as warm and insistent as a selfless lover. His hand, cupping me between my jean-clad thighs. I suck in a breath.

I want it again.

I pulse with need.

I tell myself I can't have it anymore.

I have nothing left to distract myself with, so I

finally let myself hear what Finn said. He's leaving Kendra. He claimed it wasn't for me, but if we'd simply remained nameless neighbors, I doubt he would've been prompted into action now.

I get up and pace the apartment, trying to dispel the fantasies—of him inside me, of what a life with him would look like. I pour myself another glass of wine and double-check my phone to make sure I didn't miss something from Nathan. The only thing on the screen is the time, and it's past seven now. I bite my thumbnail and call him. I wanted this to be a surprise, but it's getting late, and he should be home by now. He's good about letting me know when he leaves work after six.

It doesn't ease my concerns when the call goes to voicemail. Nathan rarely shuts off his phone, but he does sometimes put it on silent.

Like when he's visiting his dad in the hospital.

My heart squeezes as I find the number I've saved for the cancer center. Ralph's been in and out of the hospital for months, but he was supposed to be released following his last treatment. Since I missed Nathan's recent visit, it's been too long since I've seen Ralph. I should've insisted to Nathan that we go again—together.

A nurse answers. I ask if Ralph Hunt is still there. "He is," she says after a few moments on hold. "But he's asleep right now."

"So everything's okay? There's no emergency?"

"Emergency? No. Although, he doesn't seem to

be responding well to his latest rounds of radiation."

I rub my eyebrow. "Yes, that I knew. I'm looking for my husband—his son, Nathan. I thought he might've stopped by after work. Do you know if he's there?"

"Ralph hasn't had any visitors today."

I thank her and hang up. I can't enjoy my relief, because it doesn't give me any resolution. I try his office, but nobody's there. Feeling helpless, I go into the bedroom and reluctantly put on chunky socks. Nathan sees me all the time in loungewear, but I wanted to catch him off guard in our own home. But then, after another fifteen minutes of watching the candles burn down, I remove my socks to sit on the bathroom counter and change my toenail polish. I'm not sure what else to do. It isn't like Nathan to disappear, but then again, is it? Last night gave me hope, but it wasn't the breakthrough we needed by any means. Considering the way things were going before that, it was only a matter of time before he stopped communicating altogether.

Was I right to worry when he turned away from me in bed? Did last night not mean to him what it did to me? After all, the night he called me a slut during sex, he went back to being a dick the next day. And after he came in my mouth in the doorway, he didn't even wait until morning to blow me off.

So I offended him at some point in our marriage—does that give him the right to treat me like this? To leave me waiting at home without so much as a phone call? I hop down from the counter and stride through the apartment. When I stub my toe on a chair, I smudge my pedicure and curse.

With my third drink, wine sticks in my throat, turns my teeth blue. My lipstick has rubbed off onto the edge of the glass, but I don't bother reapplying it. I call Nathan again. His phone is still off.

The food is getting cold. I eat a few bites of salad before shoving the rest down the garbage disposal. Would he really have stayed at work this late? Or did he stop by the downstairs bar again? Where else could he be? I'm staring down the black drain when it hits me—and I can't *believe* I didn't realize it earlier. It's Wednesday night, and that's when Nathan bowls. Instead of relief, though, rage blazes through me like wildfire through brush. After last night, and considering the state of our marriage, he should know it's not okay to skip dinner to be with his friends. And not only did he not tell me, but he turned off his phone.

And I sat here like an idiot, worried about him.

Painting my face, my nails, thinking it would make a difference.

Wearing lingerie for him, going out of my way to get the flowers he likes, washing a blanket that was only dirty because he used it to sleep somewhere I wasn't. I grip the counter until my knuckles are white. I've had enough of this. Enough walking on eggshells around him, enough pandering to his moods.

Do I even know my own husband anymore?

Brooklyn Bowl didn't occur to me because I never would've guessed he'd choose it over working on our marriage. Over me. That isn't the Nathan I married, but it's the Nathan I have now. Maybe *The Shining* isn't even his favorite book. Maybe he doesn't care if I'm eating enough. Maybe he's used up all his kindness, and he's out there right now, laughing at me and my pathetic ribs.

I wasted an entire day on cooking him dinner, and he doesn't even have the decency to come home and eat it. For months, I've taken his bullshit and tried to make things right. For months, I've bitten my tongue.

I whirl around, knocking over the plastic salad bowl and anything its path. I yank the oven open and pull out the food. I'm so livid, so embarrassed, I lift up the heavy baking sheet to smash it on the ground, but at the last second, I freeze. Food is how I show Nathan I love him—but he doesn't want to eat what I make anymore? Fine. I know someone who does.

With a cold, untouched rib dinner weighing in my arms, I bang on Finn's door with the heel of my foot. It takes a minute until he answers, his hair disheveled, and his shirt halfway on. "Sadie?" He looks behind me and around the hall. "Jesus. What—"

"You like barbecue ribs?" I shove the food between us. "Here, have it. It's good. Or, at least, it was two hours ago when it was hot. I made it for

Nathan, but you—" A storm of emotions catches up with me. Anger heats my face. A sense of loss makes my eyes wet. "But I thought you might appreciate it more."

"Sadie," Finn says sadly and takes the sheet. He sets it on the entryway bench and wraps me in his arms. I burst into tears. All that time I spent on my makeup—pointless. All that time I spent in my marriage—wasted. Is this my fault? Did I let Nathan slip through my fingers, and if so, when did he get so far out of my reach? When did it become too late to bring him back? Did his love go away or, worse, did it turn into indifference?

"Shh." Finn lets me cry over my husband. He massages my back but doesn't hear my hiss when he kneads the shoulder blade where Nathan bit me. "It's okay," he says. "These things happen."

I sniffle. When I've calmed a little, I look up at him. "What things?"

With an amused look, he pinches his shirt and dabs under my nose.

"Sorry." I grimace. I've snotted and sobbed all over him.

He's smiling, though. "It starts small." His expression sobers. "An anniversary forgotten or a water ring on the fancy coffee table. Then it escalates over a long time. Those little frustrations become maddening. Sometimes they explode, and sometimes they just . . . fade. You stop caring."

I look at the damp spot on his t-shirt. I don't

404

believe almost three months counts as a long time. Nathan's personality changed overnight, without warning. But Finn only has his own experience as reference. "Is that what happened to you and Kendra?"

He sighs. "We were always doomed, I guess. I'm the one who forgot dates or kept not doing what she asked me to, like use a coaster. Not on purpose. I just didn't think about what made her happy. Kind of like Nathan doesn't."

His words are eerily wrong, as if he accidentally swapped Nathan's name with mine. Finn has only ever known Nathan as a neglectful husband, but I'm the one who forgets little things. I rarely throw out the coffee filter. I don't buy body wash when we're low. I eat the cherry off my sundaes first, while Nathan waits to offer his to me. That doesn't mean I don't think about what makes him happy, though. I show my love in other ways.

"But I won't be that to you," Finn backtracks, reading my thoughts. "That has more to do with the dynamic of my relationship with Kendra than with the kind of husband I would be."

My attention snags on the confidence of his statement. "To me?"

"That's why you're here, isn't it?" His question is less demanding than suggestive. "Don't come running to me when you're upset if you don't want my comfort. The best way I know how to make it better is to tell you how it can be if you choose me."

The elevator dings. My breath catches. It has to be Nathan. I wiggle in Finn's arms, but he holds on tightly. "Ask me to let go," he says. "Things will just go back to normal, and normal isn't good enough for you."

I look up at him. Not only does he want me, not only does he want *to love me*, but I want him back. Against all odds. It's rare to have found such a strong connection even once in my life, but have I found it again with Finn? I stop squirming.

6D gets off the elevator. As he passes, he doesn't hide the fact that he notices our embrace. He's been in the building longer than any of us and knows this isn't my husband.

Finn ignores him. "Come inside," he says when we're alone again.

"I don't have anything."

"What do you need?"

"For one, I'm barefoot."

"We have shoes in here." He slips his arm around my shoulder. Instantly, I'm comforted, safe, sheltered from the storm. My heartbeat calms. "Do you have your keys?"

I open my palm. The teeth have made indents in my skin.

He smiles. "What else is there? You haven't eaten, have you?" he asks.

I shake my head. "No."

"Then come in, and let me feed you."

THIRTY

Finn carries Nathan's platter of cold ribs to the kitchen. At least the love I put into them won't go to waste. Even though Finn has been in his apartment for weeks, there are still boxes on the floor. A couple cupboards sit open. I take it all in. "Finn, you've barely done anything since I was last here."

"I'm doing the best I can in a state of transition," he says flatly, as if it's rehearsed. He leaves the room and comes back with a pair of wool socks. "Sit."

One chair is stacked with photography manuals, a George Steinbrenner biography, and a DVD of *The Secret Garden*. Another is the new home of his record player, a box of Legos, and an army-green jacket. "Where?"

He comes over, lifts me by my waist, and plops me on the kitchen counter.

I giggle, and his face visibly brightens. He shoves a sock on my foot and bunches it over my ankle. It's like slipping under the covers after a long, cold day, and I don't even care if it ruins my nail polish. I realize I'm not sweating. "You fixed the radiator?"

He winks at me. "This morning. I've been in heaven ever since. This is shaping up to be the best day of my life."

I can see it in his eyes—he's temperate. Happy.

He finishes pulling on the other sock. "There. It's either that or my size twelve sneakers."

"That would be awkward."

"Yes. And this isn't at all," he says, grinning.

"It's sweet." I put my arms around his neck and pull him in for a kiss. "Thank you."

"No problem, princess," he says and goes back for the ribs. I'm grateful he walks away at that moment. I don't think I can hide my once-sweet, now-depressing memory from showing on my face.

"I'm no princess."

"Then I guess that makes you a pea."

Finn opens the microwave, but the platter is clearly too large for it. He looks at me helplessly. "Should we do half for now?"

I roll my eyes, slide off the counter, and playfully push him out of the way. "I didn't slave over dinner for hours just to zap it in the microwave." I turn on the oven. "Needs a few minutes to warm up."

"Right." He rubs the back of his neck. "I told you, the kitchen hates me."

"A kitchen is like a woman," I say, leaning back against the counter. I don't know where it comes from, so I make it up as I go. "You can't just dive in and make a gourmet meal. It takes time to explore her, to learn what she keeps in which drawers, to play with seasoning and proportions."

He stands across the room. A smile slides over his face. "So, in this example, you're the gourmet meal?"

"No—" I'm about to explain it further, but I stop. He's teasing me. "I'm just saying, don't go around banging pots and pans."

He shrugs. "Sometimes pots and pans just want to bang. Then you bring a spatula into the mix—"

"All right, I get it," I say, laughing. "Do you even know which one the spatula is?"

"Hmm." He stalks toward me, and my legs falter. The laundry room memory comes back too quickly. He reaches around me, though, and then pulls back to show me his spatula. With smiles on our faces, we look from the utensil to each other. "This one, right?"

"Right."

"Turn around."

"No. We need that to serve the food."

He doesn't budge, his expression playful but determined.

"Fine," I say and turn to face the counter. "Be gent—"

He smacks me on the ass, but it barely stings. I break into a fit of giggles.

"Feel better?" he asks.

I nod back at him, sincere. "Thank you. You really know how to cheer a girl up."

"Anytime. I mean that." He winks. "Want a tour of the apartment?"

Despite the fact that we've been intimate here, I realize I've never seen his bedroom. Just being here with Finn is making a decision, but I'm not sure I'm ready to dive in head first. "Okay . . . but—"

"Just a tour," he says, raising his palms. "Promise."

I nod, grateful he can read my mind. I stick the ribs in the oven and follow him out of the kitchen. He opens a door in a short hallway. I'm hit with a chalky, pungent smell. The tarped floor is littered with paint cans. One wall has a half-finished mural of horses. "Marissa wanted horses," he explains.

"You did that?" I ask. It's by no means Michelangelo, but that doesn't matter. It's a father's dedication to his daughter.

"She sketched it with me. Some of her stuff is here. I was going to get the rest after Thanksgiving."

I rub my eyebrow. "But not anymore."

"The house is sold, so they have to move. But—I mean, obviously, I'll help Kendra find . . ." He looks around the room a moment. "We haven't worked out any details yet."

"Oh." My gut smarts. I look into a box by the door. This is real. *Frozen*-coloring-book, Shopkins, fuzzy-pink-socks real.

"Don't," he says, looking me over.

"Don't what?"

"This would've happened eventually, Sadie. It's not your fault."

I tuck some hair behind my ear. I was a little girl once with fucked-up parents. As I got older, I convinced myself it would've been better if my dad had just divorced my mom and put each of them out of their misery. "Should you maybe slow it down a little?" I ask. "Give Kendra some time to adjust to the idea?"

He shakes his head. "She'll convince herself I've changed my mind. That's just the way she thinks. Would you want to be strung along?"

If the last few months are any indication, I don't do well with ambiguity in my relationship. "I guess not."

He shuts the door. "Not much to see in there. Or anywhere in this apartment, really." The next room is just the standard eggshell-white. To the right of a desk, three canvas photographs are propped against a wall. "These are yours?" I ask, walking in.

"I'm not pretentious enough to hang them," he says, following, "but I'm not sure where to keep them."

The first photo is a sunny landscape shot of the steps in Union Square. A teenage boy is midair and blurry on his skateboard, flying off a railing. Other kids on boards surround him in various states of movement. A woman on a step has a sandwich in one hand and an e-reader in the other. The rest of the people in the photo are using a phone, watching the teens, or having conversations. Off to the right, a man in a folding chair is surrounded by artwork with price tags. Finn has precisely captured in detail a normal day in the park off Fourteenth Street.

"This is my boss the day I quit," he says, drawing my attention to the next photo. A gray-haired man has one hand steepled on his desk. He arches an eyebrow at the camera, his mouth set in a tense line, his face a topographic map of pockmarks and wrinkles.

I glance at Finn. "You just . . . quit? And then took a picture?"

"I want to remember that day forever," he says. "I brought the camera into his office and snapped it without his permission. It's not the best shot technically since I took it fast, but his expression says everything."

"He looks pissed. And annoyed."

"He was. About my exit and the photo. I thought he was going to break my camera, but instead, he just told me to get the fuck out."

"You weren't scared to quit your job?" His ex-boss's swanky office is stark white with sharp-cornered furniture and a view of the river. He has an entire shelf of awards.

"It was more adrenaline than fear."

"Why'd you do it?"

He doesn't answer. I look back at him. "Just needed a change," he says.

"You've made a lot of changes lately."

He shrugs. "Kendra likes to point that out. I'm working on myself. I don't get why it's a problem."

"I guess when you're responsible for a young family—"

"I've never let them down," he says. "Not financially. The kind of money I was making, I was able to save a lot. I didn't buy into material shit like my colleagues did." He makes a point of looking around the nearly empty room. There are two boxes labeled *equipment* and *office*. "As you can see."

Our eyes drift to the last picture of coffee grounds piled and scattered on a familiar-looking tile floor. "Was that here?"

"Yeah." He grins. "Evidence of my kitchen klutziness. Kendra usually makes the coffee."

"So does Nathan. Even the mornings he isn't having any, he brews it and puts a mug out for me." Aside from the fact that each photo makes me feel something, there's no discernable connection between any of them. There's a stack of 4x6 prints on the desk. The top is a Terrier leashed to a park bench. The rest stick out the sides—a wrinkled finger, a rusted bike chain, a rose petal.

I realize Finn's been quiet for a while. "Sorry," I say, realizing my last comment about Nathan. "I shouldn't share so much."

"Why not?" he asks.

413

"It's weird."

"This is all weird. If we can't talk about that stuff, it'll do more harm than good to our relationship."

"That's mature," I remark.

"But it makes sense, doesn't it?"

It'd be a relief not to edit myself. I nod. "It makes sense."

He comes over and wraps me in a sideways hug. "I want you to feel comfortable enough to talk about what you're feeling. Even if it's hard at first. I understand love doesn't vanish overnight."

"Do you still love Kendra?"

"I meant you and Nathan."

"I know." I blink. Even if it makes me a little uncomfortable, I don't think I want him to stop loving her all of a sudden. It shouldn't be that way when you've been with someone so long. "Do you, though?"

His gaze shifts away. It takes him a moment to answer, as if he doesn't know what to say, or hasn't given it much thought. "Of course I do. She's the mother of my child. She's been my wife for almost eight years. But I feel something different for you than I ever did for her. Much different." He squeezes me.

The fabric of our short history is shiny, woven with new experiences, romance, lust—most of all, possibility. A fresh start. With Nathan, the threads are stronger but faded. They've been holding us together a long time. They've endured arguments, tragedies, frustrations—but also adventures and blessings. Like the time I fought him about leaving our bed the morning after a blizzard. I pouted the whole way to Central Park, laden with a scarf, knit cap, and gloves. Nathan had insisted, and I'd grumbled. Somehow he knew what a magical day it would turn out to be. We ice-skated hand in hand, admired shop windows on Fifth Avenue, and had a snowball fight that downed me, more thanks to laughter than anything. Finn and I don't have that yet. Instead, our magic is what could be, and a fresh start can be as alluring as a good memory. Neither what is nor what could be is better, and I understand what Finn means when he says different.

Finn releases me. "There's one last room . . ."

"The bathroom?" I tease.

The oven beeps. We laugh. "Divine intervention," he says, kissing the top of my head. "Let's eat. Smells fucking delicious."

On the way to the kitchen, I think about how he used the word *relationship* a minute ago. I didn't notice it at first, which means it didn't scare me.

Finn clears off the table and chairs. I get dishes and silverware. I'm familiar with his kitchen since I set it up. It's more than likely I know it better than Finn's wife does.

"What can I do?" he asks as I set the table.

"Sit," I say. "Let me serve you."

His eyes follow me around the kitchen. I get two beers. I'd rather drink more wine, but he doesn't have any, and when I think of going back to my apartment, my stomach aches.

I prepare two plates and set his in front of him. "Sorry there's no greens," I say. "I had to dump the salad."

He grabs my wrist and pulls me onto his lap. "Say that again."

I arch an eyebrow at him and think back. I know what he's asking for, but I say, "I had to dump the salad?"

He shakes his head, waiting, amused.

"Let me serve you."

"Yeah." He cups his hand between my legs. "Say it again."

I squirm as he holds onto me. "Let me serve you."

He rubs my clit with the undersides of his fingers. I inhale a sharp breath as he looks from my eyes to my mouth and back. "I can think of a few ways I want to be served."

He's hard under my thigh. I cover his searching hand with mine and move with him. It's nice. Easy.

He flips his hand over, laces his fingers through mine, and kisses my knuckles. "You should eat. If we keep this up, I can't promise we'll get to dinner."

He doesn't look at me. His self-control is thin, and it shows on his face. I appreciate that he stops to take care of me before himself, so I kiss him on the cheek. I try to get up from his lap, but he keeps me there with an arm around my waist. "You can stay here," he says. "Just don't wiggle around too much."

I smile and elbow him lightly in the ribs, but move most of my weight onto one of his thighs. "How's that?"

"We'll see." He picks up a rib and feeds me first.

I suck barbeque flavor from his fingers. "Yum."

He cleans off the rest of the meat, groaning. After swallowing, he says, "That's so worth not getting a handy."

I laugh throatily, his joke unexpected. "Liar," I say. We take a few more bites that way. My hunger is easily satisfied tonight, so I snuggle against him as he eats, but it's hard to get comfortable against his muscled chest. "I'm guessing you found a gym," I say.

"I'm at Equinox. I didn't think it'd be smart to sign up where you guys go."

I raise my eyebrows, but he can't see me. Nathan makes fun of that gym because it has the same equipment as ours, the same douchebags, and it costs twice as much. "How often do you go?"

"Right now, almost every day. I'm making up for lost time."

"What do you mean?"

"Between work, Kendra, and Marissa, I didn't exercise as much as I wanted in Connecticut." He washes down his food with beer. His body heaves as he swallows, bobbing me back and forth. He continues, "I've also been running along the East River promenade. Have you done that?"

"No," I admit. I don't add that Nathan has tried to get me to go with him, but I find jogging grueling no matter where it happens.

"Do it with me tomorrow," he says. "If you go early enough, not many people are out. It's beautiful."

"Isn't it cold?"

"Oh, it's cold as fuck," he says with a laugh, "but I'll keep you warm, baby."

With my fingertip, I trace a figure eight on his thigh. For some reason, it doesn't sound grueling when Finn suggests it. It sounds fun. "Then what?"

He doesn't miss a beat. "Then, we order all the breakfast at the diner. Enough hash browns to make us sick. We're so cute when we dip them in our sunny-side-up eggs and feed them to each other that the waitress might also be sick."

I smile hard, bursting at the seams, on the verge of laughing. "And then?"

"We'll probably have to come back here after that," he says. "We'll be full and sweaty."

"Full and sweaty?" I wrinkle my nose. "That's how you envision us as a couple?"

"Stay with me," he says. He looks toward the living room. "In the doorway, I'll strip you down to nothing and carry you over my shoulder to the shower. I'll fuck you in there. I'll fuck you in here. I'll fuck you all over the place. By then, it'll be lunchtime, and we'll go somewhere fun. You like the Museum of Natural History?"

"I guess. It's been a while—"

"It's the best one," he says. "It's just fun, not pretentious, you know? We'll get hotdogs out front and then wander around."

"*Hotdogs*?" I ask. "After all that breakfast?"

"Happy people eat a lot," he says simply.

We laugh together until his breathing evens out.

"What's next?" I ask, shifting to look at him. "Wait—let me guess. Pizza?"

He kisses me on the nose. "If that's what you want."

I turn back to the table. He's almost finished his plate, while mine is nearly full. I nod. "It's a nice fantasy, Finn. Thank you."

"It doesn't have to be a fantasy. Just say the word."

I'm not surprised by his suggestion, but what world is Finn living in that he thinks we could do that tomorrow? I love that he wants to spend the day with me, but what we're talking about is serious, and it needs a dose of reality.

"I meant because I have to work tomorrow. You know that, right? It's Thursday."

"And I'm supposed to go to Connecticut." He shrugs. "I'll cancel. You take the day off."

"All right," I concede, even though I can't since I did that today, "but then what? I can't take every day off."

419

He gets quiet. I wait for him to answer, but it becomes clear he isn't going to.

I've ruined the mood, but this could be a good thing. We need see what's behind this closed door. "What are you doing about work?" I ask.

He shifts underneath me. "If you're worried about finances, don't be. I used to manage money for a living. I'll figure it out. And until I do, I've got savings and investments."

"I'm not worried. Just curious." I rub his calf with my foot to show him I'm not nagging. "You want to make a living on your photography, right? Have you made any progress since we last talked about it? What about that job you had?"

"It's on the books," he says, a little lighter. "I'm not sure about it, though."

I tilt my head under his chin. "How come?"

"I want to do it right, but I need to upgrade my equipment if I want to be competitive. I have to turn that office into a studio. It's been so long since I did this professionally, I feel like a bit of an amateur."

I look up at him. I'm both glad and worried to see him pursuing his dream. I don't know much about the stock market, but I've heard it can crash, and if that's where his money is, I hope he knows what he's doing. It isn't easy to walk away from that kind of job stability, and I could never do it. But I remember that long-haired artist from the coffee shop, and it makes my heart swell with happiness. I kiss the underside of his jaw. "You should do it. You were great with me."

He smiles. *He* doesn't seem that worried, but he must be somewhere inside. His life has been upended. He just quit his job. He's ending his marriage. And I wonder about the little things too, like taking on an exorbitantly expensive gym membership when he has no income.

I pull back a little. "Can I ask you something you might not like?"

"Shoot."

"Are you having a mid-life crisis?"

He chuckles, pets my hair, and pulls my head to his lips for a kiss. "I love when you surprise me with stuff like that."

I wait until his smile eases away. "Are you?" I ask.

He glances at the ceiling and sighs. "I'm not even close to the halfway point. At least, I hope not."

"You know what I mean."

"Well, if that's what you want to call it, I guess I am. I don't see it that way, though. I think I was sleepwalking, and I've finally opened my eyes. I don't owe anyone my happiness, not even Marissa. If she sees me living my life for myself, then she'll know what it looks like when it's time for her to do the same."

I study his face, smooth but settling with fine lines and creases. The truth is, I've seen firsthand the changes he's going through, but it's been easy to forget his transformation started before that morning we met in the hallway. "What made you open your eyes?" I ask. "Did something happen?"

"Sort of." He snort-laughs. "I could tell you, but it'll make me sound like a *huge* hypocrite."

"I'm the last person to judge," I point out.

He nods a little and rubs my thigh. "So my boss and his partners go out a few times a year and just light up the city. They get plastered, hit the strip clubs, steak and cigars, the whole nine. And they hire these, like, escorts, you know? For the night. These women stroke their egos and their—" He stops. "You get the idea."

I swallow down the urge to gag. I can't imagine Finn and his romantic ideals getting caught up in that. I don't worry that he'll say he's treated women that way. It's not in his nature.

He shakes his head. "Anyway, if someone like me gets invited to a night out with them, it's some kind of privilege. You're expected to participate, and if you don't, you look like a pussy. And pussies don't make it to the top in a place like that. You know who told me that?"

"Not *Kendra*?"

He laughs. "Her dad. He used to be one of those guys at another firm. It was more important to him that I get promoted than stay faithful to his daughter."

I frown. "That's disgusting, Finn."

"I know it." He squeezes my knee reassuringly. "I didn't do it."

"I know. But you were invited?"

He nods. "Turning down a promotion would only delay the inevitable. That culture wasn't changing anytime soon." He goes quiet a moment, seemingly lost in a thought. "I had to accept or move to another firm if I wanted to go any higher. I asked around. Want to know what I found out? Everyone at my firm, and at other firms, hated life. They didn't come out and say it, but I knew it was true for them because it was true for me." He sniffs. "I hated my situation. Once upon a time, I believed I would create art. I believed I'd find the love of my life and do whatever it took to make her happy. Not once did I think screwing a prostitute was part of the deal. And it's not like I had to stick my dick in someone— sorry—or I'd never succeed. It was more about what it meant that I worked in that kind of industry . . . and that I was considering how to do it while keeping everyone happy."

My conscience tugs at me. He quit his job to be a better man. "I'm sorry," I say.

He sighs. "It's just a fucking disappointment when life doesn't turn out how you want. I'm doing something about it, though."

"Do you regret anything?" I ask.

"No. Not yet, at least. When I saw you again, it was like a light at the end of the tunnel. Like, if I could just get through this, I'd be rewarded."

"Or punished," I say. "Maybe you're not supposed to have me."

He shakes his head definitively. "I don't believe that. I might've done some fucked up things, but I'm not a bad person."

"Neither is Nathan."

"Maybe this is his reward too. Maybe he wants out of your marriage but feels trapped."

I swallow. Finn can't know how that word scares me, how just hearing it stings. When my dad tried to leave my mom and Andrew, she got pregnant with me. I'm the hinge that closed the door. He wasn't particularly upstanding, but he was above leaving his pregnant wife. He never got out. Their marriage is all drinking, fighting, and gambling.

Finn adjusts in his chair, and I shift on his lap. "So he's bowling tonight, right?"

I play with the collar of his cotton t-shirt. Nathan could be anywhere at this point, and it would mean the same thing. "It doesn't matter."

"Because he isn't here." Finn understands. He pulls my bottom lip down with his thumb, exposing my gums. He releases it. "When you frown, I frown."

"I'm sorry. It can't be easy for you to talk about this."

"I can handle it," he says, and adds, "to a point."

"Thank you." I peck him once on the lips. "It's getting late."

"Not that late."

I glance at the oven's digital clock. "It's almost nine."

"That clock is fast by a few hours."

I roll my eyes, grinning. "I have to work tomorrow."

"We didn't finish our tour yet," he says. "Come on. Aren't you curious?"

I can't picture his bedroom. Does it have Kendra's stamp on it? Is there an ornate bedframe to match the couch?

I'm not sure why I'm even watching the clock, because I don't want to go home. I don't want to hear Nathan's excuses, or worse, his silence. Apparently, the best I can hope for from him is a few naughty words and good, hard fuck. That's all he's given me the past few months that means anything.

Finn squeezes my hips, and I get up. He holds his hand out to me.

It's more than an invitation to see his bedroom. He's asking me to stay. To choose him. To live the life of happy people. My confidence in Nathan has been circling the drain for a while, and now I don't think I even feel it anymore. It's time for me to face the facts. I promised I'd never trap him.

He doesn't want to make our marriage work. And even if I do, I can't force him into it. Then again, maybe I don't even want that anymore.

I take Finn's hand.

THIRTY-ONE

Finn switches on a dull light, and for the first time, I'm looking at his bedroom. "So, this is it," he says flatly. It's what the space calls for. It's not the palace I'd expected Kendra to build. There's no furniture, nothing on the white walls. His bed is a sheeted mattress on the floor with two pillows and a bedspread. It's empty aside from a couple suitcases, a full laundry basket, and a lot of bare hangers.

He clears his throat. "If I'd known you were coming . . ."

My heart aches. It's not the room of a married couple. It's lonely. I try to stay upbeat, though. It won't always be like this. "It's fine," I tease. "Don't unpack on my account."

"I try—I do," he says. "But I get hot and frustrated. It makes me think of what I left at the house, and the decisions I need to make. It's easier to paint horses . . ."

I take my hand out of his and peer into the laundry basket. "Can I help?"

He tilts his head. "Really?"

"This stuff looks clean."

"It is." He picks up a pair of jeans and gets a hanger. "I just haven't put it away."

"This is New York," I tell him. I take the pants from him and fold them in half, then quarters. "Hanging space is valuable. Jeans can be folded."

"Wow," he says. "You did that fast."

"I've folded a lot of jeans in my life." I smile and stick them on a shelf. "You'll need some kind of storage, like an armoire or something."

"All right. Maybe you can help me pick one out?"

I waggle my eyebrows. His hopeful tone makes me playful, even more so because I can picture us furniture shopping on a Sunday afternoon. "We'll see."

He puts a button down shirt on a hanger and sticks it in the closet. It needs to be ironed, but I bite my tongue. Baby steps. I can bring my ironing board over. *Permanently?* I wonder.

"We could go to a flea market," he says. "Maybe fix some pieces up. I'll have paint left over."

I've never really refurbished anything, but I like the idea. I have a stack of magazines under my bed dedicated to home décor new and old. "That sounds fun."

He hangs a few more things while I create piles of jeans and casual t-shirts.

"You can stay here tonight," he says out of nowhere.

I stop folding. Standing in his bedroom, I'm surrounded by the reality of Finn and me. I can't help thinking how strange it would be to sleep next to a new man. Isn't that why I'm here, though? Why else would I be if I weren't giving in to the idea of leaving Nathan for Finn?

"I know it isn't much," he says, misreading my silence. "You deserve a real bed. I can get one here tomorrow." He pauses. "That's my way of saying you could stay again tomorrow night. I'd buy a bed—for you."

"Finn," I say, but I don't know what to follow it up with. *Okay, sure, why not?* How do I even begin this process?

He hangs another shirt in the closet, dinging the metal bar, and turns me by my shoulders. "Look at what he's turned you into these last couple months," he says earnestly. "I want to be patient, but when you cry in my arms because he can't be bothered to come home for dinner on a *weeknight*, well . . . it pisses me the fuck off. He doesn't know what he has. I want to take it from him."

There's determination is his voice and sincerity in his eyes. Right now, I want to hug and kiss and lose

429

myself in him. But do I want that every day for the rest of my life? Can I even know that after a few weeks? "Do you think it's possible to love two people?" I ask.

"Yeah," he says quietly. "Don't you?"

"I'm not sure," I admit.

I sense his disappointment, but it's gone quickly. He rubs his thumbs against my biceps. "I'm not asking you to love me tonight. All I want is a chance to show you love without conditions. I want you now—mattress-on-the-floor now. Half-painted-rooms and empty-hangers now. If you say yes, I'll fix this place up in no time. But that doesn't mean I don't want you here tonight in the mess."

I look around the room. Finn probably thinks its emptiness makes me wary, but I actually see a clean slate. There isn't anything I don't love about my own apartment—Nathan and I created it together. But that's what also makes it such a cruel reminder.

"I'm not saying no," I say, "but it feels fast."

"Not to me. My marriage is what I'm trying to save you from, Sadie. There's too much resentment there. I'm ready. Believe me, there's no benefit in drawing these things out."

Getting out of a bad marriage takes guts, any way you cut it. I'm sorry there's a child involved, and I'm sorry Kendra doesn't want this—but Finn has a point. He can do more harm to them both if he stays. Finn will be the villain no matter what he does.

He touches his forehead to mine. "So?" He kisses me softly, then runs his tongue along my bottom lip. "Will you stay, sweet Sadie? Sweet, sexy Sadie?"

I hug his neck and kiss him back. He's a beautiful and smart man who cares about me. I can feel it in his arms around my body, his lips on mine, his hands on my skin. He feeds me hope with his kiss. We can do this. It won't be easy, but don't some of the best things in life come from pain and struggle? I want this. I want to start over. Our kiss ends because I'm smiling too hard.

"Is that a yes?" he asks into my mouth.

"It's a yes."

Now, we're both grinning. He tightens his arms around my waist and lifts me up. We laugh between pecks as he walks me back to the mattress. He lays me down on it, our giddy kisses turning hungrier, harder.

"Here?" I ask, glancing around as he nibbles my jaw.

"Where else? It's not much of a bed, but I've waited a long time to have you in it."

"But have you and Kendra . . .?"

"No. Not a chance," he says, resuming his assault on my tender neck.

My breath escapes me along with my protests, and I wrap my legs around his waist. Finn and I are still new to each other, explorers mapping out each other's bodies. He doesn't know me the way Nathan does, but—I lose my train of thought when he thrusts his hips into me, his hardness stroking my clit. I hiss at the unexpected sensation and drawl, "God, Nate. *Yes.*"

Finn stills instantly, but I continue to writhe under him, my heart pounding so hard, he can probably feel it. It takes me a moment to hear my own words, to realize my mistake, and when I do, I fall back to Earth hard.

Finn lifts his head and looks down at me. "What'd you call me?"

"I-I'm sorry," I say breathlessly. "It slipped."

His eyebrows lower, and each second he stares at me becomes more charged. I shouldn't think of Nathan when I'm with Finn, but after seven years with only him, how can I not? Finally, he says, "It's okay."

It doesn't sound okay. I cup his cheek. "It doesn't mean anything, Finn."

"I know." He sniffs. "One of us was bound to do it, I guess."

I thumb his bottom lip. "Don't stop kissing me."

He angles his face away from my hand and scratches his beard. "We should probably take a timeout."

I chew on my bottom lip. "You want to stop?"

"Want to? No." He smiles. "But I think we'd better. You came here in tears, and we made a big decision tonight. You're vulnerable. I don't want to take advantage of that." Finn looks down at me openly. Adoringly. He could love me already, or maybe he thinks he has for a while. He's leaning all his weight on a moment that could've just as easily never happened. On a moment that led me to Nathan. Then led me back to Finn.

My brain hurts. Even though I was worked up a second ago, my body loosens, as if Finn gave me permission to relax. Suddenly, I'm overwhelmingly tired. I nod. "Maybe you're right."

He kisses the corner of my mouth, then my cheek. "Besides," he whispers, "sleeping with you in my arms sounds better than anything right now. Even sex."

I can't contain my smile, so I don't. My eyes already feel droopy. "It does sound pretty good."

He gets up to switch off the light. Moonlight streams through the window as I watch him walk barefoot back to the bed and peel off his shirt. I do the same, tossing mine on the floor with his. He slips in next to me and pulls my back to his front.

We don't need a blanket. He's hot, and I'm not cold. He tugs a sheet over us anyway and snuggles his face into the crook of my neck. This is messy. And strange. But it feels a little—natural. The way spending my first night in a new home should feel.

THIRTY – TWO

Even though the apartment building is heated, I shiver in the early dawn, standing in front of my door. Finn is a heavy sleeper and barely moved as I slipped out from under his arms. I left him slumped over nothing, as if I'd melted into the mattress beneath him. Or as though I was never there.

I unlock the front door quietly, even though Nathan has to be up for work soon anyway. Ginger greets me as if she were nearby. The apartment is warm, the lights still on from when I left, and thick with tension. Even Ginger is subdued.

"I'm sorry I left you alone, baby," I whisper into her fur. I prance across the tile entryway with bare, cold feet, seeking solace in the carpet, and nearly scream when I see Nathan on the couch, leaning his elbows on his knees.

I cover my pounding heart and take a deep

breath. "Jesus, Nathan. You scared me."

His bloodshot eyes track me as I walk farther into the room. "Where the hell have you been?"

It takes me a moment to remember my anger, but the evidence is all around us. The melted down candle wax and untouched tableware. The neat lines in the carpet from the vacuum. The calla lilies, stretched and open like they're laughing at me. "Where have *I* been?" I ask. "Where were *you?*"

"Right here. All night."

"Funny. Then I guess I didn't sit alone for hours, watching dinner get cold."

He shakes his head. "Don't start with me. You don't know the night I've had."

"Nope, I don't." I walk to the table and start stacking our unused plates.

He stands in drawstring pants and a Henley. "I called Andrew looking for you. I called Jill." I feel his glare as I move onto gathering silverware. "I called my dad's hospital. I was getting ready to call the police."

I glance up. "You haven't slept?"

"Slept?" He reels back. "You think I could sleep without having a damn clue where you are?"

I press my lips together unnaturally hard. He acts as though he didn't put me through the same thing— hours of waiting, agonizing, stewing. I've gone through too much trouble for his attention to have him not even bother to show up for dinner. "You weren't the only one who was worried." Ginger sticks her nose in my hip the way she always does when one of us gets loud. I pick up the dishes and shoot him a look. "But you know what? I'm not going to worry anymore. Starting now, you can do whatever the hell you want."

"What does that mean?" he asks, following me into the kitchen.

I return the forks and knives to their places in a drawer. Nathan isn't the only tidy, angry person in this relationship. "Which part?"

"I can do what I want? What, you still think I'm out having an affair?"

"No, I don't."

"Sadie, look at me."

I put the dishes in a cupboard and turn to him. He's massaging his temples with one giant hand, and I have to bite back the instinct to ask if he has a headache.

"You don't come home all night, and you're not making any sense," he says. "What's going on?"

I slow-blink at him. My simmering anger heats to a boil. For months, he's acted as though I don't exist, and he can't even handle the same treatment for one night. "*What's going on?*" I ask through my teeth. "You tell me. I'm just following your lead. Why do you get to spend the night out, and I don't? You already checked out of this relationship, and I've just realized I can do the same."

"I have *not* checked out, and you can*not* do the same," he shoots back. "We made love not even two nights ago. What about that?"

I glance away, because I know I can't hide from my face the memory of how it felt to be in his arms again. How could I have been so connected to him if there was nothing on the other side? "It didn't mean anything."

His laugh is cruel. "You don't fool me for a second. You think you could ever fake that with me? You think I don't know when your heart is wide open?"

"I think you *do* know when my heart is open," I say evenly. "And you know exactly how and where I'm vulnerable."

He shuts his mouth as the meaning behind my words sets in.

I'm not innocent, but this marriage is dead because of him. Nathan spent seven years getting me to feel safe with him, and then he turned around and used it against me. He rejected what I tried to give, physically and emotionally. Hurting me that way is worse than sleeping in another man's bed. "I'm done with this. With you." I take a few steps toward him. "Whatever I did to you, I hope it was worth our marriage."

His eyes change as his frustration vanishes. He draws his head back. "Done?"

I hold his gaze. I hold my tremble inside. I hold my ground. He doesn't get to see weak anymore. "Yes."

"No."

"Yes." He's frozen to the spot, so I go around him into the living room.

"Wait," he says, turning with me. "We need to back up a second so I can explain."

I scoff, packing up the table linens. "Sorry, you're about two-and-a-half months too late. An explanation might've helped a week ago—or even yesterday morning. You could've called me last night while I sat here alone, waiting. But I guess you were too busy in *Brooklyn* to think of that."

"I didn't go to Brooklyn. Well, I did, but not—"

I shake my head, focusing on my task. *Brooklyn* stings, as if he's talking about his mistress. "Of course you did."

He takes a placemat out of my hand and throws it on the ground. "Would you listen to me?"

I cross my arms and turn, but I can't look at him.

"I got on the L after work," he says, "but my head was all over the place. I was still mad, but being with you again felt so fucking good. I was confused about how I felt. So I stayed on the L longer than I should've, because I needed to sort it out before I faced you."

"And you decided to get off at Bedford and bowl instead."

"No, actually. After a half hour riding the subway the wrong way, I switched trains to come home, but as soon as I got on, there was an accident on the tracks. We were stuck for three hours, babe. I couldn't call because I was underground with no service."

I turn my head to the table. The L train is notorious for service interruptions, so I don't question his story. I'm just not sure why it matters at this point.

"What is all this?" he asks gesturing around us. "The flowers? Candles?"

My jaw tingles. The feeling of having my hopes crushed remains as strong as it was last night. "You were right," I say. "The other night meant a lot to me. I took work off yesterday to make you ribs and clean the apartment. I had it in my mind that we would finally talk. Figure this out."

He frowns, his eyebrows furrowing. "You didn't tell me."

"It was a surprise."

He looks around. "I would've come straight home."

"But you didn't." I uncross my arms and look up at him. "You knew how much it meant to me to have you back in bed. You said it yourself—I was open. On cloud nine. And you let me down again."

He opens his mouth, but his protests seem to die on his tongue. He looks around. "You're right. I'm sorry."

"It's okay." I swallow the lump in my throat before I continue. "Maybe it's for the best. It helped make some things clear to me."

I don't elaborate, because I see the wheels turning in his head, and I think wondering might be worse for him. After a few moments, he says, "I didn't do all this to hurt you. I'm hurting too. I've been so confused, and, yeah—I haven't dealt with it well."

"You think? You shut me out completely. You know how hard it was for me to let myself love you. I didn't want to end up in a shitty marriage like my parents, angry and resentful. And that's exactly where we are, but the worst part is that I don't even know why."

He swallows, his lips tight. "It just . . . got out of control."

"I don't care anymore. You can shove your excuses." I show him my palms. I've made my choice, and going down this path will only make it harder to tell him that. "You had plenty of chances to talk to me, and you didn't. At this point, I'm more exhausted than curious, and I just want to be done with you."

He grabs a fistful of his hair, and I don't even think he realizes he does it. "You don't mean that."

"I've had a long night. I'm going to take a shower, call in sick, and go to bed. You should go. I don't care where. Later, though, we need to talk about what we're going to do."

"Sadie—"

I turn and walk toward the bedroom.

"Sadie, wait," he says. "I know about the baby."

I stop. The baby? But there was no baby, and it's impossible that he knows about the abortion. My brother is the only one I've told the entire truth, and he wouldn't betray me. I turn back to face him. "What?"

"I know you had an abortion," he says calmly. "And I know the baby was ours."

THIRTY-THREE

My heart thuds at the base of my throat. When I had the abortion, I promised myself I'd tell Nathan. Maybe not that day, or even that year, but if our relationship made it, *one day* I'd work up the courage. Yet here we are, seven years later. I never thought he'd figure it out on his own—or that I wouldn't be there to explain it when found out. "That's what these past few months were about?"

"Yes," he says, "and no."

It makes me sad I wasn't there when he learned the truth. I understand why it would upset him, but couldn't he have come to me sooner? "You should've told me you knew."

"And you should've told me it happened."

I glance at the ground. He has a point. I kept this from him much longer than he shut me out. "I was scared of how you'd react."

"You've made huge decisions—and not just this one—without me. You don't get to pick and choose what I know. That's not a partnership."

"How'd you find out?"

"By accident. I was using your computer to research abortion clinics for one of the girls at the shelter. Around the time we went back on birth control, you'd done some searches about abortions—like whether or not having one could affect future pregnancy."

I nod. That night, I'd read probably ten articles on the subject. "I was worried that was the reason we couldn't get pregnant."

"There's no link between the two," he says. "I read the research."

I curl my toes into the carpet. Maybe not, unless that's just how life works. "But what made you think it was yours?"

"I remembered a conversation I'd overheard a couple years ago at Bell's birthday party," he says. "You and Andrew were watching Bell play in the backyard with some other kids. I was bringing you a slice of cake when you said to Andrew, 'Isn't it weird? They would've been the same age. Imagine them here together today.'"

I close my eyes, remembering the moment exactly. Nathan had come up behind me, and I'd worried he'd heard something. It was so long ago, though, and he never mentioned it.

"Andrew told you not to think like that," Nathan continues. "I didn't understand, but I never forgot that. When I saw that search, I put the pieces together. Bell was born over a year after our first date. Then there was that week, after we'd only been together a few months, when you shut me out completely. You disappeared off the face of the planet. I thought it was over. I beat myself up trying to figure out what I'd done. I was scared you'd met someone else. And then one day, you came back to me in tears and wouldn't tell me what you'd been through. I was too happy to push you to talk, afraid you'd disappear again." He scrubs his hands over his face, through his hair. "That's why you left, isn't it? You had an abortion. By yourself."

I wasn't by myself, though. My brother had taken me. We'd sat in the freezing-cold waiting room, looking at magazines without turning the pages. That's the kind of family we are—Andrew being there was enough. I didn't need him to hold my hand or assure me I was doing the right thing.

"It might sound selfish, but I did it for us," I tell him. "If you'd known I was pregnant, you would've done the right thing no matter how you felt about me."

"What would I have done?" he asks, raising his chin.

"We were young. And new. We'd only been together three months, but we had something special. I needed to know you were with me because you

445

loved me, not because you felt obligated to stay by my side. I refused to trap you."

"But you're not your mom, Sadie, and I'm not your dad. You can't just decide these things without me."

I study him. We've worked so hard not to become our parents, and yet, we've ended up like them. My parents are miserable together. His stopped talking to each other and grew apart. "If you'd come to me as soon as you'd found out, I would've told you what I'm telling you now, and the last few months could've been avoided. I don't regret what I did, and we're stronger because I made that difficult decision for us."

He shakes his head, frowning. "You're not understanding me. I'm not mad that you did it. I'm mad that you cut me out of the decision and did it alone. That you didn't trust me enough then, or the past seven years, to let me help you. To be a part of this marriage. And once I realized you were capable of that, everything else you did felt personal."

"Like what?"

"I love making you happy—you know I do. But when I found this out, I started to think of all the ways I've put you first only to have it not reciprocated. I turned down a promotion at work to be able to spend more time with you—"

"No," I interrupt. "You did that to be around for your dad."

"I did it for you," he says. "It meant more hours at the office. More workload. But when Amelia offered you a promotion months later, you took it the same day. You never even consulted me."

I wrinkle my eyebrows. "Are you kidding me? *That's* why you've made me feel like a stranger in my own home for three months?"

"All that shit piled up. You don't even know my favorite pastry—Gisele has to tell you. I try for months to get you to come to my bowling games, and then you turn around and accuse me of not inviting you. You only listen when someone else tells you about a new restaurant or bar. I talk about Park Slope all the time, but it isn't until Donna mentions it that you suddenly consider it the place to be. Then you go and make life-changing decisions without me, and it makes me wonder—would you even fucking notice if I weren't around?"

My mouth hangs open. "That's so unfair," I say. *Pastries? Brooklyn?* I can't believe those are the things coming between us. Maybe all of what he says is true, but he had plenty of chances to call me out. Instead, he let it fester, and then, he abandoned me. "Those are stupid reasons to end a marriage over."

He points at me. "And that is exactly why I haven't brought them up sooner. Do you know dumb I felt getting upset over a goddamn donut? But it's what's underneath it. Is it that you don't care enough to remember what I like? That's what's going on in my mind."

447

"But I tried so many times to get you to talk. To figure this out. Any one of those times you could've told me all this was bothering you. Instead, you shut me out, and you went too far, Nathan. I might not've been as attentive as you wanted, but this is who I was when you married me. You, on the other hand, did a complete one-eighty and left me out in the cold."

"Because I was confused and hurt."

"But at least *I* didn't hurt you on purpose." A sudden storm of emotion moves up my chest, and I need to get away from him. I've been too vulnerable for too long. He abused that, and he doesn't deserve it anymore. "You didn't love me in the dark like you promised."

His eyes widen, clearly taken aback at having the vow he wrote for me thrown in his face. *I will love you the same in the dark as I do in the light.* "Love? I never stopped loving you for a second. I hurt *because* I love you."

"That's not how it's supposed to be." I pick up the vase of calla lilies and hold it out to him. "I got these for you because *I* love. Because *I* care. Because I know they're your favorite. I made you barbeque ribs, and I dressed up how you like. I'm not a stranger. I'm your wife."

My hands shake, so he takes the vase but says, "These aren't my favorite."

"Yes they are."

"They're yours," he says. "And that's why I love them."

I frown, unexpectedly flooded by the memory of the first night we met, sitting on the beach under the stars. He asked about all my favorite things—flowers, books, cities. And to this day, he remembers them. Did I ask about his? I can't remember. "I didn't know that," I say. "So I guess it means I don't love you as much as you love me. You don't like the kind of wife I am? Then go."

"That's not what—"

I turn around and head for the bedroom.

"We're not finished," he says.

"I am. I've had a long night, and I want to be alone." I slam our bedroom door behind me, but he opens it, so I go into the bathroom, but he follows me in there too. I spin around, unbuttoning my pants. "You're no longer welcome in here. Get out."

"No." Still holding the vase, he puts it on the counter. Ginger pushes between us as if to mediate, looking from Nathan to me and back. "I made some mistakes, but so have you. I'm willing to overlook the other decisions you've made without me, but not this one. This time, I won't let you be selfish."

"I don't know what you want me to do. It's done. There's no going back." Cornered, I get into the shower fully clothed and pull the curtain shut.

He whips it back open. "I'm not talking about the abortion."

I pause to put my hand against the tile. At first, I think I've misheard him. A decision I made for us that isn't the abortion? What else could it be? But

449

then, I remember our pact. We're supposed to come to each other if we're ever tempted to cheat.

He knows about Finn. But how?

Finn and I were careless. New York isn't as big as people think. It could've been anywhere. The laundry room. Times Square. Jill might've said something to him on the phone last night.

But what makes me sick to my stomach isn't that he knows. It's that I can't tell if he's upset that I did it, or that I didn't honor our pact by telling him first. Because the least painful part of an affair is the tumble and tangle of body parts. The agony is in the guts. In the reasons behind it. When I let Finn close, I didn't choose him over Nathan—I chose myself.

I look up into his eyes. They're unguarded, even after all this. "How long have you known?"

"About what?"

"Finn."

He tilts his head and draws his eyebrows together. "Finn? Our neighbor?" In the same second that he straightens his back, I understand. Nathan doesn't know about the affair. But he isn't stupid, and by just hearing Finn's name, he figures it out. He retreats a few steps from me, shaking his head. "No."

My heart pounds as I watch the realization dawn on his face. "Nathan—"

His mouth eases apart, then cracks open as his chocolate-brown eyes dart over my face. "*Finn?*" he asks, as if he's never heard the word.

This is one of the first times in my life I can't guess his reaction. I see the tension cording his arms, but his expression is cycling through confusion, anger, despair.

"You've been . . . with . . . how long has this been going on?" he asks, gulping. "Wait. Don't tell me." He looks at the toilet paper roll, the wastebasket, the sea spray-scented hand wash. "When he took your photograph."

I wring my hands together. "Yes." I inhale. "We didn't plan—"

"When was that? *Two weeks* after he got here?" He flares his nostrils like a dragon about to spew fire. "I guess it could be worse. You could've done it on move-in day." As he stares at me, silent, a flush rises from under the collar of his t-shirt, up his neck and cheeks. "Is that where you were last night?"

Guilt I thought I couldn't feel creeps in. I can't find the right words. I don't think they exist. Even though I chose Finn last night, Nathan's obvious agony feels like a knife between my ribs. I would've had to tell him about Finn—and soon. But this isn't how I wanted him to find out. All I can do is nod.

"So you were *with* him. And then you came back here."

"Nothing happened last night," I say as if it's any kind of defense. "We didn't . . ."

His chest heaves with each breath. "I don't understand. If you didn't sleep with him, are you having an affair or not?"

"Yes, but—last night, it didn't feel right while . . ." I cover my face. "I can't explain it. You wouldn't understand. It's not just about the sex—"

"Oh," he scoffs. "No. Don't fucking tell me that."

"I was lost, Nathan. Confused. Lonely. You weren't here, and he was." I lower my hands. "I turned to him. I cried on his shoulder—over *you*, and he let me. So now . . ."

He grits his teeth, his jaw tensing, as though he's containing an explosion. "Now? Now *what*?"

It's difficult to get the words out. My decision to be with Finn is still so new. But I have to say it. I owe Nathan the truth if I expect it in return. "You know this is over," I say, tears finally flooding my eyes. My love for him isn't supposed to hurt this much. It feels like it's killing me from the inside, and it's starting with my heart in a blender. I never wanted anything or anyone other than him, but he withdrew his love to hurt me, and for what? For me, his reasons are valid, but they don't excuse his behavior. This is where we are, and it doesn't have to be this way. I have someone else now. "It's too hard."

"*Marriage* is hard."

"Don't tell me what marriage is," I say, raising my voice, disgusted. Ginger whines, nudging Nathan's leg. "You *abandoned* me."

"And you fucked someone else."

I reel back. "No. I care about him."

"So you're going to, what, walk away? For *him*? Someone you've known less than a month?"

I shake my head. "I'm sorry you had to find out like this. I was going to tell you later. But when you said you were mad about something other than the abortion, I thought you were talking about Finn."

"*Finn*?" he asks, the name slicing from his mouth. His nostrils flare, his face beet red. "You thought you could sit me down, tell me you're having an affair, and I'd just accept it?"

"No," I admit. "I figured you'd be—"

"What?" he asks. "Angry? *Furious*?" He grabs the vase. "You didn't think maybe it'd go something more like *this*?" He launches the lilies across the bathroom. The glass shatters against the wall like a crystal firework, my eardrums bursting, my hand flying over my mouth.

I'm stunned completely still, as if he threw it right at me, but Ginger panics. She takes off, skidding around the tile floor, startled.

I jump out of the shower. "*Nathan*—"

He's already after her, but she bolts for the door and slides right through glass. Shards fly from under her paws. Nathan curses, chasing her out of the bathroom. I follow, hopscotching through the mess, driven forward by her howling.

In the bedroom, Nathan has his arms around her as he tries to wrestle her onto her back.

Blood is smeared everywhere. It's so striking against the white carpet that I start to cry. I pull it together and catch one of her flailing legs for a better look, but she wriggles harder.

"Get back," Nathan says to me. "I've got it."

"No, you don't. There might be glass in there. She's bleeding a lot—"

"I can fucking see that," he snaps. "I have it. Just back off."

I straighten up and touch my trembling hands to my mouth. The fear in her eyes racks me with guilt.

"Shh, Ginge," he says, coaxing her onto her side. Her eyes dart all around the room, as if she can't see us. "Get out of the room," he says without turning to me. "She can't focus. You're making it worse."

I take a step back, more from shock than anything. To be shoved out like this when Ginger needs me breaks my heart. Nate buries his nose in Ginger's furry neck, and after a few seconds, her whines soften.

When they're both calmer, I say, "Nate—"

"Shh. It's okay," he says softly. "I just need to see your paw. Be a good girl."

She's shaking, and I just want to take her in my arms. We can help her better together, me holding her while he checks for glass. "Nathan," I try again, "Let me—"

Ginger's head shoots up, and she starts to writhe out of Nathan's grip.

"God *damn* it, Sadie," he says. "I need her calm enough to get her to the vet."

"How?"

"I'll carry her if I have to. It's not far."

"It's ten blocks," I say incredulously. "You need—"

"I don't need. Not anything. The vet won't be open yet, so call the emergency line, tell him we're coming, and stay out of the way. We don't need you."

The rock in my throat is so big, it hurts when I swallow. In a daze, I leave the bedroom, but I don't know where I'm going. *Call the vet.* I go to my purse. My phone isn't there, and I can't remember where I left it. I get Nathan's from the coffee table. From a list we keep stored in the desk, I find the phone number and let them know we're on the way.

Nathan comes out of the bedroom with Ginger in his arms. "Get the door."

"I'm coming with you."

"No. I can't deal with both of you right now."

"Nathan—"

"Christ, Sadie. I have to get a sixty-pound dog downstairs and into a cab. Can we argue later?"

Fuming, but more worried about Ginger than anything else, I walk over and open the door for him.

"Phone? Keys?" he asks on his way out.

I slide his cell into his jeans, which he somehow managed to get on while subduing her, and then his keys and wallet. "Will you call me when you know?" I ask.

He's already halfway down the hall, and I have to fight the urge to go after them. My heart aches for Ginger. For Nathan. I know he's hurt, and though my

455

instinct is to make it better, I'm not sure if I should. Or, at this point, if I even can.

I get to work early, but Howie's already in his seat next to mine, half hidden by his noise-canceling headphones. "Good look," he says sardonically and with hardly a glance.

Any other day, I'd laugh. He's right to call me out. After Nathan left with Ginger, I cleaned up the mess in the bathroom, showered, and packed a bag. My mind spun as I dressed blindly and slicked my wet hair into a bun. I don't have any meetings today, so I find it hard to care.

Opening Outlook, I start mindlessly e-mailing clients their blog features from the week before. I copy, paste, copy, paste, copy, paste until there's enough to prove I did my job—last week, at least. I should be excited that an Instagram celebrity posted a picture using IncrediBlast mascara over the weekend. Instead, I catch myself wondering whom she's getting ready for. Is she married, and if so, does she flaunt her husband like her lashes? Or did she go out with friends, teasing boys, sipping martinis? Ten minutes of scrolling through her Instagram feed, and I'm more caught up on her life than I want to be.

At a quarter to eleven, Amelia arrives from a breakfast meeting. I'm the only one unfocused enough to notice her breeze in. We're all on our second and third cups of coffee. With a once-over, Amelia nods me into her office.

Without needing to be told, I close the door to give us privacy. I've done something wrong—I just don't know what. Maybe it was simply being the first person to make eye contact with her.

"What's this?" She drapes her red, check-plaid cape and cashmere scarf over a brass coat rack.

I shift feet. "What's what?"

"Outfit. Hair." She sits on the edge of her desk. "Are you even wearing makeup? Not acceptable for this office, Sadie."

I could argue that I don't work any harder in cosmetics than I do out of them, but this is the job I signed up for. This morning, I wrote a blurb for US Weekly about a pop star who stays camera-ready by carrying lip-pumping gloss in her cleavage. "I'll visit the closet," I say, referring to a small room with emergency designer apparel and sample beauty products.

"Please do," she says. "I'd have almost preferred you'd called in sick again. Will this thing with your husband affect your work today like it has your appearance?"

I hesitate, which is a mistake.

"I recognize this. I was this," she says, wiggling a finger up and down my outfit. "The day his affair finally hit me over the head, I fell apart too, but I did it in private. Image is everything in this industry."

"I understand. I'll go change. It won't affect my work." I go for the door.

"Wait."

I turn back. "Yes?"

She looks closely at me. Despite her bluntness, I know she cares. "I hope you did the right thing and kicked him to the curb."

I let my eyes fall. Why, when I was planning to leave Nathan, does it feel like *I* was kicked to the curb?

"Don't look at the floor, Sadie. Be strong. Excuse his behavior, and he'll do it again, believe me. Cheaters are selfish. Egoists. You give him another chance, and he'll walk all over you the rest of the marriage."

I should stop her, but I'm not sure I don't deserve to hear the truth about Finn and me.

And Amelia is more than happy to be the messenger. "Do yourselves both a favor and pack your bags. Trust me. He'll beg—it didn't mean anything. He loves you, not her. Well, the son-of-a-bitch should've considered that when he had her on her back in *my* bed."

"It was only a couple times," I say defensively.

"So what if it was one time or a hundred? So what if they were strangers or if they shared their deepest, darkest secrets with each other? He made a fool of you. He betrayed you on the most basic level."

It's hard to swallow her words. She's never held much back, but I think finding a common enemy has made her more candid. How could she know I'm the one she's railing against?

"That's the worst part, isn't it? The lies? The sneaking around?" I ask, and I genuinely want to know. I want to try and understand Nathan. Why he feels I don't need him. How my excluding him from decisions made him feel left out of our marriage.

She flaps her lips with a *pfft*. "People always say that. The worst part is that he put his dick in another person."

Amelia paints a vivid picture. If the tables were turned, and Nathan had been inside someone else, I think I'd tear my hair out trying to get the image out of my mind. "I think I'm going to be sick."

"I can tell," Amelia says, happy to get in a jab whenever she can. "Now's the time to lean on your girlfriends. Shit, lean on me if you need. I don't do ice cream, but I'll kill a bottle of Glenlivet with you." She crosses her arms. "Whatever it takes, do it. Staying together never turns out well."

Because it's cold outside, the heater is turned up too high. I play with the collar of my sweater. I think of Finn, who's made the decision to leave Kendra. Then, of my brother, who's a single dad. Lastly, I remember all the times my parents brought the house down with their bickering, and how I wished they'd do whatever it took to make it stop, including divorce.

But is that Nathan and me? I thought we were the opposite of all that. I thought we were perfect. If

459

Nathan hadn't forced me to the edge without anywhere to turn, if I didn't have Finn waiting in the wings, I don't think our marriage ever would've ended. "I don't know if I believe that. There must be some couples who make it through infidelity."

She doesn't look surprised. "You think?" she asks, checking her nails.

"Maybe something like this can make a relationship stronger. I'm not saying it can ever be considered a good thing, but years down the line, if we're better off . . ."

She waits for me to continue. "What? You'll be grateful?"

"More like it'll bind us in an unbreakable way."

"I guess that could happen," she says. "Or—the next time life gets rough, he cheats again. And then what?"

"Well," I rub my palms over my hips, "it wouldn't. He wouldn't do it again."

She laughs, but there's nothing about the noise she makes that sounds happy. "That makes sense. You ride off into the sunset, never again to nag him about an unemptied dishwasher or spending too much time with his friends. Beautiful women never deign to tempt him again." Amelia waves a dismissive hand, her eyes glinting with delight. "Let his mistress deal with him. She'll be sorry soon enough."

"Is Reggie dating the woman he cheated with?"

"Of course not!" Amelia throws back her head and howls. "Two weeks in, the bastard was back on my doorstep. She probably refused to clean his shit-stained underwear. Why should she? She didn't love him. I'm better off."

She's better off. Is Reggie? Nathan won't have any problem meeting another woman, and I'll have Finn. We'll all be better off—won't we? I don't know if it's fair that picturing Nathan with someone else, with a whole new family, makes me physically ill.

"Sadie, if you hear nothing else, hear this. A man like that will never love you more than he loves himself. If he does—if he truly loves you—he'll understand that, and he'll let you go."

Her words lay heavy on my heart. Nathan has used the word *selfish* more than once over the past few weeks. Up until recently, I soaked up his adoration without apology. He liked it that way, though. Wherever we were in life, he always made me feel special, and to have him turn around and call me selfish for that hurts. But if that's what he wants—my selflessness—maybe walking away is the way to give that to him. I'm not going to change anytime soon, and Nathan is unhappy with me. Amelia might be right. My decision to leave Nathan may just be best for all of us.

THIRTY-FOUR

When the door to Andrew's house opens, I have to drop my gaze about three feet, because it isn't my brother behind it. My niece, Bell, is undoubtedly a Beckwith, with purple-blue eyes and dark hair like Andrew and me.

"Aunt Sadie," she screeches at a pitch that sends Andrew sprinting from the kitchen.

"What'd I tell you about answering the front door at night?" Andrew asks her, hitching up his sagging sweatpants.

Bell shrugs up at me. "That if I didn't recognize the person, I should kick their—"

"All right," he cuts her off, palming her small head like it's a basketball. He raises his eyebrows at me. "What're you doing here?"

I drop my duffel bag at my feet. "I needed a place to stay for the night."

"You know Nate's looking for you?"

I sigh. I haven't spoken to him since he walked out the door with Ginger, although I did call the vet before I left work. Apparently Ginger is sedated at home. "No, I didn't. I couldn't find my phone this morning. It's somewhere in the apartment."

"Let me get that for you, aunt Sadie," Bell says, grabbing my bag by its strap. It's half her size, so she drags it over the doorway.

"Did your daddy teach you such good manners?" I ask, suppressing a smile.

"No. He says you aren't a guest—you're just family. I disagree, though."

"I see." I purse my lips at Andrew. "*Just* family?"

"Sellout," he mutters.

I saw Andrew over Halloween when I took Bell trick-or-treating. So much has happened since then, though. We're not a hugging family, but I go right to him.

He opens his arms automatically. "What's wrong, Satan?"

I laugh into his chest. Andrew has always had my back, even as kids, but sometimes, he just didn't like me. Like when I spied on him and his friends. Or when I warned his high school girlfriend he was going to dump her. Instead of Sadie, those times I became Satan, his evil sister.

I pull back and look up at him. With his high cheekbones, and slicked black hair, he's a spitting image of our grandfather. He died when I was young, but since our dad wasn't much of a role model, Andrew idolized Grandpa Beckwith.

Bell sings a string of *la-las* as she drags my duffel into the guest room. "We'll talk later," I say, nodding in her direction.

He shuts the door behind me. "You hungry? I just finished dinner. Spicy kale omelets."

I unbutton my coat and follow him through the house. Against the odds, my brother has done well for himself. He skipped college to work for minimum wage at White Castle and was soon managing multiple locations in the northeast. He spent his nights learning to fix cars and restore classics from our grandfather's friend, who then retired and sold Andrew his garage.

Bell skids in behind us, scrambling onto a barstool that looks too high for her. According to Andrew, she's number one in her gymnastics class— even though I'm pretty sure the children aren't ranked. "On Thursdays, we have breakfast for dinner," she explains. "Because there are no rules."

"There are *some* rules," I say, shooting a warning glance at Andrew, "aren't there?"

Andrew shrugs. He isn't a typical father by any means, but he's the best one I know. When Bell's mom up and left them a few years ago, Nathan and I came for a weekend. Nathan took Bell everywhere he could think of to distract a three-year-old. Andrew and I stayed at the house, where I locked him inside and taught him how to cook, launder, make a bed, and clean. He was a fast learner, but he didn't have much of a choice.

I eat the eggs and groan. "You've come a long way, grasshopper. What's in this?"

He grins his signature, lady-killer smile. "And the teacher becomes the student."

I toss a crispy breakfast potato at him. He pops it in his mouth. "I'm still light years ahead of you," I say defensively. I take another bite. "I think."

"Aunt Sadie," Bell says. "I know all the words to the Rolling Stones."

I raise my eyebrows at Andrew. "Seriously? That's what you make her listen to?"

"She loves it. Don't you, Bluebell?"

She looks stressed. "I try to listen to what my friends like," she says seriously, "but when I do, I can't get no satisfaction."

Andrew and I laugh. She fights a giggle, but one corner of her mouth tugs. Andrew probably told her it wasn't cool to laugh at her own jokes. Sounds like something he'd say.

After dinner, I help Bell with her homework while Andrew washes dishes. "I'm going to call Nathan," he says, drying his hands. "I know he's worried. You want to talk to him?"

I scratch my temple. I'm not sure what there is to say over the phone. Nathan must be even more tired than I am considering he didn't sleep last night. And there'll be plenty of time to fight when I get back. "No. Just ask him how Ginger's doing."

Bell's head shoots up, but before she can ask, Andrew does. "What happened to Ginge?"

I pet Bell's silky hair and look at Andrew over her head. "Nothing. She's fine."

He raises his eyebrows as if to ask what the hell's going on, but there's no way I'm getting into it with my baby Bell in the room. She's made of innocence, and as far as Andrew and I are concerned, she'll stay that way forever.

He disappears from the kitchen but after a minute, he's back. "Sadie." I look up. He's holding out his cell. "For you."

I kiss Bell on the top of the head, get up, and take the call on the back patio. I wander into the yard, where the dead grass sticks to my socks. I barely notice. "Hi," I say into the phone.

"He can't have you."

My heart stops, and I stare out into the dark as Nathan's words sink in. "What?"

"I said," he pauses, "he . . . can't . . . have you."

"Nathan, this isn't a contest. It's complicated."

"It's simple, actually." Though there's determination in his voice, there isn't an ounce of the anger I expected to hear. "I will climb the highest mountain. I will run the fastest mile. I will carry the world on my shoulders." He takes a breath. "You think I'd sit back and let someone take you from me? I've made mistakes, but I will not let you out of this marriage for anything. I'll fight for us, and you will too, even if I have to make you."

467

I close my eyes and swallow down the lump in my throat. For so long, I wished for him to come back to me. I wandered the desert, searching for water—first on my feet, then, when I got weak, on my hands and knees. But it was someone else who gave me a drink. I got what I needed from Finn. "I'm sorry," I say quietly. "If you knew what it was like—"

"I *do* know. I've been sick with worry," he says. "I'd come get you, but Ginger needs me here."

"How is she?"

"Fine. Apparently dogs' paws have capillaries close to the surface. They bleed a lot. But the cuts aren't as bad as they looked."

"That's good," I say.

"She's sedated." He clears his throat. "I was trying to reach you."

"I left my phone there."

"I thought you were with him. I was over there for half an hour banging on his door, but the coward wouldn't open it."

I look at my socks, black shadows in the grass. It hadn't occurred to me Nathan might go looking for me. I don't even want to wonder what would've happened if he and Finn had come face to face.

"I'm not with him," I say. "But so what if I was? I'm leaving, Nate. I'm giving you what you wanted."

"You think this is what I want, Sadie? You couldn't be more wrong." He speaks frankly, as if there's no arguing with the facts. "I've had a lot of time alone today to think, and I'm sorry things got

468

this far. I didn't do a good job explaining myself. But that doesn't mean I'm ready to let you go. I fucked up, but I have a long time to make it up to you, and I will."

His words tug at my heart. Does he truly mean it, though? I can't know for sure if I'm talking to my Nathan, or the impostor I've been living with recently. "It isn't that black and white."

"Sure it is. Go be with Bell. Kiss her for me. But tomorrow, first thing, come home. Ginger and I will be waiting." He hangs up.

I lower the phone and breathe in the cold night air. My heart and my head war, but the worst part is, neither even knows which side its on. One second, my heart craves Finn's warmth, his safe embrace, while my head tells me he'll never be what Nathan is. The next, I'm thinking of all the reasons to walk away from Nathan, who hurt me on purpose, while in my depths I know—my heart beats for him.

I go back inside just as Andrew is trying, unsuccessfully, to get Bell into bed. "Come on, kid. It's a school night."

"But Aunt Sadie is here," she cries. "It's a special occasion!"

I stand in the doorway, watching them. Bell could be enough for me, couldn't she? I love her like my own daughter. I don't have to put myself through the agony each month of not being able to conceive. With Nathan, it would be a battle. He wouldn't go down easy. With Finn, though, we'd have Marissa,

469

and to him, that's enough. I ache for my own Bell or Marissa, but not everyone gets what they want. And I'm the closest thing Bell has to a mom. Shana abandoned her, and when Bell's old enough to understand that, Bell will need me more than ever.

I take over for Andrew and read Bell a story. By the time I finish, she isn't asleep, but at least she's no longer yelling. I close her door and meet Andrew in the kitchen, taking a barstool at the island as he pours me red wine. The fact that my bad-boy brother owns wineglasses makes me strangely proud.

"So what really happened to Ginger?" he asks, sliding the drink across the island.

"A casualty of Nathan's and my epic fight this morning," I say. "She cut herself on some glass, and Nate rushed her to the vet."

He raises his eyebrows, pouring himself bourbon. "You and Nate fight epically? Since when?"

I look into my glass, no idea where to begin. How to even start. Andrew and Nathan are close, and Andrew doesn't get close to anyone. They've been brothers for years now. I don't want to take that away from him any more than I want to confess what I've done.

"When was the last time you saw Nathan?" I ask.

"A couple months ago." He cocks his head. "No, wait. July fourth, actually. Has it really been that long?"

I nod, glancing up at him. "Weird, right? He loves coming over here, but the last few times, he's had excuses not to."

Andrew leans his elbows on the island. "I get it. He's busy with work."

"Not too busy for Bell."

He concedes with a nod. "True. He'd drop anything for her. Too busy for you, then?" he guesses.

I shake my head. "We've been having problems, but it isn't because of work."

"Problems? Meaning?"

"He started acting different a few months ago. Almost overnight, he became distant and cold."

Andrew spins his glass on the counter and says what I predict he will. "Cold and distant—that doesn't sound like Nathan."

"I know. I haven't mentioned it, because I kept hoping it would get better. But up until today, he barely spoke to me for months and wouldn't tell me why. Knowing the kind of couple we were, you can imagine how hard it's been for me to be iced out."

"Yeah," he says. "The Nathan I know barely leaves you alone. You know that thing about putting on your own oxygen mask in an airplane before you help the person next to you?"

I nod. "He'd put mine on first. Always."

"Exactly." He sips his drink. "So what happened today?"

"I found out why he's so upset. He knows about the abortion."

471

Andrew freezes everything but his mouth, which drops open. "From seven years ago? How?" His eyes widen. "*I* didn't tell him. Who else knows?"

"It's stupid," I say, sighing. "I looked up some stuff about abortions when we decided to stop trying to get pregnant. I think he was out of town that night, and I was drowning my sorrows in wine. I never hide anything from Nate, and I guess it just didn't occur to me to erase my history. I'm not sure I would've, even if I'd thought about it."

"And you told him it was his?"

"He knew. I guess he picked up some clues over the years, but didn't put it together until he saw that."

"Wow." He blows out a breath. "Considering how badly he wants a kid, he must be . . ."

"He actually seems okay about that part," I say thoughtfully. "He was more pissed that I hid it from him this long and that I didn't trust him enough at the time to let him be there for me."

"That's understandable," Andrew says. "But I'm not sure it's enough to give you the silent treatment for so long."

"I know. I think there's more to the story we didn't get to."

"How's that possible? What could've been more important than finding out?"

I drink more wine to bolster my confidence. "You know what Nate means to me. How perfect our marriage was."

"Was . . .?"

With Andrew, it's best to be straight. "I'm leaving him."

He sets down his glass, straightening up. "What're you talking about?"

"It got to be too much, and—" I stop. Confessing the truth about Finn isn't any easier. It might even be harder since Andrew values loyalty above all else. I'm not sure he'll understand.

"So that's it?" He stares at me. "It's just done? That doesn't make sense."

"I just—lost faith in him." I roll my lips together. "He knew how hard it was for me to open my heart to him, and then when I wasn't expecting it, he stomped all over it."

Andrew is quiet a few moments. "It's hard for me to imagine Nathan doing that," he says slowly, "but if that's really how you felt, then I can understand why you'd want to pull back."

We look at each other a long moment. Shana didn't even bother to put his heart through the grinder. She just left it behind without a second thought.

"But," he says, "now that you two know what the problem is, you guys can fix it. Get counseling. Whatever. You're too good together to let a few months shake you."

"We could have if things'd been different. If he'd told me sooner, or if I'd come clean before he found out. But it didn't work out that way, and while Nathan was busy doing everything in his power to stay away from me, someone else was doing the opposite."

Andrew tilts his head. "What do you mean 'someone else'?"

"There's a man—Finn. He moved in across the hall a few weeks ago, and . . . he and I have become close. Really close."

Andrew narrows his eyes. "How close?"

I glance down.

"*Sadie*," he says. "Seriously?"

I pinch the glass stem between my fingers and think of Finn back in his apartment, filling it with furniture for me. Or will he wait, so we can pick it out together? There's no question I'll have to leave everything behind. "We've crossed the line," I admit. "I'm having an affair."

Andrew puts his elbows back on the counter and scrubs his hands over his face. "Jesus Christ," he mutters, then pushes off the island and goes for a bourbon refill. With his back to me, he says, "Please tell me Nathan knows so I don't have to keep this a secret."

"He knows."

He looks over his shoulder. "That's why you're here. He kick you out?"

"The opposite. He wants me to come home."

"Course he does." Andrew returns across the counter from me, his forehead creased. "The guy would take any amount of shit to be with you."

I frown. "I don't know about that. You haven't seen him lately."

"Please," he says wryly and with a scoff. "The way he feels wouldn't change overnight. However pissed he is, however betrayed he feels, his love runs deep, man."

I shift on the stool. "Well, he hasn't been acting that way, and I've had enough. He made me feel like real shit, Andrew. Imagine how lonely I must've been to turn to someone else."

"That's no excuse." He looks down at his drink, torn. He's loyal, but he's also fair. "You know it's not. How did it happen?"

"To be honest, I don't even know." I swallow and put my hands in my lap. How did the affair start? It was as if I stumbled on a pebble and slipped down the side of a cliff. "It's not like I went looking for it. He made me laugh when I was sad. We got to talking, and then it just . . . happened." I pause. "It's okay if you want to take Nate's side."

"I don't want to take any sides," he says, looking thoughtful as he takes a sip. "I'm just trying to understand it from both perspectives."

I scratch my neck. Conveying my struggle in one conversation feels impossible, and I'm not sure I'm doing a good job. "Do you think I'm being selfish?" I ask. "Or that I'm a bad person?"

Andrew lifts one corner of his mouth. "You mean like Satan? I'm still deciding . . ."

I roll my eyes. I'd punch him in the arm, but he's too far away. Even though he's smiling, I see the darkness in his eyes that was often there after Shana left. "I'm sorry if this brings up old stuff."

He runs his tongue along his upper teeth. "I was just thinking about how far I've come since then. I was so angry with her for the longest time, but now . . . I'm not sure how I feel."

I study my brother. Watching him struggle wasn't easy. He's always been strong, and he's had more than one opportunity to follow in my dad's footsteps and drown his emotions in alcohol.

"I can still be angry with her, right?" I ask.

He laughs. "It took me years to figure this out, but Shana probably did the right thing. We weren't planning to get pregnant, and she wasn't happy being a mom. At the time, I told her that didn't matter— she'd gotten knocked up, and we had to grow up and deal with it. But remember how much Shana and I fought? I don't want Bell to grow up like—"

"Us?" I finish. It makes sense. He's always been a protector. When our parents fought, before Andrew was old enough to drive off, he'd distract me. He'd become a one-man zoo, mimicking animal noises. When he got desperate, he'd cover my ears and make funny faces at me until it was over. I haven't needed my big brother in a while, but I realize, maybe that's why I'm here.

He sighs. "If Shana'd stayed and been miserable, Bell would've picked up on that. And my baby's a blessing, not a burden. I'd kill anyone who makes her feel otherwise."

"So you're telling me if Shana walked in the door right now, you'd have nothing to say to her?"

"Enough about me." His mouth slides into a sinister grin, and I know—he'd definitely have some things to say to her. "Listen, you have to be happy to make Nate happy and vice versa, you know? Maybe that means sometimes you're selfish, and sometimes you're the opposite. Got to put on your own mask first."

"You're probably right, but I worry Nate puts himself second too much. And I let him."

"So tell him that."

"He thinks *I'm* selfish or I love him less because I don't know his favorite pastry or the kind of flowers he likes."

"That stuff has never been important to you. But it is to him." He looks me over. "It doesn't mean you haven't been a good wife, though. I see how you take care of him too." He cocks his hip. "When mom says things around Nathan about his job, like that she thinks it's bullshit he serves food to people who 'expect handouts for their bad choices,' you go crazy defending him. Do you think he even cares what mom thinks? No. But you turn into a rabid dog."

I frown. "Okay, but no matter what, I'll never be him. He used to bend over backwards for me on a daily basis. He doesn't forget a single date that's important to me. And when I'm sad, he knows exactly how to cheer me up. It's like he knows what I need before I do."

Andrew rolls his eyes. "Come *on*—Nathan's human. He has flaws too. You know that, right? If anything, these past few months have opened you both up to what's wrong in your relationship, and I think that might be a good thing."

"How could it be? We've been putting each other through hell."

"The man puts you on a fucking pedestal. And you do the same to him. It's about time you knocked each other off, because now you're on the ground where you should be. And that's the foundation you need to build on, not some lofty idea that you can't be happy if you aren't perfect."

"I don't think that," I say defensively.

"Yeah, you do, and I get it. You don't want to be our parents. Neither do I, which is why I work so hard to be the opposite of dad. But just because we fuck up now and then doesn't make us them."

I stare at him. I've always prided myself on my perfect marriage. Nathan knows it too. Have I built him up so much in my head that he thinks he needs to live up to that? Could I ever love Nathan any less because of his flaws? No.

I thumb the faint lipstick stain I've left on the wineglass. "I don't know what to do, Andrew."

"You love him, Sadie."

"So much. I just feel like he took advantage of that, which is something I never thought he'd do. It makes me wonder how much he's changed."

Andrew reaches across the island for my hand. Once, that would've made him uncomfortable, and he still has a hard time letting people close, but having Bell has made him softer with those he loves. Not that I'd ever say that to his face. "I know it'd be easy to walk away," he says. "It takes more guts to stay. You can fight against him while you fight for him. The marriage will come out stronger."

I inhale a shaky breath. Andrew's been single for three years. What does he know about relationships? More than I realized, maybe. Nathan said he wouldn't let me go. I don't want to be let go. And I don't want perfect if it means he's unhappy. I'd rather have him, damaged and flawed, than anyone else. Andrew's right—it's not easy or pretty, but it's the truth. I'd never forgive myself if I don't fight for him, and living that way wouldn't be fair to Finn. He'd always be in Nathan's shadow.

Andrew winces. "Are you going to cry?"

I laugh a little, and a tear slips out of the corner of my eye, but he has the good sense to ignore it. "No."

"Good." He comes around the counter. "If Bell can hold it in, so can you."

I push him in the chest. "You don't seriously shame her into not crying!"

He grins back at me as we take our drinks into the living room. "I don't even have to. She told me the other day that crying's for boys."

We laugh, and Bell comes sprinting out of her bedroom. There's a picture of Sleeping Beauty plastered on her pink nightgown. I'm grateful that despite her tatted-up, hard-hearted mechanic of a father, she's still as girly as she is. She shouts, "I won't go to bed. I won't. Aunt Sadie is here. I need girl time."

Andrew falls onto the couch with a palm in the air. "Jesus Christ, kid. Fine. Stay up all night and fall asleep on the beam tomorrow. See if I care."

She's already jumping onto the cushion between us. She chatters for a good ten minutes, and I wish Nathan were here. He'd hang on her every word. Bell winds down like a toy, her words slurring and her eyelids drooping. She lays her head in her dad's lap and her feet in mine. In the middle of a story about lecturing the class bully, she passes out.

"How're things here?" I ask, nodding at her. "How's Bell?"

"Perfection. Kicking ass and taking names, as usual."

I expect nothing less from her and no smaller response to that question from him. "School?"

"Her teachers stop me nearly every day to tell me how well she's doing."

Slowly, I raise my eyebrows at him. I don't think Andrew's that dense, but I will gladly point it out. "You don't seriously believe *that's* why they stop you."

He shrugs, settling back into the couch. "They want to talk about how great my girl is, I'm happy to let them."

"They're trying to get your attention, dummy."

He shrugs. "Whatever."

"Don't *whatever* me." That Andrew has permanently removed himself from the market is a disservice to women everywhere. Aside from the whole tall, dark, and handsome thing he's got going on, he's also smart, quick on his feet, and a stellar dad. His business is successful too. He won't hear me, though, and I wish he'd take his own advice, but he's content to live out his days doting over Bell. "You know I'm not giving up. What's the latest girl update?"

"I have a special one in my life."

"Besides Bell. What happened with that date you had last weekend?"

He sighs with exasperation. "For the last time, it wasn't a date. I went over to her house in the middle of the day to look under her hood. That's all."

"And what did you find?" Like Bell, I thin my lips into a taut line to keep from giggling. "Under her hood?"

The corner of his mouth quirks. "A busted carburetor. The thing was ancient. Float valve wasn't shutting off the flow of fuel—"

I wave my hands to stop the assault of words I don't understand and don't care to. "All right, all right. I'll back off. For now."

Andrew looks down on Bell, stroking her hair. "Have you given our conversation over Halloween any more thought?"

"About switching to almond milk?" I quip. He gives me a look that says everything. I know what he wants to hear. "How can I even think about that while my marriage is imploding?"

"Are you kidding? *Now's* the time to think about all this shit. To figure out what you really want, Sadie. What's most important." He pauses to let his words sink in. "You'd be a good mom."

Instinctively, I cross my arms over my stomach. Nathan isn't the only one who wants this for us. Andrew has been pushing me for a while to get deeper into this subject. "You and Shana barely touched, and she got pregnant," I say. "I'm sorry, but you don't know what it's like to feel so empty when you want nothing more than to feel . . . full. And then to be reminded of that monthly. Daily."

"I see. So you're finally admitting you want it again?"

I blink several times. Of course that's what he'd get when I'm trying to explain something else. "I meant before. When we were trying. Now, I'm still unsure I want it at all."

"So, what'd the doctor say? You're definitely infertile?"

I pinch my eyebrows together, my mind running over our last conversation at Halloween. I never said I'd get tested. "What doctor?"

"Exactly," he says, pumping his fist like he just schooled me. "You don't even know what the deal is, and you're flipping out. Listen to me. Step one—find out if there's a problem. Step two—go from there. You can't skip over the first step."

I swallow audibly, feeling warm just at the idea of seeing my gynecologist about this. "It's not that simple."

"How come?"

"Because . . ."

"Because being a pussy is easier?"

I gasp. "*Andrew.*"

He chuckles. "It's true, isn't it? You're scared to find out the results, so you won't go. You're scared to disappoint Nate, so you're going to give up. Just like when we were kids, and you hid under the fucking bed while Mom and Dad fought. It was cute then. Not anymore."

I clamp my mouth shut, sufficiently schooled. Andrew makes it sound so simple, but knowing the truth could change everything—not just my marriage, but my life. Am I ready for that? Could I ever be?

"She's a lot like you were, you know." Andrew admires his daughter. "Sometimes, I look at her and see you. I tried to protect you as long as I could. And when I get scared or worried about her and the

483

future, it comforts me to know how well you turned out. Even if you are a fucking pussy."

I want to be mad at him for forcing me to confront things I'd prefer to keep buried, but I'm not. In the comfort of his home, surrounded by two of the three people I love most in the world, all I can do is laugh along with him.

THIRTY-FIVE

Nathan asked me to come home in the morning, but I don't. I call into work again and stop by my gynecologist for an overdue visit. He tries to turn me away without an appointment, but after talking to Andrew, the truth can't wait. Nathan and I need to have an honest conversation about what we want, and to do that, I have to know if I can even give him a baby. Eventually, Doctor Harris takes pity on me and squeezes me in between patients.

And once I'm finished there, that's when I go home. With my duffel bag slung over my shoulder, I get off the elevator on the sixth floor, stop at Finn's apartment, and hesitate. I can't bring myself to knock. Finn is beautiful, sexy, kind. He's a father, a lover, a real man. He will never be Nathan, though.

I rap my knuckles and wait. Standing in front of 6A isn't the same as it's been the last few weeks.

There's no buzzing in my veins or brimming possibility. Finn comes to the door eventually, in the same manner as always. Hurried, caught off guard. He's sweating, which makes me wonder if the heater broke again. I don't ask. It's not my business.

His gaze drops to my duffel bag, and then he looks at me, his eyes greener than ever and round with excitement. I can't get myself to speak and kill that in him. I hesitate too long.

"Sadie—" His face splits with a grin. He grabs me, pulling me in, pressing me to his warm, damp chest. His heart beats hard, undeniable. He sighs into my hair. "You've made me the happiest man. I was in Connecticut yesterday, but I've been at it all day today, putting furniture together, unpacking boxes."

It's a killer hug, one to obliterate any before it. My body is stiff, though—and my decision solidifies. I might've thought I could love him as second place, but I can't. These aren't Nathan's arms around me. Maybe over time, they'd come close, but that's not enough for me.

Almost imperceptibly, Finn's grip on me loosens. And then he lets go. He draws back and this time, he takes a beat to study my face. His eyes roam, and his lips—the ones I could look at, touch, kiss all day— they droop at the corners.

"Finn—" I start.

"Ah, fuck," he says with a step back. He grabs the hair at his crown in a fist. "Wait. Whatever you're about to say—"

"Don't?" I ask. "That won't make it less true."

"Sadie." He comes back. Takes my shoulders. Puts his face close to mine. "You don't have to stay in a bad marriage. Divorce is scary—trust me, I know. We'll do it together, though. We will be each other's support."

"What are we going to do, Finn? Live here, with Nathan across the hall?"

"We'll go anywhere you want. Rome. Paris. The Lower East Side. I don't care."

"It won't work."

"Come inside." His eyes flicker between the elevator and my apartment door. "Let's talk."

"I'm not going in there."

"Why not?" He gets excited, his veins cording his forearms. "Because you're afraid of what's between us? If we can't be alone together, that means something."

"That's not the reason," I say. My attraction to Finn still lives, but suddenly, my love for Nathan locks over my heart, strong, protective. Finn checks the hallway again. I don't think he even realizes he's doing it. I, on the other hand, don't bother to look. If Nathan comes out now, I'd rather get caught on Finn's doorstep than hide inside his apartment.

"Nathan knows."

He pauses, blinking at me. "What?"

"I told him."

"I—" Finn blows out a breath and leans his hands against the doorframe, gripping it until they're red. "I wish you'd discussed it with me first."

I want to run into my apartment, disappear from this spot, or at the very least, close my eyes against the hurt in his face. I have to face him, though, and I can't leave any room for misinterpretation, because there's no room for him in my heart. "There wasn't anything to discuss," I say. "I wasn't planning on it."

"Why? Did he find something?" He glances at my luggage. "He kicked you out?"

"No."

"You're leaving him?"

"No."

"You're not making sense. Look..." Still looming in the doorway, he drops his head. His hair is my favorite this way, tousled, ungroomed, a bit dirty. He could use a haircut, but if he were mine, I'd ask him to wait a little longer. He raises his eyes and inhales deeply. His body broadens. "I'm not going to beg any more than I already have," he says. "But if he questions you, if he doubts you—*I* don't. I want you in my life. For good." He gestures behind me, around the hallway. "I don't think all this—ending up in the same building when we needed each other most—was a mistake."

It would be easy to give in to him. Not many people would walk away from fate or a man like this. I've made up my mind, though. I don't think I could change it back if I wanted to. "I don't know what'll

488

happen with Nathan," I say. "But I know I can't walk away."

"He's been nothing but awful to you since I've known you."

"It's complicated. If I were to start something with you now, I'd always wonder if I should've fought harder for my marriage."

"I can be patient. You don't have to give me everything today. Just say yes, and it will come."

I shake my head. "How long would you wait?"

He opens his mouth, but stops when he realizes I'm not expecting an answer. There is no answer.

"So is this goodbye?" His grip on the doorframe relaxes. "Or see you later?"

I set my bag down to take off my Burberry coat. "It's goodbye."

"Jesus." He furrows his brows. "Stop. I don't want the coat."

"It makes me feel worse." I hold it out. I realize my hands are trembling. This isn't easy. As cold as I'm being to him, there is a part of me that wants to curl up in his warmth and shut the world out for a few hours. "Please. Take it."

With some hesitation, he accepts the coat. We're close enough that I can see the gooey-honey flecks that lure me into his green eyes. He sighs, frustrated. "Will a grand gesture change your mind?"

I touch my collarbone and glance at the ground. Finn's faith in us is unshakeable. I hope he finds what he's so desperately searching for. We've become unusually close in so little time, and it sometimes feels as though we've actually known each other since those first, brief moments in the coffee shop. He's a friend I'll be sorry to lose. "Any girl would be—"

"Stop," he says. "That kind of bullshit won't help."

"It's not bullshit." I stay quiet until his focus returns to me from whatever he's mulling over. "If things were different, I'd never be able to walk away from you. Not ever. I don't know how I got up from my chair all those years ago and left you there. Maybe it was fate that made me."

He flinches. "Ouch."

"And maybe it's the reason I'm walking away now. When you find the woman who makes you happy—truly happy—you can thank me then."

He glances between my lips and eyes. He looks unconvinced, but I wouldn't have expected anything less. "Do you think I deserve to be happy after everything we've done?"

I don't have to consider it. Finn is a lot of things, and we've both made mistakes, but he's not a bad person. "Absolutely. Without question."

"Then so do you."

I curl my fingers over my chest as my heart skips—but not for Finn. For what's waiting for me in my apartment. For the happiness Nathan and I have ahead of us, happiness we deserve. "I know."

Finn takes my head in his paw-like hands and presses his lips to my forehead. We stay that way for a few seconds. Finally, he says, "I think I love you."

I grit my teeth against the lump growing in my throat. Love can be so impractical and inconvenient. I wouldn't trade it for anything, though, even if it comes from the wrong person. It is possible to fall in love within moments of knowing a person. It happened to me the first day Nathan and I spent together. "Thank you."

He releases me. "If he's ever anything less than perfect to you—"

"I will still love him," I say and mean it. "I'm beginning to see that perfection is overrated."

"Just know that you can always come back to me." He smiles sadly. "Especially if you have a dark chocolate pistachio croissant."

Our smiles are genuine, but they're quick. His familiar soapy smell tugs at my heart. I don't want to live without it, but I can. I will. He lifts his hand and mouths "bye" as he shuts the door.

The apartment is quiet. Ginger's fast asleep on her dog bed in the living room. I don't wake her, but I get on the ground to inspect her bandaged paws. On the kitchen counter, I find a note from Nathan.

2:15 p.m. gave meds/painkillers.

It's after three. Next to it is a bag of things from the vet. I read the label of Ginger's antibiotics. She'll need another dose tonight. Nathan's moved the kitchen table back from the living room, and the salad bowl I knocked over is on the drying rack. I remember my phone was next to it, so I get on my hands and knees and find it under the refrigerator.

It's dead. I go to the bedroom and plug it into a charger. My most recent missed call is from an unknown number twenty minutes ago. I sit on the bed and listen to the voicemail.

"Hello, Mrs. Hunt. I'm calling from New York Presbyterian. We've been trying to get ahold of your husband about his father." I clutch the phone as dread floods me. "Ralph's health is declining quickly, and we're afraid he won't make it through the night. Please give us a call as soon as you can."

I pull the phone way and stare at the screen. My mind goes blank. We've been expecting this, but it seemed like it would never really happen. It feels too soon. The phone is cold from being on the floor. I press it to my forehead and think. Nathan isn't here. Is he already on his way? Where else could he be?

I call and speak to a nurse. "Ralph Hunt?" she repeats when I ask how he's doing. It's quiet except for typing in the background. "Are you a relative?"

"Daughter-in-law."

She makes a thoughtful noise. "You should get here as soon as you can."

"Have you reached his son? My husband?"

"Not yet," she says. "Can you find him?"

492

Nathan told me last night he'd be waiting for me. He could be at work, but I can't envision him sitting at his desk today when both Ginger and I need him. He was here an hour ago. Knowing Nathan is struggling, there's only one other place I can think of that he might be. A place he goes for clarification, answers, and to remind himself of the important things. "I'll get him there," I say.

"Great. Then we'll see you soon."

I check to make sure I have no recent messages from Nathan, but he knows I didn't have my phone. The only ones are from yesterday when he was looking for me.

I try his cell. After the fourth ring, I reach his voicemail. "You have reached the mailbox of six-four-six—"

His phone is on, but there's no reason he'd be out of touch—unless he's where I thought he'd be. The soup kitchen. When he serves food, he always turns his ringer off. I grab my phone with the charger and my purse. Ralph is alone—Nathan is alone. It's my responsibility to bring them together. I run downstairs and into the street, flagging down the first taxi that passes.

"Where to?" the cabbie asks.

"Family-kind soup kitchen on Sixth and Fifteenth."

I don't even have to tell him to hustle, because he slams on the gas pedal. During the drive, I pinch the bridge of my nose and compose myself. Nathan will need me to be his rock. Since Nate's mom moved away, he and his father have gotten much closer. This won't come as a surprise to Nathan, but that won't make it any less difficult.

When we arrive, I tell the driver to wait at the curb. The late afternoon is crisp and gray. There's a line out front of the shelter, mostly young men and women, some with children. Through a window, I spot Nathan behind a banquet wearing an apron and a smile. If he's happy in this moment, I don't want to take that away—we've hurt each other enough recently. I have to dig deep for the strength to break his heart again, but it's there. Out of time, I unearth it as I open the door and go inside.

THIRTY-SIX

Nathan is somehow both commanding and gentle. He cuts turkey like the head of the household, but he smiles at each young woman and child coming down the line of food.

"Nathan," I call out, and people turn to look at me.

He squints at me, setting down his knife. "Sadie?"

"We've been trying to reach you."

He comes around the bank of food and stops in front of me. "Who?"

I need to touch him as I tell him, so I fist the fabric of his apron and pull him a little closer.

A corner of his mouth quirks. "What's going on?"

With a deep breath, I say, "It's your dad."

His face falls. "Why? What happened?"

"Nothing yet." I look him in the eye. "But we need to go."

He stares at me, but he doesn't see me, his gaze distant. "My dad? But we—we need more time."

I shake him by his apron, and he blinks a few times. "Now, Nathan. We need to go now."

He nods slightly and then hard. "Yeah. Okay." He unties the apron and tosses it on a table as we walk through the dining hall. On our way out the door, I reach up to snatch a hairnet off his head, and his static-charged hair stands on end.

He follows me to the cab idling out front. Nathan gestures me inside first, a gentleman, no matter the circumstances. I slide only as far as the middle. "New York Presbyterian."

Nathan gets in beside me. "Go fast. My dad is . . . is . . ." He looks at me.

"He's alive," I say. "They don't know how much longer, though."

He shifts his gaze out the window. I slip my fingers between his, and he turns back to me. With our hands interlocked, he kisses my knuckles. "You're here."

I slide closer to my husband until I'm practically in his lap. I touch his jaw. There's a layer of stubble from the past couple days. "I'm here."

"I had no idea about the affair. If I had, I would've stopped it."

"We don't have to talk about that now."

"I would've done everything differently."

496

I tilt my head, curiosity getting the best of me. "You would've? Like what?"

"I should've come to you when I figured out the abortion. I didn't, because I was afraid of the decision I'd have to make."

"I don't understand," I say. "What decision?"

"You don't want children."

I part my lips and frown. I don't know what I expected him to say, but it wasn't that. I've been struggling with this a while, but I've barely said it aloud. "How do you know?"

He shakes his head. "I've sensed it for some time. Comments here and there. The distance in your eyes when it comes up. And that day we went back on birth control, when you were out of the room, the gynecologist told me not to worry too much. He said a lot of women who have trouble conceiving convince themselves they don't want children."

"I mentioned it to him," I say, glancing at our hands in his lap. There's no right way to tell Nate that because I might not be capable of giving him what he wants, I don't even want to try. "I've been having second thoughts."

"I thought you'd say that. This is what I was talking about in the bathroom. I won't let you selfishly decide something this big without me." We sit in silence for a few blocks. Our palms are clammy from clutching each other. "And that's why I couldn't bring myself to tell you what was wrong these past few months," he continues. "I knew if you told me

497

you didn't want children at all, and I couldn't convince you, I'd have to make the hardest decision of my life."

From the way my chest aches, I know I understand the gravity of his decision. He'll tell anyone I'm the love of his life. But is that enough for him if I don't want to be a mother?

"By making the choices you have in the past without me, I couldn't trust that you'd even count my vote."

I squeeze his hand, not to comfort him, but because I feel like I'm floundering. "I made you feel unwanted."

"Not unwanted—*unnecessary*. And I shouldn't have shut you out, but I wanted to come in to the discussion with a clear head. Not when I was angry or hurt."

"But we're supposed to be able to get hurt and angry together. You didn't let me be there for you for that decision. You've made huge decisions without me too, Nathan."

He swallows. "I see that now. It's okay to be scared. It's not okay to be a coward, and I was, and I'm sorry."

When I see the remorse on his face, I just want to be close to him. I lean in and nuzzle his neck, breathing in his musk. I can feel his fast heartbeat. He's nervous. Or scared. Forgiveness isn't hard to find, because I've wanted to give it for so long. I've wanted to move past this with him. He was the one holding onto things that couldn't be changed. "I forgive you," I whisper into his skin. I feel him here. Home. My Nathan. That's why I can say the words and mean them. "Can you forgive me for not telling you about the baby?"

He nods. "Yes. I was never trying to be your enemy."

"I wanted the baby, but it was the wrong time for us." My chest stutters when I inhale, and I squeeze my eyes shut against the tears to keep talking into the warm space between his jaw and neck. "I want one now, but I'm afraid I can't give you that. I can't stand to disappoint you month after month, possibly even years."

"What's the alternative? We don't even try? We break up?"

"I don't know."

"You chose me once over a baby," he says. "Would you do it again?"

I swallow. There's never been any question that Nathan wants this, but I have to as well. I can do it a lot of different ways—naturally, or with medical intervention, or by adopting—but I have to want to be a mother for myself. Not because he wants me to. "I choose you, and I want you to choose me back. Even if I can't give you what you want most in the world."

He cups his hand against my cheek, keeping me there. "I love you, Sadie. You're what I want. You can close off your heart, but don't forget—I know how to

499

tear you open. I've done it before, and I'll do it again and again until you realize I will never, ever let you abandon me. And I will never, ever abandon you."

It isn't until we walk into Ralph's hospital room that the reality of what's happening hits me.

Nathan's aunt greets us with mascara under her eyes. We each take a turn to hug her. "I just got here," she says.

Ralph is gaunt and the color of his hospital-green gown. He already looks halfway underground. He slits his eyes open and nods. I want to turn into Nathan's chest and hide and cry. Ralph and I aren't father and daughter by any means. The way Nathan was the last few months, cold and distant, is how Ralph has been his whole life. But he's still family.

"You don't got family of your own?" he asked me at *dinner once, while Nate was in another room.*

I wiped my brow. Ralph and I hadn't spent much time alone. "I do."

"They're no good? Nathan gets bent out of shape when I ask."

"He's protective."

"Maybe he thinks I'm going to try and be a dad to you. I'm not. Not that kind of guy."

"It's okay," I said. "I have a dad. Not a very good one, but Nathan and I have learned to live with what we got."

"You saying I'm not a good dad?"

"I think you are, actually." It was the truth. The man couldn't tell Nathan he loved him, but I knew he did by the way he looked at him. Nathan had always blamed his dad for ignoring his mom so long, she'd had no choice but to go away. "Seems to me like maybe some things got mixed up along the way."

Ralph eyed me closely. "He thinks I didn't love his mom. I did. Too much. It was hard to watch her fall out of love with me."

"So you pushed her away instead," I guessed.

"She would've stayed no matter how she felt," he said, looking away from me. "Now, she's happier. Lives in California with some guy who has money." I thought that was the end of it, but before Nathan returned, Ralph said, "If you ever think he's falling out of love with you, stop him. Before it's too late."

I don't think Nathan will ever understand the space Ralph put between himself and his wife, but I do. For whatever reason, he couldn't make her as happy as he thought she deserved. Even if I understand it, I don't want it for us. Nathan and I will have to work harder to be happy with ourselves so we can be happy together. To communicate, especially when it feels impossible.

Today, Ralph doesn't seem well enough to speak. He's alive, though. Nathan hugs his dad for a few long moments. He tells him he loves him, sits, and holds his hand as I hold Nathan's.

Ralph falls back asleep, even though we've only been there five minutes. Nathan slouches back in the

501

chair but doesn't take his eyes off Ralph. "I should call my mom."

"I'll do it," I say. "Stay here just in case."

His expression is blank as he looks up at me. He pats his lap. "Sit with me?"

I smooth his hair back and kiss him on the forehead, his skin warm under my lips. Familiar. "I will. After I make the call."

I pull up his mom's contact information on the way to the cafeteria. She answers my call right away. "Sadie. This is unexpected. Everything okay?"

"Yes," I say. "Well, no. Ralph is—" I pause.

"Oh." Neither of us speaks for a few seconds. "I wish I could be there."

"We know."

"How's Nathan?"

I find coffee and pour three cups. "As well as can be expected."

"Sadie." She sighs. "Take care of my boy. He'll try to be strong for everyone. I'm so happy he has you there."

I stare into the black coffee. I almost wasn't here, but I am. It makes me grateful I made the hard decisions I needed to—today, yesterday, and in the past. I did it to protect Nathan, but now I that I've seen the damage of my one-sidedness, I don't want to make any more without him. "I'll take care of him."

"Have Nathan call me when he's made arrangements."

"I will. Talk to you—"

"Wait—Sadie?"

"Yes?"

"Tell Ralph . . ." She pauses and whimpers. "Just tell him I love him. Tell him I never stopped."

I lean a hand against the counter. I can hear the emotion in her voice, but I can't distinguish if it's regret, grief, or something else. "Is that true?"

"Part of me will always love part of him. Those parts are distant memories, but they're there. I suppose those wounds'll be fresh tonight."

I nod. "I'll make sure he knows."

We both hang up. Since Thanksgiving is next week, I get turkey sandwiches, cranberry juice, and chocolate pudding. The four of us eat Ralph's final meal together, and though the mood is somber, we share what we're thankful for. For me, it's not just Nathan, but also his forgiveness and understanding. I'm thankful to Nathan for a love so unrelenting, he continues to fight for me. And to myself, for letting him. For finally finding the strength again to let myself want what I know can hurt me.

THIRTY-SEVEN

Nathan and I get in a cab as the sun rises through the skyscrapers. He leans his elbows onto his knees. "I have to make some calls."

I rub his back. "I'll take care of it."

"He has a burial plan."

"I'm already looking into it," I say. While Nathan and his aunt stayed with Ralph, I got to work on how to proceed after the death of a family member. There are a lot of details, and I want to take as much as I can off Nathan's plate.

Nathan's shoulders sag. He drops his face in his hands and inhales a stuttering, sobbing breath. Nathan has shed few tears in my presence. All that comes to mind is the day I walked down the aisle and the time he took a spiked ball to the crotch during beach volleyball. I scoot as close to him as I can get and hug him tightly from the side. He opens his hand for mine and holds it to his wet cheek.

This is my Nathan. *My* Nathan doesn't hold back or withdraw. He loves and regrets, fears and hopes, with his whole heart. I'm happy to be reunited with him, and as hard as the past few months have been, we're going to come out stronger. But in this moment, I can't think of anything worse than watching him submit to his pain. I bury my face in his shoulder and weep with him.

Ginger greets us at the door. I came home briefly after dinner last night to check in on her, and it's almost time for her next round of medication.

"I'll take her downstairs," Nathan says, picking up the leash before we're even through the door.

I snatch it from him. "No."

He raises his palms as if he's been caught doing something wrong. "What was that for?"

"*I'll* do it." Nathan is back to taking care of everything and everyone. He measures his love by how much weight he can shoulder, and that has to change. "Then I'll feed her. I'll check her wounds. You need rest. Let me help you."

He lowers his hands. "All right. Geez. No need to get grabby."

"Yes there is, Nathan." I pace the tiny entryway. Ginger watches me, back and forth. "I want you to listen to me, because it needs to be said. Going forward, things need to be said, not just tucked away for later."

"Yes," he says slowly. "I think we've proven that."

"I love how you care for me. I don't ever want that to stop. You have to let me return the favor, though."

"Okay."

"I'm not finished." I face him. "You came into my life, swept me off my feet, and never put me back down. With that, you set a precedent. Sometimes, you have to let me take care of you. When things get to be too much, tell me. Ask for help. You have to put your own mask on first."

He angles his head. "Mask . . .?"

"The pedestals," I continue. "They're over. Gone. We're on the ground now, and that's a better place to be because it's firmer."

He furrows his eyebrows. "You lost me. Maybe you're the one who needs to rest."

I sigh. "Andrew explains it better. I'm trying to say we aren't perfect, and we have to own that."

"Oh." He straightens up a little. "You want perfect, though."

"No, I don't. Not anymore. I want us, the flawed version. I'll never be the perfect wife, you won't be the perfect husband, and when we accept that, I think we'll both be happier. Not perfect, but happy."

"I never asked you to be that. *I* don't want perfect. You have to recognize that if you screw up, you can't hide because it's easier. You can't make decisions on your own so you won't burden me." He presses his lips together. "When you're lost, don't turn to someone else."

"And don't leave me out in the cold again." We stare at each other. I say, "I need your warmth, even when you don't think you can give it to me. What do *you* need?"

"I need to be a father."

I suck in a breath. I've heard *I want* from him. I've heard *wouldn't it be great*. When it comes to having a family, Nathan is vocal, but he hasn't yet said *I need*.

He takes my shoulders. "I know you're afraid. So am I. It doesn't have to be today or next year or three. But I need to love something outside of us. I have so much to give, and you—oh, God, Sadie. So do you. When you stop holding back, you are so loving."

I feel my face scrunching. Loving? Does he think so? He believes in us. In me. And I do want that—to stand by his side and raise our child together.

"You might even want it more than me," he says, "and that's why you're so terrified. If we can't conceive, we'll do something else. Do you think I'd have any less love to give if we adopted?"

His grip on me is firm. I flex my hands in and out of fists because I feel like I need to take a step back and I can't. This is a different kind of intimacy. Just like Andrew, when Nathan says it out loud, I know it's true—I *am* terrified. It doesn't shock me that he probably knew before I did, but it doesn't make it any easier to hear.

He lets go and backs away. "There're clean bandages and medication on the kitchen counter. I'm going to rest now."

By the twitch of his lips indicating a smile, I sense he thinks he's had some kind of victory—even though I haven't agreed to anything.

While Nathan naps, I clean Ginger's wounds. "I'm sorry you got hurt," I tell her. "But it's better now, isn't it?" She tilts her head. Tenderly, I wrap her paws in fresh bandages. A child is far more accident prone than a dog. Inevitably, bad things will happen. Nathan believes in us, though. I can handle the heartache and disappointment of failing to have a baby. It's watching Nathan go through it that worries me. I decided not to want kids to protect him, but I can't make those kinds of decisions without him anymore. "He takes good care of you," I murmur, "and I guess I do too."

Once Ginger's fed and walked, I open the refrigerator. When Nathan wakes up, I want to comfort him with something so delicious, he can't be sad. He lost his father today, so it has to be good. I decide to make the apple caramel pie I was planning for Thanksgiving.

I make the crust and put it in the fridge to chill, then slice some apples. When I've prepped all I can, I move to the couch. Armed with hot cider, I take Nathan's computer in my lap and call his aunt.

Together, she and I make a list of everyone to contact about Ralph's passing. We discuss what needs to be done over the next few days.

As I hang up, I notice a voicemail from yesterday, so I hit play.

"Good evening, Sadie. This is Kim from Doctor Harris's office calling about your fertility exam. Please contact us to schedule an appointment and discuss the results."

I lower the phone from my ear and stare at the screen. During the chaos of yesterday, the exam had slipped my mind. Schedule an appointment? Doesn't that always mean bad news? I glance at the closed door to our bedroom. Nathan thinks he can put himself through this, but does he really know what we'd be getting ourselves into? Will he be as adamant about it a year down the line, several doctors' appointments in, countless dollars spent?

I put the pie in the oven, barely paying attention to what I'm doing, and almost burn myself. The truth is, now that I've decided, I need to know. I won't be able to focus on anything else. Whatever the results are, Nathan and I will deal with them together.

I go back to the couch and return the call. As the phone rings, my nerves catch up with my brain. Each passing second brings more doubt. Nathan is already dealing with the death of his father. I don't know if this would be the best or worst time to break the news of my infertility. After several seconds with no answer, I remember that it's Saturday. I'll have no choice but to wait through the weekend after all.

I go to end the call when a voice on the line stops me. "Hello?" a man asks. "I mean—Doctor Harris's office."

"Doctor Harris?" I ask, surprised.

"You've got him."

"It's Sadie Hunt. I'm so sorry. I got your message and completely forgot it was the weekend."

"If only all my patients were as excited to see me as you," he teases. "I'd never go out of business."

I smile. "I'm really sorry. I know I was a little pushy yesterday."

"It's all right. You aren't the first. But I can't give you your results over the phone. You'll have to come in—*with an appointment*," he stresses. "Right now, we're closed. You just caught me passing through." He sighs. "I don't know what my wife is referring to when she says I work too much."

"Thank you. I'll come in. Or, you could just give me a hint."

"Sadie . . ."

"I don't want to keep you. It's just—Nathan and I have had a rough few days, and if it's bad news, I want to get it over with. But if it's not . . . it could really help."

He sighs. "Right. Let me pull up your file and see what we're dealing with. Give me a moment." The line goes quiet. While I wait, I pick up Nate's laptop from the coffee table. The *Brooklyn* folder on his bookmark bar catches my eye. I click it again, and again, the long list of apartment listings pops up.

"Sadie? You there?" the doctor asks.

"I'm here."

"Great. As I said, I can't give you your results over the phone." He hums into the receiver. "However, if you were to ask me a hypothetical question, I could answer that."

My heart begins to pound, and I cover it to keep it from bursting through my chest. Do I really want to know? Suspecting I'm infertile is one thing, but knowing I am would start Nathan and I on a whole new course. "Um." I swallow. "Hypothetically—if I were to have sex this weekend, could I get pregnant?"

He laughs robustly. "That's not quite the question I was expecting. Listen, I'm looking at my computer screen right now, and I like what I see."

I roll my lips together and brace myself, convinced there's concern in his voice. "But?"

"There's no but. Of course, in a hypothetical situation where the physical exam and blood test results look good, one could then proceed to more invasive tests to gain more confidence."

I loosen my fingers, which I'd curled into my chest. My blood feels like it's gushing through me, as if a dam broke somewhere in my veins. Good? Everything is *good*? "Are you sure?" I ask.

"Would I hypothetically lie?"

A spontaneous smile takes over my face. My relief is physical, my limbs liquefying, my breath coming easier. I'm tempted to wake Nathan right away and tell him things might actually be *good*. "Do you think this person should get more tests?" I ask.

"Hmm. If she and her husband have been trying less than a year, here's what I would suggest she do— relax. Remove unnecessary stress from her life. Start keeping a journal of what she does each day and how she feels. How her body feels. Know what I mean?"

I hesitate. "Not really. I've never kept a diary."

"Don't think of it as a diary. It's more of a log with notes about your—her—feelings. Record what she eats, how she exercises, when she has sex. Stay healthy. When she's ready, she should go off birth control and enjoy her husband."

I wrinkle my nose. "That's it? That's how someone gets pregnant?"

"Well, not technically. Should I go into more detail?"

I laugh for what feels like the first time in days.

"Now you've got the idea," he says, a smile in his voice. "Your body reacts negatively to stress, Sadie. When we talked about your past abortion, you sounded a bit . . . hopeless. Resigned to the fact that because of a decision you made ages ago, you've ruined your future. I've heard this before, and I recommend talking to someone about that. Speaking with a therapist will help you sort through some of the issues that may be blocking pregnancy."

Months ago, I'm not sure I would've believed there could be any connection between my fears and my inability to get pregnant. Now, though, I already feel lighter for having shared the truth about the abortion with Nathan. "Thanks," I say. "She will definitely look into therapy. She might even . . . buy a diary."

"Good," he says cheerfully. "And, listen, if none of that works and she doesn't get pregnant in the next six to twelve months, there are more tests that can be done, starting with her husband."

I'm about to thank him again when I stop. Did he say husband? "I'm sorry," I say. "What do you mean?"

"Well, his sperm could be the issue. It'd be unlikely, considering the hypothetical spouse has gotten his wife pregnant in the past, but it doesn't hurt to check him out."

I sit back against the couch, my mind spinning. I see myself here in my apartment, open-mouthed on the phone, as if I've left my own body. I don't know why it never occurred to me that Nathan might be the reason we can't have children. Instantly, I'm furious with the way I've berated and punished myself. If Nathan were infertile, I wouldn't love him any less. I'd never leave him because of it. I'd still be honored to adopt a child with him. The truth becomes crystal clear to me—Nathan and I are in this together until the end. I want to give him a family, but even if I can't, I won't let him go. Nathan asked if I'd choose him over a baby again, and I still would.

"Thank you, Doctor Harris. You don't know what this conversation has meant to my hypothetical self."

"Happy early Thanksgiving, Sadie," he says. "Tell Nathan the same."

I hang up the phone, feeling as giddy as a child with a new toy. I click on the first link Nathan has bookmarked. It's a three-bedroom apartment in Cobble Hill that's slightly out of our price range. The description tells me it's *ideal for a young family* and *in a quiet neighborhood* and *within walking distance of schools.*

Next is a house in Dyker Heights. I click through every link. The folder makes sense now. When I'd seen it before, I'd assumed Nate was looking for his own place. These are all for families. Nathan spends time in Brooklyn because that's where he wants to be. Near his friends. In a family-friendly neighborhood. Somewhere long-term.

I don't care that it's the weekend. I choose a few of my favorite listings and make some overdue phone calls.

I sneak into the bedroom where Nathan's sprawled on his back. One arm reaches toward my pillow. It would be wonderful to crawl in next to him, but he needs his rest. I dig in my nightstand drawer for the remainder of my year's supply of birth control and take it into the kitchen. I push every pill through the foil into the sink, crumple the wrappers, and toss them in the full garbage before tying it off.

With my keys in one hand and a Hefty bag in the other, I go into the hallway. I've only taken two steps toward the trash chute when the door to 6A opens. I freeze in place, my instinct to flee firing off, but it's too late. I brace myself to see Finn for the first time since I dumped him, but it's Kendra who comes out. She has my Burberry coat thrown over an NYU shirt that looks several sizes too big.

She stops and looks over at me. "Shit. Did you hear all that?"

"What?"

"Never mind. Sadie, right?"

My throat is suddenly dry, but my hand sweats around the trash bag. I nod. "Right."

"Any chance your adorable husband has a single brother?" Her expression sours. "I find myself suddenly available."

Since she appears more annoyed than angry, I wonder—does she know about me? She isn't exactly lunging, claws out, like I would expect. "No, he doesn't," I say. "I'm . . . I'm so sorry, Kendra."

She shrugs. "My luck, he'd be a cheating bastard anyway." She waves and takes off for the elevator. "See ya."

Finn flies out of his apartment and starts down the hall after her. "Kendra, hang on. We still have a lot to—"

"Eat shit," she throws over her shoulder. "And I'm taking the bitch's coat. If anyone deserves Burberry for getting fucked, it's me."

She boards the elevator, leaving Finn staring after her. With a hand on his hip, he drops his head for a few silent seconds before turning back for his apartment. He stops abruptly when he sees me. "How long have you been standing there?"

I shift on my feet. The garbage bag crinkles louder than seems possible. "I saw all of it."

"Perfect," he mutters. He has twenty-six days' worth of beard and new black circles under his eyes to go with it.

"You told her about us?" I ask.

"Not exactly. It was a surprise visit. There was evidence . . . the coat, for one."

I walk cautiously toward him. "I'm sorry."

"Me too."

"One day, though, you'll see—this is a good thing. It's better to be honest with her now—"

"You're going to talk to me about honesty?"

I close my mouth.

He sighs, rubbing his eyes with the heels of his hands. "This wasn't how I expected things to go. It was easier when I thought you'd be by my side for—"

My apartment door opens behind me, sending my heart into my throat. I close my eyes, hoping I'm imagining that Nathan has just come into the hallway.

When nothing happens, I look over my shoulder. Although Nathan's eyes are puffy from sleep, they're shrewd and sharpened above my head—at Finn.

"Nate—" I begin, holding out my free hand.

517

Ignoring me, he beelines for Finn. Nathan is by no means violent, but all at once I see the tension in his muscles, the balling of his hands, the grit of his teeth. I drop the trash to catch his arm, but he's already past me. He raises his fist and clocks Finn straight across the jaw. I cover my mouth, gasping as Finn retreats a few paces, one hand clutching his face.

Nathan shakes out his fist, flexing it.

"Oh my God," I say, unable to conceal my shock.

"It's okay." Finn squeezes his eyes shut and works his jaw side to side, wincing. "I deserved it. But if there's more coming—"

"I feel sorry for you," Nathan cuts him off.

Finn pauses. His green eyes go foggy as he looks from Nathan to me. "You should."

I want to tell Finn and his broken heart that he'll meet his own soul mate—a woman who thoroughly belongs to him in a way I never could. A woman who, unlike Kendra, won't hold him hostage if she doesn't get what she wants. I can't promise him that, though, and he isn't my concern anyway. He'll have to figure it out on his own.

Nathan turns around. He doesn't look at me, but he puts his arm firmly around my shoulders. "Come inside."

"The trash—"

"Leave it."

THIRTY-EIGHT

We're barely in the apartment when Nathan grabs my bicep and pulls me to him. "I want you."

I glance at his hand on me, red and possibly swelling. "You need ice."

"I need *you*, Sadie." He leans in, his breath brushing my cheek. I can see his pulse racing at the base of his neck. "Now."

I blush furiously at the growl in his voice. It's been too long since he looked at me with this much love—this much *lust*. My insides coil and tighten deliciously. I look away, bashful, as if I have an enormous crush on my own husband. I sort of do. "You can have me," I say, wrestling my arm from him. "Right after I take care of your hand."

We stare each other down. He narrows his eyes like a lion that's spotted its next meal. I take a step back. He takes one forward, bouncing on the balls of his feet. I bolt for the kitchen with him hot on my heels. I manage to grip the handle of the freezer right before he captures my waist and lifts me off my feet.

I devolve into peals of breathless laughter as he half swings, half tickles me. He sets me down facing the counter, my back to him, then slides his hands under my sweater. I close my eyes. Listen to our labored breaths. Appreciate the splash of chills over my skin. He tugs my top over my head, dropping it on the ground. My hair crackles with static while he combs his fingers through it. He unhooks my bra, tosses it, and reaches around to open the fly of my jeans. Seconds later, my pants and underwear are halfway down my thighs.

He runs his hand over my collarbone and rests it at the base of my throat. My heart pounds like it's the first time a man's ever touched me. Nathan reaches forward and picks a birth control pill out of the sink. "Is this . . . what I think it is?"

I turn in his arms and place my hands on his cheeks. He draws his eyebrows together, two wrinkles deepening between them, as if he's concerned about what I'll say.

"Let's make a baby, Nathan."

His expression eases with relief. He takes my hand and trails kisses from the inside of my palm up my forearm. With his big, enveloping arms, he hoists me by my waist. I shriek with surprise when my bare ass hits the cold countertop. Flour and sugar, leftover from my baking, bite into my skin. From this position, I get to watch his dance, the feverish way he rips open his fly and hops out of his pants and underwear. He reaches behind him to yank his t-shirt over his head.

And then, finally, but also swiftly, he's sandwiched between my knees. He cups the base of my head and kisses his way up my neck until his mouth devours mine. Our tongues slip and slide faster than I can keep track.

He pulls my hips to the edge of the counter, and I wrap my legs around him. Teasing me, he traces the head of his cock up and down my slit. "I don't think I can take it slow right now." He presses in a little and groans. "Just to touch you with only my dick and feel how wet you are . . ."

I bite my bottom lip as he stretches me, slides inside me. He's lost his dad, and he almost lost me too. I can feel his hunger, and I want to feed him. "This is a new start for us. Promise me, Nathan."

He lifts his head to look at me. Sunlight filters through the kitchen window. His pupils constrict, his eyes a piercing almond-brown. "This isn't a beginning or ending. It's just where we are. We have a long and happy life behind us—ahead of us too."

I dig my fingers into his shoulder as he breaks me open. With each heartfelt word and deliberate thrust, he rubs my sweetest spots. I'm practically purring. "Okay, Nathan. I trust you."

"You want this baby?"

"I want this baby."

He rears back, and I brace myself to take all of him, but the oven beeps. We freeze. He checks with me, an adorable expression of suffering and indecision plastered on his face. He knows I might want to stop. I don't. It feels like sunshine after the rain to have him inside me again. But, there'll be a price if we don't. "It's caramel apple pie," I tell him. "Your call."

He winces, as if I just slapped him. "I have to choose between pie and sex?"

"Warm and yummy," I say. "I even got vanilla ice cream."

He looks sidelong at the oven. "For the pie or the sex?"

I giggle and push him off me. He acts reluctant, but he smells the same delicious baked apples and homemade crust I do. "It'll just take a minute," I say and hop off the counter. "Otherwise it'll be ruined."

As I get out the oven mitts, he grabs an apron from the side closet and ties it on me. "Hot food and naked skin don't mix."

I bend over to check the pie and predictably, Nathan's hand rounds the curve of my behind. "Mmm," he hums. "You're all the dessert I need."

"Get me a cooling rack from the top cupboard, will you, babe?"

He slaps my ass. I gasp with the unexpected sting. "You've got flour on your buns," he says. "And it's making me hot."

My motor is still running too, the throb between my thighs deeply unsatisfied. I place the dish on a trivet he set up. "It just needs to cool off." I tease him as I toss the mitts aside, "Maybe I should let you cool off too."

"Oh, I'm cool as a cucumber," he says, scooping me up again. He plants my floured buns in the same pile of powder, takes a step back, and looks me over. He's tall, lean, and hard everywhere. His sculpted shoulders. His muscular thighs. His pink, engorged cock, still glistening with traces of me.

"Nate," I scold. Heat rises up my chest. "How will we ever make a baby if we don't cross the finish line?"

He smiles slowly. "It's just—you, in your apron. And the flour in your hair. You're so beautiful, Sadie. It's been too long since I told you."

I get flustered under his praise and look away. Tucking my hair behind my ear, I hide my smile. "You're the one who's beautiful."

He comes to me and turns my face to him by my chin. He pecks me hard on the lips and pulls back. Holding my gaze, he squats down to push my knees apart and my apron up. He kisses my pussy like he did my mouth, once, fast and hard, and then looks up at me with a shit-eating grin.

"What?" I ask warily.

"Tastes just like caramel apple."

I shove his shoulder, but he holds firm. My laughter dies when he goes back for more. He sucks my clit between his teeth, then dives deep. I open my mouth toward the heavens, enjoying every nuance of his exploration. I grab onto anything I can—on one side, the sink faucet, on the other, the edge of a cupboard. "Oh my God, Nate. Where have you been with that tongue?"

He eats me out like I'm Thanksgiving dessert. In a way, I am. I smile as I moan. With a particularly pleasurable flick of his tongue, I grasp his hair. He stands up, licking his lips. "Now for the main course."

It isn't the first time Nathan has seduced me with cooking terms, but with his hair sticking up from where I pulled it and the irresistible smile on his face, it might be the cutest. He hauls me to the counter's edge. The apron rides up, exposing me. We both watch as he takes his shaft in his hand and presses the tip against me. There's nothing cute about his cock, or the way it fills me. Once he's inside, he takes my hips and slides me onto him, steady but fast. He grits his teeth until he's buried to the hilt. "God, Sadie. What was the matter with us? This is where we belong. It's so clear."

My only response is to arch my back. He grabs one of my tits through the ruffled top of the apron and squeezes. The ceiling blurs as my body submits to Nathan's hard, commanding thrusts. He moves his hand to my mouth, his fingers pressing inside, urgent. I suck on them as he takes me faster, rougher. He uses his wet thumb to circle my clit. I've been on the verge so long, it doesn't take much for me to capture my orgasm. I shut my eyes. My pussy closes around him, sucking him deep. He groans so passionately, it's his primal sounds that take my climax to the next level and drive me wild.

When I'm spent, I wrap my arms around his neck, my legs around his waist, and give my body over. He slams into me, his thrusts powerful and assertive. "I love you," he breathes on my neck. "Only I can love you this much."

I answer him by hanging onto him more tightly. I meet his need and take him painfully deep. I tell him with my body what I can't with my words—*I'm sorry I ever doubted you.*

"Fuck, my, God, yes," he rages. His muscles are alive with tension. Veins cord his neck, forearms, temples. His last drive is the deepest, and he comes, claiming me from the inside out.

He hugs me frantically, feeling the backs of my shoulders, gripping my waist and hips. He digs his fingers into my skin as if to make sure I'm real. "Sadie."

"Nathan." I squeeze my arms around his neck and rub my smooth cheek over his scratchy one. "I'm here."

He exhales into the crook of my neck, relaxing. When he straightens up, I loosen my hold, but keep my arms around him. He pushes my hair off my face, then kisses me. Slowly, our lips part, and I slide my tongue along his. He angles over me, trying for deeper. "Let's do it again," he rumbles with his whole body.

I laugh into his mouth. "All right. But can we move to the shower? There's flour in my crack."

He captures my bottom lip with his teeth and grins. "I'll meet you in there."

I slide off the counter and cross the apartment to our bedroom. In the bathroom, I flip on the shower. As I'm untying my apron, the trashcan catches my eye. It's stuffed with calla lilies, and a couple of them are spotted with Ginger's blood. I steady myself against the counter as the echo of shattering glass sounds in my ears. Ginger's howling. Nathan's crestfallen face. I grip the edge until my knuckles are white. It all could've gone a different way.

It didn't.

The once-beautiful, now-ugly flowers are a part of our imperfect history. I look up at my reflection. White flour stripes my temple, my hip, my forearm. My hair isn't just messy, but also greasy, and my makeup has been cried, rubbed, and fucked off.

Nathan enters behind me. He picks up where I left off, sliding the apron straps off my shoulders and setting it aside. He, too, has seen better days, with his day-old stubble, wayward hair, and a patch of sugar on his chin he got while eating me out.

I tilt my head up and back to look at him. "Come here."

He leans down, and I suck the sugar off his jaw. Just like that, my horrible last memory in this bathroom is replaced with sweetness.

He wraps his arms around me from behind and hugs me with unrestrained strength. His love floods my system like a drug—instant, pleasant, warm. "I've missed you," he says. "I love you."

"I know." My lungs burn for air as he crushes me to him. "Look at us."

Our eyes meet in the reflection. He smiles with a wink. "What a mess."

Neither of us moves. This is comfortable, our naked bodies glued together, the shower steaming over, the rhythmic sound of water beating the tub floor. Tonight, in bed, I'll tell him about the conversation with my doctor. I'll tell him that on Sunday, we have an appointment with a realtor in Park Slope. Right now, though, I just want to stay in the simplicity of our moment, memorizing its imperfections and the way it feels to be back home in Nathan's arms.

TITLES BY
JESSICA HAWKINS

SLIP OF THE TONGUE

NIGHT FEVER SERIES
NIGHT FEVER
NIGHT CALL
NIGHT MOVES
NIGHT EDGE

THE CITYSCAPE SERIES
COME UNDONE
COME ALIVE
COME TOGETHER

STRICTLY OFF LIMITS

ACKNOWLEDGMENTS

To my team: my editor, Elizabeth, who pushed me to my limits to make me, and this book, better. To the designer, Sarah, and the photographer, Tyler, for the most stunning, mind-blowing cover I couldn't even dream up. To Katie, who took this story to the next level with her in-depth proof & beta read—all under a tight deadline. To Nina & Jenn with Social Butterfly PR, along with Give Me Books & Gossip Girls PR for their dedication to spreading the word about *Slip of the Tongue*. And to every blogger, everywhere—you do more for indie authors than could be conveyed in an entire book, much less a sentence.

To Lisa, Bethany & Amber, not only readers but friends, not only bloggers but superheroes, for keeping me sane with your relentless support and love—morning, noon & night, and to the rest of my street team for keeping me on my toes . . . and more importantly, motivated.

Speaking of motivated, nothing lights a fire under my ass like my peers and colleagues. A special thank you to Carter Ashby & Louise Bay, who prop me up every day just by existing, and to RS Grey, Lisa Suzanne, Liv Morris, and many other authors for being examples and, of course, friends. To the authors who took time to let me peek behind the curtains by sharing their self-publishing experiences and then to those who generously agreed to read and blurb *Slip of the Tongue* when I was afraid to ask, and lastly to the scaffolding of the support system, AS101 and BFFs for all the tips, guidance, and laughs over the years.

CONNECT WITH JESSICA

Stay updated & join the
JESSICA HAWKINS Mailing List
www.JESSICAHAWKINS.net/mailing-list

www.amazon.com/author/jessicahawkins
www.facebook.com/jessicahawkinsauthor
instagram: @jessica_hawkins
twitter: @jess_hawk

ABOUT THE AUTHOR

JESSICA HAWKINS grew up between the purple mountains and under the endless sun of Palm Springs, California. She studied international business at Arizona State University and has also lived in Costa Rica and New York City. To her, the most intriguing fiction is forbidden, and that's what you'll find in her stories. Currently, she resides wherever her head lands, which is often the unexpected (but warm) keyboard of her trusty MacBook.

49778030R00319

Made in the USA
Middletown, DE
22 October 2017